I0646449

Ian McKinley

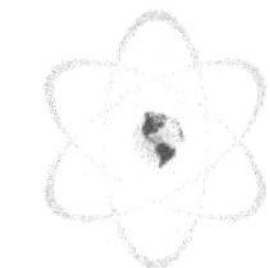

2017, TWB Press

www.twbpress.com

Chemotroph

Edited by Terry Wright

Model image by goldeneden from shutterstock.com

ISBN: 978-1-944045-49-1

chemotroph (kē′mō-trŏf′) 1. An organism that manufactures its own food through chemosynthesis as opposed to photosynthesis, generally harmless. 2. A martial artist using performance-enhancing designer drugs, generally extremely dangerous.

1 ...thorn in my side

Bruce sat in a bay window, looking out over the partially submerged town of Hamilton while he inhaled the local Bermudan clone of Jamaican Blue Mountain coffee. *Life is certainly not at all bad,* he mused as he watched the mismatched combatants slugging it out on the lawn below. A tall, slim blonde wearing a smart-suit leotard swept a long bo – a Japanese fighting stick – at the head of a small red-haired girl who appeared to be completely naked.

The redhead back-flipped out of range, only to be confronted by the bo scything towards her at waist height as her opponent charged in. To the evident surprise of the taller woman, the waiflike redhead spun forward, blocking the stick halfway along its length with an upraised foot. The crack of contact sounded like a gunshot, and the shock almost shook the weapon from the blonde's grasp.

Bruce winced. *Combat implants. The miniscule redhead, Engel, was more dangerous barehanded than many combatants would be when armed to the teeth. Not that the willowy blonde, Eva, was any newcomer to martial arts*. The competition was much more balanced than it looked size-wise. The smaller Engel had ignored any opportunity to follow-up on her momentary advantage and dropped into a crouch to allow the taller Eva to recover.

Eva stood with the bo held two-handed against her right ear then exploded forward with a savage cut towards her opponent's neck.

Engel looked frozen to the spot, and then, when it seemed that avoidance was impossible, blurred into a turn that allowed her to grab the stick as she twisted under Eva's arms. This would have led to a throw or wristlock, but Eva had clearly anticipated the move. She released the bo and caught Engel in a stranglehold, which lifted her off the ground.

Small Engel wriggled like a snake and rained blows from her elbows and heels into Eva's ribs and legs. The *Smart-Fabric* smart-suit she wore seemed to be holding up well, hardening to steely rigidity on the instant of contact. Although hampered by the loss of flexibility caused by these protection measures, Eva was able to drop forward to fall with her full weight on top of Engel.

The momentary stiffening of the entire suit on impact with the ground was enough hindrance for Engel to squirm loose of Eva's grip and establish a lock on her exposed right wrist. With a squeal of pain, Eva attempted to roll free but, within a second, was immobilized with her face pressed into the dew-damp grass. Engel sat on Eva's back but her smug look of victory suddenly turned to shock, and she jumped clear with a curse while rubbing her buttocks.

"Static charge fibers," Bruce mumbled as he stood

and leaned forward to watch the fight more closely. He had heard about *Smart-Fabric* with this option but didn't know that it was already commercially available.

Engineers must have sorted out the risk of electrocuting the wearer. The smart-features would probably be sub-vocally controlled, which would be easy to hide given the suit's polo neck.

Engel was clearly not amused. A rain of kicks knocked her larger opponent back to the ground, and every time she attempted to clamber up, she got knocked down. The smart-suit's active panzering was clearly getting in the way, so Eva deactivated it in the middle of a flamboyant series of back roundhouse kicks, enabling her to grab a rapidly moving foot as she was kicked backwards. Although her grip on the foot seemed firm, she was unable to get any hold on the rest of the leg while the girls fell together to the ground.

Bruce's interest increased as the wrestling on the ground grew increasingly scrappy.

Engel's body, with the exception of her hands and feet, was evidently coated in some kind of grease, which prevented Eva from finding any kind of immobilizing hold. Eva had countered by making her smart-suit texture as smooth as possible, so the entire bout began to look like mud wrestling but without the mud. This was made particularly bizarre by the camouflage feature of the smart-suit, which displayed a confusing picture of flesh as the couple rolled over each other.

It looked like the battle had reached a stalemate until

Eva, still grasping Engel's foot, managed to slide her free hand up Engel's leg and secure a grasp on the strings of her tanga, which was so brief Bruce had previously been unaware of its existence. Twisting her fist to secure the grip, Eva had enough leverage to pull Engel's heel backwards and force a savage knee-lock, which made Engel slap the ground in defeat, but not before her underwear snapped and Eva rose to her feet, waving the minute souvenir of her victory.

As a finger sensuously caressed his right earlobe, Bruce jumped in surprise, almost spilling the dregs of his coffee.

The Amazonian frame of Professor Angela White squeezed up against him as she peered out the window. "Did Eva manage to hold Maria off?" She set a few folded white towels on the windowsill.

Eva was Angela's daughter and Maria Maiden – aka Engel – was Bruce's partner in the extremophile sampling business. While Angela started a monologue on the dangers of underestimating modern materials technology, Bruce pondered on the weird position he found himself in.

Despite having met the three women only six months previously, they now lived together like a family – admittedly in a kind of exotically incestuous manner. Even in the liberated moral environment of mid-21st century secular Europe – which seemed to counterbalance the Orwellian controls on the populations of the many fundamentalist regimes – the rapid development of the relationship between the four of them was unusual.

Maybe something to do with lonely people being forced together under dangerous circumstances, some kind of self-imposed Stockholm-syndrome.

Engel had appointed herself his partner only after having failed to block his first meeting with Professor White. In fact, formally, Angela was still his employer.

He glanced appreciatively at her curvaceous, Rubenesque form – squeezed into a skin-tight tube, as usual, which clearly showed she wasn't wearing underwear and left little else to the imagination.

Not the common image of a Nobel-laureate boffin.

He had learned the secret of Angela White's serendipitous rejuvenation after she'd recruited him for his first extremophile sampling escapade. While working on microbial colonies that were adapted to life under extreme conditions of temperature, radiation and chemotoxicity, she'd discovered a mutant strain with an internal repair system so efficient it made them effectively immortal. Even more amazingly, their longevity and ability to facilitate rejuvenation was transferable to higher organisms.

Even at this early stage, Angela's elixir attracted the attention of a network of organizations that were either opposed to it or desired to posses it for themselves. During an industrial sabotage attack that destroyed her laboratory, she had injected herself with the sole sample of microbial extract to avoid it falling into the hands of her opponents. Unintentionally, she became the personification of the dreams of her pharm sponsors. She appeared to be in her mid-thirties when, actually, she was seventy-five years old.

Unable to recreate her original discovery in the laboratory, she recruited Bruce to obtain samples of microbial populations that had already been exposed to relevant extreme conditions for periods of decades or more. Their first sampling trip to the site of the Fukushima reactor meltdowns in Japan had been carried out successfully, despite numerous attempts by adversaries to block their path.

Unfortunately, most of their samples had been lost during the destruction of their Glasgow base and, although now recovering well, Eva had been seriously injured in the fracas. Nevertheless, enough material remained to show that the extremophile microbes present were similar to the type that Angela was looking for, even if not advanced enough to exhibit immortality traits.

A further sampling trip was being planned with the additional hope that the microbial extract would help speed Eva's recuperation. Or, at least, that was what the girls thought. Only a couple days before, Angela had confessed that treatment of Eva's damaged left optic nerve was not able to prevent continued degeneration, so she could easily lose sight in that eye. Considering the horrendous facial trauma she had suffered, Eva was relatively lucky, but the close-knit team was committed to doing anything possible to ensure her full recovery.

Within the next few weeks, they would set off on their second extremophile sampling trip. While Eva had been healing, this had been an implicitly taboo subject. Now, however, it was difficult to justify putting the project off further.

He smiled at the pair on the lawn, Eva gamboling around, swinging her trophy at a height just above the pursuing Engel's reach.

Clearly time to get the extremophile sampling team mobile again.

As he recognized a question in Angela's tone, Bruce pulled himself back to the present. "Sorry," he mumbled. "What was that?"

"These smart-suits...do you think we should order a set for us?"

"I don't see what use we'd have for them. It's fine for the girls out there, but these fights are like chess puzzles. What if you put the latest smart-suit up against a greased-up ninja? Completely academic, though a smart-suit could be worthwhile for Engel's kind of penetration or burglary jobs where the camouflage option could be useful. In that case, of course, she'd unlikely carry a big bloody bo with her. Also, in a fight, the camo can be quite confusing, but she'd give up that advantage while brandishing such an obvious weapon. The suit is also pretty warm; fine for colder climes, but you wouldn't want to wear it for long in the tropics, which is about the only place you're likely to encounter people fighting in the buff."

Eva ran into the room, tossed the remnants of Engel's tanga to Bruce, and stopped to loosen the neck of her suit and peel it down to her waist, exposing a pair of beautifully formed breasts covered with sweat.

"See what I mean?" He smiled.

"Okay, point made," the professor conceded and threw one of the towels to the heavily perspiring blonde.

Eva had just wiped her torso down when redheaded Engel stomped into the room – obviously completely unconcerned about her lack of clothing. "Luck," she shouted. "Pure Luck. I don't know why I put on those stupid fuckin' knickers."

"Wouldn't have helped you anyway," the blonde responded. "If you hadn't been wearing them, you'd just have exposed something else I could have grabbed hold of."

Too much information.

Bruce grimaced and broke in before the argument turned into a second round of combat. "Engel, what kind of grease were you using? It clearly doesn't rub-off or spread to your hands and feet."

"It's a buckyball body-paint," Engel responded, noticeably brightening up with the chance to avoid a post-mortem of her defeat. "I found it on a porn site. The sales holo was hilarious. Three guys and a girl coated completely in this stuff trying to get it away. Maybe we should all try it sometime," she added with a grin.

"High tech version of the Mazola parties of my youth." Angela sighed. "There seems to be no advance in science and technology that can't be somehow used for sex. Anyway, we can try that later," she concluded, apparently accepting Engel's scurrilous suggestion at face value. "In the meantime, how are the plans coming along, lad? Where are we off to next?"

Bruce had to close his eyes for a few seconds to cope with this shift in the topic of conversation and moving into an area that had been taboo while Eva was recuperating. "Based on the latest results from the few Fukushima samples that we managed to hold onto, I guess resampling that location is unlikely to give us what we're looking for." He glanced at the statuesque brunette professor, who nodded. "Our aim is to get cultures that have been exposed to extremely high pH and radiation for as long as possible."

The professor provided more details. "Within these mixed cultures, the key organisms seem to be the ones at the bottom of the food chain. Chemotrophs. Microbes that extract the energy they need to grow from chemical reactions," she expanded, noting Engel's look of confusion.

"In particular, we need to focus on SRBs, sulfate reducing bacteria. They're not normally found under hyperalkaline conditions, but it's not unknown either. In fact, there were some early studies in Jordan—"

"Angela," Bruce interrupted her before this turned into another of her extended monologues. "That still fits with our original profile. But what about the opposition? We still need to move as surreptitiously as we can." He raised an eyebrow in Eva's direction. "That Glasgow bomb certainly stirred up a hornets' nest, caused a lot of serious action by the Big Boys over the following few months."

"Also within GRW," Angela added, referring to the pharmaceutical giant that sponsored her work. "They've had a major clear out. Top management got shocked to the core when they realized how badly they'd been infiltrated. Mainly in security section, of all places."

Bruce turned to look out of the window. "At least here we've been clear of it all. Do you think we could have vanished completely from their radar?" He was referring to the loose network of organizations that had grouped together to try to sabotage Angela's project.

Eva chipped in, "I believe we've lost them for the moment and that the pharm side of the opposition may well back off completely. However, the national groups are a different kettle of fish. Even a multinat has limited control over the actions of governments in places like India and the craziest of the Muslim fundamentalist countries. Even worse, the drive is probably coming from intelligence groups within these countries, and the governments involved may have little idea of what is going on." She casually tossed the now rolled up towel at the redhead. "What this boils down to is that we can expect at least as much trouble as before. If anything, given that they've had more time to organize and we've got to assume stories about our last trip leaked out, I'd say probably worse rather than better."

Angela broke in before Bruce could respond. "Maybe you're a little pessimistic, dear. Remember we're still running a lot of disinformation activities of our own, and we've seen no sign that anyone has tried to duplicate our Ichi-effu sampling. We also officially killed off our own Flynn and Drndarski identities in the explosion." She referred to the pseudonyms used by Angela and Eva to help conceal their earlier work.

Bruce took his turn to speak. "We really have no idea, but let's assume the worst. So, should we go to the office and have a look at the options for where, when and how? I could concentrate better if the girls were wearing clothes." He passed Engel the remnants of her underwear.

"Excellent idea," Angela said. "Anyone for coffee?" she asked over her shoulder as she led the way to a spiral staircase that led to the extensive work room, which formed the attic across the entire length of the converted villa, officially registered as a marine biology research station.

***

Fifteen minutes later they were sitting in massive leather chairs around an oval table that appeared to have been carved from a single block of oak. In stark contrast to the low-tech table, a holographic display appeared suspended above it, displaying a ranking of options following Bruce's last review of potential sampling sites.

"Since we first did this, I've been able to dig up a lot more info on the original sites and added a few more obscure possibilities. So, we've got..." a list of files glowed lurid green, "...old reactors, meltdowns, weapon sites, waste repositories, ore bodies...and now I've added contaminated sites.

"The reactors have all been assigned second priority or lower. The best prospects involve really old, first generation beasts, which have either been sealed prior to decommissioning or have been disposed-of intact. There are a few reactors dumped with full fuel loading, which would be the best options in terms of continuous high radiation exposure—"

"You're surely joking, Bruce," Angela interrupted. "Nobody could simply dump a nuclear reactor."

Bruce set down his coffee mug and used a virtual pointer to highlight the sites that had been placed in the *reserve / reactor* box. As each site was highlighted, a range of pictures, diagrams and lists of key data flashed into existence in front of each seat.

"You'd think so, wouldn't you? So far I've found forty-three, and that's counting only those that contain at least some fuel. All marine power plants and almost all military. I think that a couple of the nuclear icebreakers listed were, at least formally, civil ships. They are sub-categorized here as accidentally-sunk and un-recovered in green, deliberately scuttled in red, and disposed of within a special facility in blue.

"We can eliminate most of these by considering either our preference for warm, highly-alkaline conditions or else simple practicality of getting samples from the deep sea options. If I could think of a way of getting near them, however, there are a couple of these that would be very good options."

The flickering pictures froze to show two similar-looking Soviet nuclear submarines. "Scuttled in the Sea of Japan back in the '80s, fully loaded reactor core and the entire active area stabilized with cement grout prior to sinking." More color graphics appeared. "Some old IAEA estimates of temperatures...the water at the disposal depth of about twelve hundred meters is around five degrees Celsius but the radiogenic heat should keep the core a fair bit warmer. A bit on the low side, nevertheless, but otherwise good options in terms of pH and time."

Bruce looked around the table with a smile. "The bad news, of course, is that this area has been used for decades by the military for dumping all kinds of radioactive and toxic shit. It's a rigorous exclusion zone under twenty-four-seven satellite surveillance by the UN."

"Finally, we have three more submarine reactors." The graphics morphed into an animation of the dismantling process of a massive Soviet nuclear submarine. "Due to failure of fuel elements left stored in the core and very high levels of resultant contamination, the entire block of hull containing the reactor was sealed, grouted with cement, and dumped in a clay-lined trench." Rather grainy video footage showed this unwieldy process, under the supervision of people muffled in massive parkas.

"All three reactors are at the same location in North Russia," a map of Russia gradually zoomed-in to show increasing local detail, "which is a national disposal facility for Cold War military waste. Unfortunately, this was planned as a permafrost site and, since global warming kicked in, is a bit of a political hot potato. The Yanks are being pushed by the Norwegians to pressure the Russians to remediate the entire site. The Russians know where a lot of bodies are buried on the other side of the Atlantic...on the military waste side, I mean, and so the Amis have got to be careful not to push too hard. A good reserve option, but maybe now would not be a good time to plan a visit."

Before he could go further, Angela broke in. "Bruce, lad, this is all very fascinating, and I'm sure you could entertain us for hours on all the unsuitable sites. Why don't we cut to the chase? What do you reckon is our best bet?"

"I'll second that," Engel added rudely.

Bruce looked around in exasperation but gave in with a sigh. The holo-display flashed and simplified to a map of Europe. "Bure— "

"Who're you callin' a boor?" Engel glared at him. "I think you're too fond of the sound of your own fuck'n voice. If you'd just— "

"Bure," he shouted as the map zoomed in on France and centered on a town of this name, somewhat to the south east of Reims.

"Oops, sorry," Engel whispered meekly.

The display now began to expand with details of the facilities at this location.

"A repository?" Angela asked. "I thought you weren't very keen on them?"

"I've been looking for the combination of high-activity waste with cement or concrete but, for many good technical reasons, this is usually avoided in modern designs. However, I found this well-hidden in old archive material."

A 2-D plan ghosted in front of the extensive 3-D layout of the *West-European Regional High-level Waste Repository*. French-language legends were rapidly replaced by English as the auto-translate demon picked them up. Bruce's pointed finger caused an area in the old plan to expand: the *Spent-fuel Disposal Demonstration Site.* Expanding the equivalent area of the repository layout showed nothing at all marked. Highlighting the area and searching all openly available information in the repository database resulted in nothing more than a note that this was an abandoned testing area.

"Now the French civil nuclear program was never particularly open, pretty typical of the countries with military programs overlapping in lots of places. The Bure site was also particularly sensitive due to lots of local opposition to repository siting in the late 20th and early this century. Remember, France used to be a big agricultural power in Europe with a major wine industry in those days. Bure was planned as a French national repository for waste from reprocessing. France was also big in the reprocessing business—"

Engel cut in. "Do we really need the history lesson?"

"You certainly do...and the others need a bit of background to see where the problems come in."

She slouched in her chair.

Bruce continued smoothly. "France was pushing old, messy, wet reprocessing technology, but many insiders could see that it wasn't commercially sensible. Many other countries had already decided to directly dispose of spent fuel. This was for financial reasons, like the Scandinavians, or to minimize risk of weapons proliferation, like the Yanks. So the wily Frogs decided to keep fingers in both pies and set up a test of a direct disposal design in a corner of the underground lab they'd built to characterize the Bure geology."

A series of further graphics and animation sequences appeared. "You couldn't say that this was a secret project. It just wasn't publicized much."

Angela nodded knowingly, being well aware of similar procedures to lower the profile of sensitive work in the pharmaceutical industry.

"As you can see from the specs, the test couldn't have been better for us. High-burnup uranium-plutonium fuel, MOX they called it, in thin-walled steel canisters. These were emplaced in holes backfilled with cement grout...although, for the life of me, I can't think why. Anyway, the radiation field, temperature and pH readings from the first decade of monitoring data look spot on." The data streams were highlighted in 3-D color graphics.

"Things get a lot more difficult to follow in the '30s, although there was definitely some kind of accident. Reading between the lines of the few vague documents I've been able to excavate, I'd say some local flooding followed by the collapse of a monitoring tunnel. There were initially high radioactive noble gas measurements, so at least some of the spent fuel containers must have failed."

"Come on, Bruce," Angela interjected, "surely you're

not saying that a major accident in Europe's biggest repository was covered up?"

"At the time, it was a French repository. And, remember, it was the '30s. The French economy was falling apart and infrastructure was collapsing due to Greenhouse weather. Nuclear was booming but, more and more, with fourth generation reactors; small, modular, inherently-safe technology from the Far East rather than the old-fashioned, high energy-density monsters developed in France. The French government simply couldn't allow the investment in Bure to be lost. The accident was thus buried, both literally and metaphorically, in obscure archives and under a vast quantity of concrete. Just like the 1F storage caverns, when you're suffering from terminal cancer, leprosy and plague, the odd ingrown toenail doesn't receive a lot of attention."

"I'm not sure I'd class a leaky repository as an ingrown toenail," Angela commented dryly. "But, anyway, how do we get our samples?"

"That's the problem," Bruce conceded. "I don't have a clue as yet. I was hoping that you might have some ideas. You said before, in Glasgow, that you had looked at repositories."

Eva called up one of the pharm files and raised an eyebrow in Angela's direction. Following a nod of approval, she opened the file and sorted through the Bure subdirectory. "This was an option we examined in detail at the start of the project. Apart from anything else, it was convenient for our Basel team."

A similar 3-D layout of the repository appeared, which differed mainly in a color-coded mesh that had been superposed on the underground workings. "The monitoring network shown here includes all the water sampling lines: active in green, inactive in red and planned in yellow. We have contractors who could obtain material for us from any of these. After a bit of analysis, however, we decided that we wouldn't get much out of them."

"I can guess why," Bruce said. "Firstly, there is probably almost bugger-all water to sample. That clay is tight as the proverbial crab's arse. Secondly, any water sampled is probably only slightly alkaline, and I wouldn't be surprised to find a few acid waters due to pyrite oxidation. Finally, of course, the samples would contain only natural levels of radioactivity."

Eva smiled warmly and threw up a short study execsum. "Three out of three, not just a pretty face."

Bruce continued. "That clay-rock is just about completely impermeable. You'd wait millennia to pick up anything of interest. It's the usual shit, monitor where you know nothing will be seen, for PR purposes, and stay well away from the dodgy bits. Even with a bit a flooding, the spent fuel area will be almost as bad. Distant monitoring won't show anything at all. We need to core within centimeters of one of the waste packages. Ideally, a damaged one."

"Should I switch in the Basel team?" Eva asked. "They probably have a lot of local contacts."

"Maybe not yet," Bruce shot back. "As we learned

before, the fewer who know anything about this, the better."

"Okay, Bwana, what do we do now?" Engel piped-in as she fidgeted restlessly.

"I don't think this'll be a quick in-out like Fukushima. We'll probably have to spend some time locally to check out the situation on the ground. I'll chase up some names to get a site visit organized. Who's coming?"

All heads turned to Angela. "I've been thinking about this. Physically I may be in my thirties, but I'm not sure my old brain could take another jaunt like the last time. On the technical side, Eva can cover everything that I could contribute to this caper."

Bruce nodded in relief and was about to congratulate her on a wise decision, when she added, "However, I know that my calming influence could help prevent you from acting too rashly." She leaned to clip Engel playfully on the side of the head in response to her exaggerated roll of the eyes. "So, how about this for a compromise? We travel to Europe together and set up a local base of operations within striking distance of Bure. I stay out of any sampling work, but I'll be on hand to offer the fruits of my long and widespread experience."

Bruce thought for a moment, but couldn't see any reasonable objection to Angela's suggestion. "Okay, sounds good. I'll sort out somewhere in Switzerland."

"Anywhere," Engel added, "as long as it's not that dingy flat in Baden."

***

By the evening, Bruce had some of the logistical details sorted out. As they sat around the lounge, sipping a pre-prandial Fino and watching the sun set amid storm clouds over the distant remnants of the old naval dockyard, he outlined his suggestions.

"I think it would be easiest for me to go first. I'm well overdue checking out things at Hasliberg, anyway. It shouldn't take me more than a couple days to sort out some accommodation and secure transportation routes. If I leave tomorrow, we could be settled down in snowy Switzerland by the weekend."

"You'll need only internal transportation," Angela reminded him. "We can use secure pharm transportation as far as Basel."

Bruce tried to find a problem with this option, but was forced to concede the very fact they were now in a GRW safe house implied a certain minimal trust. As long as there were no internal leaks, it was certain that an international pharmaceutical giant could probably move people into Switzerland as quietly as he could.

"And, anyway," Angela continued, "why can't we all stay at your place at Hasliberg? It's big enough, isn't it?"

"Certainly, but not very convenient for France."

"As long as you're not worried about your housekeepers," Angela added, inexorably aware that she had now caught the attention of the two girls.

"Housekeepers? Housekeepers? What's all this about,

you dirty Beast? You've never mentioned anything of the sort to me," Engel claimed, storming to his chair and straddling one leg.

"You never asked," he responded hurriedly, struggling to change the drift of the discussion. "Montreux or Gstaad might be better, lots of rich celebs, so very, very tight."

"Stop waffling, lad." Angela was now in full matron mode. "A couple days should be enough for you to clean the place up a bit and hide the bimbos. I'm really looking forward to seeing your mountain abode."

Bruce could see when he was onto a loser and nodded. "Okay. Okay, no probs. In that case, there's no point hanging about. I'll pass on the pharm travel option and use the black money route via NY. That gives me..." a pause as he quickly flicked through a set of travel windows, "...a ten o'clock flight tomorrow morning."

***

After dinner, Bruce opted for an early night and headed off for his bedroom located on the ground floor. It formed a buffer between that used by Angela and the massive twin room shared by the girls. He had completed his evening ablutions and was wandering around in his birthday suit, making a pile of the few items he wanted to take with him to Switzerland. Suddenly, the door opened and Engel strode into the room.

"Okay, let's get this over with," she commanded, catching his hand and drawing him towards the bed.

Turning him to face her, she suddenly pushed hard with both hands against his chest, causing him to hit the back of his knees against the bed and crash onto the hard mattress with a loud grunt. Grinning, the small woman grabbed the hem of her flimsy sundress, pulled it over her head in a single, fluid movement and threw it casually to the floor. For a second she just stood naked in front of him, posing with hand on hip.

Despite his familiarity with Engel's body, any fresh glimpse of her hairless mons inevitably caused an intake of breath. She was so small and compact that she could be taken for a girl in her teens. *As long as I don't notice the calluses due to the armored implants in her hands, feet, elbows and knees. Or look into her eyes, which betrayed experience that could only be earned over decades.*

Engel placed her hands on his knees and somersaulted over his prone body to land in a kneeling position, with her armored knees digging painfully into his shoulders. "How about skipping the foreplay tonight..." Bruce started to suggest before she spread her knees and a rather sweaty quim dropped onto his face.

There's got to be worse ways to die.

He struggled to bring his hands to her waist. Tiny hands grabbed his and twisted, forcing him to grunt with the pain of the wristlocks.

I taught her that bloody lock.

"Okay, no more Mister Nice Guy," he warned, drew his head back, and gently set his teeth around the engorged fold of flesh on offer. A shock of pain drove his head into the mattress. "Ah, fuck," he screamed. "What the fuck're you playin' at? Would've served you fuckin' right if my teeth had clamped shut."

"Worry not, dear Beast," she murmured into his ear. "Based on extensive experimentation on Eva, I can tell you for sure that your mouth had to open, no matter how hard you tried to do otherwise."

Turning his head, he sunk his teeth into his torturer's inner thigh. His head slammed back into the bed. "Fuck."

"Told you so," she whispered smugly. "Have I ever told you that you're so Scottish when you're angry?"

With a mental shrug, Bruce decided to make the best of his present position. First he restricted himself to slowly moving his head back and forward, rubbing his nose along the sides of an increasingly wet cleft and starting to circle the hard, pink button emerging at its upper end.

Gently does it, one false move and she'll pull my bloody arms off.

Following a couple of almost subliminal moans, which issued from deep in her throat, Bruce cautiously leaned his head further back and started to work with his tongue. The outer lips were salty with sweat but, deeper within, a richer more organic taste greeted him. *A bit like nectar,* he thought reverently before sticking his tongue as far inside her as it would reach. Her hips slowly began to grind from side to side and he sucked rich flesh into his mouth, squeezing gently with his teeth while strobing the end of his tongue over her rigid clitoris.

The moans were deeper now and almost continuous.

Two options now, I either take advantage of her present state to reverse the wristlock or just go with the flow.

Resisting the temptation to score silly macho points, he gently drew his hands free of her grip and slid them between her legs to increase his options for stimulating her.

Several minutes of fingers and tongue and she was squirming uncontrollably on his face. Grabbing her thighs, he lifted her into the air and, ignoring her cries for him not to stop, rolled over to drop her onto her back, forcing her legs towards her head, and then pushing her knees down until they were almost touching her ears.

Plough, yoga sleep position, he noted as he moved down again between her legs. *If this is a sleep position, then it's no wonder they ended up with some bizarre contortions in the Kama Sutra.*

While he was repositioning her body, Engel seemed to have calmed down a bit, but she now responded instantaneously to the slightest touch of her flesh. With tongue, nose, lips, teeth and fingers, sometimes gently stroking, sometimes roughly penetrating, he brought her repeatedly to the brink, but stopped in every case before she found her peak.

She tried to reach in with her hands, but he forced them back. Now she was begging, "Go, go, go, you bastard. Cunt. Fucker."

He drew away and whispered, "You sure do know how to sweet-talk a man," then dropped back and gave Engel the *Full Monty,* ramming fingers roughly into both orifices while mauling rubbery flesh with teeth and tongue.

In contrast to the noise earlier, Engel was now almost silent, her neck arched and mouth open in a soundless scream. Her entire body trembled, and her breathing became a rapid sequence of inelegant grunts.

Her body went completely rigid for about ten seconds, and then she whipped her legs up to lock his head between her thighs. "Mmm, mmm, enough, stop," she murmured.

He grabbed her thighs to ease the pressure on his ears, but continued to lick as hard as he could. "No, no, oh...yes," she screamed while she writhed like an eel. Orgasm after orgasm wracked her frame as he fought to keep a hold of her sweat-slick body. Finally, she managed to wrench free of his face and throw herself, panting, on the bed. "Enough now, Beast." She commanded. "Stop. Heel."

"Heels are fine with me." He grabbed her feet and twisted her onto her back, and then held her legs wide open. "My turn now." He lunged forward and thrust his penis into her gaping vagina.

For such a small woman, there was no shortage of space. Cavernous: a cavern brimming with warm liquid honey. His thrusts made wet slurping sounds as she raised herself up to push against him. He tried to find a rhythm. Lack of friction was causing him to soften, forcing him to thrust faster and faster to maintain his erection.

Suddenly her fingers had joined his penis, and

maintaining hardness was no longer a problem. He was now straining to hold back an orgasm that was causing his body to shake. He looked down to see a pair of bottomless blue eyes, which opened wide as she bit his left nipple. The next thrust pushed as deep as possible and seized into rigidity while he came in a series of contractions that originated deep within his pelvis.

Spent, he released the grip on her ankles and sank slowly on top of the girl, amazed that someone so slight could support his weight so easily. He rolled onto his back, pulling her with him onto his chest.

She curved her back, poked two pointy elbows into his chest, and laid her chin in her hands. "That's not bad for a start," she purred. "I have decided to shag you into the deck, just to make sure you don't get into any mischief with these fuckin' housemaids of yours. Ready for round two?"

"Sorry, I'll have to take a rain-check on that. I doubt you could raise my erection with a lorry-load of chocolate-covered lesbians."

"Trust in me, trust in me," she hissed. "Lots of orifices to try yet. Every single one a guaranteed winner."

***

About a half hour later, as she prepared to leave, a sore and totally exhausted Bruce had to admit that she had been absolutely correct.

She turned at the door. "So, you're off in the morning?"

"Yup. And all being equal, I'll fit in a day or two skiing, as well."

"Break a leg," she sang before switching off the light and closing the door.

Well, that's it; we're committed to getting the show on the road. Hopefully our sponsor's retaliation for the bombing of the Glasgow Uni research center will ensure that our opponents don't consider such extreme measures again. But the prize, and potential threats, are so huge that I'm sure there are some operators who won't be deterred. We're doing it for Eva, but last time we were badly mauled. Can we really be sure that any benefit will be worth the risk?

2 ...I'm so lucky

Standing at the edge of the drop-off from the summit of Vrenelisgärtli, Bruce was not sure this run was a good idea. Riding up in the chopper, with the first touches of winter sun painting a pink blush on the peaks of the Glärner Alps, he figured the runs mapped out seemed straightforward. *If anything, maybe a bit tame.*

First break in the weather after at least a meter of new snow revealed everything was covered by a smooth carpet of perfect white. Glarus itself was buried under five meters, even though it was only the middle of December. He was sure that there must have been a good ten meters of base below the latest powder here at the top.

Bruce keyed in his helmet display and watched the descent route ghost itself over the view in front of his face. He shuffled forward another few centimeters, aware that at least a third of his two-sixty skis was now hanging over empty space. Glancing quickly to his right, he caught a glimpse of Tom, also tottering on the brink but with an idiotic grin on his face. As Tom snapped his poles together, the lead-in to *Selling Jesus* blasted through Bruce's helmet and he jumped over the edge even as his balls attempted to opt out of this obviously insane act of suicide. A second of confusion as his mind and gonads rebelled, but the rest of his body was already committed, and then the adrenaline rush let the old, reptilian brain structures, where unthinking animal reflexes resided, take over completely.

A couple of meters of free fall and then the fat, isomorphic-cermet skis ploughed into the bottomless powder and threw him back to the surface of the fifty degree gradient slope in an explosion of white. Even in zero visibility, an artificial horizon and target route glowed in three dimensions within his faceplate, but Bruce's body was already carving the first turn based only on the clues provided by gravity and wind-rush. He flew into clear air for a second, only to disappear again into the cloud thrown up by Tom's skis.

A second turn blind, a third in dazzling clear air, and then speed and gradient – helped a lot by his long fat skis – combined to catapult him onto the light crust the wind had formed on the deep powder. Turns were now getting harder as velocity increased as Bruce powered down the fall line. While the Doppler readout in the corner of his vision blurred towards seventy k, the volume of the Skunk Anansie track ramped up towards eardrum-bursting levels. Despite this wall of sound, the rumble accompanying Bruce's tenth turn could not be missed; not so much registering in his ears, but more through his spine.

Bruce vaguely recognized the sick feeling of his withdrawn testicles trying to find refuge in his throat.

"Only part of my body with any sort of sense," he subvocalized while dropping into a racing crouch and arrowing in the direction indicated in his helm by a wide red flashing path extending towards a crag on his left.

Small irregularities in the slope were now battering the base of his skis, sending shocks of pain through his knees and threatening to throw him off his escape line. Suddenly it felt as if a couple of flat hands had been placed on his buttocks – pushing him forward with a force that threatened to tip him on his face.

If this's just the leading edge of the avalanche shockwave, then it's a real monster.

Screaming pain in his legs seemed much less important now; Bruce's focus was entirely on forcing his body into the most aerodynamic crouch possible.

Now, not only was the air thickening around him, but turbulent blasts were pushing from both sides, and the snow below his feet vibrated. Just at the instant when it seemed certain he would lose it, all pressure disappeared as he raced past the edge of the avalanche and into the lee of a massive crag. Hardly daring to breathe, he gently leaned into a gradual turn to lose some of the murderous speed he had built up.

Although the numbers were slowly dropping now, a glowing max of 102.5 kph was still hovering at the edge of his vision. "Fuck me." He breathed.

More than ten k over my best ever, a boot in bum by a powder snow avalanche will do that.

He slowly eased a little out of his crouch, allowing air

resistance to add to the breaking effect of the curve that was now taking him into a traverse across the slope. A wide turn in a spray of sparkling wake brought Bruce round to face the wall of white that showed the path of the avalanche he had so narrowly escaped. A sigh of satisfaction was cut off by an explosion, which managed to penetrate even the volume of the Skunk Anansie track.

Glancing upwards – a risky maneuver in itself at his present speed – Bruce froze at the sight of the top of his protective crag falling towards him in a riot of rocks, trees and blocks of ice.

"Fuck, fuck, fuck, fuck, fuck..." he screamed while he forced his aching legs into the tightest turn possible. The speedo, which had bottomed out at sixty, began to climb upwards as Bruce dropped back close to the fall line. More worryingly, however, the optimal route arrow had vanished.

The shelter of the crag was my programmed escape zone and the option of the fucking thing falling down wasn´t a scenario we considered when planning this jaunt.

Even though this slope was not much more than about thirty degrees, Bruce's speed was ramping up rapidly, but not rapidly enough to get him out of the way of the icefall rushing his direction.

He leaned hard left with a force that made both knees pop and sent a shock of pain throughout his entire body. He was now heading directly for the trees that filled a gully at the edge of the otherwise bare slope. The logical part of his brain was screaming: *Trees. Not good. Not good.*

Regardless, his body clearly considered trees a softer option than bloody big rocks.

The shockwave from the second avalanche-cum-rock-fall was just beginning to push him to the side when Bruce rocketed between two trees, hit a bump that sent him into the air, and then smashed through foliage. With the first hard impact, his suit went rigid as the smart alloy mesh lost its plasticity. He saw rather than felt the skis snap from their bindings and spin off in opposite directions. Emergency mode killed the music system, so he could now hear the sounds of breaking branches over the roar of the rock-fall. He was still well above the ground when a wall of snow hit and everything went black.

***

Bruce became aware that he was drifting in and out of consciousness. For a while he was too dazed to really be sure of what was happening, but gradually memory returned, along with the feeling of cold and the beginning of panic in the claustrophobic darkness. "Light," he called and was rewarded by a faint white glow from the instruments within his helmet. As far as he could see, his faceplate was intact and the air still seemed fresh.

His breathing slowed a little as relief began to soak in.

My ski kit's cutting edge but, in an avalanche, even the toughest body armor can get completely shredded. As long as I'm in one piece and have air, though, all I need to do is wait to be dug out.

"Status," started the systems review. Scrolling text

was typically precise about things he already knew: suit; rigid phase, L ski; missing, R ski; missing, L pole; missing, R pole; missing... The critical burial data block was, however, absolute gobbledygook: dbs; <0m, snow hardness; oor, air content; oor…

Due to the rockfall that initiated the avalanche and the trees in the gully, I'd expect some out-of-range readings. But the depth-below-surface of less than zero clearly indicates that the entire sensor system's totally screwed-up.

At the end of the review came a list of modules not available – either non-functional or not installed. First of these was *Medrep*, reminding him that he had decided against the emergency medical analysis option.

It's not just a matter of cost; I just couldn't imagine when I'd need such a thing. Either you're reasonably okay and you don't need an expensive kit to confirm this – or you're knackered in some way, which is best left to some medic to sort out.

Bruce closed his eyes and tried to localize the pains that were beginning to penetrate the wall established by initial shock.

Left ankle, well no surprise there, it takes a lot of force to spring those bindings. Ribs, left shoulder – again to be expected, as I'd have had to hit hard to initiate the suit phase change. Last, but by no means least, the beginnings of a brutal headache. Can't expect to hit trees at about eighty k without being shaken up a lot. There's only so much that an armored suit can do.

No sense in being a martyr. "Painkiller, medium strength." A dermal patch released the drug into his neck. Within a few seconds, the pains began to fade.

Bugger waiting; let's just see what kind of state I'm in.

Although not recommended and hence not audio-cued, he searched with his chin until he found the lever that would send a current through his suit's armor layer, causing it to regain plasticity. "I just hope that I don't have a fuck'n ton of rock lying on me," he muttered before he pushed the lever.

His body sagged immediately and something jammed painfully into his side. He almost pushed again to reset the suit but noticed the change in light penetrating his visor. Cracks of searing whiteness appeared, bright enough to cause the plastic to darken. Carefully, he shook his head and most of the snow caking the faceplate broke loose.

Reflexively, Bruce grabbed at the branch that appeared in front of his face. Rather than being well buried, he was wedged in the fork of a tree about fifteen meters above the ground. Snow and rocks had caused a lot of superficial damage to foliage, but the sturdy conifer had weathered the avalanche well.

Forcing his left hand to loosen its grip, he wiped the last traces of snow from his visor and looked around. He was well down the gully, in the middle of a thirty-meter wide swath of debris. A haze of light powder still remained in the air and rushes of secondary snowfalls from the heavily laden trees to either side of the avalanche path were occurring at irregular intervals.

Although it hadn't helped me at the time, a dbs less than zero is, in fact, technically correct, Bruce conceded with a wry grin.

He nudged the *heads-up* switch in the panel beside his chin and flicked though the menu until his path record appeared. The smooth curves of the ski run broke into the jumble of his descent into the gully. The timer, which was still running, logged his time at his present position as just under five minutes. *Must have been unconscious for about three minutes,* but he admitted to himself that he really had no way of judging just how long he had spent simply paralyzed with fear in the dark.

Anyway, now that I know that I'm okay, where the hell's Tom?

A quick scroll through the coms menu showed that his buddy was still in default send-only mode. As Bruce accessed the signal, he was rewarded by the sound of panting breaths and grunts of pain. Despite his situation, Bruce couldn't help smiling; from anyone else, he would consider such sound worrying, but he had heard Tom skiing before and knew that this indicated only that he was still racing to be first to the Heli-pickup at the bottom of their planned run.

Less than a minute later, with a triumphal, "Yes," the comm opened up. "Leader of the pack calling all laggards and layabouts. Anyone out there? Are you just resting your lazy ass or should I send someone up to dig you out?"

With a reluctant sigh Bruce confirmed he was okay and described his situation to his increasingly amused pal.

"Up a bloody tree? At least you don't have to worry

about getting eaten by bears," Tom responded cheerfully.

Bruce considered reminding his American buddy that there were no bears in Switzerland – and damned few in North America for that matter – but decided that it would probably just encourage him to take the piss.

In any case, couldn't most bears climb trees?

"What about sending the Heli up to get me?"

"Ah...there's the rub. The wind's getting up and the tourist choppers are grounded, but they'll probably do a rescue. Should I send one up?"

"No way," Bruce shouted. "Do you know what a rescue costs?" A rhetorical question, as anyone attempting x-sports was repeatedly warned: all accident insurance was void as soon as they even kitted up for a rescue. It wasn't just that the rescue would be incredibly expensive, there would also be no attempt to recover a top-of-the-range pair of skis, which should have been lying about somewhere in the vicinity.

"Okay," Bruce continued. "I'll get myself out of this tree and call you back with a sitrep within a half hour or so. You could get yourself some breakfast in the interim."

"Nul problem," came the unconcerned reply. "I'm already en route to that restaurant where we left the buggy, Adler I think it was. Maybe see you there soon."

Shit, maybe that was a bit rash. Too much instant macho response and not enough thinking things through. "I've got a rendezvous," Bruce murmured to himself. "And still don't know how to get down from this fuckin' tree."

Realizing that he hadn't really emphasized to Tom

quite how high up he was, Bruce admitted that he only had himself to blame. He was starting to think about how Tom would respond to the helmcam shots when it occurred to him that he was just trying to divert himself from his real problem.

Well then, think about this as a technical challenge, he commanded himself. *Idiot stuck up bloody tree...about fifteen meters of smooth trunk of fifty centimeter diameter between said idiot and rock-strewn avalanche debris.*

Two obvious solutions – jump down or climb down. The former would certainly be easiest and his suit armor would certainly help protect against injuries.

Even then, there's a limit to what its rigidity can do, so landing on a hard surface from my present height isn't going to be pleasant. On the other hand, if I land on a very soft bit, I could be easily buried deeper than I can dig myself out. Then I'd certainly need a rescue. And that could take a while if the wind is getting up.

Climb down then.

Looking to the ground, he could feel his grip involuntarily tighten. A minute of silent contemplation and then he gave his helmet a token bump off the trunk in front of his face. Finally, his neurons powered up.

He was wedged in the fork of some kind of conifer. Above the fork, branches were spaced at regular intervals, including the one he clung to. Below the fork there were only a few stumps and even these were confined to the upper couple meters.

Releasing one hand after another, he reached down

and pulled the levers on his boots that released the inbuilt crampons. *Just as well I'm wearing touring boots rather than on-piste kit*.

Using voice commands to work through the options available, he overrode the settings and placed the suit in deep burial mode. This would be needed for the normal case of being hit by an avalanche. From the menu, he selected *dig* and added *enhance,* which activated a muscle performance stimulation derm behind his neck.

After a considerable amount of wriggling about, he managed to get his left leg into position to kick the toe spikes into the tree trunk. The ceramic spikes easily penetrated full length into the wood. Gingerly, he transferred his weight onto this foot and lifted himself from the fork of the tree. First left, then right, he released his grip on the branch and hugged the leftmost trunk above the fork. The fingertips of his gauntlets were shaped for digging snow but gripped the trunk securely. A further series of awkward twists and then he was able to kick his right boot solidly home.

"Left hand down, right hand down, left foot down, right foot down," he commanded sub-vocally. His body was not convinced, however, and remained motionless. Bruce could feel sweat sting his eyes and trickle from his armpits. Within a minute he could feel his knees begin to tremble and, defeated, sank his weight back into the crotch of the tree.

"Fucking Jesus Christ all bastarding mighty." Then, realizing that Tom may be listening in, added, "a little prayer does help."

More than prayer was needed here, he concluded and, with a sigh, used the voice commands to return to the deep buried mode and selected the flashing red *sissy* option. Intended for anyone who, not unreasonably, panicked as a response to being buried by an avalanche, this activated a dermal patch containing an extremely strong tranquilizer. By definition, anybody sensible enough to panic under such circumstances would be unlikely to go avalanche skiing in the first place – hence the derogatory label. Just to ensure that it could not be missed, this option immediately displayed SISSY in lurid pink letters across the brow of his helmet. Despite his precarious situation, he dreaded the slagging-off he was going to get from Tom.

Maybe jumping would have been the better option after all.

This concern melted away as the trank hit and a feeling of relaxation and contentment washed over his body like a cool shower.

Watch it. This stuff's intended for keeping you calm while immobile, not for acrobatics in the treetops.

Regardless, he happily lifted himself free of the fork and clambered a few steps higher to position himself for the descent.

"Left, right, left, right..." he chanted cheerfully while he stepped downwards, completely unbothered by even the small slips that often resulted from the shaking movements needed to release the toes of his boots from the soft wood.

Maybe it'd be better to try to kick more gently. The spikes're certainly strong enough to support me on a fraction of their length.

Sure enough, a couple of steps went much easier. On his third step, however, he felt his upper boot pull loose and jerk him backwards into free air.

Contact with the ground was almost instantaneous. He lay unmoving while the mild shock passed through his chemically damped senses. In some hidden corner of his mind where logic was still operational he cursed the trank.

The spikes would certainly hold my weight on a fraction of their length in rock-hard ice – but not in bloody wood. Just as well, I was almost on the ground before I started mucking about.

The spacey feeling of confidence and happiness was just too dangerous for the present. He rolled onto his stomach and clambered unsteadily to his feet on the rough, sloping surface. The snow had set rock-hard and the crampons sank only halfway into a surface layer of powder.

That's one question answered.

He unlocked his visor, screwed up his eyes at the blast of unfiltered whiteness and took a few deep breaths. Pulling off his right glove, he noticed that the hardened fingers of both gauntlets were coated with sticky sap. He un-zipped a breast pocket and drew out a flat wallet. From the range of pharms present, he selected a small pink rhomboid of sissy-nullifier and swallowed it with a gulp.

As with many fast-acting nullifiers, its action seemed to concentrate the effects of whatever the primary pharm buffered against. The effect was known as *the law of conservation of hangovers* as a result of the some of the very earliest nullifiers, which focused on alcohol. As the drug kicked in, Bruce started to shake as a wave of pure terror hit. He retched once, and threw up on the snow – thankful indeed that he had opened his visor. He fought against a bladder that threatened to burst. "No, no, no," he grunted with gritted teeth.

Enough of this bloody message on my helmet, no way am I going to piss myself into the bargain.

After frantically unzipping his fly and prying out his dick, Bruce pointed at the tree that he had just descended and christened it with a steaming stream of urine. Leaning with one hand against the trunk for support, he sighed in relief, this simple pleasure momentarily drowning out the other miseries of the nullifier.

Quickly shaken dry, he rushed to zip up.

It's too bloody cold to leave flesh exposed to the elements.

Although the gully was sheltered from the wind, loose powder blew overhead, indicating the wind was indeed getting up as promised.

Closing his visor, he called up the search routine. A map of the gully centered on his present position showed both skis below him, a pole somewhere to his left as he looked uphill, and the other pole at the very top of the gully.

How the hell did it get there? In any case best sacrificed, he concluded, painfully aware that his strength-enhancer would keep him going only for a limited time and that he would be completely drained when it wore off.

***

The first pole was no problem; its tip actually protruded from the snow within twenty meters of his present position. Using this for additional support, he started to follow the avalanche route downwards, fighting his way through tangles of branches and occasionally sinking waist deep into powder that had been sheltered from the main flow. After fifteen minutes of slow progress, he spotted a line of yellow ribbon indicating the presence of a ski. Dragging on the ribbon produced no result, so he was forced to dig for a further ten minutes to locate it wedged under an exposed root. The long fat ski proved to be more of a hindrance than a help in the tangled undergrowth, so Bruce finally settled for dragging it while he descended the gully farther. His remaining ski was easy to find - sitting on a surface of undisturbed powder on the gully side, above the avalanche track. Even though it was only ten meters or so, pushing up the steep slope through the waist-deep powder left Bruce panting.

The bloody enhancer is definitely beginning to wear off.

The effort of clearing an area where he could adjust the skis and lock them onto his boots reduced him to a panting wreck.

Thank God at least it's dry powder.

He retracted the crampons.

I doubt that I've the strength for the additional faffing about that would be needed to clean off sticky snow.

Although designed primarily for high-speed descent, the skis also included full touring mode. Pushing one lever altered the fabric of the base while a second released the heel of the binding. Wishing now that he had a second pole, Bruce cautiously started to work his way along a contour that would take him to the rim of the steeply dipping gully. The monster skis did a good job of keeping him on top of the powder but made zigzagging around the trees and rocks dotting the slope a frustrating and tiring job.

Slogging along with his attention concentrated on finding an optimal route through increasingly dense trees, he became aware of his proximity to the rim only when the fall of light powder took on a more horizontal direction.

The good news is that I'm almost clear of the trees; the bad news that the wind's now much stronger and the sun's only a diffused glow behind a blizzard of light powder.

Only then did he notice how much duller it had become – finally realizing that his visor had gradually turned from an initial polarizing grey to a light yellow, which maximized contrast in low visibility conditions.

A few more minutes of struggling and Bruce was clear of the trees completely, now huddling below the crest of the ridge to keep out of the wind. He felt completely drained and the stink of ammoniacal sweat stung his nose. A fruitless suck on the nipple within his helmet then confirmed that his pouch of isotonic drink was empty.

As he pondered his options, Tom's cheerful voice broke in, "What Ho, Snow Bunny. How goes it? Still sitting up in a tree?"

Bruce glanced at the elapsed time readout. "About bloody time. Call this a half-hour? I could have died of exposure in the last sixty minutes."

"Don't be wet. Anyway, you're always telling me that only the good die young. In which case, you've got decades to go..." There was a pause before Tom continued, "...and there was this really cute waitress..."

"I don't believe this, I'm fighting for my life and you're chasing totty. I bet you didn't even check if she had a cute friend for me, you inconsiderate bugger."

"I didn't think you'd be needing the friend, dying of exposure as you are. Actually, while I think of it, what's keeping your flabby ass up that hill? Now that I've had my breakfast, thoughts are turning to a pre-lunch pint."

Insult added to injury. Bruce groaned, aware that his mouth was bone dry and the thought of a beer just made things worse.

He drew himself up and felt his spine crack.

This conversation is just what's needed to drive on a competitive, macho type of idiot. Just like me.

He grimaced then locked his bindings, set the base of his skis to downhill texture, and pushed himself into a traverse that brought him face-on into the howling wind.

"What was that, Bruce baby, you okay?" For the first time there was a slight air of concern evident in the American's voice.

"Absolutely perfect." Bruce lied. "Be with you in a trice. You can get in a pint for me."

***

Visibility was almost nil when Bruce turned closer to the fall line to compensate for the braking effect of the wind, which was blowing even harder now that he was on the fully exposed slope. With great care, he carved his first turn and almost fell forward as the blizzard kicked him in the back. His knees creaked as he crouched and rose into the second turn, hitting a wall of snow that seemed to have the consistency of treacle.

After a half dozen turns, the fear of falling – or, more accurately, the fear of the effort required to recover from a fall – began to fade. The fire in his calves and thighs drove exhaustion aside, and he was actually enjoying the run.

Fantastic equipment is all very well, but there's something primeval about this kind of pure survival skiing. The key's simply to stay upright and get downhill with minimum effort. The heads-up map certainly makes navigation easy in this high mountain terrain, but the body has to be capable of responding automatically to the constant changes in slope and snow texture. I can do this.

A long traverse with the wind at his back allowed him to review his options. Below was a steep, forested slope that would take him directly to his goal. Alternatively, traversing farther would take him to a wide, gentle slope that would bring him down to the valley bottom, but require a trek of a kilometer or so to the restaurant.

Coming to a halt, he checked the forest option at

higher resolution. A wide firebreak ran down for about five hundred vertical meters, dropping onto a forestry road that gently wound down directly to the Adler.

Absolutely perfect, if not for the fact that my knees are already shaking with exhaustion and the various pains that I've tried to forget are getting worse.

His left foot, in particular, was throbbing ominously.

Two clear options: a strong painkiller and another mild performance enhancer and then down the easy slope or a max enhancer, gritted teeth and the forest. Whatever, both options require manual over-ride of the safeties that prevent dangerous cumulative use of such strong drugs.

"In for a penny..." Bruce muttered before selecting the max enhancer. This would certainly deaden pain responses a little but, due to the danger of causing severe damage to already stressed joints, it would be crazy to combine it with any more analgesic.

Within thirty seconds, the full effect had kicked in and he felt ready to go. He tried to ignore the pain associated with his first turn as he carved downhill towards the ride. As he passed between the walls of trees lining the firebreak, the wind dropped completely and visibility improved markedly. The slope was steep but the firebreak was wide, giving the impression of a ski piste.

Down – up and turn – traverse, down – up and turn – traverse, down – up and turn – traverse…

He carved down the slope in a series of wide turns that used the full width available. The plumes of powder thrown up by each turn formed a cloud that he sailed into two turns later.

Down – up and turn – traverse, down – up and turn – traverse.

The movements were hypnotic and helped him to ignore the gradually increasing pain associated with each turn.

Down – up and turn – traverse and fuck! Into midair?

Only now did he notice a drop of about five meters onto the forestry road.

"Skis together, tips up," he had time to mutter before he thumped into deep powder with a shock of pain that almost made him sick. Although almost sure that there was no way that he could stay upright, the powder he landed in was a little heavier, providing the support that allowed him to fight his way to a teetering balance as he burst through a cloud of snow and forced a turn to avoid shooting off the edge of the roadway.

A sigh of relief before he carved the first turn of the road's switchback descent turned into a gasp of pain when he dropped into a crouch to fit under a tree that was leaning across the road. "Keep it together, you dozy bugger." Bruce cursed himself under his breath.

Even a road descent under these conditions is tricky enough to give me serious problems if I lose concentration for even a second.

Even though the gradient was now less than ten percent, the fat skis kept him moving fast over the light crust on the fresh powder. To minimize effort, Bruce stood up during straight runs, so that air braking kept his speed under control. He carved turns to follow bends in the road, using the profile of the skis to do most of the work. Despite this, he had to make rapid turns to find gaps under two further leaning trees and struggled to land from an inadvertent jump caused by a tree that must have fallen before the last snow. The pain from his ankle ramped up with each of these maneuvers and he was aware that his teeth were so tightly clenched that they ground together with every jolt of his body.

Finally, he carved a turn into a wall of blowing snow. He had now cleared the woods and had about a kilometer more of road as it snaked down to the valley floor.

I could shorten the distance a bit by leaving the roadway and cutting directly towards the guesthouse. But, by now, the pain's so intense that I don't dare attempt anything associated with an increased risk of falling. The road is the devil I know; there could be any kind of shit that could give problems with a short-cut under such low visibility conditions.

It transpired that even finding the track of the road would have been tricky in some places without the map that ghosted over his visor. Despite that, the absence of the hurdles of fallen trees allowed Bruce to let his speed creep up so that it took less than a minute until he had started on a final straight schuss, which would take him directly to the Adler car park. Through the haze of pain he had the satisfaction of noting that this had been a perfect descent route, which should take him directly to the door of the restaurant.

The road ended in a wall of snow that had been

ploughed from the car park. Bruce curved onto the rim of this wall and slid down onto the packed snow within. The park had space for at least a couple of dozen vehicles, but only three were present, sitting diagonally opposite, close to the Gästehaus entrance. He skimmed gently to the green six-wheel-drive van, which towered over the other two cars, and snow-ploughed to a halt. With a grunt of relief, he dropped his single pole on the ground and bent wearily to release his bindings.

Stepping out of the skis, he almost fell to the ground when a shock of agony shot up his left leg. "Painkiller max," he grunted as he swayed in place, supporting himself with two hands clinging to the roof-rail of the van. Nothing happened; even the over-rides would not allow the auto-dispensers to administer more drugs. With a grunt, he struggled to pull the small wallet from his pocket and then removed a red pill. As he dry-swallowed it, the sickening pain subsided rapidly, but a remnant throb from the vicinity of his left ankle refused to vanish.

Not a good sign.

He limped towards the door of the restaurant.

***

The front door led into a brightly lit hallway with a row of coat-hooks on the left wall, a long shelf on the right and a large umbrella stand. Bruce recognized Tom's ski poles as the sole contents of the stand. He unlatched his helmet, lifted it off and, grimacing at the message it presented, placed it carefully on the shelf, facing inwards.

Pulling off his gloves and clipping them onto rings at his hips, he then limped through the folds of a heavy leather curtain into the restaurant.

It was a typical mountain Gästehaus, a cavernous room paneled in dark wood and sporting all kinds of kitschy decorations: cow bells, wooden skis, backpacks for carrying cheese, ancient posters advertising Swiss resorts... One wall was covered entirely with pennants, bells, medals and assorted pewter-ware won by the local Jodelverein. In a far corner, two ancient worthies sat at a circular Stammtisch, deep in conversation with a matronly waitress. Despite reasonable familiarity with Swiss-German, Bruce could understand not a single word of the broad dialect spoken.

Tom was sitting at the nearest table, his suit unzipped and unpeeled to the waist, legs were stretched out with his boots propped up on his helmet and gloves. He lifted a half-full beer mug in greeting, "Well, well, well, the Snowman cometh. What took you so long? I was just about to start on your pint." He pointed at a full glass opposite with a distinctly flat head.

Bruce sank onto a padded bench with a grunt of relief, lifted the beer to his parched lips, and downed most of the contents in a single, slow swallow. As the cold liquid reached his stomach, the reality of the end of his ordeal crystallized and caused him to slump back in his seat. "Now that might be just about the best beer I've ever tasted."

"Good God, you must be in a bad way...it's bloody

Calenda. Anyway, I'm dying to hear all your excuses for having messed up an absolutely classic run. I'll get in another couple of beers and something to nibble on."

"Another beer and a couple packets of something salty would be a good idea," Bruce conceded. "You'll love my story, but we'll postpone details until later. I think I should pop into a hospital asap to get my leg looked at." He stopped, sat forward and let out a loud belch.

"One effective way of catching the serving wench's attention," Tom noted as he waved in the direction of the three locals who had all turned at the noise. "Let me order and then you can tell me all about your tree climbing exploits."

Over the next half hour, Bruce outlined the basics of his adventures – playing up the difficulties involved and failing to mention the horrendous cocktail of drugs that he had consumed.

Tom clearly considered that the source of the entire sequence of problems was Bruce's initial route selection, breaking left rather than the option to the right favored by himself, so he was not very sympathetic. Bruce's argument that Tom was the one who had originally programed the left route met little sympathy. "Can't put your trust in tools, old chap, got to go with that mountain-man instinct."

Bruce, as last down the mountain, picked up the tab and, with a wave in the direction of Stammtisch, limped after Tom through the curtain towards the door. With a gasp of horror, he noted that Tom was reaching to lift the lone helmet from the shelf. "It's okay, I'll get..." Bruce started, but it was already too late.

As Tom turned the helmet and caught sight of the lurid message, he dropped theatrically to his knees, punching the air in delight. "Yes. Yes, yes, yes. Oh, you are not going to be able to bullshit your way out of this, Bruce baby. I'll just hold on to this until we can get the helmcam download; wouldn't want any details to be accidentally scrubbed, would we?"

God, can I cram any more mishaps into a single day?

Bruce groaned.

Tom held the door and waved Bruce through, chuckling loudly. Bruce rolled his eyes and hobbled towards the van. The wind was now gale-force and it was snowing heavily. Bruce threw skis and pole into the back of the van through the side door while Tom unzipped his suit-top completely, pulled off his boots and placed them in the back of the passenger cabin, alongside his gauntlets and both helmets. Bruce was in the process of climbing awkwardly onto the passenger side of the front bench when Tom finished closing the Velcro on his trainers and powered up the wagon.

Bruce had restricted himself so far to opening the front of his suit, despite the warmth of the restaurant. In the cab of the van, although it was not much cooler; he found himself shivering and zipped it to his neck. His foot was passing again from discomfort to sharp pain and he decided against even attempting to remove his boots.

The view through the front windscreen was limited

to the warp-drive of snow flowing hypnotically into the headlights until the active radar kicked in. In combination with the GPS, a false-color outline of their view in the absence of a blizzard ghosted on top of reality, allowing Tom to drive out of the park and turn left onto the deserted road, following the instructions for Glarus Kantonsspital as indicated in lurid green text at the top of the screen.

They drove in silence for a kilometer or so, until they joined a larger road and started to see other cars. *Auto Available* now flashed in the middle of the screen and Tom immediately flicked the autopilot switch on the left side of the steering wheel and then sat back with a sigh. As the auto engaged, the com unit began to chirrup.

Bruce pressed the flashing red button. "You have one message," it announced, some bleeping and then Engel's voice burst out. "What ho, Beast. Have you finished playing about in the snow yet? We've just arrived in Hasliberg. How about getting your hairy arse here, pronto?"

Bruce groaned as Tom looked at him with caricature wide eyes. "Don't ask," he muttered. "This is just proof that disasters come in threes." He sank back with a sigh, closed his eyes and tried to use yoga breathing exercises to reduce the waves of agony pulsing from his leg.

I realize this jaunt could be dangerous, but I didn't think my troubles would start so soon. Surely this isn't a bad omen...

That was his last thought before he lost consciousness.

3 ...Missundastood

Bruce woke gradually – less waking, more slowly drifting towards consciousness. He opened sticky eyes and strained to focus on almost featureless white surroundings. He was lying in a high bed and seemed to be wearing some kind of white nightgown.

This is really weird; I never wear anything in bed.

He took a deep breath and felt a twinge of pain from around his ribcage. He twisted a little to try to raise his shoulders from the mattress but felt the restricted movement of his left leg. Craning his neck to look downwards, he could see that his leg was lifted at an angle of about thirty degrees from the vertical. He closed his eyes.

Can't really feel anything definite below the waist, except maybe a vague throbbing from my left heel. Also, I don't have my usual early-morning, full-bladder hard-on.

Over the next quarter of an hour, memories of the ski run from hell gradually began to return. At first it seemed more like remembering a dream but, as the details filled in, he had to admit to himself that this was just wishful thinking.

I'm really not looking forward to finding out how Tom's

going to publicize my ignominious performance. The bloody helmet with SISSY all over it is probably hanging on the wall of some pub by now. Fuck.

His reverie was disturbed by the sound of a door opening. Pushing himself weakly onto his elbows, he glanced around the rather bland white room. He was facing a blank wall that contained only a large display panel showing only a faint profile of what could be a snow-scape by moonlight. The entire left wall was a continuous cream curtain and the right was featureless, with the exception of the door.

An attractive, chocolate-colored woman wearing a white uniform entered. *Asian, maybe Indian or Pakistani.* As she approached the bed, he looked closely at her smiling face. *Maybe a bit of racial mixing helped to form her fine, delicate features – not just pretty, actually very beautiful.*

"Good afternoon, Doctor Roberts. My name is Naomi. How are you feeling now?" she inquired in perfect BBC English.

"Not too bad, considering," Bruce croaked, noticing for the first time his dry throat. "Would it be possible to get a drink of water?"

"Of course." She reached forward to pour water from a flask into a glass. As Bruce twisted to follow her movement, he spotted that his watch was sitting beside the glass on a previously unnoticed table, which sat level with his right ear.

The nurse moved her left hand out of his range of vision and the back of his bed began to rise up with a soft humming noise. He sank back when it reached an angle of about sixty degrees, took the frosted glass gratefully and drank its contents in a single swallow. "More?" she asked, but he shook his head with a muttered, "No, thanks."

"Doctor, do you want to see the details?" she asked. Before he could answer, the screen on the facing wall had already lit up with a range of color figures and tables of data. Conspicuous on the left side were a couple of rotating tomograms of a left leg, from the knee down. The data to the right seemed to be mainly blood chemistry.

"Could I look at the tomograms in more detail?"

They immediately expanded to sit side-by-side, filling the entire screen. "Before and after," he sighed.

"Very unusual to break the leg so far down in a ski accident," the nurse commented. "It started off as a clean break and, if you had managed to get to us immediately, with a bit of immobilization and bone growth accelerators, you'd have been right as rain. As you can see from the NMR and terahertz overlays, continued movement has mashed things up a bit. Your boot was the only thing holding the bones together. By the time you arrived here, swelling was so bad that we had to cut the boot off."

Bruce groaned. Those had been an extremely expensive pair of boots.

"In fact, it was only the designer drugs that allowed you to keep going," Naomi continued. Tables of data replaced the rotating legs. "You know, of course, that such powerful pharmaceuticals should be used with great care. You can't eat them like Smarties." She was clearly giving him a ticking-off.

"The combination of painkillers and performance enhancers allowed you to not only muck-up your leg, but also caused an imbalance in your entire blood chemistry. It wouldn't have surprised me at all if you had ended up with cardiac arrest, thrombosis or something similar. There are traces of some other drug residues that we haven't identified as yet," a number of GCMS peaks were highlighted in red, "but these seem to have played only a minor role."

That would be Sissy and anti-Sissy.

The nurse continued as if she hadn't really expected any input from him. "You were unconscious when you arrived at casualty. I'm sure these drugs would have been enough to knock you out but..." she frowned in his direction and a further list of analytical data was highlighted, "...the beer was the final straw."

The legs reappeared on the screen, with the right-hand after image highlighted. "As you can see, we had to put you under the knife. After we got the worst of the swelling down, Doctor Berner opened you up and cleaned the mess out."

A series of gory holographic images jumped out of the screen, showing a number of procedures being carried out on a leg exposed to the bone by a twenty-centimeter long incision.

"The doctor likes room to work," she explained in response to his horrified glance.

Most operations still used conventional keyhole

techniques but, since the arrival of rapid skin sealing agents that produced no scarring, there had been a recent revival in large-scale invasive surgery.

"It's a belt-and-braces job," she pointed out. "Glue plus a supporting porous ceramic sheath. Your leg should now be considerably stronger than it was originally."

"That's good news."

"But there's bad news." She looked at him in a quizzical manner.

"And the bad news is..." he encouraged her.

"Now you're awake and the surgical anesthetic is beginning to wear off. We have buffers that are stabilizing your blood chemistry..." a graph showed the time profile of several blood components, "...so the doctor refuses to allow any use at all of strong painkillers until you hit the norm line." She pointed at the graph. "That would be sometime tomorrow, I'd guess. As I remember it, his exact words were 'Let the stupid Scottish bugger suffer, maybe then he won't be so daft next time'. He's English, you know."

Okay, a bit of pain, I can stand that, so it's not too bad. Thinking of pain, though...

"My friend, who brought me in, is he still about?"

"I think he left after we completed the first check-up. We've been keeping him informed, though." Noticing Bruce's frown she pointed to the time axis on the graph. "You have, after all, been out for over forty-eight hours."

***

An hour or so later, after a light meal that his body couldn't decide if it was breakfast, lunch or dinner, Bruce realized that he couldn't postpone things any further.

This bloody leg is beginning to pass from discomfort to real pain, so a counter-irritant is called for.

A clock at the edge of the screen read six pm.

Lesser of the evils first.

He decided to call Tom – who, on what must now be Monday evening, should be home from work.

After a few seconds of connection muzak behind alpine landscape wallpaper, Tom's grinning visage appeared. "What Ho, Lord of the Trees. How're things in the wild, decadent Kantonsspital? Hot and cold running naughty nurses? I would guess that you must be about ready to raise some hell now, after your long rest."

Bruce briefly summarized his situation, playing down the drug complications but painfully aware that Tom had probably already received a full report directly from the hospital. He obviously hadn't heard about the painkiller ban, but limited his response to an expressive "Ouch."

After some general chat about the dangers of hospitals and the logistics of sorting out Bruce's van and kit, which was now in Tom's garage in Zurich, Tom noted that he had downloaded Bruce's helmcam and emailed the file on to him. "Some fantastic shots," he commented. "That crag coming down was really great and your loopy attempt to go through the forest was a wipe-out classic. The tree descent was also a beauty."

For the first time, the young American looked almost

serious. "You should have said how high up you were, though. You could have broken your bloody back if you'd fallen from higher up. In any case, why the hell did you climb? An abseil would have been much easier."

Noting Bruce's look of confusion, he continued. "Let me guess, you buy the very best, top-of-the-range touring suit and you don't even read the instructions."

Bruce was now looking distinctly sheepish, well aware of his rather casual approach to high tech sportswear.

"Cuff pockets, both arms?" he hinted. "Twenty-five meters of monofilament in each, about a gram per meter with a load capacity of a ton or so. Good old Brucey, never take an easy option if there is any possibility of making life much more difficult for yourself. Now, in fact, if you'd gone for my descent route..."

After another ten minutes of having his wounds salted, Bruce managed to break off, excusing himself with the need to call home.

"Anyway," Tom finished, "now that you're patched-up, how about Andermatt next weekend?"

"Maybe," Bruce answered just before he broke the connection. He laid his head back and massaged his neck with both hands.

I wonder if Tom knows that 'maybe' is Japanese for 'no way'?

The pain in his foot was getting worse. *Now's the time,* he concluded and called his chalet in Hasliberg.

The connection was almost instantaneous and a

smiling Eva appeared on the screen. "Bruce. Great. How are you? I'll get the others." Before he could answer, she moved off to the left, shouting something that the directional mike couldn't pick up.

Seconds later, three women faced him. They were crammed together on an overstuffed, leather armchair.

Contrasting appearances matched by contrasting facial expressions.

Petite, red-haired Engel perched on the left arm was scowling angrily. In the middle, Angela provided a complete contrast – brunette and statuesque, with her heavy breasts threatening to burst the fabric of the tight dress she wore. Angela's brow was creased with a look of concern. Tall, slim, blonde Eva was now draped over the right arm of the seat. She appeared completely relaxed and smiled warmly "So, Bruce, what've you been up to?"

Before he could draw a breath, Engel butted in. "What a bloody tosser. We can't leave you on your fuckin' own for ten fuckin' minutes without you fuckin' somethin' up."

Attack the best form of defense here.

"Thank you, darling, for those kind words," he interrupted. "You know, sympathy becomes you...makes you look so cute."

Engel jumped to her feet, only to be pulled onto Angela's knee by the hem of her short skirt and a hand clamped over her mouth. "Stop bickering, children," the professor commanded in her schoolmarm voice. "We got a brief call from your friend Thomas, along with a couple of video clips. I take it the tree-one is yours?"

Bruce groaned, which was taken as a cue to continue. "As we're trying to maintain a low profile, I didn't contact the hospital, so I'm not sure of the extent of the damage. Could you send me your file please?" A copy had already been logged on his personal medfile, so he nodded.

"Good, so let's hear all about it." She settled back, releasing the smaller woman, who remained on her lap, glaring fiercely at him.

Bruce shortened the story as much as he could but, from the detailed interrogation he received, it was clear that the women had his helmcam vid playing in parallel. Angela was particularly concerned about his response to the various drugs, which made it clear that they had also managed to hack into the full record of the run, which was automatically included as an encrypted hyperlink to the video sequence. This option was compulsory in Switzerland, to support the enquiries that resulted automatically from any fatal accidents in the mountains.

When Bruce concluded a short summary of his present medical status, there was a short silence.

"Well, hell mend ya." Engel jumped to her feet. "Serves you right for being such a tool. I hope it's really sore."

Angela ignored her. "I can scan through your file and then check with Basel. I'm sure we've got some beta-test painkillers that you could use without any risk of complications. We also have some new ultra-fast tissue regenerators."

"Thanks a lot, Prof, but, as you already noted, we're supposed to have our heads down here. It's only one night. I'll be okay." Bruce sank back, hoping Angela hadn't noted that his hands were clenched in fists, his nails digging into his palms.

He arranged for Eva to collect his van and, all being well, pick him up from the hospital en route back to Hasliberg. He agreed to call back the following morning to confirm when he would be released then broke the connection to a chorus of good nights.

Without the distraction of the call, the pain was excruciating. *That's my excuse,* Bruce tried to convince himself while he entered the code that allowed him access to the backdoor into his chalet security system. Working through a few menus, he quickly opened the link to the video surveillance of the living room. The image was as crisp as the communication link.

The three women were enjoying a post-prandial cognac. Eva sat at the end of a long, black, leather settee, with Engel's head in her lap. Engel was sprawled ungainly on her back, staring into the shadows between the spotlights scattered about the high ceiling.

Angela sat opposite in a massive armchair, her laptop on her knees. Bruce's blood chemistry data streams were displayed holographically, floating in mid-air over the coffee table. "No lasting damage done," she announced, "but it amazes me that he could stand, much less ski, with that cocktail of drugs. And that's not even considering the mess his leg was in."

Engel twisted to stare into the flames of the open wood fire. "Yeah, he's a tough bugger," she conceded, seeming to have gotten over her anger. "And, of course, he's a Scot living in Switzerland." In response to Angela's quizzical grunt she continued, "I checked how much a rescue would cost. The tight-arsed beast would have crawled down on broken bottles to avoid parting with that kind of dosh."

"Surely not? With the payment from the first sampling trip he has plenty of money."

"You may, indeed, be a very smart professor and know loads about almost everything," Engel said smugly, "but you don't know much about Scotsmen."

Fuck, completely correct! This is just adding insult to injury.

With a scoff, he disconnected the link and dimmed the room light.

How bad can a bit of pain be?

***

The pain ramped up continually until it was so intense that he could not imagine anything that could take his mind off it. He closed his eyes and tried to focus on his breathing, using a yoga relaxation technique.

Slow breathing, relax, ignore the pain – no don't even think about pain, only breathing, slower deeper.

Time dragged and the pain just seemed to get worse. Sometimes he was sweating and sometimes shivering, but the pain just got worse. The breathing would work for a while, but then he would lose concentration and the full weight of the pain would break over him like a wave of broken glass.

Time stretched like elastic. He did not dare open his eyes to check its progress, but he was sure it was not passing fast enough.

There's got to be a pain saturation level – after that, things will just get numb. And then maybe sleep. I'm exhausted. Lying here suffering is more tiring than skiing down the bloody mountain.

But there was too much pain, not a hope of dropping off regardless of how knackered he was.

Hours, weeks, months of pain – and then he heard the door open. He lay rigid, muscles clenched in knots. A silent prayer: *let it be morning, for fuck's sake, please let it be morning.*

He opened his eyes and looked into her beautiful brown face as the nurse smiled at him. "It's nine o'clock, Doctor Roberts. I've got a nutritional drink for you."

"Yes, yes, yes."

"I'll just set it by your bed," she continued. "I'm just going off shift now, but the night shift personnel are available at all times. Just push the buzzer here."

He closed his eyes and pushed his head hard against his pillow. "*Fuuuuck!*" he screamed, under his breath, as the pain ramped up and up and up.

4 ...I love nuclear power

Low winter sun was full in his face as Bruce leaned on the rail of the balcony and squinted in the direction of the facing mountains. The valley below was filled with clouds, forming a frozen sea of blinding white. Diamonds of light sparkled in the snow below the chalet, and meter-long icicles hanging from the balconies above were dripping. He took a deep breath of the frigid air, aware of the contrast between his front, which was getting warm, and his back, which was distinctly chilly.

An arm slipped round his waist and a large frame squeezed against his side. He glanced round to see that Angela was wearing a gigantic baggy Aran sweater that came to mid-thigh but had bare legs and feet.

"Jesus, you must be freezing," he gasped. "Don't you want some trousers or something?"

"No, no, I'm fine," she cooed. "Just taking advantage of this beautiful day. So how are you feeling now, my dear Doctor Roberts?"

"I'm just perfect." He had been in Hasliberg two days, during which the weather had been a continuous whiteout. His leg had initially been immobilized in a light cast, but this was more to keep Angela happy than any strict medical requirement. He had put up with the cast for one day then decided it had to go. It was just too bloody uncomfortable. "Your painkillers were great, but I haven't taken any for twenty-four hours." *And didn't have them when I really needed them,* he added silently, memories of his night of infinite misery in the Kantonsspital still raw in his mind.

"What about this view?" He pointed his finger along the panorama. "Meiringen is below us, hidden by the cloud. Opposite is Rosenlauethal. Just through the gap there you can make out the Eiger-Mönch-Jungfrau group. To the left would be the beginning of the Susten Pass and more or less straight ahead is Grimsel."

"Grimsel, that's where the lab is, right?"

"Yup! Run by the Uni in Innertkirchen. I've taught a few courses there."

"I never took you as the academic type. A teacher, huh?"

"Nothing regular. They have courses on all kinds of topics associated with waste cleanup and disposal. I've mainly helped out with fieldwork. Anything for dosh, you know."

Angela pulled his elbow. "Well, you can see too much beauty, but the cold is going for my bladder. Let's get in before I wet myself. Breakfast time."

The girls were already sitting around the breakfast-bar in the large rustic kitchen. They were sharing one of his karate gis. The jacket drowned Engel's small frame; the hem came down to her knees. The trousers were baggy on Eva, but the length was good. *Not that many people would notice*. Bruce tried hard not to stare at her bare breasts. Angela perched on a stool and pulled her jersey over a pair of rather blue, gooseflesh knees.

"Mornin', Beast," Engel greeted him. "So now we finally see some of this mountain scenery you've been telling us about. Not bad."

"It's really spectacular," Eva added. "I can understand why you chose to live here."

"You could even take us skiing. If you weren't such a spaz, that is." Engel grinned mischievously.

"Anyway, now that we can see where we are thanks to the storm being over, what're we going to do?" Angela poured a mug of coffee for Bruce and then one for herself.

Bruce inhaled the aroma. "Actually, skiing might keep the girls out of trouble for a bit."

Engel rolled her eyes. "Us? Trouble? Pot calling the kettle black arse."

Ignoring her, Bruce continued. "It's certainly a shame to miss out on such great weather. You and I, however, are descending into the murk to have lunch with an IWU bigwig. All we need to do before then is to come up with a credible story to explain our interest in Bure."

"Maybe I'm being a bit dim here," Eva spoke up, "but how will a University in the Swiss Alps help us get into a repository in France? Apart from anything else, I thought it was some kind of EU repository...and Switzerland's about the only country between Canada and Siberia that hasn't joined that club."

"Yeah, I suppose the name is a bit misleading. It's less

a conventional university than an outstation for a sort of international training network. There are hundreds of different universities and R&D organizations involved. The EU is probably the second-biggest funder of the IWU, after the Far East if you sum up all their input. If we want to try the academic route into Bure, this is definitely the best way to go. It's just coincidence that it happens to be on my doorstep."

"And who is it we're meeting?" Angela asked.

"An old mate of mine called Dumbledore: Professor Dumbledore McLachlan."

"You have got to be kidding me. Nobody would inflict a kid with a name like that."

"Yeah, Genghis McCann, Roland Butter kind of thing. His mother was totally addicted to some kind of kids' book. As you can imagine he prefers to be called Dee, or even Dum, at a pinch."

"Harry Potter has a lot to answer for," Angela muttered, rolling her eyes.

***

Despite Bruce's encouragement, the girls had decided to postpone skiing until sometime when they could all be together and insisted on joining the lunch date. Bruce suspected that they were actually thinking more of their bodyguard role.

At least, they're less of a magnet for attention in cold-weather gear.

Following his insistence that they were kitted-up for a

walk in sub-zero temperatures, all three women piled into the van. They were clad in heavy trousers, jackets and boots.

The drive from the chalet to the Brünig Pass summit on the packed snow of a secondary road was a sugar-frosted Disney fairyland. The screen polarization darkened to cut out the UV glare, but light sparkled from all sides. High altitude ice cast a rainbow halo around the sun, which blazed from an otherwise clear sky. There was a fair amount of traffic on the road, but most of it was heading in the opposite direction.

Late-start skiers, heading for the slopes, where I'd quite happily be on a day like this.

At the pass, they turned left onto the main road, which was completely snow-free. Bruce explained that the heat-pumps used to keep the main roads clear in winter had the unplanned benefit of also cooling the black ceramic surface during the blistering summers, thus reducing the injuries that had previously been caused to tourists crossing roads in thin shoes or, even worse, bare feet.

A few hundred meters from the junction, they hit the top of the cloud and quickly passed into thick, dark fog. Bruce switched onto auto and let the van navigate its own way along the increasingly busy road. A couple of kilometers farther, the van emerged from the base of the cloud, revealing a view over the floor of the steep-walled valley. The windows were now completely transparent, and the snowy landscape appeared bright despite the thick cloud cover.

"Where exactly are we having lunch?" Angela inquired as she scowled a GPS map readout.

"Meiringen, a pub called the Sherlock Holmes. It's beside the Holmes museum."

"Ah, that Meiringen. Reichenbach Falls, Moriarty and all that kind of stuff."

"The very one. In the summer you can take a little funicular up the Falls to see the spot where the fatal encounter took place. Now, in winter, there's nothing to see, as the entire place is well buried in snow."

"Sherlock Holmes was a story, wasn't it?" Engel enquired while leaning over the seatback. "I don't see the connection."

"Don't worry about it," Angela responded. "You have to be particularly strange to make a pilgrimage to the place where a fictional character died."

"There's probably a lot of God-botherers who'd disagree with you," Eva chipped in, which led to a three-way discussion on the probable existence, or otherwise, of Jesus Christ, Mohammed, Buddha and a range of other assorted Gods and prophets. Engel sighed theatrically as she gazed out the window, completely ignored by the others.

The argument lost steam by the time the van cruised into Meiringen, stalemated by information from web searches that could be used to support both opposing cases. Bruce took over manual control and drove directly into an underground car park near the town center. A labyrinth of underground walkways bustled with lunchtime crowds; a minority wore normal clothes and the majority, lurid winter sports gear.

Bruce led the women to an escalator that took them up to the almost deserted street level. Snow was piled high on roofs and in small gardens and parks, but the pavement was clear and generally dry, steaming gently where water dripped from eaves or light powder drifted from heavily-laden trees. The air was dry and very cold; it crackled in the nose with every inhaled breath.

The pedestrianized roadway was lined with shops, bars and restaurants. Engel's attention was caught by a shop with a window display that included every variant on the theme: *knife,* ranging from minute cigar-cutters to six-foot broadswords. She pointed at a center display of ceramic and molecular-crystal switchblades and fighting knives. "Surely you can't just buy these weapons in a bloody gift shop? There's some seriously dangerous kit here."

"Nul Problemo," Bruce responded. "Remember, this is Switzerland. You can buy just about anything, but don't even think about using it within the national border. Criminal penalties are brutal, especially for foreigners. They'll ship this kind of stuff anywhere for you. It's up to the purchaser to check possession with local regulations. Caveat emptor."

"Jesus!" Engel now had her nose against the window and was shading her eyes to see inside better. "There's handguns, rifles, all kinds of shit in there."

"Very big with the Amis. You can buy a genuine Uzi and have it immobilized. As long as there's a certificate to guarantee that it can't be fired, you can import it into the States."

"Now that seems really daft to me." Engel turned from the shop window. "I'm not keen on firearms, but they're useless if they don't work." She joined the others strolling along the road.

Midway down the street, they reached a snow-covered garden in front of the grandiose Hotel au Savage. Beside it, an incongruous fake Tudor-English mansion was labeled *Holmes Experience* in gothic text. The party entered through an air-curtain and felt circulation return to their cheeks as they entered the heated environment.

A short corridor led to a busy central courtyard that featured a life-size bronze statue of *The Great Detective,* complete with tweeds, deerstalker and pipe.

Angela looked it over, unimpressed. "It wouldn't have the same effect if it portrayed him shooting-up, I guess."

A Japanese couple who were videoing each other by the statue stared at her, aghast.

Gift shops, a Baker Street museum, a multimedia show, a theme restaurant and an English-style pub surrounded the courtyard. In contrast to the restaurant, which was packed, the pub looked almost empty. "More of an evening place," Bruce commented, as he held the door for the ladies.

The pub was dimly lit, with dark wood walls and

roof covered with every possible kind of pseudo-antique Anglo-tack: horse brasses, agricultural implements, beer advertisements, football scarves, road signs... In a far corner, a dartboard and a pool table completed the picture.

"Kitschy," Angela commented as she led them to a table in a niche with a window that looked out onto the empty street.

Engel tailed Bruce as he went to the bar to get drinks. A tall, blonde barman in a leather apron greeted them with an anachronistic, "G'day, mate," delivered in a broad Ozzy accent.

Bruce ordered two pints of Beamish and two cüplis of Swiss sekt. As he watched the hypnotic process of tan emulsion settling into a base of pitch black topped by a cream-colored head, he was shocked back to reality by a heavy hand clapping him on the back.

Bruce spun around in time to get a blocking arm in front of Engel, whose right leg was already cocked back. "Big Dee," he exclaimed in delight, turning the block into a handshake. "How're you doing? It must be about a year since I've seen you...or is it longer? Anyway, absolutely perfect timing. What're you drinking?"

Engel stared impolitely at the tall, skinny newcomer whose head brushed the fake rafters of the low roof.

Bruce could almost read her mind as she sized him up and tried to link this image to a top-level academic.

She must feel minute, facing a man about two-ten tall with hands like shovels.

Wearing an open brown leather dustcoat over denim

jeans and shirt, he looked like an escapee from a spaghetti western rather than some kind of professor. Only a pair of heavy walking boots took away from the cowboy theme.

Bruce turned back to the bar to order a pint of lager for his friend, noting that it was Calenda on draft, which caused a strange flash of déjà vu. "Oh, let me introduce my colleague Maria. Maria, Professor Dee McLachlan."

The tall professor started as if Engel had appeared out of nowhere. "Absolutely delighted to meet you, my dear," he greeted her warmly in a very English accent then lifted her hand, and bending from the waist, touched his lips to it. He held on to her hand for a further couple of seconds, subtly drawing attention to the fact that his index finger was longer than her entire hand. When he straightened up, Engel was left staring into a polished belt buckle that was almost exactly at her head-height.

Bruce handed the lager to Dee, the cüplis to Engel, and picked up the pints of stout. He led the way back to their table with a cheery, "Come and meet the others."

Angela was already standing as Bruce approached. As he placed the beers on the table, she reached past him and introduced herself. "Professor McLachlan, I presume. Great to finally meet you. My name is Angela Smythe."

"My pleasure, Professor Smythe." And the hand kissing procedure was repeated. "Please call me Dee. Bruce has told me a bit about your work."

"And this is Eva," Bruce interrupted. Again the hand kissing, but this time it seemed a bit more drawn-out than before. Only when the lanky professor drew himself upright could Bruce see that Eva had opened her jacket, revealing a tight, polo-neck ski shirt, which would have been provocative enough without the mesh panel that ran diagonally across the front. Eva's left breast was revealed in its full glory, with a protruding hard nipple like a cherry on the cake.

Seeing Bruce's discomfort, Engel caught his eye and slowly started to unzip her own jacket, revealing an increasing expanse of naked flesh.

Fuck, fuck, fuck, he cursed to himself while he directed Dee to sit with Angela using one hand and zipping Engel's jacket to the neck with his other, and then he squeezed onto the bench beside her.

Next time I lock them in the bloody chalet, he promised himself.

The professor was quite oblivious, however, torn between Angela's questions about his work at the IWU and glances across the table at the silent, smiling Eva. Bruce sat back, sipped his pint with a sigh and then passed out menus.

The pub food on offer was a strange amalgamation of English and Swiss. Ordering was simplified when it was agreed just to get ploughman's lunches for everyone, which eventually turned up as a cheese board with a selection of Swiss mountain cheeses accompanied by a basket of bread, a bowl of apples and a jar of Branston Pickle.

Dee was obviously enjoying Angela's attention, although he did have a short break to check Bruce's availability for a couple of field trips during the next academic year. After the remnants of lunch were cleared away and they settled down to another round of drinks, Bruce started to steer the conversation onto the reason for their meeting.

"So, Dee, as Angela's been telling you, the pharms are gradually getting forced into deep geological disposal for some of their nastiest wastes. She would like to link up with the IWU, but her big bosses aren't keen. Really worried that it's the thin end of the wedge and that they're finally going to have to spend some serious dosh on waste management."

"Why worry now?" Dee grumbled. "They've managed to drag their heels for the last five decades."

"Anyway, with or without approval, Angela would like to start building links by setting up some joint projects. If all goes well, collaboration could just end up a fait accompli. I've worked with her on a couple of projects now and offered to act as middleman, co-supervising these post-doc students." He nodded at Eva and Engel.

"What kind of project did you have in mind?"

"The pharms have a lot of experience in shallow sites and some in disposal...I suppose it's really dumping...in deeper disused mines. We thought to extend work where they have special expertise, in this case geo-microbiology. Applying this to a deep disposal environment would be useful for everyone involved."

"What were you thinking of, chemotoxic or radioactive? Chemotox is much easier to find a partner in."

"Actually we were thinking nuke, specifically Bure. It's deep and there are plenty of older areas where the environment should have recovered from operational perturbations. Also it's very convenient from Basel."

"Do you really need to do any field work? We've got lots of sample material kicking around in the IWU and we've got access to plenty more. Rock, water, whatever. If you just want to play underground, you can do just about anything you want at Grimsel."

"Yeah, it's certainly a bit gratuitous, but the key point from our side is to show we can access resources through the IWU that we couldn't get otherwise. We could use our own pharm links to get archive samples or get onto chemotoxic sites. Bure would be something completely different."

"Mmm, I suppose that's a point. It'd be good to finally get the Swiss pharmaceutical industry fully committed here, which might even help to break the international logjam." McLachlan put his elbows on the table and placed his chin on his fingertips. "It should be doable..." his eyes lost focus and he continued in a rather dreamy voice, "...if we can dream up an appropriate training course. IAEA or NEA would be best. Something that would take a group of students into one of the old disposal areas."

"Safeguards?" Bruce suggested.

"No, that wouldn't work. All the reprocessing waste is exempt from safeguards supervision. There's a fair amount of plutonium in some of the intermediate wastes, but there's no way a bunch of students would get close to that stuff. No, unless we managed to have a look at the old spent fuel test site..." He faded off when his eyes refocused and he realized that he was staring directly at Eva's exposed breast.

Bruce fought to hide a smile. "Spent fuel? I didn't know there was any in Bure." He sat back with his head cradled in his hands as Dee outlined the disposal test project, which Bruce had unearthed only a week before.

I knew it. If there was anyone in the world who would know all of this stuff it'd be the IWU boffin who taught, amongst other courses, a module on `History of Radwaste Management in the EU`.

"It all seems perfect, but surely doing some sampling there is going to be sensitive, to say the least."

"Ah, that's the great thing, there's none of the young guys in the Bure operational team who have any idea about it. I had a wander past the site during a visit a couple years ago. There are all these signs, *unstable rock* and *no drilling* and the like. Most are even in bloody French. But nobody has any clue at all what is in there."

Now we need to back-off a bit.

Bruce struggled to hide a smile. "This is getting a bit convoluted, Dee. If they don't know...or won't admit that there is any spent fuel there, there wouldn't be any point in a bunch of IAEA trainees doing inspection tests. Even if we managed to sneak some samples, we couldn't report the work without causing problems for the IWU."

"True, true, Bruce old man." He returned to frowning

at Eva's boobs. "Shame, though, I'd really like to have a look myself at some samples from that area."

Hook and reel in. "Of course, we could always do safeguards background measurements. If we log a sampling run near, but not too near the old spent fuel test, we can sell it as testing equipment and methodology in an area where there should be no signature of fissile materials—"

"That's it. The very dab. Anyone who has no idea what's in there, should have no problems with that, after all, it's a conspicuously blank area at repository depth. The couple folk who do know what's going on will know that we know and should appreciate the sampling location was chosen to minimize the chances of causing problems. Best for them to grin and bear it rather than risk IAEA asking for a formal inspection. This should work and would be a really nice project for some of our jungle-bunny IAEA students."

He glanced round apologetically, "Sorry, I mean students from some of the developing countries. It is a big problem for the IAEA," he explained. "Small, inherently-safe power plants are cheap and cheerful and ideally suited to the poor countries in Africa, Asia and South America, which have been hit so hard by greenhouse climate changes. These reactors are just about idiot-proof, but there's always a little bit of radioactive waste handling. Local training options are meager at best, so thousands of these guys end up heading for the IAEA every year. And a lot end up at the IWU.

"Anyway, back to this project. I'll see who we have in Innertkirchen at present and suggest an advanced project for a couple of our star pupils. It'll take a few days to nail down, as any suggestion of preferred treatment usually ends up in a bun-fight. I'd try to limit it to about a half dozen from the IAEA who could cover all the isotope measurements. Your students can do the bugs."

"I assume that you'd come along, Bruce." He waited for a nod. "But what about yourself, Angela?"

"I'm much more the lab type. Bruce can keep the girls under control on his own. Would you also go along, Dee?"

"We would certainly need someone else from the IWU." He pondered for a moment, then: "I don't really see why not." He glanced surreptitiously at Eva. "I haven't been farther than Grimsel for ages." He flicked through an organizer module on his rather bulky wristwatch. "There's a nice window between Christmas and New Year. If we get our skates on we could make it. We have a lot of non-Christian residential students hanging about the place, but no formal teaching. Bure is open for the entire period, of course, but the emplacement operators are on holiday and so it's actually the ideal time for visitors."

"But we don't want to ruin your holiday," interrupted Angela, to Bruce's annoyance.

"Christmas...humbug! Totally over-commercialized version of a pagan festival that was highjacked by the bloody Christians. I always volunteer to keep things ticking-over during Christmas...and also bloody Easter. I much prefer to take my holidays when everyone else is at work. Much better idea."

"It's going to be a rush," he continued. "We should aim to get all required kit together and have a dry run..." he consulted his organizer, "...which needs to be early next week. That doable for you, Bruce?"

Bruce glanced at Angela and, seeing her nod, confirmed that he could fit in with any time suitable for the IWU.

The tall professor stretched, which almost allowed him to touch the ceiling from a sitting position. "This should be jolly good fun," he stated in a contented Oxbridge accent.

Bruce sat back to finish his pint while Angela proceeded to swarm over the smug Englishman, complementing him on his idea and thanking him effusively. Eva remained silent, but he noticed her winking at the bemused professor when she caught his eye, causing him to choke on the beer he was drinking at the time.

Out of the corner of his eye, Bruce noticed Engel surreptitiously starting to slide her zip lower. He looped an arm round her shoulder and crushed her to his side. "Cool it," he whispered. "Any more of that and I'll put you over my knee."

"Yes please, Beast," she whispered back. "Would you like to tie me up first?" She looked straight into his eyes and, very slowly, licked her lips.

Thank God she's not really my student. I'd end up in jail. At least she's no longer playing with that bloody zip.

They finished their drinks and agreed to meet again

over the weekend, when more of the details had been sorted out. Bruce suggested dinner at his house, inviting Dee to bring his wife. The professor was vague on his wife's availability while casting a furtive glance at Eva's nipple, but he certainly seemed keen on the idea of dinner.

At the door of the pub, the men shook hands, and Engel's hand was kissed. When Dee approached Angela, she proffered her cheek and was rewarded with a typical European triple kiss. He repeated this with Eva, holding her upper arms lightly as touched his lips to her right cheek, left, right again. When he stood back, releasing her arms, she moved to his side, deliberately drawing her exposed nipple along the back of his right hand. His eyes opened wide as she zipped-up her jacket and with a cheery, "See you soon, Professor McLachlan," headed for the street.

Bruce, Angela and Engel waved as the tall frame walked onto an escalator, almost tripping as it took him downwards, and then turned to follow the slim blonde.

***

The sky had started to cloud over when they reached the chalet, and gigantic snowflakes were silently falling by the time afternoon faded into dusk. Later, as they settled around the log fire for a pre-prandial drink, Bruce reviewed progress. He was still annoyed at the girls' antics over lunch but, reluctantly, had to agree with Angela that it hadn't seemed to discourage the good professor. In fact, the planned trip seemed just about perfect.

His original intention had been to try to use the IWU only as a contact to help organize their small sampling trip. The IAEA cover was much better, and active participation of an IWU staff member would certainly make things much easier. The tricky bit would be ensuring that they could get the samples they wanted without raising Professor McLachlan's suspicions.

Angela was still worried about the sampling process. "Getting to the site is all very well, Bruce, but surely you can't just drill into a highly contaminated area as if by mistake. You'll set off alarms everywhere."

"Yeah, that's where we're going to need some special kit from your people. We'll set up the project to simulate sampling in a suspect site with full radiation-protection paraphernalia. The IAEA work will be done with one of the old Grimsel mechanical drills. The seismic intrusion alarms will be switched off before we start, but the passive tomography will show up the drill like a searchlight." Bruce called up a holo display from his laptop. "In parallel, we'll use a state-of-the-art laser to core into the vicinity of some damaged fuel. If we do it right, then if anything at all is picked up, it'll just look like an echo from the other drill.

"Here's our optimum drilling line," he pointed, as a red trace appeared running from an access tunnel past the old test site. "This runs past each of the waste packages. We just keep going until we hit radioactivity. It's a bit tricky, trying to ensure that we get well into the high radiation field but don't pick up too much actinide activity. Whatever, the core might be pretty hot –

radioactive I mean – with a fair amount of volatiles. We don't have all the remote handling kit they had at Tokai but, anyway, I think it's doable.

"The samples will all be packed in shielded containers for later analysis. Of course, the tricky bit will be that we will inevitably have some surface contamination on ours, but I've got an idea about that." He didn't elucidate further, just sank back into the sofa with a smile.

"And you think you can do all of this without Dee noticing?" Angela prodded.

"I think that's where Eva comes in."

The blonde turned from the holo projection in surprise.

"Having shown your ability to distract poor old Dee over lunch, you're just going to have to divert him while we're sampling."

"Wait a minute here," Eva growled out. "I'm the one with the technical experience to do the sampling. If you just need a bimbo, then Engel's available."

Engel bounced on the sofa with glee. "Ah, but I don't have udders like you. The prof is certainly into the bovine sort of bint." With a crack, Engel blocked a jab to her face with a panzered elbow.

Eva stomped off in the direction of the kitchen, massaging her hand, ignoring the others' laughter. Even Angela was amused. "Serves her right for acting such a tart in Meiringen. Although," she continued in a dreamy voice, "he was very tall. I wonder if other parts of his anatomy scale with his hands."

Bloody Hell, he groaned aloud as Engel expanded on her experience of the relationship of penis size to other male attributes, *they're as bad as each other*.

5 ...she's a dove, she's a fucking nightmare

Bruce worked over the weekend to set up equipment for the test run at Grimsel. An experimental area had been reserved for Monday afternoon and the planned dinner postponed until after the test. Bruce was a little surprised that Dee had confirmed that his wife would join them: in a decade of occasional collaboration with McLachlan, he had never before met the woman.

Tom had called on the Saturday morning with suggestions for a ski-tour, but Engel had intercepted this. As she stood shamelessly naked in front of the camera, rubbing a towel over the short red stubble covering her head, she had, with a straight face, reported that Bruce was still in the bath with the other two women. At the time, he had actually been working out in the small gym in his basement. Unsurprisingly, Tom hadn't called back.

Monday morning dawned in a blaze of light. Not only the glare from the sun reflecting from snowy mountains and the cloud filling the valley but, despite an apparently clear sky, the air full of glittering microscopic ice crystals sparkled. After breakfast, Bruce went through the work program in detail, with particular emphasis on Engel's sample handling. Angela would help at Grimsel, as would be expected for a professor with a couple of inexperienced students. Bruce would handle drilling and borehole sealing while Eva was responsible for core recovery and decontamination. Again, as a dry run, she would attempt to divert McLachlan during the critical sampling phase, if this was required.

Just after ten o'clock, they piled into the van and drove into the overcast valley, arriving at the university complex about half an hour later. Angela was surprised at the compact size of the facility: a two-story administrative block, a neighboring four-story glass-faced block containing lecture halls, laboratories, meeting rooms and workshops and a scatter of residential accommodation for staff and students.

The party passed through registration in the admin block and was guided to a conference room by a matronly secretary who spoke sultry French-accented English. They were served coffee and had just settled in deep green-leather swivel chairs around a circular table when the lanky professor exploded into the room, followed by five students. While more coffees were served, the students were introduced. A thin, very black man of indeterminate age from Ghana, who was almost as tall as McLachlan, contrasted with a short chubby New Zealander with pale freckled skin and a shock of untidy red hair. The three women were all around one-seventy tall and dark-haired; a lithe, muscular-looking Fijian, a thin Indian and a heavily built Egyptian. Bruce couldn't help staring at the last of these who, unfortunately, looked like a swarthy man in drag. *Not helped by her rather prominent moustache.*

All five students were wearing white suits with crossover breasts, which made Bruce think of dentists. McLachlan explained that, because of the risk of contamination, everyone would be wearing disposable clothing during the exercise. For the active sampling, they would take a crawler up to the test site rather than the usual winter visitor access by cable car. A hologram of the sampling site appeared over the central table: a tunnel that had been used a decade previously for tracer experiments using a range of radionuclides. The following briefing was comprehensive and covered the sampling, site cleanup and subsequent analysis protocols. Eva and the five students took copious notes on palmtops; Bruce kicked Engel under the table and glared at her until she half-heartedly pretended to type into her notebook.

At midday, they broke for a light sandwich lunch served in the meeting room. Bruce was disappointed to find drinks restricted to milk or fruit juice. He pointedly ignored Angela's mouthed, "What, no beer?" as he sipped his milk.

After lunch, Dee took Bruce off to a changing room while the smiling Fijian – confusingly called Eve – took the three women off in the opposite direction. *Engel and Angela, Eva and Eve; why couldn't one of them be called Ingeborg or Priscilla or even Betty or Judy?*

The sampling party met up again in an underground garage where the students bustled around a massive red tracked vehicle. The New Zealander, called Dave, climbed a ladder and pulled himself into the driver's seat. The engine started with a low, almost subsonic rumble, which caused buzzes of resonance from various parts of the cavernous garage. While the others filed up a ramp into the back of the snowmobile, McLachlan waved Angela to the ladder in front of him and followed her up to the passenger side of the driver's cab.

As last to enter, Bruce pushed a button that withdrew the ramp and sealed the back entrance. He followed the others through a windowless laboratory module and then a sliding door into a bright cabin with three rows of benches, each capable of seating four or five people. A glass partition separated this module from the driver's cab. Both sidewalls and the roof were completely transparent, although numerous scratches and patches of mud limited the view.

The vehicle rolled through a long tunnel and emerged through an automatic door into a snow-covered forecourt that was crisscrossed with wheel and track marks. Dave steered the giant snowmobile effortlessly onto a road that was marked only by the presence of snow-poles at both sides and what looked like a skidoo track along the middle of the deep fresh snow. The truck did not take up the full width of the road, but Bruce guessed it would not be able to pass anything bigger than a langlaufer without leaving the roadway.

The run to the lab took three quarters of an hour. The driver held speed almost constant, slowing only for the steep ramps of snow that had formed at the ends of several tunnels, a few of the tightest bends and transit through the snow-buried village of Handeck. As they motored up some of the steeper stretches of road, Bruce was uncomfortably aware that they were driving at a level well above the crash barriers that guarded the road in the summer, when it was open to the general public.

After passing below the face of a towering concrete dam, the snow-mobile drove straight towards a rock face which, almost at the last moment, slid aside to allow them to pass through a short tunnel and into a large cavern. Engel turned quizzically to look at Bruce, who explained. "Tourist area – at least in the summer. To minimize visual impact on the scenery, all possible structures are built underground and access routes are made as unobtrusive as possible."

The truck turned in place and reversed up to a concrete shelf. By the time Bruce had walked to the back of the vehicle, the door was already open and the tail of the truck formed a bridge to the concrete dock. Angela, Dee and Dave had to climb down to the floor of the garage and then up another ladder to join them. Dave was panting noticeably from these exertions. "It's the altitude," he explained weakly while he opened a door and led them to a smaller tunnel containing an ancient minibus.

Again Angela and Dee joined him in the cab while the others clambered into the back and slid along the hard benches that faced each other across a narrow central aisle. The van drove through another automatic door and then rattled for about ten minutes along an unlit, rough-walled tunnel. Their eyes had almost become accustomed to the low, yellow light provided by the insipid headlights when they passed through another door – dimensioned like an airlock – into the actinic glare of fluorescent lights along the roof and walls of a white-painted, smooth-walled cavern.

Bruce jumped out of the bus, stretched and wandered over to join the others, who were inspecting a row of packages lined up on one of the side workbenches.

Dee was distributing kit. "Okay, Bruce, here's your poncey new drill. Our old brute is already set up in the tunnel. Eva: core liners and your spectrometer. Maria and Professor Smythe: sample boxes. Christ they're heavy. I'll give you a hand with those. Dave, split our samplers between the others and you take the mass spec."

Bruce slung the drill over his shoulder and, with a grunt, turned to follow Dee through yet another door into an antiseptically white room. Here everyone put on white overshoes and gloves and Dave was obliged to spit out his chewing gum. They then filed through an inactive monitor, which looked like an isolated doorframe, over a sticky mat and through an air-curtain into the active experimental area.

Dee led the way along well-lit, circular tunnels that had been drilled through the hard granite. The walls were smooth bare rock except at junctions, which were less regular and sometimes covered by a layer of shotcrete. Two of the students were pushing a trolley found at the tunnel entrance. It rolled easily along the flat concrete floor but one wheel squeaked in an extremely annoying, nail-on-blackboard, kind of a way.

One more air-curtain and they emerged into a dead-end tunnel that was packed with equipment; cables, pipes and, dominating all else, an antique drilling machine painted bright yellow. Dee and Dave worked together to organize the rest of the students, while Bruce drew the others as far as possible towards the less-cluttered end of the tunnel and set up his laptop on a free space on top of a large refrigerator.

Speaking softly, although this was hardly required given the scream produced by the mechanical drilling rig, Bruce organized his team. The laser drill was glued to the wall at a position indicated by a laptop-projection and then the borehole profile was downloaded. The rest of the drilling operation was automatic, with the only action needed being feeding in the one-meter lengths of light carbon core-liner. The laser was set to melt the borehole surface and bond the liner onto the core, but some rock volatilization was inevitable. The vacuum unit started to pick up activity after eight meters of drilling and the measured count rate, mirrored by clicks that gradually merged to a continuous buzz, climbed steadily as drilling progressed.

Dee was drawn over by the noise. "Good grief, that's a bloody fast drill," he commented as he looked at the hologram displaying work progress. "My guys have only managed a couple of meters so far."

"Why don't you get some newer kit then?" Bruce

responded on cue. "The IWU has enough cash."

"Cash isn't the problem. What's the point in training these guys with a laser when the best they've got back home is probably worse than that heap of shit?" He indicated the yellow monstrosity with a nod. "It's always easier to re-learn to use better kit. Going from state-of-the-art solid-state to steam-powered Heath-Robinson mechanical is a hell of a lot more difficult." He stomped back to his students with a small shake of the head. Bruce grinned, having heard this spiel many times before.

Bruce checked with Eva, who assured him that all activity from the vacuum unit was being picked up by the trap, which was being shared by the exhausts from both drills. The laser switched off when it reached the target depth of thirteen meters and the team prepared to recover the thin pencils of rock core.

As each meter length of core was withdrawn, Bruce took hold of it in two-handed clamps and Eva cut it loose with a laser guillotine. Bruce then placed the cores in a box that, when closed, coated them entirely in diamond-like carbon. Engel retrieved the coated cores and, again using grips, transferred them to shielded carrying units, each of which held five cores. Finally, Engel downloaded sample identifiers to the memory of the carriers, sealed them and checked for surface contamination.

The guillotine was set to separate a millimeter thick disc during each cut. Eva used forceps to transfer these discs into the portable gamma-spectrometer. The ten-minute count was the step that limited the rate of core recovery. After counting, the disks were ejected – already DLC-coated – into a shielded sample bottle. When the last disc had been counted, Angela screwed a lid onto the bottle, checked that the surface was clean, and moved it to lie beside the core carriers.

Sampling had gone like clockwork and Bruce's team had unglued the drill and completed decontamination of it and the spectrometer almost exactly three hours after the start of drilling. Bruce finished by injecting a fast-setting resin to plug the hole and then they wandered over to see how the others were getting on.

McLachlan stood close to the air-curtain, observing and making notes in his wrist organizer. Dave was helping the tall Ghanaian – whose name was something like M'boto but everyone called him Mob – operate the drilling rig. They were sampling at a depth of only six meters, but were forced to pull out every ten centimeters or so when the sample barrel jammed. Eve extracted small columns of core and passed them to Rehana – the slim Indian – for sub-sampling and sealing in a thermosetting plastic sheath.

Selected small discs of core were passed to the Egyptian – Nariman – who was struggling with the plasma mass-spec. "The bloody machine is broke," she complained in heavily accented English. "It doesn't give to me the correct answer."

Bruce looked over her shoulder at the holo-spectrum, the peaks of which the library program was identifying when she pointed to them. "Bloody, bloody uranium," she continued, "it has the wrong bloody number."

Bruce was about to say something when he noticed that Dee had his finger to his lips, making a faint shushing noise. "What's up with your spectrometer, Nariman?" the professor asked.

"I have a big 233 uranium," she growled. "Not a 235 or a 238 or the other one – but a 233. I think it should be 238, but the bloody machine will not correct." Bruce watched as she tried again to force the analysis package to recalibrate and her peak assignments were rejected. "Bloody, bloody machine."

"Anyone else with any ideas?" McLachlan inquired and was met by blank stares. "Dave?" he looked at the rotund Kiwi, who was a post-grad carrying out his Ph.D. at the IWU, rather than being on a 6-month training course like the others.

"There's nothing wrong with the spec, Dee. The 233 measurement's kosher." He reached past the hirsute Egyptian and changed the display. "It's no wonder that Nariman's confused, though, look at the uranium ratios. I'd guess that could be weapons-grade, if anyone ever made bombs out of 233. The Swiss don't have a weapons test site here, do they?"

Nariman glared at him, mumbling under her breath. "Not confused, bloody machine is broke."

McLachlan smiled at Bruce's team. "Eva?" Bruce was amused to see the Fijian start nervously and then sigh with relief when she realized that the question was directed elsewhere.

The tall blonde smiled back. "I'm afraid it's not really fair for me to answer, as Bruce briefed us on the history of the site this morning." She continued as McLachlan made a rolling gesture with the index finger of his right hand. "Well, this is an old tracer test site. Most recently it's been used for short-term tests with simple tracers but, originally, they ran long-term tests with actinides. I'm pretty sure U-233 was one of the tracers used."

Dave groaned and slapped himself loudly on the forehead. "I knew that. Shit. I can't believe that I said weapons tests. What a prune."

"Anyway," the tall professor concluded, "I think we have enough core now. Let's get things cleared away."

Bruce helped clean up the yellow rig while Angela took charge of Nariman, who had managed to thoroughly contaminate her gloves. Engel lugged the heavy sample containers through the air curtain while Eva drew Dee into conversation, looking directly into his eyes as she quizzed him on early tracer tests at the site. McLachlan should have been double-checking the inventory of activity in each of the containers, but failed to even glance at Engel as she negotiated her way past him.

***

It was after five o'clock and already dark when the snowmobile emerged from the test site and crawled onto a road lit only by the truck's powerful headlights. Under these conditions, their speed seemed even greater, and the invisible drop-off at the side of the road looked even more threatening. Bruce sat back and closed his eyes, listening to the chatter of the students and Nariman's litany of "Bloody, bloody machine."

In the IWU garage there was a further contamination check of the containers and then Dave carried Bruce's over to his van. Bruce changed quickly back to his street clothes, but the girls were delayed after Nariman's hands and arms were found to be contaminated and required repeated scrubbing, a process Angela supervised.

McLachlan waved when they finally climbed into Bruce's van "Cheerio. See you for dinner at about eight."

As Bruce gained the main road and switched to auto, the three women started to talk simultaneously. Angela then took the lead. "There's something not right about that Egyptian woman. It's not even that she's bloody, bloody useless," she mimicked Nariman's mantra, "but she must have really tried hard to get as contaminated as she did. I know we go through all the radiation protection stuff, but that's really just as a backup. The sampling protocol should keep all radiation pretty well contained."

"Yeah," Engel added, "I saw her rubbing a sample in her hands before she put it in her bloody, bloody machine. She was trying to hide what she was doing."

"Surely not," Angela broke in. "She was told that all handling was to be done with forceps."

"This wasn't handling," Eva confirmed. "She was rubbing samples between her gloves. I saw her do it a couple of times."

"Mmm, I wonder what would have happened if I

hadn't done the contamination checks," Angela stated.

Bruce wracked his brain to find some kind of explanation for this bizarre behavior. "I don't know what's going on, but we better keep an eye on those students – especially the hairy Nariman. We can try to find out more about them this evening when Dee comes round."

***

Immediately on their return to Bruce's chalet, Eva and Angela headed straight for the kitchen to start dinner preparations, leaving Bruce and Engel to lug their sample containers to a new industrial-sized refrigerator that had been installed in his garage only the previous week. An open crate, plastered with lurid radiation, chemotox and biohazard warning signs, sat beside the fridge. This would hold the containers for transfer to Bermuda via Basel.

Ignoring the activity in the kitchen, Bruce climbed the stairs to the attic-level and was pleased that Engel followed him into his bedroom. Kicking off her pumps, she sat on the bed and watched him strip. She followed him into the bathroom, but he was disappointed that she didn't join him in the shower but instead perched on the toilet. As he started to lather his short hair, Engel explained what was bothering her.

"It's not just the hairy Arab, the wee Packie's not right either," she started.

"She's not a `Packie`, she's Indian," he corrected.

"Whatever, wee wog of some kind. She tea-leafed a couple of samples. Just tiny bits, mind you. She was sealing them and putting them in a wee tube. I think she slipped it down her knickers. I watched her as we were changing and there was all the fuss about cleaning up the bearded Arab. Nice tight wee body the wogette has, but no sign of the tube. Bodily cavities, I reckon," she murmured salaciously.

"This isn't good, but we can't change things now. The setup for Bure is just too good. Talk to Eva, but it's probably best not to worry Angela about it. If you keep an eye on your wogette, Eva can do the Arab, and I'll look out for the others."

"Eva's also got the big English streak of piss," she reminded him.

"No problem for a woman of her caliber, I'm sure. The main thing will be to ensure that she doesn't give the streak of piss a heart attack this evening."

"Or get him divorced," she added then padded out of the bathroom.

***

Bruce dressed for dinner in light cream-colored linen trousers and a matching short-sleeved shirt. Slipping his feet into black kung-fu pumps, he stalked downstairs. The kitchen was now empty, and the hum of a convection oven was almost drowned by noises coming from the other upstairs bedrooms. It sounded like the girls were arguing about clothes and Angela was trying to moderate.

He rolled his eyes to heaven in a theatrical manner before setting up *Carmina Burana* as background music. *Oh*

Fortuna built up in waves while he wandered the kitchen and served himself a chilled Fino.

Just before eight o'clock, the women piled downstairs. All were barefoot. Angela wore an ephemeral black tube that coated her buxom figure like paint from mid-breast to mid-thigh. *And not very thick paint at that.* He sighed. Engel had on a short miniskirt and a brief halter-top, which seemed quite modest by comparison.

Most surprisingly, Eva sported a baggy tee shirt featuring a hologram of a smiling Dan Dare on the front. A pair of turquoise running shorts complemented her bizarre fashion statement. Bruce was aware that, from behind, the shorts would present a beautiful view of the tall blonde's buttocks.

Well, she'll be perfectly presentable if I can just keep her facing forward.

The women were in the process of sorting out drinks when the driveway sensors activated the video that showed an approaching all-terrain sports car. Bruce ordered the door garage open and set off downstairs to meet his guests.

The car crawled slowly into the free space beside Bruce's van, accompanied by a flurry of blowing snow that was gradually cut-off by the closing door. Like a spider, Dee folded out of the gull-wing door at the driver's side of the low-slung car. There seemed to be more arm and leg than could possibly have fit into such a confined space. He stood and stretched, easily touching the garage ceiling. The passenger door opened and he walked round to help his wife, calling out, "Hi, Bruce. Great place you've got here. It looks huge."

As his wife emerged, Bruce was amazed to see that she was only a couple of centimeters shorter than the professor and even thinner. *Distinctly skinny, in fact.* Like her husband, she was clad entirely in denim. In fact, the couple appeared to be wearing identical chisel-toed, embossed-leather cowboy boots.

"Bruce, let me introduce Rebecca." McLachlan propelled his wife forward and Bruce stretched up to triple kiss her cheeks.

"Delighted to meet you after all this time." Bruce inspected her sharp features and noted the streaks of grey in her paged black hair.

"And I'm glad to finally meet you," she responded in an incongruously deep voice while looking directly into his eyes with a sparkle that belayed her otherwise plain appearance.

Bruce guided the pair upstairs and introduced them to the others. The uncertain girls shook hands, but Angela crashed through protocol and triple-kissed them both. "This is the Swiss way, isn't it?" she offered by way of explanation.

Angela led Dee into the living room while Bruce followed with his wife, leaving the girls to fetch drinks for their guests. Bruce and Rebecca sat on one sofa while Angela and Dee settled on the other, facing them across the intervening coffee table.

Dee was obviously trying to avoid staring down

Angela's cleavage, which amused his wife. "She's very young to be a professor," she whispered to Bruce. "I'd have never guessed it looking at her. She's a bit more – I don't know – flamboyant than your average academic."

Bruce moved quickly to change the direction of this conversation. "Angela's certainly anything but average. But what about you? I'd guess from your accent that you're German, somewhere in the south, although your English is perfect."

"Well spotted: Bavaria, München." Her eyes sparkled. "I knew you were Scottish, but I'd say West Coast, Glasgow?"

"Right on the button," he responded, impressed. "Anyway, how did you end up in Switzerland with old Dee here?"

The sparkle in her eye had become a gleam as she leant towards him in a confidential manner. The front of her shirt opened, revealing a very flat breast and a huge nipple, like a giant acorn. "We actually met in a Reeperbahn bar. I was a dancer and he was a post-doc in the new Hamburg Max Planck Institute. We were married two weeks later." She sat back with a grin, evidently enjoying Bruce's gob-smacked expression.

Well, well, well, just goes to show you can't judge people by appearances.

He had always had fun working with Dee and enjoyed the few social evenings they had spent together, but he'd actually considered him a bit prudish.

Although, then again, he has always had a wandering eye.

He noticed McLachlan's focus drift back to the fabric straining to retain Angela's huge breasts, like a moth drawn to a flame.

Engel handed Rebecca a glass of English Champagne and then dropped, with a flash of white knickers, into a nearby armchair. Eva handed Dee a Fino and squeezed down on the other side of Bruce. As Dee sipped his sherry and listened intently to something Angela was saying, Bruce noticed him glance towards Eva and then immediately start to choke.

Angela clapped him heartedly on the back, almost spilling his sherry and causing her breasts to bounce.

Like the proverbial blancmanges on springs.

He tore his eyes away from this disconcerting sight and glared suspiciously at Eva. Obviously aware of his attention, she looked straight at him – a paragon of blue-eyed innocence.

Definitely up to something, although I'm damned if I can see what it is.

After the aperitif, Angela led them to the dining table situated in a wide niche to the side of the kitchen. A bottle of Gavi de Gavi sat in a cooler in the middle of the table and a little vegetable amuse-bouche graced each place. Bruce was seated at the head of the table, with Rebecca and Engel beside him. Dee faced him at the other end, between Angela and Eva.

Angela tasted the wine with an inelegant sniff and gulp then poured for everyone. When she reached towards Bruce, he had to force himself to refrain from pulling up her top, as it looked certain that her tits were going to fall out at any moment.

Dee seemed to be having problems concentrating. After coughing over another sip of wine, he had taking to closing his eyes every time he drank. It was very nice wine and Angela was certainly distracting, but Bruce was sure that Eva was up to some sort of mischief. Before he could check further, however, Rebecca caught his eye and asked him about his story – how did a Scot end up in Hasliberg?

The conversation rolled on easily. Engel and Rebecca turned out to have a shared love of Ireland and, of all things, body enhancements – although Engel's interest in combat implants didn't quite match Rebecca's fascination with cosmetic implants, tattoos and piercing.

To accompany the fois gras, the women opted for a sweet Chilean wine while Bruce and Dee tried a Newfoundland Pinot Noir. Angela joined the men on the Pinot to go with the seared tuna main course, while the others tried a Lithuanian Sauvignon Blanc. With the final cheese plate, everyone was drinking something different, as the previously opened bottles had been polished-off. Dee moved onto port while Bruce went for a thirty-year-old New Zealand Cabernet Sauvignon.

During this final course, conversation drifted to work and Angela asked about the students.

"Dave's a good lad," Dee started, counting them off on his fingers. "He's been with us almost eighteen months and should easily finish his Ph.D. project in another eighteen. Really good with technical kit and works well with the jungle..." he caught a glimpse of his wife's raised eyebrow and stuttered, "...eh, well, trainees from developing countries. Mob seems competent enough, but he's extremely quiet: never says a word if he can avoid it. He started at the same time as Eve, three months ago. She's also reasonably good, but much more friendly and chatty."

His brow creased. "I don't know so much about the other pair. They were foist on us by IAEA only when we informed them about the Bure sampling last Friday. It's bloody typical of the IAEA to do things like that, although I must say that they rarely move so fast."

Bruce and Engel exchanged a meaningful nod.

"I really wanted to look at them – and your team of course – in Grimsel today. By the way, I must really complement your girls. They're really on the ball." He glanced at Eva, seemed to lose the place, and then continued uncertainly. "The little Indian seems to know what she's doing. Again a bit quiet, but she picks up stuff so quickly that I'm sure she's done it before."

"Then there's the Egyptian bint." He sighed. "Bloody, bloody useless." Everyone laughed with the exception of Rebecca, who looked mystified.

"I'm seriously thinking about sending her packing, but you know what these sodding North African Muslim states are like – they'll scream bloody murder. The easier way is probably just to bring her along, but not let her touch anything. She can do the videoing."

Bruce laughed at this, knowing that everything done in Bure would be caught on security cameras and could be downloaded at their convenience. He was not happy about the presence of either the Egyptian or the Indian, but he could appreciate Dee's point of avoiding an international incident out of it.

While Bruce pondered the potential problems posed by the students, he missed the start of a heated discussion between Angela and Rebecca. Rebecca suggested that they leave, while Angela tried to persuade them to have coffee and digestifs and stay the night.

Knowing how difficult it was to stand up to Angela, Bruce was unsurprised when the McLachlans eventually gave in, under the condition that they could leave by seven thirty the following morning.

Angela cleared away the cheeseboard debris while Eva served coffee. When Eva turned behind Engel, he heard a small gasp from Rebecca as she spilled a few drops of coffee onto her place mat. Bruce quickly wiped these up with his napkin, staring in suspicion at Eve, who was now walking towards the kitchen with a flash of beautiful tanned buttocks.

No doubt about it, she has a truly fantastic bum.

He noted that Rebecca was also following the tall blonde's progress with flashing eyes and a wide grin.

Nevertheless, there's definitely something that I'm missing here.

They adjourned back to the living room, carrying their coffees with them. Engel and Eva served a small Calvados to Bruce and large Cognacs to everyone else. While Bruce sipped his drink, he noted that Engel had caught Eva from behind and, holding her elbows, slowly turned the taller girl in front of him. As Dan Dare's holographic face, with characteristic zigzag raised eyebrow, turned to half profile, for an instant it vanished and he was presented with a completely unimpeded view of Eva's outstanding breasts. All that was left of the hologram was the single word Dare. Almost before he could register it, Eva had turned a little further and Dan was back in his full glory.

Due to his previous suspicions, Bruce managed to hide his reaction to this exposé. Engel had clearly timed it with the intention of making him choke on his drink. Rebecca had, however, clearly seen what was going on and her grin was reaching Cheshire Cat proportions. She leaned toward Bruce and whispered. "That's a very well-endowed young girl. I must say, though, the students I see through the IWU don't seem so...frisky might be the word."

She looked deep into his eyes and, with a hungry look on her thin face, continued thoughtfully. "It must be fun for you having these three visit you. Do you do a lot together?"

Shit, this woman is perceptive.

"We've been working together quite intensively for six months or so," he answered cautiously. "This involved a fair bit of travelling, so I guess we've gotten to know each other a bit better than usual during student projects. As you've seen, Angela encourages an informal working environment, and I must say I get on fantastically with all three of them."

"I bet you do." She raised an eyebrow.

Bruce carefully steered Rebecca towards the general conversation on past and present holidays. The environmental chaos, economic disruption and social unrest associated with climate change had destroyed much of the tourist industry that had boomed at the turn of the century. Despite this, there were enough well-off people looking for a break to keep the top end of the holiday travel market afloat.

Even in Switzerland, academics like McLachlan were not so well paid. They did, however, have the perk of international travel associated with projects or conferences, which could serve as the basis for an attached holiday. With the advent of cheap full-immersion holo-conferencing, it was getting harder to justify such jollies, but academics were nothing if not imaginative.

Dee expanded on his plans for a fortnight in Thailand, following some international symposium in Bangkok. He had already set up a detailed itinerary, including beach resorts, jungle trips and visits to archaeological sites. During the meeting itself, he had also planned an exhausting schedule of visits to the main *Wats* and other Bangkok sites.

As he drew to the end of his list of attractions, his wife grinned. "Not forgetting the naughty bars in Patpong," she added mischievously.

Dee rolled his eyes.

It was almost eleven thirty when Angela went

upstairs to clear out her bedroom for the McLachlans – setting out toiletries and moving some of her own stuff into the girls' room. Five minutes later they said their goodnights and Eva led their visitors upstairs.

After they vanished from sight, Engel bounced up from her seat and plonked herself on Bruce's knee. "Pretty wild couple there. Rebecca may be skin and bones, but I reckon that she'd give you a good seeing to. It's funny about old Dee, though. I thought that, with the titless missus, he'd be into slim, willowy types like myself." To illustrate the point, she pulled the halter-top to one side to show off a small but beautifully formed breast.

Deliberately leaving the breast on show, she continued. "At a pinch, maybe, somebody tall like Eva. She may be a bit bovine..."

Bruce pinched her bottom in response to this totally unfair comment.

"Ouch. But anyway, even I would admit she hasn't the worst arse in the world." Now she waved her hands to express her amazement. "But who is he salivating over? The old, fat prof." She squeaked in response to a further nip. "Come on, Beast. I know you're into matronly types, but look at the contrast. Becky's got a chest like an ironing board and Angie looks like she's got a couple of Zeppelins stuffed up her shirt. It's not normal."

"It could be intellectual, you know. Lots of men are attracted by bright women."

"Aye, right! Name one. What attracted him was the Grand fuckin' Canyon. Any closer and he would have fallen in. And we'd have had to send you down on a rope to get him back out." She finished with a laugh.

Despite himself, Bruce couldn't help grinning at the image conjured up by this description. He took Engel's small, flat nipple between finger and thumb and rubbed thoughtfully. "It could be nipples, you know, really big ones."

"Could be, Beast, for a titless wonder, you could hang your hat on her nips. I wonder if she was feeling the cold or if it was just the sight of your sexy bod. More likely my sexy bod," she ruminated. "I'd bet that woman would be into anything – man, woman or beast." On the last word, she nudged Bruce in the ribs with a painfully sharp elbow. "Or maybe it's the jewelry." She noticed Bruce's mystified look and laughed. "I don't believe it. She talked about it half the night and had her shirt undone to the waist and you didn't see a thing. Too much wanking, Bruce my boy, you're going completely blind. Her nipples! You can't have missed her bloody nipples."

"Well, they were certainly big. And brown, I guess she must—"

"And pierced, you blind bugger, pierced. She had some kind of big ring through the left nip and a bar-and-chain on the right. Serious chunky stuff there. She must have fun with security metal detectors."

Bruce closed his eyes, and tried to think back. He certainly caught enough glimpses of tit. The large nipples were like the ends of his index finger but, for the life of him, he couldn't remember noticing any jewelry.

That's it, no more self-abuse. Then again, maybe that's a bit rash – at least cut down a bit.

"Best not to think about it, Beast. Anyway, you've enough on your hands without anything else." She looked meaningfully at her own nipple, which was now hard and erect.

"I suppose this isn't the time or the place." He reluctantly released her nipple and re-covered her breast while listening to the sounds of people wandering about upstairs. "Maybe later?" he suggested hopefully.

"In your dreams." She laughed, jumped up and pulled him to his feet.

Right enough.

He smiled as he followed the flashes of white tanga upstairs, *but that's the self-abuse resolution right out of the window.*

***

Bruce was lying in bed and beginning to drift off when the light came on in response to the door opening. He lay with his eyes closed, faking sleep. *Engel or Angela? Maybe fifty-fifty? No, probably Engel, the nipple massage must have worked,* he concluded as a body slipped into bed beside him and the lights dimmed.

He jumped with shock as a deep voice whispered, "Stop pretending, Bruce, I know you're wide awake." A long, thin hand slid down his chest and clasped his half-erect penis.

"Rebecca! What's going on? What are..?" His

protestations died as her lips traced the route followed by her hand.

The mind may be confused, but the body's raring to go. This woman knows what she's doing.

A second hand cupped his balls and a long finger stroked his anus. He gave a mental shrug and ran his hand down a knobbly spine to grasp a skinny buttock.

That which can't be cured must with patience be endured. Although not much sign of patience on her side, Rebecca seems like a woman in a hurry.

His orgasm went on and on while she continued to work on him with mouth and hands. *Like shagging a fucking vacuum cleaner,* he thought irreverently, while his spine arched and his head pushed into the pillow.

He sank back, sweat-soaked and drained while lips slowly traced their way up his front to finish pressed against his own. Her tongue forced into his mouth, opening it for a sticky, salty kiss. The sheets were pulled back and a long, bony body slipped on top of him and started to grind against his groin.

"I'm sorry," he apologized, "that finished me off. That's the problem with such a fantastic blow-job."

"Not a problem," she growled. "A challenge."

She moved her chest until a thick, hard nipple pressed against his. Then his nipple rubbed warm metal. She raised herself on her arms, allowing him to slide his hand along her thin flanks, over a prominent ribcage to grasp her nipples. Her breasts had been noticeable only in terms of slightly smoother skin over her upper chest.

He squeezed the nipples hard and then felt for the ornaments. With the ring in one hand and the chain in the other, he pulled down experimentally and was rewarded by a low moan.

"Does that hurt?" he asked in concern.

"Yesss," she hissed, pulling her body backwards to increase the tension. In the faint light from the windows, which formed the wall of the room leading onto the balcony, Bruce could see the dark shape wriggling above him. *Like a fish caught on a hook – or, more precisely, two hooks.*

To his surprise, he could feel his dick hardening again.

I don't believe it, I'm not into all this kinky shit – or skinny women for that matter.

Or so he tried to convince himself.

Rebecca quickly spotted this development and started to grind a very wet groin against him. As rubbery flesh rubbed against his swelling penis, he again felt metal.

Pierced down there as well, why am I not surprised?

She raised her hips and then dropped onto him. When his dick slipped into a very well lubricated cleft, he felt more metal rubbing on either side.

At least another two piercings.

He remembered Engel's metal detector comment and smiled.

She then started to bounce violently up and down, as if intending by brute force to ram his prick as deeply into her vagina as possible. He had looped a finger through the little chain hanging from her right breast, but had difficulties holding on to the ring through her right nipple. Despite her passion, on the couple of occasions when he lost his grip, she stopped her exertions immediately and remained panting, body quivering until he had recovered his hold. Then off again full speed.

She kept grinding on and on and on. Bruce began to feel increasing pain from the metal rubbing against his dick, despite the copious quantities of lubricant present.

I can't keep this up.

He pulled hard on the small chain and, when she was forced forward, he craned his neck upwards. A large nipple touched his lip and he grabbed it with his teeth. As his teeth sank into the engorged, rubbery flesh, her body twitched as if electrocuted, and she screamed.

After a second of rigidity, during which he relaxed his grip, her body jerked upright, which pulled his head painfully forward as the metal bar caught in his teeth. His grunt of pain was drowned out by another scream as she slammed down onto his penis. The scream turned to a series of grunts while she twisted rapidly from side to side, confounding his efforts to work his teeth free. Nails like talons raked his back. Another high-pitched scream and she dropped forward, her chest on his face.

He worked his mouth free of her tit jewelry and tasted the salt of blood in his mouth. He assumed that the blood was his own, but conceded that her nipple could well be in a bit of a mess. As if reading his mind, she raised herself slowly and rubbed the nipple against his nose, which resulted in a small gasp.

"Mmm," she purred deeply while twisting her body. "Here, bite this one."

A rock hard teat pressed into his mouth; the ring hit his lower front teeth. Bruce couldn't hide an audible groan.

6 ...glory days

As the door opened, Bruce woke instantly. The room was lit by the first traces of early dawn light. A pixy-like face peered in, showing a mock look of concern. "Anybody still alive in here? It sounded like pigs were being slaughtered all night."

Bruce groaned, closed his eyes and pulled the sheet over his head. A few seconds later it was rudely wrenched out of his grip and dragged to below his waist. "Christ. It looks like a slaughterhouse right enough." Now there seemed a trace of real concern in the voice, "What the fuck were you up to? Did she beat you up and rape you?"

Bruce sneaked a look through half-closed eyes and saw what she meant: the sheets and pillow were liberally spotted with blood. He surreptitiously ran a finger over his mouth while Engel clinically examined his exposed wedding tackle.

Split lip with some crusted blood and a chipped front tooth.

He winced when Engel lifted his member between finger and thumb and peeled back his foreskin, uttering a meaningful "Yuck. That's totally foul, dick cheese or whit! And your wee willy is scraped to bits. Did she work you over with a cheese-grater?"

No sense in trying to put it off further.

Bruce levered himself up on his elbows to look at the damage for himself. Not a pretty sight, he conceded, shriveled, red-raw and covered by a thin coating of something that was flaking-off like dandruff. Even more like dandruff was more of the same stuff matting his pubic hair and extending up to the fine hair on his belly. There was some half-remembered quote in the back of his mind.

Either we made love or I was raped by a jar of honey. It was some character from a comic. Spider-something. Not Spiderman – somebody with a mutant cat.

The voice cut through his reverie. "I don't know what you're grinning about, you daft tosser. If I was you, I'd get that thing well seen to. Wire brush and Dettol would be a good starting point." She drew the sheet back up over his face. "I'm just away to cut-off my hands in case that stuff's fuckin' contagious."

On hearing the door close, Bruce threw back the sheets and rolled out of bed. He checked the time – just after seven.

I should get down before my guests leave, but it's very tempting to hide out for the next half hour. I'm not sure how I'm going to face Rebecca, or Dee, or any of the others for that matter.

Turning towards the en-suite bathroom, he caught sight of a side view of his body in the full-length mirrors on the wardrobe doors. Curved rows of scratches ran from his shoulders to just above his hips. Twisting nearer for closer inspection, he could see that, while most were just angry red scrapes, a few had gone deep enough to draw blood.

Fuck. I've been in fights where I've come out looking better than this!

He took a long shower-shave and then applied cream to his throbbing dick and, to the extent he could reach, the scratches on his back. Inspecting his face in the mirror, he scraped a crust of dried blood off his lip and applied a sealant.

Back in the bedroom, he pulled out shorts and a t-shirt from a drawer, dressing quickly and taking particular care to carefully position his sensitive prick while he pulled on his underwear. Bracing his shoulders, he glanced once more at the soiled bed, grimaced, and left the room.

All the others were seated round the breakfast-bar, chatting animatedly. The view through the window was crystal clear. The first pink glow of the rising sun touched the mountaintops and flooded the living room with a rose light that competed with the overhead spots in the kitchen. His entrance was a complete anti-climax, a rustle of *good-mornings* and a mug of coffee shoved in his direction.

Angela was discussing coffee blends with Dee while Rebecca was trying to find a date to take the two girls skiing. The skinny woman glanced in his direction as he reached past her for a gipfeli, but her acknowledgement of the previous night was limited to a sly wink.

It appeared that the McLachlans had already finished their breakfast and had been waiting on his appearance to take their leave. Bruce put down his coffee and led them to the garage. The three women trailed after.

While Dee clambered in behind the wheel, Bruce helped Rebecca into the passenger side. As he bent to kiss her cheeks, he was rewarded with a view of both prominent nipples. No worse for wear, he noted, and all jewelry intact.

How on earth could I fail to see it during dinner?

He was still wondering about this as the car drove out into a glare of white.

He waved briefly and turned to face three enigmatic, Mona Lisa smiles. Angela took him by the hand and led him back upstairs. "Now just what was going on last night?" he started. "What were you three..?"

Angela turned and put a finger to her lips. "Don't ask, don't tell." She dragged him back to the table and handed him his coffee mug.

As the tall brunette leaned over to top up Eva's mug, her top pulled down slightly and Bruce spotted what looked like scratches on her back. *Do not go there,* he commanded himself, as he tried to concentrate all his attention on breathing the fine aroma of his coffee.

***

Taking Bruce's van, Angela and Eva left mid-morning to transfer the samples to Basel. They would remain at the pharm for a few days to carry out some quick tests, which should confirm that viable microbial colonies were preserved during the sample handling process. Then, just in case there was anything of interest, they would send sub-samples on to the Bermuda lab.

During their absence, Bruce worked to set up the logistical details for the Bure trip – now set for the following week. Despite worsening weather, Bruce dragged his langlauf skis out every morning, spent an hour or two fighting though blowing snow and struggling to find the markers that showed the position of the deeply buried loipe. On two occasions, conditions were so bad he needed GPS to find his way back home.

Engel was amused by this blatant masochism. She confined her fitness activities to working out in Bruce's small gym. She spent a couple of restless days before coming upon a crossbow buried amongst Bruce's sports kit. Thereafter she set up a target range in the garage and spent hours practicing.

The first time Bruce went down to watch, he was amazed at the clutter of boxes and other obstacles lying around. Engel was standing still, wearing a black, silky body-suit, crossbow held at her side. Suddenly she exploded into action, diving over a box and rolling smoothly to a crouched firing position. The bolt thudded into the upper edge of a large archery target, having passed through an intervening plywood board.

As she reloaded, rapidly working the lever that slowly tensioned the bow, she turned to him with a feral grin. "This is a great wee toy, Beast. You could do someone some serious fuckin' damage wi' this. No chemicals, no electronics – fuckin' magic."

Firing from the hip, she whirled like a black tornado. Her back roundhouse kick sent flying a tall box usually used for transporting skis. The bolt just clipped the left edge of the target and ricocheted off a couple concrete walls, causing Bruce to duck involuntarily.

Too dangerous here.

He retreated upstairs.

She's much best left to her own devices.

***

The microbiologists returned to Hasliberg on Thursday, which was Christmas Eve. The weather was terrible. Gale-force winds blew snow and reduced visibility to almost zero. Despite this, Eva reported that the drive had been easy – even if a bit slow. Much of the route ran through tunnels and the rest of the main road was protected by high snow-barriers. Only the last few kilometers from the pass summit had required manual control and, even here, the GPS / radar combination made navigation along the almost empty road straightforward.

"The only tricky part was finding the garage door, hidden behind a wall of snow," she conceded. "That and getting in around all the crap that's down there." She glared at Engel, who smiled sweetly back at her.

Following his refusal to be talked into a Christmas Day ski run with Tom, Bruce had endured a half-hour of slagging from his buddy. This despite a dire weather forecast for the following day. Finally, Tom allowed himself to be mollified by an invitation to Christmas dinner. With a grin, Engel suggested that they could also invite the McLachlans and was rewarded by a glare from Bruce.

***

On Christmas morning, Bruce awoke to slightly improved weather conditions; still snowing hard, but without the high winds. With marked reluctance, he dragged himself from bed and padded downstairs to his sports kit room. To his surprise, Eva was already there, dressed in a silver one-piece suit. She raised one expressive eyebrow while she scanned his naked body from head to toe, but limited herself to a cheery "Good Morning."

Bruce mumbled a morning greeting while he scrabbled in a drawer for thermal long-johns. After dragging them on, he turned to the tall blonde. "Well then, you fancy a yuletide plod through the snow? It's going to be chewy out there."

"I'm going stir crazy here. I haven't walked outside since Meiringen. Back home in Bermuda, I run just about every day. I just need to get outside."

"I know what you mean," he responded as he wriggled into a skin-tight ski suit, "but don't say I didn't warn you."

Carrying skis and poles, he led the way into the garage and, following her nod, opened the door. The pair pushed their way through an air curtain into soft, thigh-deep snow. They both rapidly pulled over hoods with integral visors and Eva pulled up a collar that covered her nose.

A bit of over-reaction as the temperature isn't much below freezing.

After they struggled into their bindings, Bruce set off over his buried garden towards the high poles that marked the position of the loipe. To his surprise, the trail looked like it had been laid out within the last hour or so, with the parallel rail marks for classical langlauf clearly marked.

Typical Swiss, snowing like hell on Christmas and still someone goes out at six in the morning to set up the cross-country ski trail.

Bruce crossed one set of tracks and turned right into the second. He pushed off with both poles and immediately went into a crouch when the path dropped down the side of an open field and then into the forest. Within the trees, the track leveled-out and Bruce rose into smooth gliding strides that sent him speeding along. Out the corner of his eye, he could see Eva holding position just behind him on the flattened area of the skating track.

Although he acknowledged that the skating technique was faster and more efficient, Bruce stuck to classic langlauf. This was partially because the traditional skis were better for slogging around untracked routes, like those he had been skiing on during the previous week, but mainly due to his limited skill and the difficulty of the undulating loipes on the Hasliberg.

He had never previously skied with Eva, but he remembered that she had once spent a winter somewhere in Canada. A middle-of-nowhere place in Manitoba, where almost everyone was of Icelandic descent. It sounded pretty awful, but Eva had glowed whenever she described skiing over frozen lakes lit only by the Northern Lights. Each to their own.

When they came to a long, gradually curving climb, Eva overtook him as she powered upwards. Bruce tried to keep up, pushing on his poles with all his might, but almost toppled when he was momentarily distracted by the view of her muscular thighs and buttocks in the skin-tight suit. The silver form pulled farther ahead, seeming somehow unreal – too perfect. *Like some female cyborg in a Japanese manga or anime science fiction epic.*

Eva's figure was soon lost from sight. Bruce crested the hill, which took him out of the forest and onto a traverse along an open hillside. The snow had eased a little and he could now see for about five hundred meters. His companion was gone, but Bruce could easily follow the alternating diagonal slashes in the fresh snow.

A couple of kilometers in the open and then her track followed a fork in the loipe, which turned sharply to the right and dived into deep forest. Bruce shot down the path, which had narrowed considerably, standing with knees only slightly bent to take some advantage of air resistance to limit his acceleration.

A sharp left turn came into view and Bruce lifted his right ski from the track and used it to reduce speed and help him negotiate the bend. He immediately replaced his right ski and reversed the procedure to fight his way around the following right turn. As he struggled to keep upright, he was painfully aware that Eva's tracks had been completely parallel for the descent, with deep cuts for both turns.

She must be moving really fast.

The trail became even steeper; a straight run that was complicated by a series of bumps. Bruce again used one ski as a brake between bumps, but he could see from the long gaps in Eva's spoor after each summit that she was using them as jumps. As the profile of the loipe flashed through his mind, he felt a sinking in his stomach and struggled into a full snowplough, using both skis to decelerate as hard as possible.

He had almost slowed to a stop when he reached the crest of the last and largest bump. He stepped round to bring his skis perpendicular to the slope and cautiously sideslipped towards the right-angled turn at the bottom of the slope. The turn lay at the junction of the firebreak, which the route had been following, and a forestry road, which the loipe would now follow in a long climb up to a point close to where they entered this wooded section. The loipe was set out to allow less adventurous skiers to take a short cut to avoid this entire tricky descent section.

"Fuck," Bruce cursed as he saw the virgin path curving upwards. He battled his skis though the soft, heavy snow that formed a wall blocking the continuation of the firebreak. As he began to slide forward and his skis sank to mid-calf in the fresh snow, he saw the deep imprint of Eva's landing and the parallel tracks that arrowed down the center of the ride. Bruce slipped over to enter these tracks and his speed increased considerably.

Not a good idea to rush into things hereabouts.

He braked with his left ski in an attempt to keep his speed down to a fast walking pace.

What the hell is the bloody girl up to?

He frowned as he skied onwards.

Surely she knows she's missed a turn. Why not stop and turn back?

The slope flattened out and Bruce brought his skis together in Eva's tracks to keep up his forward speed, coasting over a small rise before he frantically snowploughed to a halt. The perfectly parallel tracks became a gouge that ended in a hole in the snow just as the firebreak appeared to end. The hole looked as if it were cut with a knife. Bruce could see a silvery shape in the depths of the hole and could now make out muffled calls for help.

It was only about twenty meters to the edge of the cliff. Bruce cautiously sidestepped to the end of the tracks and quickly snapped loose his bindings and stepped out of his skis. He could now see that Eva was lying face down in the snow, her arms dug in deep above her head. Below the waist she was hanging freely off the edge of a precipitous drop, which continued beyond the limits of his restricted visibility.

"Hang on," he shouted, unnecessarily, as he tried to edge closer, his smooth-soled langlauf boots slipping on the steep slope. Only the poles kept him upright. At this sound, Eva cautiously arced her head upwards, exposing a white, terrified face. Even this slight movement caused her to slide slightly, resulting in a squeak of horror and her face pressed back into the snow.

Watch it. One wrong move and we're both flying. And it's not the falling that's the difficult part; it's the fucking landing.

The thought helped him fight down the beginning of panic while he carefully reviewed his options.

He could call for help, but that would certainly be quite some time coming under present conditions. Unlike Vrenelisgärtli, which had been a stupid macho decision, now he had no choice but to sort out things himself. No mountain touring kit available now, just sports langlauf gear. With a start, he realized that he did not even have his usual emergency drug kit. After all, he had just been going for a little ski around the house.

No time for recriminations.

He forced himself to concentrate on what he had to handle. Carefully twisting round, he reached for a ski that he drove, back-end first, as deep as possible into the snow below him. He repeated the exercise with the second ski, and then pulled his hands through the wrist-straps of his ski poles. Hooking one stick into the wrist-strap of the other, he then wedged it behind the skis. Holding the free pole by the basket, he slowly moved closer to the fallen girl, kicking his heels as deeply as possible on each step.

At full stretch of his left arm, he sank to his knees and groped around with his right hand until he caught hold of Eva's elbow. "Grab my arm," he shouted in response to her involuntary twitch of surprise. A panicked wriggle served only to dislodge his grip and start an inexorable slide towards the edge. He grabbed at a flailing forearm and the pseudo-sharkskin palms of his gloves fought for a grip on the smooth fabric of her sleeve.

A scream cut off as she slipped a little further and was transformed into sobs that wracked her body as she scrabbled with both hands to find some kind of purchase in the soft snow. Another jerk and he was holding only the back of her glove, feeling her fingers slip through his grip, joint by joint.

They both screamed as her hand slipped free. Bruce grabbed frantically and gasped as he caught hold of something that almost wrenched his shoulder from its socket. Glancing down, he saw that he had a hold of Eva's ski pole, which was still tied to her wrist. Her hand was now clenched around the wrist-strap, holding the weight of her entire body, which dangled over the edge of the cliff from armpit level.

"Your other hand. Other hand," he screamed as her body twisted. "The pole, grab the pole."

One more wrench to his shoulder as her left hand grabbed the strap just above her right. Both arms now lay in the snow and she looked through a snow-covered visor directly into his eyes. "Come on," he encouraged her. "Can you climb up a bit?"

The girl made no attempt to answer, but Bruce saw the muscles in her arm tense as she gently began to wriggle her upper body over the lip of the cliff. Her arms were bent to right angles to pull herself up to mid-chest level. Then she stopped and muttered. "Now it gets tricky."

With a rapid movement that seemed somehow reptilian, Eva slid her left hand upwards to lock in place on the shaft of the pole. She froze, holding her breath with eyes closed. Slowly, she inhaled and stared at her hand, as if to check that it was still there. Then she looked at her right, as if to command it to release its iron grip. This time it was a slow twist to release her wrist from the strap and reach up to just above her left hand. Her head then sank down for a moment, appearing to kiss the strap that had saved her life.

A couple of slow breaths and then her muscles tensed again and she started to writhe upwards again. A long pull and she was lying on her belly.

Just about where she was when I first found her.

Bruce grimaced, feeling the pain in his arms begin to bite through the adrenalin analgesic, which had kept his mind otherwise occupied until this point.

One more pull and she was clinging to his wrist and forearm. "Hold tight." He grunted as he released his grip on the pole and twisted slowly to transfer his hold to her wrist. They sighed in unison.

"Now, my belt," he commanded as he began to pull her towards him. Bruce's arm was beginning to tremble, but he noted that Eva was also pulling hard, wriggling her body upwards. With a sudden jolt, her body slid forward and her left hand hooked onto his belt. He glanced down to see that Eva was now clear of the drop, her legs bent at the knees and skis in the air. *Shit, I'd forgotten about those.*

No wonder she was having so many problems climbing up.

A bit more straining and Eva had a good hold on his belt with both hands. Although the wide belt was cutting into his waist, he sighed with relief when he was able to turn and take hold of his ski stick with a second hand. Slowly, still on his knees, he pulled himself hand over hand until he reached his buried skis.

With one arm around his skis, he helped support the girl as she twisted to bring her skis at right angles to the slope and shakily come to her feet. His grip tensed as she slid a little, downhill ski touching her fallen stick. They both stared in silence as it slid over the edge and disappeared.

Eve stood catching her breath while Bruce extricated his own skis and spent several minutes clearing snow from his bindings and boots. Finally, secure in the skis, Bruce extended one pole to the pale girl and, when she confirmed a secure grip, led her sidestepping up the slope.

As soon as they reached a relatively flat patch of snow, Bruce slid to her side and wrapped an arm around the tall woman, crushing her to his side. They stood silently for a couple of minutes until the tremors of her body gradually died away.

"I'll call up the mountain rescue," he announced. "I'm not sure if they could get a chopper in here with this visibility, but they should be able to get a snowmobile to us within twenty minutes, half hour tops."

"Wait a minute, Bruce," she demurred, wiping the last traces of snow from her visor. "I'm not hurt, there's no reason to make a fuss. I'm a little bit shaky at present, but that's only the aftereffects of being scared totally shitless. And a bit cold," she admitted, "but that'd sort itself out if we got moving."

Bruce looked her over skeptically. "I'm not sure about that. You look totally shagged."

"Okay, Bruce, what would you do if it was the other way round? If I'd just dragged you off a cliff, would you call for help?"

"If I thought I really needed help, I'd definitely call for it regardless of..." he ground to a halt as she smiled wanly at him, the first reassuring sign since he had found her – he glanced at his watch – just over ten minutes ago.

Only ten minutes, Christ, it felt like ten-times that.

"Okay, okay," he conceded. "Let's give it a whirl. You take my poles and stay in my tracks. No speeding."

She looked like she was going to refuse the ski sticks, but one glance at his communicator was enough to force her to back down.

Without poles, Bruce struggled to find a regular rhythm but, despite this, Eva was clearly having difficulties keeping up. By the time they reached the marked loipe, both of them were breathing heavily. Bruce turned left onto the gentler ascent, but stopped on hearing Eva's loud cry.

"Fuck."

My very word for it.

Eva so rarely swore that he guessed something must be wrong. He stood in place as she skied up to him, still mumbling to herself.

"I never even saw this bloody turn," she explained. "It was such a brilliant run down and I was really going for the jumps. I noticed that the snow got a bit slower, but I never even spotted that the loipe had disappeared. Until the precipice, that is, you don't get many of those on cross-country paths."

One mystery explained.

He shrugged and led on uphill. At the top of the long ascent, Bruce cut right at a fork, which brought them back to the original junction that still showed their earlier tracks. Now they were reversing their original route.

Well, instead of a planned twenty k circuit, we've probably covered no more than about eight. Nevertheless, I feel as if I've just run a bloody marathon. Terror does, indeed, take it out of you – even if the fear is about the risk to someone else.

When they neared the house, Bruce began to relax and felt tension fade, leaving only dull aches in the muscles of his arms and shoulders. He stepped out of his skis and supported Eva as she almost fell out of her bindings. Carrying both sets of skis, he led the way into the garage, followed by the silver-clad girl who, even on the concrete floor, was supporting herself on the ski poles.

Bruce tossed the skis carelessly to one side and helped Eva sit down on the bench in the kit-room. As he turned to run upstairs for help, she grabbed his hand. "Please, Bruce, don't mention this to the others. You know how Angela is after my last...accident." Even Eva was loath to mention the violent incident earlier in the year.

"Just give me a bit of time to get my head together."

Bruce stripped off his suit and, standing in a very sweaty pair of long-johns, chucked it into the fresher. Seeing the girl slumped with her head in her hands, he helped her to stand. He peeled back her hood but, as he started to unzip her suit, she turned away from his hand.

He regarded her in surprise, noticing that she was blushing. She stood silently for a second and then, in a low voice that was almost a whisper, she sighed. "Let me do this myself. It's not very nice. I was really, really scared. I can't remember ever being so frightened. Not good on a full bladder..."

Bruce felt himself blush as he realized her predicament. "For Christ's sake," he blustered. "Where's the problem? Happens all the time on ski tours."

At her raised eyebrow he continued. "Well, not unknown anyway. If you don't let it bother you, I won't let it bother me. Trust me, I'm a doctor."

"You're a bloody Ph.D., not a real doctor," she mumbled but allowed him to draw the zip down and help her out of the suit. In actual fact, the sweet smell of fresh urine was dwarfed by the ammoniacal stink of sweat.

"I don't know what you're going on about," he commented. "You don't smell anything like as bad as I do." He chucked her suit into the fresher and she threw a now transparent pair of briefs after it. Shrugging cheerfully, he followed these with his own very whiffy long-johns.

In the rather basic basement shower, he soaped her

back while she stood passively under a jet of hot water. After a couple of minutes without a response, Bruce proceeded to wash her hair and then the rest of her body. Even with her eyes closed and body sagging with exhaustion, she was a stunningly beautiful woman, and he strained to stop his body from expressing his arousal. He tried to concentrate on her imperfections, stubble in her armpits and around her trimmed blonde pubes, but it really didn't help. Only when she began to shake with silent sobs, did his slowly building erection wilt.

He washed himself quickly and drew her out of the shower.

No hot air blow-dry available here.

He grabbed a towel and gently rubbed her down. A very quick dab at his own damp frame and he led her back into the kit room.

"Something here you fancy?" He waved vaguely at some of his martial arts kit, which was hanging in an open wardrobe.

She grimaced at a bright yellow kung-fu top and instead rummaged in a drawer until she found a pair of running shorts and a baggy t-shirt that advertised some brewpub in Vail. She pulled on the t-shirt and shorts and smiled when she glanced down at the text on her chest: *Bitter as Love.*

Good, she's definitely looking a lot brighter.

As if to confirm this, she grinned at him. "Lovely though your willy may be...I'm not sure it's what the others will want to look at during breakfast. How about the lurid pajamas?"

Bruce also decided that this option was not quite ideal and rapidly drew on a light karate suit. Taking Eva gently by the hand, he led her upstairs.

***

Once again Bruce had the feeling of anticlimax entering the kitchen. Angela was already sitting in the lounge, deeply emerged in a newssheet hardcopy. "Good morning, kids. Have a nice ski?" she greeted them cheerily, without raising her head.

Engel, perched on a stool by the breakfast bar, rolled her eyes. "Fuckin' nutters, goin' out in this weather. Need your fuckin' heads looked at." She sipped her coffee and returned her attention to the tower she was constructing with playing cards.

Bruce poured coffee for them both and nuked a half-dozen gipfeli. The smell of fresh bread made him realize how hungry he was and he sorted out a platter of assorted cheeses, meats and fruit from the contents of his massive fridge.

When he placed the wooden board in front of Eva, Engel's tower toppled and she turned to him with a glare.

"Come on now," he defended himself, "it's a solid block of granite. You're not saying that putting this food on it knocked your cards down?"

"In any case, it's a table for having breakfast at, which is why it's called a breakfast bar. Now, on the other hand, if this was a card table..." Eva stopped with a grin when she received her own glare from the little redhead.

Eva and Bruce ate a hearty breakfast, which attracted Engel's attention. "You guys are grumfing away there like fuckin' horses. I hope you weren't up to any hanky-panky out there in the snow."

"Of course we were." Bruce pointed to the whiteout conditions outside the windows. "It's no problem actually, after you build the igloo."

"You're forgetting killing the polar bear," Eva added. "It wasn't really a problem to beat it to death with ski poles, but skinning it with Bruce's Swiss army knife took a bit of time. But it was worth it. You can't beat red hot passion on a bear skin."

"That wouldn't have made us so hungry, but there was this pack of nymphomaniac girl guides we met on the loipe. It was all a bit crowded in the igloo, but we were just lucky that it was a bloody huge polar bear."

"And then there was..." Eva made to continue, but Engel bounced off her stool, demolishing her latest tower and stomped off to the lounge.

"Fuckin' smartarses," she mumbled under her breath as she bounced onto a sofa and picked up some of the discarded sheets from Angela's paper.

Bruce reached over to stroke the back of Eva's hand. "You look fine now. All okay?"

Eva smiled warmly at him. "Yes, I'm absolutely great. I'm even thinking that we should go out again tomorrow. Getting back in the saddle sort of a thing."

"It's a date," he promised. "Next time I'll show you a

profile of the route before we start off," he added, apologetically.

"No problem, next time I'll follow you, like you told me to this morning. Even if you're very slow." She grinned and squeezed his hand.

***

Tom arrived at five, having taken the train to Meiringen and the cablecar to Hasliberg. Even though it was less than a couple of kilometers, Bruce picked him up with the van as the wind was again blowing strongly.

Bruce led him to the bedroom usually used by Angela to allow him to change out of his cold-weather kit. Surprisingly, there was no trace of the women when Bruce returned to the lounge and busied himself sorting out wine bottles and glasses.

Tom joined him within minutes and allowed himself to be talked into a pre-prandial glass of Irish Riesling. Bruce looked him over – light grey baggy cotton shirt and slacks and matching grey espadrilles.

Must be a special show for the women, can't think of any other time I've seen him in other than jeans and a lurid t-shirt.

They settled down into armchairs and the inevitable light-hearted verbal sparring commenced; the American trying to draw out more details of their last ski adventure while Bruce strained to change the topic of conversation.

A clatter on the stairs announced the arrival of the women. Bruce had a distinct feeling of foreboding before he drew Tom forward to introduce them.

First to appear was Angela wearing a tight tube in a metallic shade of scarlet, which made Bruce think of fire engines.

As usual, she looks as if she is going to burst out of the top, but otherwise not too bad.

As if reading his mind, she span around at the bottom of the stairs, revealing a completely transparent back panel to her dress which extended far enough to show the top of the crack of her bum. It also revealed a large mistletoe tattoo at the base of her spine.

Bruce introduced a bemused Tom, who shook hands awkwardly with the tall brunette. Angela grinned mischievously as she pointed above his head. A sprig of mistletoe, which could have been the model for her tattoo, hung from the ceiling.

Where on earth did that come from?

Angela drew his ski buddy into a wet kiss then drew back with a cheerful, "Merry Christmas," as the girls came downstairs. They wore matching white halter-tops and low-slung denim shorts. White tangas were pulled high over their hips. The tall curvaceous blonde and the elfin redhead were indeed a dramatic sight, Bruce had to admit.

He glanced at his pal and was surprised to see the startled look on his face.

A real case of rabbit-in-headlights.

He looked at the girls more closely and could not hide a gasp. The tangas seemed to be genuine enough, but the rest was body paint.

Tom had already met Eva when she picked up

Bruce's van, and she introduced Engel to him while Angela dragged Bruce under the mistletoe for a deep kiss. Immediately afterwards, he was being kissed by Eva. He ran his hand down her back: nothing but the feel of warm flesh.

Whatever kind of body paint they're using, it's subtle stuff.

After Tom had been comprehensively kissed, he was dragged to a sofa and seated between the two girls, opposite Angela. Bruce was dispatched to the kitchen to fetch champagne for the women and, by the time he returned, they were trying to outdo each other in blatantly flirting with his friend.

After their aperitif, Bruce led the women to the table, which was already set with little dishes of caviar, lemons, sour cream, toast and a magnum of champagne in a massive ice bucket. Tom excused himself and rushed upstairs while the women organized the seating arrangements.

Tom returned with a parcel wrapped in gaudy Paddington Bear Christmas paper and bound with a scarlet ribbon. "Just a little thing for old Bruce," he explained. "I'm sorry that I didn't bring something for the rest of you."

"Funny that," Bruce responded, "looks not unlike what I have here." He reached below the table and pulled out a similar sized parcel – this one wrapped in ancient-looking newspaper and tied with an old, frayed piece of climbing rope.

The men grinned at each other and exchanged

presents while the bemused women looked on. Tom went first, roughly pulling the rope and paper free to reveal the box of a thirty-year-old Islay malt. "You shouldn't have," he exclaimed in surprise.

"It's okay. I didn't." Bruce laughed while his pal opened the box and withdrew a bottle of beer.

"Good one." Tom showed the bottle to the women: a North English microbrew called *Old Fart*.

Bruce carefully unwrapped his parcel and opened a plain box to reveal another beer bottle. "Great minds." He laughed, displaying the American stout *Arrogant Bastard*.

The girls were greatly amused, although a smiling Angela rolled her eyes theatrically and sighed. "Boys' humor."

"Actually," Bruce continued, "I do have something for the women, which can be from both of us." He dived below the table and appeared again with a couple of minute parcels, both of which were again wrapped in newspaper. He handed one to Angela and tossed the other casually to Eva. The women looked at each other while they cautiously peeled off the duct tape holding the scrappy paper together.

Angela held up a small thong with a Santa Clause pattern, while Eva showed a matching item with a snowman theme. "Very Christmassy," they agreed.

"But that's not all." Bruce leant over and pressed a button hidden by a bow in the back of Angela's tanga. Everyone laughed as a clear, although rather tinny, version of *Rudolf the Red-nosed Reindeer* emerged from the thong.

Eva peered at her own present and found the button. The strains of *Frosty the Snowman* added to the amusement at the table.

"Thank you very much," Angela said. "Nobody has ever given me musical underwear before."

"That was very thoughtful." Eva stretched over the table to kiss his cheek and give him a close-up view of her mammary paintwork.

"Unfortunately, I could only get a hold of two pairs of singing knickers." Bruce looked at Engel and saw her trying to hide a look of disappointment. He teased her with a moment of silence before again reaching below the table then emerging with a larger box. This one was packaged in a ripped carrier bag and held together by considerable amounts of drab green insulating tape.

Engel grabbed the present from his hands and savagely ripped off the covering. She looked stunned, as a tin box was revealed. "Scottish full butter shortbread?" She looked at Bruce who was chortling merrily. "What's so bloody funny?"

Sensing more to the joke, she peeled off some sealing tape and opened the tin. "Bruce! You bugger." She shot from her seat, rushed round the table and threw her arms round his neck.

As he responded to her kiss, he was very aware of how little clothing the compact nymph in his arms was actually wearing. Engel clearly noticed and rubbed a hip against his growing erection.

Looking over the close-cropped red hair, Bruce was

relieved to see that attention was focused on Engel's present, which was being shown round by Eva. The little, one-handed crossbow looked like a toy, but Tom pointed out the smart alloy bow could be tensioned by a conventional mechanical system or by disposable power-packs. A sheet of warnings, in half a dozen languages, emphasized the penetrating abilities of the thin, DU-tipped bolts.

After the presents, dinner was a boisterous, alcoholic affair. Tom clearly enjoyed being the focus of attention and the target of the increasingly outrageous behavior of the girls. After a few glasses of wine, Bruce also felt more relaxed and enjoyed having his friend bear the brunt of their games.

Their favorite was trying to shock him into choking on his drink, which Bruce remembered from an earlier incarnation in a Hong Kong bar. Here, however, the American proved to be amazingly good at timing his swallows to confound their efforts. He would swill wine in his mouth while they were building up to some outrageous display or comment and quickly gulp it down when they were least expecting it.

By the time they adjourned to the lounge for coffee and digestifs, the girls had quieted down a little and Angela was earnestly chatting to Tom about his work at the University. Although he was an engineer, his research in nanotechnology had a number of surprising overlaps with her microbiological studies, especially on the analytical instrumentation side. The girls were now bracketing Bruce on a sofa, Eva with her head on his shoulder while she silently followed the nanoscience discussion and Engel sitting in full lotus, with her back against him, while she studied the crossbow manual.

About eleven o'clock, Angela looked at Bruce and announced, "Hot tub! I reckon that would be just the thing to relax us before bed. What do you think, Bruce?"

"Shit, I'm really sorry. I've got an old tub on the balcony, but it hasn't been used in ages. If we filled it now, it'd take about five or six hours to heat up. I could set it up for the morning, if you like."

"Don't be silly, lad. I wouldn't be asking you if we hadn't sorted things out already. Let's go." She levered herself up and turned to pull Tom to his feet.

"Well, okay." Tom twisted to catch a hint from Bruce on how to react. Correctly interpreting the shrugged shoulders and palms raised to the ceiling as an indication that everything was beyond any man's control, he allowed himself to be led upstairs.

***

Angela started to pull the dress over her head as soon as she entered Bruce's bedroom. She waved at the en-suite bathroom, "Through there and onto the balcony. Switch on the air curtain to stop the room cooling down. We need to shower to get rid of this paint first."

Tom was rooted to the spot, watching the statuesque woman strip and, after throwing her single garment carelessly onto the bed, stride into the bathroom.

Engel slid in front of him. "What's up, Tom? Need some help?" She had already started on the buttons of his shirt and had pulled it open before he could offer more than token resistance.

"Mmm, this is more like it," she growled in appreciation as his body-builder's torso was exposed. "Have a look here, Beast. This is what you could be like if you'd start training your flabby arse." The look of panic on Tom's face seemed to fade a little as the complement registered.

Difficult to look frightened and chuffed at the same time.

The sight of Eva pulling off her tanga then distracted him. The absence of the small triangle of material exposed blond pubes, completely destroying the illusion of the body paint. Somehow she managed to look even more naked than Angela had been.

Better get out of this kit and into that tub sharpish.

He grinned, feeling the first twinges of tumescence.

As Engel bent down to help Tom remove his shoes, Eva pulled the small redhead's thong down with a fluid movement of her left hand and slapped the bare bottom thus exposed with her right. With a squeal, the small girl whirled round, caught hold of her tall opponent and threw her onto the clothes-strewn bed.

Bruce dragged off his clothes as quickly as possible and followed Angela. He left his bemused friend stripped to the waist, flies undone, wearing one shoe and nailed to the spot by the sight of the two naked women wrestling on the bed.

Angela had washed off the fake tattoo and had opened the sliding door onto the balcony, which was lit by red and green lights instead of the usual white spots. The balcony was sheltered by the overhanging eves of the house but, nevertheless, was covered by about thirty centimeters of snow. Snow-covered steps to the left led into the hot tub, which was still covered by its insulating lid. Bruce pressed a button by the door and the lid slid back, immediately hiding the balcony in a cloud of steam.

"I should clear the snow away," Bruce said, turning to go. "I've got a shovel in the basement."

Angela grabbed him by the elbow and pulled him towards the door. "Don't be such a poofter," she cried, dragging him through the blast of the air curtain and onto the balcony. The cold air on his body hardly registered, but the knee-deep snow was a shock. He quickly staggered after the brunette, who scampered up the steps and plunged inelegantly into the steaming water.

At first, the water seemed unbearably hot when he stepped into the bath. His legs tingled as he slid deeper, eventually ending chest-deep, sitting on a wide ledge. As he settled down, Angela slowly surfaced in the middle of the pool and scraped her face clear of a tangle of shoulder-length hair. She slid into position next to him and pointed silently above his head. Suspended above the center of the tub was a wreath of holly and mistletoe.

The deep kiss with the voluptuous, naked professor seemed to last an age. Bruce caressed her heavy buttocks with one hand while he slid the other up to stroke a hard nipple. Before things could progress further, he was shocked back to the present by an outbreak of curses when Engel burst through the door onto the balcony.

"Fuck, fuck, fuck." The petite woman bounced from foot to foot and then ran halfway up the steps to the tub and then stopped with an evil grin on her face. With perfect timing she scooped an armful of soft snow and flung it to explode over Eva when she followed her through the air curtain.

Engel's "Yes," as her naked body dived headfirst into the tub was drowned out by a wordless scream from the tall figure while she tried frantically to wipe off the snow sticking to her wet body.

As soon as she cleared her face enough to see, Eva rushed up the steps and plunged into the tub, sending a spray of hot water in all directions. After about twenty seconds, her head emerged and, even in the limited visibility due to steam and the colored lighting, Bruce could detect a dangerous glint in her eyes.

Engel had managed to slide her slim frame behind Angela, exposing only a grinning face. As Eva started a lunge in that direction, Bruce reached out and wrapped his arms around her. He had to use all his strength to hold the wriggling girl, but had to admit that it was not an unpleasant task as her naked body squirmed against his.

Gradually she calmed down and caught sight of Angela's pointing finger. She looked upwards and then smiled, relaxing completely. Sliding round in his grasp, she grabbed his head and drew him into an open-mouthed kiss.

Bruce first drew back in surprise, but quickly reacted to the probing tongue by opening his own mouth. A few moments of very wet kissing and then the girl broke contact and nuzzled his earlobe. “What were you doing there anyway?” she whispered. “Was that wrestling or foreplay?” while her hand closed on his erection.

Once more, just as Bruce was beginning to drift into a fantasy world, he was brought back to earth with a bump. This time it was a rather embarrassed cough and he glanced up to see Tom emerging onto the balcony, clutching a pile of bath towels.

“What a very sensible lad.” Angela stood and waved him toward the tub. “Throw those towels on the window ledge there and come and sit beside me.”

Tom got to the top of the steps, before hurling the towels at the window ledge and trying to step into the pool at the same time. No doubt due to a combination of embarrassment about the erection he was trying to hide and his eyes being glued to Angela’s massive tits, the towels missed their target, and he tripped on the top step. He splashed into the pool, half-caught by the large brunette and ending up with his head squeezed against a breast that was about the same size.

Bruce and the girls burst into peals of laughter.

Apparently oblivious to his discomfort, Angela dragged Tom to sit beside her. He had hardly recovered his breath when it was mistletoe time and he disappeared in a flamboyant embrace.

Bruce settled deeper into the hot water with a contented sigh. Eva lifted his right arm and wriggled to find a comfortable position with her head against his shoulder. Engel settled on his other side, her thin back pressed against his side, facing Tom. The water reached the middle of his chest but was lapping Engel's chin.

Tom had his head in Angela's shoulder and seemed to finally be relaxing, listening to her monologue on the therapeutic effects of hot water and the historical development of communal bathing as a social institution. He had just closed his eyes, possibly to minimize the distraction presented by the large breasts floating in front of his face, when he jerked upright with a shocked stare at Engel.

Bruce reached over with his left arm, took hold of a right nipple and squeezed. "Leave the poor lad alone. If you give my ski buddy a heart attack, I'll never forgive you," he whispered in her ear.

"What? Me? I never did nothing." A face with a look of teenage innocence looked up at him. "Well, not much anyway," she added with a salacious smile that made her appear instantly ten years older. A small hand slid up his thigh and gently squeezed his testicles.

The hot bath, maybe complemented by Angela's lecturing tone, had a soporific effect, sending the others into deep relaxation approaching a snooze. In Bruce's case, he could feel himself beginning to doze. He had no idea how much time had passed when Angela suddenly announced, "Wakey-wakey. Time to get out, before we all end up looking like prunes."

Grabbing Tom's hand she dragged him to his feet, so that he was face-level with her solid buttocks while she clambered out of the tub. She was certainly on the big side, but Bruce had to admit that her generous curves had a primeval sexual attraction.

Not quite a Paleolithic Venus, but certainly going in that direction.

The girls were much more interested in Tom, who seemed to be discomfited by their obvious attention. When he stepped out of the bath, Engel gave a piercing wolf-whistle, while Eva commented in a stage whisper, "Nice, tight buns."

Angela handed the blushing American a towel, not bothering with one for herself. She pulled him towards the air-curtain, "Come on, lad. Get in out of the snow." Pushing him into the bathroom, she turned to the others, "Just going to give this young chap his Christmas present. Don't wait up." She disappeared with a smug grin.

Bruce felt a twinge of jealousy. Tom was in for a Christmas night of passion and red-hot lust, whether he wanted it or not.

I just wish there was some way that I could tell him Angela's age or relationship to Eva. That'll be a shock to start Boxing Day with!

"What are you grinning about, Beast?" Engel slipped onto his lap. "Just because old fatarse has nabbed the hunk, it doesn't mean that I'm going to satisfy your perverse cravings tonight. I'm not that desperate." She twisted round and, to emphasize the point, kissed Eva passionately. Bruce watched in fascination as the kiss dragged on, inches from his face.

Finally breaking off, the androgynous redhead climbed quickly from the pool and bent to pick up a towel.

"Come on, Blondie..." As she straightened up she was cut-off by a massive snowball, which hit her full on the face.

"Fuck," she screamed while she staggered towards the door and was hit once more between the shoulder blades. The air curtain muffled further cursing.

The tall blonde sank back into the pool and settled herself on Bruce's knee. "Revenge is, indeed, sweet. What is it they say – 'a dish best served cold'? Mmm, yes." She snuggled against his chest.

Bruce wrapped his arms round her muscular body and sighed with inner contentment.

If it wasn't for the fact that Eva's a lesbian, this could be the start of a perfect night.

They sat silently for a couple minutes before an elfin face peered cautiously through the air-curtain. "Okay, Beast, I've changed my mind. Dump that fat dike in the snow and get your hairy arse in here. You're in for the shagging of a lifetime." The head disappeared an instant before a snowball slammed into the doorframe.

Eva turned and offered her hand. "Come on, let's get in. She rarely manages to stay angry for more than ten minutes. You never know, if you're really lucky, you might actually get the shagging of a lifetime."

Bruce got out of the tub, picked up the remaining towels and quickly scampered through the snow to the bathroom. After he closed the door, replaced the tub lid and switched off the lights on the balcony, he could hear scuffling noises from the bedroom. He dried himself in the shower hot air blower and tiptoed into the bedroom.

The two girls were in bed, under a very rumpled sheet. Eva drew it back and waved him to join them. "Have you ever had two girls sitting on your face while they make love to each other? I've heard some guys are really into that kind of stuff. You might enjoy it."

I haven't. I was. I would.

***

After foreplay beyond his wildest wet dreams, Engel was as good as her promise.

It wasn't just the shagging, it was her lesbian lover watching that made this bizarre and, at the same time, erotic beyond belief.

He glanced over at the two girls sleeping at his side.

But now, is it post-coital tristesse or the coincidence of two potentially lethal accidents that has me worried? We haven't even started the tricky bit of this caper, so surely it's just bad luck. Still, given the savagery of our opponents, we can't afford to let our defenses down.

7 ... fairies wear boots

Tom had, without a lot of persuasion, agreed to stay on for Boxing Day – having emerged sheepishly only in time for lunch. Although it was still overcast, that afternoon he took the girls skiing while Bruce and Angela struggled with the logistics of importing radioactive materials into Switzerland. After two hours, they conceded defeat and changed their plans to a private veetol jet transfer from a pharm warehouse in the French suburbs of Basel directly to Bermuda.

Tom was adapting rapidly to the Bohemian lifestyle of the Hasliberg chalet and, en route to the post-prandial hot tub, was the one to initiate a snowball fight with the two girls.

He may have a doctorate, but he has a lot to learn.

Bruce smiled, enjoying his friend's surprise as the boyish redhead threw him to the ground and held him immobilized with one hand while the tall blonde buried him in snow.

After a soak in the bath, Tom was first to leave. As he left the pool he held his hand out to the well-endowed professor and silently raised his eyebrows.

"Seconds away, round two," Angela announced happily while she clambered out, treating the others to a self-satisfied smirk. "Just off to watch Coronation Street," she called cryptically before she disappeared into the bathroom.

By December 27th, the weather had cleared completely and the sun rose on a blinding snowscape. Tom managed to drag himself out of bed in time to join Bruce and Eva on their early morning langlauf, but he was not in top form, trailing far behind the others.

"Too much bed and not enough sleep," Eva commented with a smile.

With obvious reluctance, Tom left after breakfast. He refused the offer of a lift and elected to walk to the cable-car station in order to take full advantage of the beautiful scenery. "Best Christmas I've ever had." He slapped Bruce on the shoulder. Brief kisses from the girls and a longer kiss from Angela and he was ready to go.

Bruce stood on the balcony, watching his friend fight his way through fresh snow to reach the snow-ploughed road. At the road, Tom turned to wave and was hit almost simultaneously in the forehead and chest by soft snowballs. Two giggling girls clattered up the stairs from the basement and defused his retaliation by the simple action of pulling up their t-shirts. The bemused American dropped his snowball, waved and walked off with a grin and a definite spring to his step.

***

The details of the Bure trip had been finalized with Angela as far as was possible, so Bruce called Professor

McLachlan to confirm that everything was also set from the IWU side. Bruce then loaded the van while the women finished packing. After a light lunch they set off for Basel.

The drive to the Brunig pass was beautiful but, after turning onto the main road to Lucerne, most of the time was spent in tunnels or sections where their view was blocked by high snow barricades. Beyond Lucerne, the clear blue sky was gradually blocked by high clouds until everything became grey and drab.

In Basel, they turned off the highway at the sign for the Hauptbahnhof and, suddenly, Bruce remembered their last drive along this route seven months previously.

My God, it was only May this year and I hardly knew these three at that point.

He glanced round at the women in turn.

Now it seems like I've been with them half my life.

Bruce took manual control and Eva threw a heads-up route on the windscreen. After weaving through the ugly industrial area, he drove into a tunnel that led to a blank wall and stopped in front of a row of security monitors.

Angela spoke into a com unit, and suddenly the floor sank as an elevator dropped them down two floors. A heavy door opened, allowing Bruce to drive into a short tunnel. Like an airlock, a second door in front of them opened only after the first had sealed closed with a solid-sounding thump.

"Seems a bit different to when we left the last time," Bruce commented.

"These guys tend to concentrate more on keeping

people out rather than in," Angela answered. "Also, security has been tightened a lot since May. There was quite a bit of bad blood between the big boys for a while."

Angela appeared to have satisfied all the security requirements, however, giving them a clear run through a labyrinth of tunnels until they climbed a spiral ramp into a huge hanger.

A large cargo plane was parked alongside a couple of smaller jets at the back of the hanger. Bruce drove straight past them and parked next to the group of people who were standing around a sleek executive jet, which was warming up near the open doors. Eva directed a couple of young men in light blue uniforms, who took some of the luggage from the van while Angela was greeted by an older man in an old-fashioned grey suit who, in turn, introduced her to a tall woman in a pilot's uniform. Bruce and Engel stood at the side of the van and moved forward only when Angela was ready to board the plane.

Each received a motherly peck on the cheek as Angela wished them luck. "Just get the samples as quickly as possible and get back to Bermuda. Give me a call if you have any problems at all."

Eva received a longer kiss. "Look after yourself, girl. Love you," she added in a soft voice before she turned, followed the pilot up the steps and disappeared inside.

Bruce climbed into the van and waited while the girls waved at the departing jet. When they joined him, their mood was distinctly subdued. Angela leaving was a sign that things were getting serious and, even though there had been no indications that anyone was paying any attention to their activities so far, they had to be prepared for the worst.

And Basel was where it started getting physical the last time.

Following Eva's directions, they emerged from the pharm after following a different, much shorter route. After a few hundred meters they joined a main road, with signs already counting down distances to the French border.

At the border, Bruce hardly had to slow down to drive his Swiss-registered vehicle into France. As they passed through the little town of Saint Louis, he mused that, despite half a century of the absence of a formal frontier between France and Germany, these border villages and towns were archetypal French. In much of the rest of Common Europe, by contrast, a homogenization process had rendered population centers completely characterless.

Passing the Greater Basel flood barricades, which extended as far as the airport, the road ran along a levee that was supposed to protect the Alsace plain from the summer floodwaters of the Rhine. North of Mulhouse, however, the evidence of repeated failure of the system was evident despite the layer of snow. Abandoned villages and ruined farms were common on both sides of the busy road.

Engel was surprised at the desolate appearance of the region and broke the silence that had reigned since Basel.

"What's up here? It surely can't be so fuck'n difficult to build a dyke."

"It's not just a matter of dykes," Bruce responded. "The high waters and spring rains make flooding inevitable here."

"Although that's not really the key problem," Eva added. "If it was simple flooding, they could grow rice or other flood-tolerant crops. It's the mining that went on in this area in the past and later dumping of waste in abandoned mines. The entire area is contaminated to hell with heavy metals, organics, you-name-it. Clean up would cost hundreds of billions – and the EC doesn't have that kind of spare cash. Cheaper just to abandon the worst contaminated regions."

"It's a shame that a lot of beautiful villages have been lost, but there are still some nice places at the edges of the Vosges Mountains. How about if we stay somewhere like that tonight?" Bruce suggested.

The girls agreed willingly and Bruce took the next turn off the autoroute, which led onto a much quieter road running west to the edge of the plain. As they drew closer to the hills, which gradually emerged from the grey sleet, there were more signs of life in the farms and increasing numbers of rugged-looking greenhouses that, even during the day, glowed faintly from internal lighting.

Turning north onto a small road, which a snow-covered sign claimed to be a *Route des Vins D'Alsac*e, Bruce drove for fifteen minutes before turning onto an even smaller side road leading to the walled town center of

Riquewihr. He drew into a covered car park beside the main gate, which allowed only pedestrians through the wall, then accessed the local accommodation database. "There's a nice old place here with a room free, a double with a pullout single. How about that?" he asked rhetorically, completing the booking at the same time.

Each carrying a shoulder bag, they walked from the covered park into the light sleety-rain that fell on the maze of narrow cobbled streets within the wall that still surrounded the medieval town center. Despite the weather and time of year, a few tourists were wandering around, recording the sights and buying tacky souvenirs from the numerous shops and street-hawkers.

Their hotel was only a hundred meters or so from the arch that granted entrance through the ancient walls. From its façade, it could once have been the townhouse of some nobleman, but the grand hallway was now a bit dilapidated, giving an air of faded splendor. Registration was entirely electronic, but a bored clerk sat behind the check-in desk watching TV on an ancient flat-screen. He looked up when the transaction was completed and an antique key-card was issued but, noting their light luggage, restricted himself to a grunted *B'jour* and returned to his TV.

Bruce led the way up a grand staircase and along a high-ceilinged hallway lit by old incandescent bulbs in shabby chandeliers. Dark paintings in ornate gilt frames hung between massive bedroom doors, decoratively carved out of some kind of dark wood. Stopping at the door numbered 106, he pushed the perforated plastic card into a slot above the handle and was surprised to find that the somewhat ill fitting door then opened smoothly. He guessed the lock must be about fifty years old. Entering, he looked around and then realized that the lock might be the youngest artifact present.

Engel pushed past him and jumped up onto the massive four-poster bed. She lay back spread-eagled, almost lost in the thick duvet. "Wow," she exclaimed in surprise. "There's a mirror on the roof of this fuckin' thing."

Bruce bent over to look. Sure enough, the threadbare pelmet around the four bedposts concealed a modern mirror and some hidden light source.

Probably the honeymoon suite.

Engel was clearly delighted with the bed. "Pity the old prof isn't with us. Plenty of room here for some wild and kinky bonking. What do you think, Beast?"

Eva turned from the large double window, which led onto a small balcony overlooking a drab little courtyard. "Which old prof? My mum or the tall one with the metalliferous wife?"

"Both, I guess," the redhead answered thoughtfully. "I suppose there's probably enough room. The mirror might not be a good idea for the Beast, though. He'd probably faint if he was able to watch whatever it was that scrawny bag-of-bones did to his poor willy."

"What about Tom then?"

"That'd be a good idea as long as the old prof – your

mum of course – wasn't around to snaffle him. I wouldn't mind jumping his fuckin' bones, I'll tell you. I just don't see what he sees in old, fat women. Must be like that Greek bloke."

"Oedipus?"

"The very one – mummy's boy. He does, however, have a very nice, tight butt."

Bruce tuned out as the girls continued an increasingly intimate discussion of his friend's physical attributes. He wandered around the room and found a modern holovision unit concealed in the top half of an antique cabinet, complete with a mini-bar in the bottom. An otherwise empty walk-in wardrobe contained a small safe and a dispenser of marital aids.

Definitely the honeymoon suite.

He continued his tour and inspected three very faded sketches of female nudes.

At one time these would have been rather nice.

The girls quickly unpacked their luggage into a massive chest of drawers. Bruce restricted himself to extracting a small toilet bag, before his satchel was tossed carelessly onto the small single bed that sat, rather incongruously, in the corner of the room.

Although it was already getting dark and still sleeting, the girls readily agreed to a walk round the town. The variable level of street lighting increased the historical feel to the maze of little streets within the ancient walls. The larger streets were clear of snow, indicating some kind of heating, but the smaller lanes and alleys merely had snow brushed to one side and were made treacherous by piles of slush, where snow had recently slipped from the roofs above.

Fewer tourists were evident and many of the souvenir shops had closed. The streets were, however, busier with locals and many of the small butchers, bakers, grocers and wine shops were doing a roaring trade. The bakers seemed to be particularly busy and the smell of fresh bread wafted through the air.

In less than an hour, they felt that they had seen enough and adjourned to a cavernous bar in the basement of a building that looked as if it might once have been a church. Bruce guided the girls to an alcove by the door, as far as possible from the other patrons, a group of locals who sat round the bar, wreathed in a cloud of cigarette smoke.

Like many of the Mediterranean countries, smoking of carcinogenic tobacco was still very popular in France, despite the existence of substitute smoking materials that were almost risk-free. While it was true that most cancers – and other associated problems like heart disease – were easily curable, Bruce could not understand why anyone would want to inflict such serious medical treatments on themselves. Plus, he hated the stink of cigarette, pipe and, especially, cigar smoke.

A world-weary barmaid took their order surprisingly quickly and returned with two hot-chocolates, two Cognacs and a twenty-five centiliter pichet of local Riesling for Bruce. She raised an eyebrow when the girls poured the spirits directly into their creamy chocolates, but departed without a comment.

They killed time over their drinks, examining some rather gruesome instruments of torture hanging from the walls and ceiling. The girls competed with each other to imagine how Rebecca McLachlan might introduce such tools into her S&M love life and what the possible consequences on Bruce's anatomy might be. By the time they left, the morose cloud that had descended on the group in Basel had vanished completely and they now looked the part of friends on holiday, without a care in the world, while they compared menus outside restaurants to choose a location for dinner.

Bruce felt that the meal itself was a bit heavy going – especially as the girls had insisted that they all had *Choucroute Royale Garni*.

No matter how well disguised by French chefs, this remains sauerkraut and fatty pork, as far as I'm concerned.

Nevertheless, it was accompanied by an excellent, if very expensive, Riesling from a local vineyard.

Wine production in the Alsace was a small fraction of what it once had been and confined now to the foothills of the Vosges Mountains. Greenhouses and root heaters protected the vines during the hard winters and artificial irrigation was often needed in the heat of summer. The resultant wines were still of high quality and, due to their rarity, commanded high prices and were rarely found outside the region. This had to be distinguished from a lot of cheaper wine that was sold as Alsatian but was produced from imported grapes.

The girls both elected for Mouse au Chocolat for dessert, while Bruce chose a portion of Munster, washed down by a half-bottle of a heavy Corsican red wine. Neither of the women was prepared to try the smelly cheese with its slimy orange rind but, as far as Bruce was concerned, this was certainly the highlight of the entire meal.

After dinner they wandered aimlessly through a labyrinth of slippy lanes for a half hour. Sleet turned to light snow and unheated cobbles became coated with a treacherous layer of ice. Selecting on the basis of minimum smokiness, they sat at the counter of a small bar and finished the evening with coffee and Calvados.

Despite lights glowing from several room windows, Bruce had to use his plastic key to open the front door of the hotel. The reception area was now deserted, although faint music drifted from a doorway that seemed to lead into a bar. "Early start tomorrow," Bruce reminded the girls, diverting them from further investigation of the source of the music and herding them towards their bedroom.

They hung up damp jackets in the gigantic wardrobe and pulled off their winter boots. Bruce then stripped and headed for the en-suite bathroom while the girls began to argue about sleeping arrangements.

"It's fuckin' obvious to me. I'm the AC / DC one here, so I go in the middle."

"Poor old Bruce needs his beauty sleep, so it'd be

better if I was in the middle. If he has any energy for self-abuse, then that'd also be very much better, as he'd obviously get off with much less effort while looking at me."

It's going to end up wrestling on the bed pretty soon now.

He smiled and closed the door behind him.

The shower was something out of the previous century, which was limited entirely to spraying water from above. He dried himself with a thick, soft but rather grey towel and found an electro-mechanical razor in a cupboard under the sink. Somewhat cautiously he drew it through his stubble and was surprised to find it did a reasonable job. A splash of the provided aftershave, a rinse with tooth cleanser and then he was done.

Two rather disheveled girls regarded him from the bed. "It's agreed," a triumphant Engel announced. "I'm in the middle." She bounced off the bed, pulling the tall blonde behind her. They stripped off trousers, shirts, knickers and, in Eva's case, a sports bra, and carelessly dropped their clothes on the floor.

Before the tall blonde was dragged into the bathroom, she turned to Bruce. "Get into bed. Maria's going to show me how to give the perfect blowjob." With a salacious grin, she disappeared.

Bruce threw back the cover and climbed onto the bed. He lay in the middle of the expanse of white sheet, looking critically at the figure reflected with perfect clarity by the mirror above. Not quite a six-pack, he thought critically, pinching a roll of fat from his stomach. Maybe more of a small beer barrel. *Must do more regular training*, he decided for the umpteenth time.

His critical listing of the different points of improvement needed in order to transform himself into a veritable Adonis, which he was disappointed to note was already running into double figures, was interrupted by the reappearance of the women.

Eva wandered around the bed and clambered in on the other side while Engel, in a typically perverse way, climbed painfully over Bruce to wedge herself in the middle. She then twisted downwards and grabbed a hold of his cock. He lifted himself onto his elbows to see what has going on, but was pushed back into the pillow. "Watch the action in the mirror. That's what it's there for."

Indeed, when he lay back, Bruce realized he could see everything going on in the mirror, although there was a momentary feeling of disconcertion due to the unaccustomed perspective of looking vertically upwards at himself. Both girls were now head-down on the bed. Engel was stroking his already erect dick with her left hand, while she cradled his balls with her right. She was whispering a running commentary, with breaks only when she ran her tongue along the length of his rigid member.

Eva was squeezed against the smaller frame, her cheek touching that of the redhead while she looked on in rapt attention. Almost unconsciously, she was cupping a small breast in her left hand, slowly rubbing an erect nipple between finger and thumb.

By listening carefully Bruce could make out most of

Engel's instructions, "...now under the head here. Get the foreskin right back and lick all around. It's nice now after a shower. In the morning it can be a bit cheesy – you know, like that fuckin' stuff he had for dinner."

The blonde wrinkled her nose and gave a snort of disgust.

The commentary died away when she took his prick into her mouth and started to suck him deeper and deeper, the rhythm synchronizing with the movements of her tongue and hands.

Bruce's breathing became deeper and faster; his spine arched in ecstasy. Just as he was about to come, Engel drew back and explained, "Now the critical bit...make like a vacuum cleaner." He groaned as she proceeded to do exactly that, sucking hard while a long drawn-out orgasm caused him to gasp out loud.

While his body shook, Engel continued to suck on his slowly softening penis. Eva looked horrified. "Yuck. You're not really swallowing that are you? That's totally disgusting."

The redhead completed her ministrations and twisted round with a grin. "Tastes tart but very good for you. Full of proteins and vitamins and all kinds of good shit. You should try it." She grabbed the blonde's head and tried to force a kiss, while the taller girl fought her off.

"No way. No chance. I can't believe I've ever let you kiss me before. Never again. You're a dirty..." Eva's protestations died away as Engel gradually moved her attention down the shapely body and finally ended up kissing a lower pair of lips. "Mmm, yes. That's good. Just there." She began to slowly rock her hips from side to side.

Her head blocked his view of the action in the mirror but, by craning his neck, Bruce could watch Engel working the tip of her tongue over a swollen vulva. Then she used her fingers to spread the wet folds wide open, and sparkling blue eyes looked up at him while she gave a smug grin. "Now, on the other hand, this is really tasty. Who gives a fuck if it's good for you or not." She then returned full attention to the exposed, gaping pink flesh.

Bruce felt his erection grow while Eva was brought to a screaming series of orgasms. By the time she had started licking Engel's hairless quim, he felt ready to burst and couldn't restrain himself from the few strokes of masturbation needed to make himself come. He was aware of Engel watching him, which somehow made it even more erotic. Without a word she rubbed a finger on his sticky stomach and, with a mischievous grin, shoved her finger between her legs, If Eva noticed at all, it appeared to have no effect on her noisy cunnilingus.

Despite the fascinating floorshow, Bruce dozed off shortly after Engel had reached a very noisy climax. The girls were still at it in a soixante-neuf variant.

Where do they get their energy?

That was his last conscious thought.

***

It was probably about an hour later when pressure on his bladder caused Bruce to wake. Careful not to wake the girls, who were buried in a heap of bedding at his side, he slipped out from the sheets and padded off to the bathroom, able to navigate by the faint streetlight penetrating the windows. His feeling of unease was back, a grim foreboding of danger in the near future.

It's not like last time, there's no way the bad guys can possibly know what we're up to. Then again, I was sure of that last time too – and tragically wrong then.

8 ...going underground

Bruce woke to a grey light seeping through rather grimy lace curtains and turned to smile at the two girls sleeping at his side. They were covered only by a sheet and were lying face-to-face, noses touching and arms wrapped round each other. Engel was snoring gently.

How the hell can anybody sleep like that?

He smiled before carefully slipping out of bed to avoid disturbing them.

After completing his morning ablutions and dressing, he woke the girls by slowly drawing down the sheet that covered them. The sight was almost enough to draw him back into bed.

Engel's eyes had opened the instant the cover moved, and she stretched with a yawn.

He gently slapped a very comely backside. "Come on now, time to get moving. It's bug sampling time."

Fifteen minutes later they were breaking their fast on thick, oily coffee and rich, buttery croissants. This was served in the bar area by the same TV-watching clerk who had been in reception the previous afternoon. The only other people present were a middle-aged couple: a rather tired looking man with a bald head and a grey beard sitting with a short blonde woman wearing very tight trousers and a ski-shirt that revealed muscular arms. Probably heavily into some kind of sport, Bruce guessed, wondering what would lead to the well-defined biceps evident every time she lifted her coffee cup.

Engel shocked him out of his reverie by kicking his ankle. "Stop staring, you sad bastard," she whispered. "Middle-aged men and old women with big tits," she muttered in Eva's direction.

True enough, Bruce conceded to himself.

The woman has rather large, well-shaped breasts, but there's no way either girl will believe that hadn't been what caught my attention.

After breakfast, it took only a few minutes to pack their luggage, and shortly afterwards, they were back on the road, driving through a grey landscape that was poorly visible through wet, soggy snow. Bruce followed the wine route as far as Strasbourg and then joined a six-lane autoroute for the rest of the circuitous route via Metz and Nancy.

To Bruce's surprise, the repository turn-off was actually signposted on the motorway and at all subsequent junctions on the secondary roads that led to the site. It was just after nine thirty when they arrived in the car park in front of a large visitor center. Already several coaches were parked in front of it and, as he watched, another drew up and disgorged a load of school children. He had no idea what on earth they could be doing here on a Sunday during the school holidays.

Beyond the center, they came to a small blockhouse signed *Reception* in English and *Réception* in French, followed by a long list of other languages in much smaller letters. Bruce parked under the shelter of a transparent awning and led the girls into the building.

Inside, he entered a single room with a row of five booths, each manned by two uniformed staff, mainly young women. Two security guards lounged by the door. Only one of the booths was busy, with four business-suited Japanese.

Typical make-work jobs to increase acceptance by local communities.

Bruce stepped into the nearest free booth.

Their visit was already registered, so all that was required were confirmatory retinal scans. Identification bracelets were distributed, which gave a green glow when locked in place and would be valid for two days. The bracelet would also allow entrance to the guest hostel, which they were booked into for one night. Bruce confirmed the location of their meeting with the Director of Science and that Dee and his students had arrived the previous evening.

Back in the van, the route to the main administration building downloaded automatically from the bracelet to the navigation computer. Bruce drove to the indicated visitors' entrance, where they had to pass through three security fences, each with its individual checkpoints. At the second of these, they had to leave the van while it was comprehensively scanned. These measures seemed a bit draconian to the girls, but Bruce knew that the site had, in the past, been a regular target for terrorist attacks by eco-nuts, anti-nukes, French nationalists and many more.

The route planner directed Bruce to an almost empty garage below the Admin building. As they took an elevator to the eighth floor, Bruce tried to guess what the hundreds of people who must work in this edifice actually did.

Leaving the elevator, a tinny voice from his bracelet directed Bruce to a small meeting room, which bustled with people. Bruce immediately identified Dee, towering over the four students, who were seated at the far end of a long conference table. Dee waved as soon as he saw Bruce and hurried to join him, the faithful Dave trailing in his wake. "The Gods are indeed smiling on us, Bruce old man. The Science Director is down with the latest Singapore flu and his deputy is on holiday in Kenya."

There had not been a flu pandemic since the early 2020s and, since then, such diseases were easily treatable. Nevertheless, the limited access of large parts of the global population to modern medical support and the highly contagious nature of many recent flu variants usually resulted in isolation for a couple of days for anyone unlucky enough to catch a novel strain.

"Why's that good news?" Bruce enquired. "Isn't that likely to delay things?"

"Not at all, m'boy, not at all. The director would have had to give us the big welcome, introduce staff, invite us to lunch, all that toss. Basically, I suppose, the poor bugger doesn't have much else to do. There's not a lot of science going on in this joint. Projects for local school kids and grants to sweeten-up French academics, but no science, per se. It's a lucky escape, I'm telling you. We can just sort details out with the techies," he raised his chin in the direction of a couple of sullen-looking men in white overalls, "and get cracking."

The extremophile team members were rather taken aback by this sudden development. Nevertheless, determined not to look a gift horse in the mouth, Bruce hurried the girls to the conference table where Dee was already getting his students organized.

Dee took full charge of the project briefing, confirming that the local staff had received all deliveries from the IWU and had already transferred everything to the sampling zone. Ventilation in that area had been increased and all power and communications links checked. The projection holo over the table showed a live time feed from this location to confirm this point. Because the old test site was completely separate from any of the current active areas, a buffer zone with changing and decontamination facilities had already been set up at the point of entrance from a main access tunnel.

The senior technician, Jean-Baptiste, had evidently met the professor previously. He assured Dee that they would provide any assistance required for the training exercise, but was evidently much relieved to be asked only to provide transportation.

"No point in you lads getting all kitted up and

hanging around for hours watching us. You can do that just as well from the comfort of your control room up here." The professor winked at Bruce and whispered, "Big football match on today. Watch these guys cheer up."

Dee's prediction came true immediately, as J-B grinned with evident relief and gave his partner a covert thumbs-up. Final details were quickly organized, and the group trouped to a large elevator that took them directly to a basement garage. A small twenty-seater bus was waiting for them, and the team clambered in while J-B reconfirmed the transport route with Dee and Bruce, plotted as a red-line on a small holo-display that sat where a driver might be expected in a manually controlled vehicle.

J-B retreated off the bus and waved as the doors closed, and the bus rolled smoothly forward into a well-lit tunnel. After about a hundred meters, the bus slowed to allow a massive door to slide aside, allowing entrance to a huge cavern containing a strange device, looking like a heavy, isolated doorframe, anomalously sitting in its center.

The bus drove slowly through this portal while Dee explained that this was the inventory check – logging all radioactivity going into the repository. "All scans here are logged by the IAEA, with a special check on fissile material. When we leave there will be another check, which is an even tighter scan to ensure that these nasties stay put.

Bruce and Engel had positioned themselves to watch the IWU students while Eva sat beside the lanky professor.

Both of them noticed the Egyptian girl squirm uncomfortably while they passed through the scanner and Engel whispered in his ear, "The hairy Arab is definitely not kosher."

"I suppose that's one way to put it," Bruce whispered back, as suspicions about the Egyptian student's bizarre behavior in Grimsel began to build a somewhat worrying picture.

Maybe this is what's been bothering me for the last few days?

"When this Nariman was being cleaned up at the IWU, what actually happened?"

The bus had passed through another massive door and into a large two-lane tunnel that spiraled gently downwards while Engel answered, eyes closed as she strained to remember details. "We had already been through monitors up at the lab and her hands were okay after we got rid of her contaminated gloves. Down at the institute, there was a full body radiation monitor and another scanner...sonic or something. I don't think they were supposed to find anything. Just part of training for the students, like the stuff the prof was talking about a minute ago."

"Okay, but what happened when you got a reading from her?"

"We had already stripped off working clothes and were wandering around in undies, not a pretty sight in the Arab's case...big baggy passion-killers with tufts of pubes sticking out everywhere—"

Bruce gently elbowed her ribs.

"Okay, okay. The Nariman creature was last through the monitor and set off an alarm. Angela and the Fijian girl checked her out and found some traces of activity on both her upper forearms, so they scrubber her down and then sent her off for a shower. God, when she dropped those knickers, I have never in my life seen such a fuckin' hairy—"

"Right, right, I can guess. But did she go though the other scanner?"

Engel hesitated, eyes screwed up. "You know..." she answered slowly, "I don't think she did."

***

After about a couple kilometers on the spiral ramp, the road entered another large cavern, which must have been about five hundred meters long, with tunnels leading off to the right at fifty meter intervals. The bus drove past all of these and smoothly drew into a much smaller tunnel at the end of the cavern. The vehicle stopped and the route map was replaced by a holo of J-B. "You are now entering the test area," he explained before a door opened to allow the bus access to an airlock section.

After the first hatch closed, a second opened, and the bus drove into the experimental access drift while J-B continued, "I'm afraid this is pretty old and not up to the level of the repository itself. Anyway, it's perfectly safe and I hope you can get all you want. Call me if you need anything. Ciao." He vanished and the route map reappeared.

The tunnel was indeed a marked contrast to the gleaming white, antiseptic cleanliness they had experienced so far. Unpainted concrete walls were dirty, cracked and, in several places, covered by colorful slimes. After only about a hundred meters, the bus stopped in front of an air curtain that blocked off the tunnel and the doors opened.

Dee led the way off the bus, turning to extend a helping hand to Eva, but ignoring his other students. As the others filed off, they grouped around the tall professor, who was now standing with his hand on the shoulder of his Kiwi student. "Okay, ladies and gentlemen, we are now ready to start our exercise. The main thing to remember is that this isn't a game. We are in a real repository, full of real waste. Although this is an experimental area, there's high burnup MOX just a few tens of meters through there." He waved a shovel-like hand in the general direction of the air curtain.

"You can now think of yourselves as inspectors for the IAEA or local government or greenies or whatever, who have got to examine a suspect site. You're going to take some samples for testing in a careful and quality-assured manner, because these might later be the basis of national or international court cases. Most importantly, however, you're going to sample with all precautions needed to ensure safety as I can't guarantee, even in this exercise, that you won't hit high activity zones."

As he finished, the professor raised an eyebrow in

Bruce's direction. Engel moved to his side, rising on tiptoes to whisper into his ear. "What's going on, Beast? You and that Dee are up to something."

"Don't worry about it, just something to ensure that we have fewer problems with our samples. If you're going to worry about anything, concentrate on Nariman."

Bruce and Engel followed the others through the air curtain into an area of tunnel that looked much better, the walls and floor being covered with some kind of white plastic coating. Within this area sat two large trailer units set up as changing rooms. Dee led the men into one, while the Fijian student, Eve, had been delegated in charge of the ladies.

After the students had disappeared from sight, Bruce strode quickly to the frame of the monitor that was set up for radiation scanning after sampling. As he hoped, it was a multimode scanner, with only the radiation detectors activated. A simple remote hack from his palmtop put sonic, terahertz and x-ray scans online, with output downloaded directly to his own image analysis software. While he hurried to change, Bruce smiled to himself.

The trap is set – just a case of getting the rat into it.

Fifteen minutes later, the group was fully kitted up in disposable overalls, shoes and gloves. For the sake of completeness, Dave also issued light helmets with integral emergency visors and facemasks. Dee then led the way through a second air curtain into the tunnel zone where the sampling would take place. The tunnel walls had not been coated in this section and preparation restricted to installation of bright lighting, special ventilation and extra power supplies. The actinic glare of the lights emphasized the fact that the area had clearly been unused for a long time, with stalactites extending from the concrete roof and algal mats growing on the walls and floors in areas of water seepage.

The sampling zone extended for about twenty-five meters, before the tunnel bent at right angles to the left. An extremely rusty chain-link gate prevented further access. This bore an *Access Inderdit* sign, which was only just legible. It was difficult to see beyond the gate, as the tunnel section was unlit, but reflections from pools of water on the floor confirmed Bruce's earlier suspicions that there had been flooding problems in this area.

The equipment from the IWU lay on transportation pallets along the right wall of the tunnel. Dave and Mob concentrated on setting up the old mechanical drilling rig, while Eve and the two IAEA girls organized core barrels and sampling equipment.

Bruce took responsibility for setting up his lightweight drill, after first spraying the target area of tunnel wall with a sealant that also acted as a surface disinfectant. The drill itself was first glued to the wall and then sterilized, along with its surroundings, by a burst of hard UV. Orientation of the drill was set up by Eva, working from Bruce's laptop, while the liners and sampling kit were neatly stacked in place by Engel.

Dee watched the process with interest, peering over Eva's shoulder to examine the drilling profile. "You're pretty close to the waste there, mate," he pointed out to Bruce. "All the same, your team certainly seems up to it." With a sigh, he turned and plodded back to check on Dave's progress with his rig.

As soon as Dee's back was turned, Eva quickly modified the drill line that was being set up. Bruce winked at her to confirm the settings. This would pass within centimeters of the concrete-filled holes containing the waste, rather than half a meter as previously indicated. *Poor old Dee would've had a heart attack, had he known.*

As soon as the drill was ready to go, Bruce left the girls to get on with it and moved over to stand with a frowning Professor McLachlan. "So, Dee, we're ready to rock and roll. How goes it with you?"

"Dave and yon Mob laddie are doing really well, work nicely as a team and can even master that shitty old bugger of a drill." He nodded as they finalized alignment against a holographic projection. "Your Eve here is very careful, even if a bit slow and, um..." He was evidently searching for the name. "Rehana, yes. She's very competent. In fact, I'm not really sure why she's on this course. But Nariman..." He groaned. "Actually, where the hell is the bloody woman?"

"I saw her disappear back towards the changing room a couple of minutes ago. Maybe off for a pee. Should I have a look?"

"Be obliged if you could, old chap," he shouted over the noise of the drill starting up. "I'd better wait here until they get through the tunnel lining, at least. You never know when you might hit rebars or some other shit in these old tunnels."

As Bruce passed through the translucent air curtain, he spotted the Egyptian student rummaging through the small packs that the students had brought with them. She jumped up with a startled gasp when she suddenly heard his approach. "Bloody camera!" she spluttered. "Video thing. I mean holo thing. For the bloody record taking."

Bruce smiled. "I saw it earlier lying on the floor and put it across there." He pointed to an object that resembled a huge knuckle-duster that lay on a bench used for removing overshoes. As he was partially blocking her route, the student was forced to walk through the monitoring frame in order to collect the device. Turning once to scowl in his direction, she then stomped off back into the sampling tunnel.

"And without a word of thanks," Bruce murmured while he pulled out his palmtop and checked the scan, rotating the holographic image at face level. First the terahertz scan showed an unclothed Nariman.

My God, what a bush indeed.

He grimaced and quickly moved to the sonic – x-ray synthesis. The image processor had already identified anomalies from her stomach region, which stepped up in magnification on his command.

"Oh, shit." The software confirmed his first guess. While he hurried back towards the sampling area, his thoughts raced.

Absolutely fucking typical case of the law of conservation of luck. Every bit of good luck, like the sampling being so incredibly easy, has got to be matched by something bad. In this case, something incredibly bad.

***

Bruce returned to the sampling area and watched silently as Nariman stamped around the two drilling rigs with the camera held at arm's length. Although she looked inelegant and bad-tempered, Bruce noted that the recording was being very professionally done, the camera moving around to ensure that no action was blocked by the busily working students.

Now this is something she really does know what to do.

Bruce frowned as his worries increased.

The IWU students were making much better progress than at Grimsel – possibly having benefited from the first exercise, or maybe just because the rock being drilled was much softer. The drilling exhaust traps were still measuring activity at background levels and they were about to remove a first length of core – a complete 1-meter length.

He meandered farther to check on the microbiologists, who were doing even better. The laser had already penetrated 15 meters and stopped after encountering first traces of artificial radioactivity. Enough to show up on Bruce's sensitive monitor, but not yet high enough to set off the exhaust trap alarm. Surreptitiously, Bruce closed a valve that diverted the laser exhaust through a cryogenic trap, which was disguised as a conventional shielded core container, before joining the common line shared with the IWU drill. He nodded to Eva, who restarted the drill.

After an hour, radioactivity levels from the laser exhaust had peaked and were beginning to decline. Bruce was happy that they had drilled through the plume of releases from a failed waste package and hence stopped drilling and started with core recovery. As previously agreed, Eva removed core only very slowly, exaggerating the radiation monitoring, surface decontamination and logging procedures. Engel was equally careful with core sealing and packaging, taking time to smile sweetly at Nariman, whenever she wandered by with her camera.

Bruce sidled up to McLachlan, who was listening to the complaints voiced by Dave – apparently also on behalf of the silent Mob, who towered behind him. "But Professor, breakfast was a long time ago. I'm starving here. My stomach thinks my throat's been cut—"

"Yes, yes, lad, I know. But it'll take ages to get cleaned up, drive out, find something to eat, back in, kitted up again. We'll lose hours. We could be done here in a couple of hours. Three at most."

The rotund Kiwi looked like he had received a death sentence. "I'm starving now," he grumbled before guiding his tall companion back to the drilling rig.

Bruce followed the frowning scientist out of earshot. "I think we've got what we need – should we start the test now?"

"Excellent idea." The professor looked instantly

cheerier and coded something into his palmtop.

Immediately the radiation readings on the exhaust monitor began to climb slowly and the ticking, which had been an unnoticed backdrop to all of their work, began to get more rapid. The Indian student was the first to notice and glanced suspiciously at the monitor, which was now at the very top of the permissible background range. "Is that all right, professor?" she asked shyly.

"What do you think, Dave?"

While the worried-looking student peered at the details transferred to his palmtop, the background limit was exceeded and a shrill alarm went off.

All the students froze, before turning, wide-eyed to stare at the monitor. Bruce glanced at Eva and Engel, who looked equally shocked, but were staring worriedly at him. The first movement was again the slim Indian, who called out, "Cesium 137! We must have hit a leak. We should get out of here!"

Dave looked horror-struck. "Fuuuuuck," he exclaimed before looking over at the skinny professor who was leaning against the far wall with his arms folded. He looked even more shocked for a moment, but slowly started to recover as the reality of the situation began to dawn. "Wait a minute, folks. This is just what could happen during any sampling work. Mob, stop the drill. Rehana, what are the levels like?"

The sudden voice of command seemed to have reassured the students, with the exception of Nariman who was visibly shaking, although continuing to video the evolving incident.

"The levels are just above background and 137 only," Rehana answered clearly, completely recovered from her earlier shock.

"Okay, switch off that bloody alarm, button on the top there. There's no danger at all. This is what you might get at the very front of a plume. I guess we don't need to go further." He glanced at his supervisor and was rewarded by a cheerful nod. "So we just need to get this last bit of core out, bearing in mind that it could be quite hot. We can't rely on the exhaust monitor here to give the whole story."

"Good, good, good. Well done, Dave lad. Okay, you can get on with it, but carefully. Just, while you're at it, have a think about the setup. We'll have a wee chat about it later."

McLachlan turned to Bruce. "That was a bloody good idea of yours. I thought they were going to shit themselves. Even your dream team looked like rabbits in headlights. I'm going to enjoy watching the vid of this." He glanced around, evidently looking for the Egyptian. "Buggeration. Don't tell me she's off again. I hope to hell she got everything recorded before she ran off to the loo."

"I'm on it. You'd better watch your core recovery." Bruce slipped through the air curtain after glancing over to note that Eva and Engel were rapidly packaging core while everyone's attention was elsewhere. Some of this was hot enough to be picked up by the exhaust gas monitor, but the alarm was off and nobody was taking any notice of it, now that drilling had stopped.

The control area was empty, with no sign of Nariman. Bruce silently moved to the ladies changing trailer and eased the door open. Again no sign of anyone, but a toilet door at the end of the changing room was ajar. As he crept towards it, Bruce could make out the figure of the student sitting on the toilet seat while she watched a holographic replay of the surprise exercise. She was deep in a conversation with someone, which, given their present location, indicated some very sophisticated coms gear in this camera.

"Here it is again," she said as the moment of the alarm going off replayed. "This is the only time that we have seen any kind of radioactivity here. There was much more at Grimsel. I have no idea what they are doing here."

Bruce noted that Nariman's strong accent had disappeared and her English had improved dramatically.

There was a delay as she listened to some response, too directional for Bruce to pick up, and then the holo shifted to the microbial sampling team. "See, as I told you. They finished drilling without any activity at all. All background." The view zoomed onto the exhaust monitor. A delay and then a zoom-in to examine the laser drilling rig in detail. It zoomed in farther, tracing the exhaust line.

Oops, here we go.

"What? Bloody monitor. Bloody, bloody monitor."

The holo winked out.

Much more like the old Nariman, he thought while he moved to the side of the door. As the Egyptian stormed out of the toilet, he punched her on the side of the head with all the force he could muster. She dropped like a log. He crouched down beside her and slapped a derm on her neck. This was one of Angela's specials, which she assured him would keep anyone out for at least a couple hours, regardless of what kind of protective pharmware they were loaded with.

He quickly dragged the unconscious woman to a bench and laid her along it. As fast as he could, he pulled the disposable clothes off her, until she lay in her passion-killer knickers and an elasticated vest. The second locker he tried contained her clothes and he awkwardly dragged them onto her slumped form, thankful that all were on the baggy side. Finally, with a grunt, he heaved her over his shoulder and carried her to the bus, where he dropped her heavily onto the rear bench seat.

Wiping sweat from his brow, Bruce strode back to the sampling area and waved Dee over. "It's not very good with little Nariman. Women's trouble I think."

"You've got to be joking. In this day and age? Surely there's no civilized..." Dee trailed off.

"Yep." Bruce nodded. "Fundamentalist Muslim of some form. Believe that it's God's wish that women suffer The Curse. I've given her a painkiller and she's dozed off. Out like a light, actually, probably not used to such strong medicine."

The skinny professor shrugged. "Well maybe for the best. At least it keeps her out of the way. Anyhow, your team seems to be pretty well finished and my crowd has managed to master the apparently contaminated core." He grinned. "I think we can move out pretty soon. Dave and Mob have volunteered to come back and clear up the drills. Anything to get to food as soon as possible."

The rest of the tidying up went smoothly and the extremophile team was already back in the bus before the other students had started to change. As they looked together at the sleeping Egyptian, Engel could restrain herself no longer. "Right, now out with it. What the fuck's going on? First the contamination, which almost had me peeing my pants, I may add. Then the disappearing Arab, who's now doing a Rip-van-Winkle impersonation. You've definitely been up to something."

"The contamination is the easy bit. I talked big Dee into staging a special test, simulating the effect of drilling into a highly active area."

"What do you mean simulating?" Eva broke in. "The bloody monitor alarm went off with all the cesium stuff. I thought we were going to get nabbed."

"No, no, it was all simulated. It was a hack into the monitor to give a pre-programmed signal. We cleared it with the control room boys in advance. I'm sure they were watching all the fun...as long as it didn't clash with the football. It actually was a good exercise for them, and the Dave lad did well. Admittedly, I think he would have panicked more if Dee hadn't given the game away by his casual manner. Whatever, it served the main purpose for us. Nobody paid the slightest interest to the monitors afterwards. If that hadn't worked, Eva would have had to distract Dee while I hacked the monitor. That would've been tricky, though, as the monitor has a failsafe analogue readout, which is clear to anyone who knows what to look for."

"Nariman's a bit more difficult. I just couldn't imagine why she would try to contaminate herself at Grimsel. Just as we were coming in today, however, I noticed that she was worried about scans. It seems the fuss at the IWU did the job of diverting everyone's attention, so that she managed to avoid being scanned."

"But nobody was taking any notice of the scans," Engel interrupted. "The wee Indian bint sailed right through, even though she was definitely carrying something. Did the bloody Nariman really have so much to hide?"

"She did indeed. I'll show you the scans later and tell you all about how I got them, but the bottom line is that the girl is a walking bomb. I can only guess that she is either on some kind of suicide mission or it's to take care of the evidence in case she gets caught."

"A bit extreme for the latter," Eva commented. "I thought spies had cyanide pills or a more high-tech equivalent thereof these days."

"I've been thinking about that," Bruce responded. "Remember the story your mother told us about the original sabotage at her lab. It was just a break in, but the guy torched himself – and the entire lab – when he got caught out. Sounds a lot like the same team."

The girls looked at each other in silence. Once again

they had relaxed and let their guards down a little.

The sampling was like a game and we were having fun together. Casual sexual relationships are increasingly common, as old traditions like marriage begin to disappear from many western cultures – but the relationship I've built up with these women - is unusually intense. I can't think of any time I've ever had anything similar, even with one woman.

But now our game is crashing up against reality. Our opponents aren't playing by any civilized rules and are not only prepared to kill, but even to commit suicide in order to reach their goals.

For the first time, Bruce actually began to feel sorry for the unfortunate Egyptian girl. How on earth could she get so drawn into a cause that she'd consider killing herself while still in her mid-twenties?

Rather somberly Bruce continued, "Anyway, we should be okay as long as Nariman is out cold. All the same, we're certainly going to need some help here. I don't like doing it, Eva, but I guess we're going to need to switch in your pharm support. Can you raise them from here and get them to sort out some kind of medical pick-up for Nariman. If they can do that, we have a few minutes to make up a story to ensure that she doesn't get taken to the medical center on site. I dread to think what would happen if they attempt to scan her."

On Eva's nod, Bruce retreated off the bus to join the professor and the rest of the students, who were cramming various pieces of kit into their packs and stowing a small DU shielded container containing their sub-samples into the luggage space in the boot of the bus, beside a similar container with the microbial samples. The main cores would be picked up later when the lads returned to recover the drills.

Bruce would have very much preferred to take all his samples with him, but things were going too well to make a fuss. He checked with Dee. "That seems like a job well done. It's pretty late for lunch, but I'm sure we can get something in the site restaurant. It may be an EU repository, but it's France after all. Anyway, my treat. These pharm boys have oodles of dosh, so we could live it up a bit."

Before the professor could respond, Dave, who was standing by his elbow, let out a heartfelt, "Yes," causing them both to grin.

***

Returning to the surface, with all required scanning, went smoothly. The only worrying point was the final full-body scan to log fissionable material. Bruce argued that this token gesture was fairly pointless for Nariman, who had been kept well away from all radioactivity. With a shrug, McLachlan agreed to let her sleep while he cleared it with a pair of patently uninterested control-room operators.

Back in the main garage, Bruce found that both the IWU van and his own truck had been neatly lined-up beside the bus parking area. They may not be the cheeriest guys on the planet, Bruce reflected, but the repository blokes certainly were efficient.

Probably keen to get rid of us as soon as possible.

Bruce stored his subsamples carefully in the boot of his SUV and returned to the bus to pick up the unconscious Egyptian. While he struggled to carry her from the bus, he took care to avoid bumping her head, again pity for this tragic figure overpowering his original feeling of hatred of anyone threatening him and his friends.

As Bruce staggered from the bus, he called to the professor, busy organizing storage of his own samples. "Dee, I'll take the girl to the medical center. She really doesn't look too good. You just go to the restaurant and get started. We'll meet you there."

With evident relief, Dave nodded enthusiastically, and the professor took the hint. "Okay. That's fine with me. Just make sure all records are copied to the IAEA. They can get sticky about things like this."

The normally silent Indian student piped up. "I'll go with you if you want, Doctor Roberts. I guess I knew Nariman better than anyone else."

Bruce turned in surprise to Eva, who was holding open the door for him, but even more surprised to hear her answer for him, as he tried to gently place the unconscious girl in the back of his truck.

"That's a good idea, Rehana. Maria can go over for lunch with your bunch." She nudged a bewildered looking Engel towards the IWU van and whispered, "It's fine. I've just got a reply back from the pharm. Rehana is one of ours."

"What?" Bruce started in surprise, bumping his head as he drew back out of the car. "We didn't give your pharm any details of this sampling trip." He looked suspiciously at Eva, "Did we?"

"Definitely not," she replied defensively. "As far as they were informed, we were having a holiday in Switzerland. Angela and I took the opportunity to use some special analytical facilities in Basel, and our samples were then shipped to Bermuda. The story should have been reasonably watertight. Nevertheless, the GRW guys tell me that Rehana has been covering us and will take over the extraction of Nariman."

Still somewhat bemused, Bruce allowed himself to be shepherded behind the driving wheel while Rehana squeezed between himself and Eva on the front bench seat. As they slowly wended their way through the checkpoints and out into the main visitor car park, the small Indian girl filled in the details.

"Because of your past links with the IWU, we have had a demon monitor all their communications since you were first brought into this project, Doctor Roberts. Personally, I've been on this job only since June. The security group has been completely gutted, and it's all new folk looking after Professor Flynn." Rehana shuffled uncomfortably, aware that the pharm security section had been the cause of most of their previous problems, which had resulted in Eva being seriously injured. It was also clear that the operational security staff would only know

Eva and Angela by their original Glasgow identities: Drndarski and Flynn.

"Anyway," she continued, "the IAEA project coming so soon after you arrived in Switzerland rang bells, and I got inserted to cover you. If you had informed us what you were doing, we would have told you all about it."

Definitely on the defensive. I guess there's probably a lot of politics behind this.

"I was especially sent to cover the Egyptian girl, who we knew jumped ahead of the queue following high-level pressure from a number of strong Muslim governments. I've had six months to get up to speed on technical background here, but this Nariman is security or military with a couple days crash training, at most."

Bruce felt somewhat embarrassed, shown up yet again by the ability of clever profilers to anticipate his moves.

Must really find out more about this profiling shit and how to get round it.

"But what was stealing the Grimsel samples all about?"

"You noticed that, did you?" She smiled. "It was really for Nariman's benefit. She clearly knew something was up, but didn't know who was involved. It could have been that you were a smokescreen and I was really doing the work. In fact, I'm pretty sure that was her conclusion after she saw me pocketing a sample immediately after the alarm went off."

"I was watching fairly closely at that time," Bruce

broke in, "and saw nothing. You looked as frightened as the others."

"The alarm certainly caught me off guard, and I might have been a bit worried...I don't really have much hands-on experience with radioactivity, but as soon as Dave calmed down, I got a scraping of the previous core while Nariman was videoing in the background." She rummaged in a pocket and produced a small phial. She shook it to show a number of small beads. "Half a dozen sets of scrapings, sealed in a DLC matrix. The pelletizer is a modification of the core-coating unit that we set up specially. I wouldn't be surprised if Nariman hadn't already discovered it."

"Okay, that explains quite a lot." Bruce briefly described Nariman's holo and the associated communication that he had overheard. "You certainly managed to mislead the Egyptian operative, but her controllers seem to be a bit cleverer," he concluded. "So what do you propose to do now?"

"We wait here for a bit. A support team will join us..." the Indian girl looked at her palmtop, "...in about ten minutes or so. They'll take Nariman off our hands, and records will show that she was only logged in at the medical center here and then immediately transferred to the hospital in Strasbourg. There'll be an unfortunate road accident en route."

"Is that really necessary?" Eva interrupted, plainly distressed by the idea of such a cold-blooded killing.

Bruce admitted to himself that he felt the same way.

It's one thing to experience violence in the heat of combat, but this is something different. Evil, somehow.

Rehana was not particularly enamored by the idea herself, but she stuck to the company line. "It would be nice to handle her some other way, but this girl is dangerous. If she was sure that she had obtained all the information on our work or that she would be able to remove the key actors from our side, I'm sure that she wouldn't have hesitated to take us all out. If she had actually realized that she had your entire team at Grimsel, you would never have left the tunnels."

Bruce felt suddenly nauseous when he realized their close escape – *more by luck than by judgment*. He glanced at Eva whose white face and clenched knuckles showed that she felt a similar shock.

***

They sat together in silence for several minutes until, earlier than scheduled, a lurid orange ambulance raced into the car park, sirens wailing and lights flashing, and drew up beside them. Two white-clad orderlies jumped out and waved at Rehana, who evidently recognized them. Only then did Bruce and the girls climb from the truck.

After a mumbled greeting to Rehana, the large men eased the sleeping Egyptian from Bruce's back seat and onto a stretcher, which was quickly slid into the back of the ambulance. The doors slammed shut and, only a minute after arriving, the ambulance sped away towards the exit.

Bruce stood between the girls with an arm on Eva's shoulder while he watched the ambulance pull onto the main road. It had just completed this maneuver when, with a deafening concussion, it exploded in a ball of flame.

Reflexively, Bruce pulled the tall blonde close to him and scrambled after the Indian girl into the back seat of his car to avoid the debris that was raining down. After he slammed the door and shook his head to clear the ringing in his ears he stared at Rehana, who, despite her chocolate complexion, managed to look pale with shock. "Now what the fuck was that?"

"The unfortunate Miss Sayed." The unexpected American drawl caused Bruce's neck to whip round painfully to look straight into a gun pointed directly into his face. "She wasn't much bloody use, but she went out with a big bloody bang."

Through his confusion, Bruce recognized the speaker.

The old baldy guy from the hotel breakfast room.

Sure enough, he could make out the small, muscular blonde standing outside. Also, at an almost subconscious level, he spotted from his choice of words that this man must have been working with Nariman.

Probably the person she was talking to when I overheard her.

"Now don't even dream about doing anything silly, Doctor Roberts," he continued. "I am most definitely not somebody to be messed about with. I am going to tell you what to do, and you are going to do it exactly as I specify. *Capisce?*"

Bruce nodded and pulled Eva to his side, while the small Indian cowered behind him. The hefty blonde woman slipped into the driver's seat and the car set off. The bald man ignored seat safety warnings and remained kneeling on the front bench with his gun immobile a few centimeters from Bruce's nose.

As the car curved towards the marked entrance to the car park, completely ignoring no entry signs, Bruce could see that most attention was focused on the blazing wreck at the exit. Already emergency vehicles were emerging from a garage behind the repository security fence. Nevertheless, they were not the only ones making a hurried escape. A coach full of visitors followed in their wake.

The car turned onto the main road, heading away from the burning ambulance. To Bruce's surprise, however, the car drove only about five hundred meters along the tree-lined road before turning sharply into the courtyard of a small motel. Only two other cars sat on the slushy expanse, close to the block labeled as reception. The woman drove past these and parked in front of a drab two-story block situated diagonally opposite reception.

"Out," the American commanded gruffly.

Bruce pushed the girls out the door, which had been opened by their driver, and followed them into the motel room. In the room, Bruce pulled Eva to his chest and, unconsciously, rested his hand on the Indian security agent's shoulders while he looked around.

Typical, drab, chain motel. You find them everywhere in

the world now – same appearance, same facilities, same smell. However, the sophisticated communication kit lying on the glass-topped coffee table is far from usual.

Momentarily forgetting his present predicament, he peered at the holo that seemed to be very high-tech hackware following a frequency-hopping, highly encrypted signal. The Basel identifier, which popped-up regularly, appeared to confirm his guess, that this was interception of an internal link from Eva's pharm.

"Make yourselves at home." The American waved in the general direction of a faded sofa. "We'll have to wait it out here for a few hours until the dust dies down. McLachlan has already been informed that you guys are okay and has been told that you can't get back into the site due to the security clampdown. They're eating now and think you're doing the same."

"Oh, yeah," he added as an afterthought, "nobody knows anything about the exploding Egyptian as yet." The American glanced as his silent companion, who grinned.

Bruce felt a twinge of remorse. He had completely forgotten about Nariman.

Not just the sad waste of a life, but a death that's a joke to the people she works with. Then again, is the pharm employing me really any better?

Breaking this morose chain of thought, Bruce realized that he had more pressing matters to attend to. "It's clear enough what you're after, but you have the samples so what're we doing hanging around here?"

"Don't be silly, Doc. We know that the main samples

are still underground and will be picked up later today. We also know that your Miss Maiden is also still there. Things have been extremely confusing since we lost our contacts inside GRW, but you are definitely at the center of things. Miss Maiden too, if she really is who we think she is."

Bruce's head was spinning, as the implications of this new input began to crystallize.

Firstly, this guy seems to be fairly well informed and a member of one of the major organizations involved – not a simple contract grunt, like Engel was when I first met her. Secondly, Nariman had been working for him, but merely as an expendable pawn. He'd been pulling her strings all along. Thirdly, their profiling was sophisticated – but concentrated on Engel and myself. The disinformation associated with the deaths of Flynn and Drndarski seemed to have worked.

As he thought about it further, he wasn't sure if the last point was good or bad news.

If this guy recognizes the value of Eva as a hostage to gain access to the key player in this entire game, the rejuvenated Professor White, his interest in Engel and the samples will surely wane. On the other hand, Eva's apparent lack of value puts her under a more immediate risk.

Bruce looked into the eyes of the man facing him.

Cruel and merciless, a complete contrast to his general appearance. In a tweed suit, the man would look the epitome of an aging civil servant.

"So," Bruce started, "how are you going to get a hold of the samples? They'll be dispatched to the IWU in an

IAEA transporter."

The bald man laughed. "Come on now. Do I really look like some kind of hick? Sure the IWU samples will be sent back, but your cores will go with you directly to Basel." He smiled smugly and sat in an armchair opposite, resting his gun against his thigh.

Ah, yep, fourthly – he has another contact in the IWU team. I wonder who it could be?

***

After two hours of sitting squeezed between the two girls, Bruce was uncomfortable and getting extremely hungry. Fear only lasts so long, now he was getting very seriously pissed-off. Both girls had been allowed a visit to the toilet, in each case accompanied by the blonde who, as yet, had still spoken not a single word. The American had not allowed them to speak to each other and refused their requests for food or even something to drink.

Suddenly the American jumped to his feet. "Okay, folks. We're now ready for the next step. The communications block that the repository crowd set up is now down and coms should be back to normal. We're going to have a talk with McLachlan."

Two hours shut down; it must have been total chaos in the control room. I guess they have some kind of protocol for terrorist attacks, and this must have kicked it off. I wonder if they caught their football match before all this hell broke loose.

Bruce said, "I'll talk to McLachlan, but I need to talk to Maiden first."

"You'll do what I tell you, when I tell you to do it." The man was clearly annoyed. "Don't try to be clever, because I'm not messing about here." To emphasize his point he turned slowly, aimed casually and his gun gave an almost silent *phut* as he shot the Indian agent in the stomach.

She doubled over and screamed, which dropped off sharply as the blonde woman touched a control on the coms unit.

"Anti-sound," the man confirmed. "She can scream and shout as much as she wants." He seemed amused as he watched the girl writhe in agony, tears pouring down her face while blood seeped around the hands clenched to her stomach.

Bruce realized he was standing, shouting at the man sitting calmly in front of him. "Enough, man, for fuck's sake. Jesus fuckin' Christ. I was only trying to tell you that it's obvious to McLachlan that I'd call Maria first. He knows us pretty well. I assume you're trying to keep this whole fucking thing low key, and you don't want him to think anything's wrong. He's going to be already concerned about this explosion and worried about poor fuckin' Nariman. If you're going to do this softly, you've got to listen to me."

The American was completely unruffled by this outburst. "All righty, Doc. You're convincing me. You should have said this before. But in any case, you shouldn't be taking the Lord's name in vain, no matter what. Be careful with that," he warned as Bruce stared at him in complete amazement.

Fucking totally loopy Christian nutcase psycho.

He struggled to calm down and looked behind him at Eva, who was cradling the small brown woman in her arms. Her ashen, tear-streaked face looked up at him in absolute horror.

Christ, it was only six months ago she was shot. She really shouldn't be here.

"Okay, okay, let's just calm down here. What do you want me to do? Just let me know what you want, and I'll get it sorted."

"All right, Mister Fixit. I want the IWU vehicle to drive Miss Maiden and the samples out and bring them here. You can tell them that supercritical Sayed..." he smiled at his feeble attempt at humor, "...is feeling a bit better and is waiting here to be picked up. Just park there, beside your truck, and come right in."

Fuck, fuck, fuck, fuck, fuck! Bruce raved as this worst-case scenario was presented.

This fucker's going to take out the whole IWU group. He's not someone to tie people up and leave them behind. I don't even dare argue with him.

Bruce strained to grasp at any kind of escape plan.

"Let me use my palmtop and I'll do it." Bruce struggled to control his breathing, searching for inner calm and focus.

In response to a nod he drew the unit out of the pouch on his belt. Weeping and groans of agony died away completely as the anti-sound was stepped up in a narrow beam to allow Bruce to call Engel.

"Just up the volume now, boy, so we can all hear what's going on," the killer commanded.

The connection was made instantly; Engel must have been waiting for his call. Before he could speak, her amplified whisper rang through the room "Christ's sake, Bruce, what the fuck's going on? Old Dee here's really starting to worry—"

"Okay, Maria." Bruce broke in before Engel could give anything away – or annoy the American with her colorful use of the vernacular. "This has got to be quick. Eve and I are fine, but poor little Nariman's feeling a bit stotious, so we'll wait for you in a motel by the gate. If you can get all our samples into the IWU van, you can get a lift with them out here and then we can swap them for the two students. Is Professor McLachlan there?"

Engel gave him a hard stare, but answered evenly, "Okay, Bruce, that sounds fine. The professor's standing beside me now. Here he is..."

"Ah, Bruce, good to hear you're fine. What the bloody hell's going on out there? Car bomb they seem to be claiming. It's a total shambles here, as all the bosses are on holiday and the young lads are totally out of their depth. They just closed everything tight and waited until a director finally turned up."

Bruce broke in before McLachlan could get fully into his stride. "Pretty crazy out here as well, Dee. We had to take Nariman out as she came to and wouldn't allow herself to be examined by a male Christian doctor." Bruce kept on going while the professor muttered his misgivings about the IWU getting involved with any kind of fundamentalist regime – *Muslim, Christian or any other brand of bloody God-botherer,* as he put it.

"We've got her bedded down in a little motel just by the gates, Relais Comfort or something like that, but she seems a lot better now. If you bring out Maria and my samples, you can pick up your two here."

"I know the very place you mean. What room are you in?"

Bruce looked wildly at the bald American, who was struggling to remove a key from his pocket, while keeping his gun clearly pointed at Bruce's head. "I can't remember," he improvised, "but you can't miss it as my truck is parked directly outside and it's about the only car in the park."

"Righty Ho. The boys should have all the kit back here in half an hour or thereabouts, so we should be with you in...maybe an hour. See you then. Toodle pip!"

Bruce switched the palmtop off, returned it to its pouch and dropped heavily onto the settee beside the girls.

"You've got what you wanted. Can we do something about this poor girl now? She's in agony."

"It was a bit too much chit chat, but you did fix things as you promised. The least I can do is fix the girl." With that he leant forward towards the writhing girl and coolly shot her though the forehead.

Bruce froze, shocked to the core by this gratuitous act of violence. Eva stared in horror at the gore from the back of the dead girl's head, which had splashed on her arm. With a whimper, she jerked her hands free, bent at the waist and vomited.

Bruce could also feel bile rising in his gorge, but he fought it down. Horror was already turning to cold hatred.

This evil fucker has to die before anyone else gets hurt.

"Well that sure is fixed." The psychopath grinned at his silent accomplice. "I can guarantee one hundred percent that she'll feel no more pain from now on."

His look of satisfaction was sickening enough, but Bruce was even more horrified by the look, almost of hunger, on the face of the heavily-built woman while she examined the pattern of blood, brain and scalp sprayed over the back of the settee.

Bruce drew Eva to her feet and led her to sit on the side of a double bed, as far as possible from the Indian girl's corpse. Eva's body shook as silent sobs wracked her. When he used the sleeve of his jacket to wipe her mouth, he noticed that her eyes were glazed. *She's going into shock.* He pulled her head to his cheek and whispered, "Eva, Eva love, relax. Just don't think about it. Pull yourself together. You're going to have to help me here. We have got to nail this cunt before he kills us."

The American watched silently and then rose slowly to his feet. "Enough cuddling there, you two. Show a bit of respect." He grinned and blew imaginary smoke from the muzzle of his gun. "It's going to smell a bit in here, so move it." He gesticulated with the gun, and Bruce turned to see that the small blonde had moved silently behind him and was holding open a connecting door to the next room.

Bruce pulled Eva up and led her into a room that was identical, but laid out as a mirror image to the one they had just left. Eva moved like an automaton while he guided her, with his arm tightly round her shoulder, to sit as indicated on another faded settee.

Here we go again.

Bruce scowled while he stroked the distraught girl's hair. *Here we go again, but now only Eva can be used as a threat to me if I need to be cowed. And only an hour before this place turns into a slaughterhouse, in any case.*

***

The American seemed increasingly agitated and rocked on his feet while he looked down at his captives.

For all his cool appearance, he's burning an adrenaline high.

"Now we talk." The drawl betrayed no sign of any emotion. "You know what will happen if you shit me." He waved the gun in Eva's direction, giving the strong impression that he was aching to use it again.

Bruce hugged the girl tighter, glad that her eyes had closed and she appeared to be switched off from the entire situation. "What do you want to know?"

"What you're doing here, who you're working with, where you're based? You know, all that kind of shit."

Bruce realized that there was no way he could risk a lie. Much better to give as much detail as possible and hope he could hide critical information by omission. "I came to Switzerland a couple of weeks ago, but had a bit of a ski accident which—"

"You can skip all of that. You were picked up as soon as you appeared at your house in the Alps. You've been near the top of our search list since you disappeared six months ago, and then you just breeze up home. You were very lucky, though, your little ski accident should have been enough for you to call out a rescue heli. We would have been able to get you fully wired then." A feral smile lit up his face as Bruce goggled in confusion. "Rocks don't always fall down by themselves, sometimes they need a little help."

"You couldn't possibly have known about the ski trip," Bruce interrupted. "We decided on it only the night before. I was using a Swiss secure comlink: there's no way you could hack into that."

"No need to, smart guy. Your American friend can't keep a secret. Pillow talk."

"I didn't know Tom had a girlfriend."

"Didn't say nothing about no gal. Your buddy's a fag."

Bruce almost forgot where he was in the light of this stunning revelation. *Homosexual and bisexual relationships are common enough but, after the last few days in Hasliberg, Tom clearly isn't straight gay. But maybe bi? It's possible but I can't think of previous indication that he swung in that direction.*

"Now how about we stop wasting time here? You

just need to know we've got you well covered. Look, I'll help you focus," he continued. "You were at your house with her," he gestured with the pistol in Eva's direction, "Maiden and somebody who's supposed to be a professor. You visited the waste disposal institute and set up something with this McLachlan guy. You went up to get samples in the Alps and now here, which confirms what we already thought – you're looking for something radioactive. Let's start hearing more about that."

Too dangerous to waffle here, he decided, so briefly summarized the first extremophile sampling trip, finishing with, "...and that was the explosion that killed Professor White and all of her key staff. Maiden and I were lucky enough to be evacuated to Bermuda, where we've been preparing for another sampling trip. We know now what samples are needed and the boffins in Basel will do the science." He waited with baited breath to see how the killer would react.

"Yes. I knew it was something big. Now I can see why all these Muslim nutcases are so keen to put you out of action. Their first reaction, whenever we seemed to be getting close, has been to blow everything up. My boss, however, wanted you and the samples. She must know what's going on. She is a very, very powerful lady and very, very rich. Also very, very old. She'd pay anything for this stuff." He looked extremely pleased with himself as he dropped into the facing armchair.

Bruce could almost see the wheels turn in his captor's head as the man tried to work out how he could make most use out of this new knowledge.

At least Eva and Angela seem to be out of the picture for the moment. On the other hand, with the information he now possesses, there's little incentive for the psychopathic bastard to keep anyone alive.

***

After about half an hour, Eva drifted off into an exhausted sleep. Bruce was anything but tired; his brain raced, going over events since their kidnapping again and again. The bald killer was clearly someone who enjoyed his work. He could easily have carried a laser, which would be just as effective but totally silent and produce neatly cauterized holes that reduced any mess.

This guy likes bullets. He likes the mess and the gore. The smell of the kill.

Bruce watched the way the man unconsciously stroked the pistol with his thumb.

He loves his fucking gun. Although obviously American, he probably couldn't survive in the States with their draconian handgun controls. So what would this guy's weaknesses be?

The woman was much trickier. She had managed to avoid saying a single word, but Bruce had the feeling that this wasn't because she was mute. Just taciturn, he guessed. Unlike her companion, she carried no visible weapon and stood most of the times with her arms folded, showing off her wide shoulders and heavy biceps. Nevertheless, she radiated a definite air of menace. She moved silently, smoothly, like a panther. But most of all it was her eyes – cold and calculating and showing any emotion only when Rehana was shot.

Would definitely not want to come home to that one with a broken pay packet.

He gently shook Eva awake and stared into her confused blue eyes. "Got to go for a leak, love. Wake up now."

Bruce held the tall blonde while she slowly remembered where she was and started to weep. "Keep it together, girl. We'll sort it out. Please help me here," he whispered while he rubbed her neck before settling her against the back of the settee and standing up.

"Excuse me," he cautiously addressed the bald man, who was obviously annoyed to be disturbed from his plans of wealth and power. "I need to go to the bog..." he noticed the look of confusion, "...to the rest room. I really need a pee."

The American sighed theatrically. "You gotta go, then you gotta go." He raised an eyebrow at the silent blonde, who simple nodded. "Just go through there. I really hope you ain't shy, because I'll be watching you."

Bruce entered the small bathroom indicated, which contained a shower, toilet, bidet, double washbowl and a towel rack crammed into the small space. He heard the door close behind him and the muzzle of the gun poked into his neck, pushing him forward. Perfect. Bruce unzipped his flies.

Although he really did desperately need to pee, nervous tension held him back.

Come on, for Christ's sake go!

He could hear the man behind him shuffling uncomfortably. Finally, with a gasp, the flow began and urine splashed noisily into the pan.

Bruce steeled himself, breathed in deeply and then whirled around to spray the jet of yellow fluid against the horrified man's trousers. "What the hell..?" he started in disgust while he tried to step back from the warm liquid soaking into his crotch, cut off as Bruce's fist crashed with all the force he could muster into his throat.

Gasping, the killer pulled the trigger, but Bruce already had control of the smaller man's wrist, directing his shot into the ceiling. Bruce kicked savagely into a rather soggy groin and, with a loud grunt, the killer folded like a jackknife, exposing a neck just asking to be hit. Grabbing what little white hair was available above an ear, Bruce scythed the edge of his hand against this target and was rewarded by a satisfying crack as the killer's neck broke.

Bruce gasped for breath while he stared at the prone figure, suddenly seeming just like a little old man. Remembering the Indian girl, however, Bruce hopped into the air and stamped down with his entire body weight onto the side of the wheezing man's neck. There was a very wet, squelching noise and the sound of breathing stopped.

Bruce stood frozen for a second while he strained to calm down from this explosive adrenaline rush. He was gradually aware that his penis was still hanging out the front of his trousers and looked down while he pushed the still-dripping member back into place. Suddenly his neck was seized with a grip of steel and he found himself hurtling through the air into the bedroom.

"Didn't even get a chance to do up my flies," he mumbled as his body reacted automatically with a rolling breakfall that brought him back to his feet – although almost falling over the coffee table in the cluttered room. Bruce quickly glanced at Eva, who was cowering at the edge of the sofa, before turning to face the small blonde woman who was casually walking out of the bathroom.

They stared at each other for several seconds while the woman slowly peeled off her jacket to reveal the bulging ski shirt. Bruce fumbled his own jacket off, pulling out the wallet containing his designer chemware and selecting a blue rhomboid of Angela's super-slowdown. The woman simply watched him, the slightest traces of a smile on her hard face.

What on earth is she doing? She really must be a couple of pennies short of the full shilling.

The slowdown cut-in and Bruce felt confident as he slowly edged forward.

I'm faster, stronger and all my senses are enhanced. This poor woman has no chance.

Her lack of movement was disconcerting as Bruce moved within range. *I've also the advantage of reach here.* He feigned with his right fist then kicked at her knee.

Despite his accelerated reflexes her hands blurred as she slapped his kick aside, knocking him off balance. He staggered back as pain shot up his left leg. It might well have broken if not for the reinforcement from Glarus Kantonsspital, he realized. Glaring at the blonde with respect that was slowly tending towards fear, he dropped into a fighting crouch and waited for her to come to him.

Unhurriedly, the small woman walked forward until she was well within his reach and stopped. No chance of Aiki-stuff, using her momentum against her, he had time to muse before she span like a top and a back roundhouse kick sent him flying through the air to end up sprawled on his back on the bed. His chest was on fire. He prodded tenderly; ribs well bruised, probably cracked, maybe broken. With a groan he rolled off the bed and staggered to his feet. His impassive opponent merely stared and then slowly began to walk towards him.

Bruce backed away, struggling to concentrate through the pain.

This fucking woman's just taking it easy. She must be seriously enhanced, faster even than Engel, and could probably have finished me off during our first encounter in the toilet.

Then it dawned on him.

She's actually taking her time, playing with me, making it last longer. Like a cat with a mouse, she's enjoying this. That's why she let me take the slowdown, to make the fucking fight last longer.

Bruce glared at his silent opponent, now really frightened. He had never imagined ever encountering someone like this in real life.

Just like one of those...

Realization dawned, "Gladiator," he exclaimed.

The woman's face lit up with a smile and Bruce could not hide a groan. *Fucking gladiators!* Since the drop in gun-crime in the USA and the increasingly powerful roles played by fundamentalist religions supporting – and supported by – entertainment networks, combat sports had become more and more extreme. Silly, but violent, wrestling, demolition derbies, and audience-participation fight games evolved into the present circuses, where ultra-enhanced gladiators of both sexes fought in blood-soaked arenas. Of course, with modern medical technology, the horrific mutilations and dismemberments inflicted were rarely fatal – but accidents happened and dozens of gladiators were killed or suffered irreversible brain damage each year.

As with ancient Rome, Bruce had always considered such circuses as a sign of a society in terminal decline and was glad that they were banned in most of Europe. Nevertheless, they were very popular – and even more extreme – in some Asian countries and available on the entertainment networks everywhere.

Bruce shook as he assessed the consequences of this revelation.

Basically, I'm stuffed! Engel on drugs might have a chance, but I'm totally outclassed by this pocket dreadnought.

He sidled round the sofa, noting absently that Eva was huddling in a corner of the room, well out of their way. *Sensible girl.* He whipped a heavy vase from a chest of drawers and threw it straight at the gladiator.

With a look of distain, the blonde snatched the vase from the air and threw it right back at him. The movement was so fast that he had no chance to react before it smashed into his face. He was momentarily blinded by shards of pottery and a pain that shot through his head, bringing tears to his eyes.

That's my nose gone now.

Blood flowed freely down his face, mainly from his smashed nose, but also from a number of minor cuts on his face and scalp. The woman's eyes gleamed.

She's clearly enjoying herself.

As he backed off further, keeping out of range of his opponent, Bruce bumped into a standard lamp. With a gasp of relief he whipped it up and smashed the light shade loose. The heavy base had remained in place, so Bruce was now holding a long metal tube, the upper part of which was still glowing brightly.

The gladiator looked pleased, lifting the settee and casually throwing it on top of the bed to clear some space. This was followed by the coffee table, lifted with one hand and hurled to smash against the far wall, sending a squealing Eva scrambling for cover from the shards of flying glass.

Bruce kicked at an armchair, attempting to help clear some room. The bulky chair hardly moved.

Again a smile as the woman lifted the chair, hesitated, and then hurled it at the frightened girl, almost hitting her before she rolled for cover into the bathroom.

The moment the chair was thrown, Bruce moved to

the attack, swinging the rod two-handed towards the gladiator's exposed neck. A crack rang out like a gunshot as the blow was blocked against a raised forearm. "Fucking panzering," he cursed under his breath, drawing back into a defensive position and noting the dent on his metal bo.

Rapid blows to left and right, each resulting a similar block, and Bruce drew back to inspect his increasingly battered weapon. Changing tactics he feinted to the left, then drove the end of the pole like a rapier towards her stomach.

For an instant Bruce thought he had her, but the blow stopped with a jolt, which almost dislocated his wrists, when her left hand blurred to grab the still-glowing end of the tube. Maybe now, he hoped, as he twisted the pole to lock the fighter's meaty wrist. For the first time he saw a twinge of pain while she struggled to retain her hold against his much superior leverage.

Bruce's satisfaction was very short-lived when, to his surprise, she turned forwards to grip the pole also with her right hand and, with a grunt, lifted him clear off the floor. His grip loosened in surprise and he fell backwards when the pole flew from his hands. Retaining his balance, he felt the shock when the pole crashed into his already aching ribs.

Though blurry eyes he could see the woman's wide grin as the pole whistled towards his left ear. He half-rolled, half-fell to the right. Swaying on his feet, he was knocked backward as the light stand, thrown lengthwise, smacked into his chest. Back-pedaling, he attempted to grab it, but it fell at his feet, When he crouched to recover the weapon, the front of his neck was seized and he was pulled forward onto his knees.

"Mmm..." was the first noise Bruce had heard from this woman as she stared into his goggling eyes.

Using both hands, Bruce strained to stop the slowly building pressure as her thumb and fingers crushed into the side of his throat. Pale blue eyes looked directly into his while her breathing became deeper – not with exertion, he noted absently, but with pleasure.

She's going to get off ripping my fucking throat out.

He redoubled his efforts and felt his shoulders pop with the strain. He was choking and beginning to lose strength when she pulled his face forward and pushed a rock-hard nipple against his bleeding nose. Her eyes gleamed as further tears of pain rolled down his cheeks.

Her fingers had broken the skin of his neck when the nipple again pushed against his nose. The pain was beginning to transform to blackness when suddenly pressure ceased and he dropped backwards onto the floor, writhing as he fought for breath. He was helpless for several seconds until his vision began to clear and he could see the gladiator lying beside him, her head in a lake of blood. Only then did he notice Eva standing like a statue, face like marble, staring blankly at the gun held tightly in her hand.

***

Bruce sat beside Eva on a corner of the bed that was relatively clear of shards of glass, holding her around the shoulders and speaking softly. "You've done really well, girl, really well. We've got to get going, though. It's going to get chewy here pretty soon. Will you be okay? I could really do with your help. Yet again," he added with feeling and was rewarded by a wan smile.

"Okay, now can you get your pharm team in here to clean things up? Despite the carnage here..." He got up and peered through the lace curtain. "...we don't seem to have attracted any attention, but we can't be sure. We need to blow Dodge pdq."

The tall blonde straightened up with a sigh. "The place is bound to be crawling with our folk by now. It was our ambulance that blew up after all. Unfortunately, it's probably also crawling with folk we don't want to meet up with. I would normally recommend getting a large security detail to pick us up, but I'm not so sure now."

Bruce was relieved, not only by the girl's signs of recovery, but also by her clear thinking. "You're dead right there. I get the strong impression that this pair weren't part of the main effort. Definitely involved, but with their own agenda. Others out there may not be as clued up on us, so linking up to your pharm crew might only attract attention.

"Okay, let's check in with Engel first."

He pulled his palmtop and again was answered immediately. This time, however, Engel limited herself to a cautious, "Hello?"

"It's me. It's okay now. We can talk."

"Thank fuck," Engel responded with evident relief. "What the fuck was that all about last time, with the wrong names and all the Glaswegian gobbledygook. I was worried sick..." She hesitated for a breath, though hating to drop her favored Ninja-warrior image, "...anyway, I thought you were in some kind of serious trouble. I've been driving the folk here crazy, pestering them to get the finger out. What's been going on?" She stopped suddenly, apparently now noticing Bruce's battered appearance on the monitor. "And what the fuck happened to your face?"

Bruce sighed. "We've had a spot of bother, but we're both okay at the moment. I'll tell you everything later, but now we need to be moving asap. What's going on at your end?"

"I'm in the garage now. Our stuff is lying by the van and the IWU crowd is getting theirs packaged for transport. They should be back in ten, maybe fifteen minutes. That soon enough?"

"Nope, but this is even better than I hoped. Throw the container with the hottest core in the IWU van and UV burst the rest. Then drive out and take the road signposted for Metz. After a bit I'll flash you and you can dump the van. Clear?"

Engel's training showed. No questions and only a muttered, "The big prof ain't going to be happy about this," before she cut the link.

Bruce turned to Eva, who was looking a bit better and had been closely following his conversation. "Right, let's get into the car and..." he stopped as she rolled her eyes.

"You aren't going anywhere dressed like that. In fact, neither am I." She looked with disgust at the traces of blood and vomit on her jacket and trousers. "We've got to have at least five minutes until Maria gets through all those checkpoints. Let's move it."

Bruce followed the shapely blonde towards the door but she waved him back. "You just get those clothes off and rinse away the worst of the blood in the shower. I'll be back in a tick."

In the toilet Bruce first dragged out the body of his unknown assailant and threw it onto the assorted wreckage of furniture at the side of the bed.

At least it's out of sight for Eva.

He then stripped off his clothes, wrinkling his nose at the urine soaked trousers. When he entered the shower he caught sight of himself in the mirror above the sink. Blood caked his face and was still dripping from his nose. Both eyes were bloodshot and the lids were beginning to swell, an indication of the blackening to come. His throat was bruised and scraped and his ribcage was already turning a gaudy purple.

"Stop admiring yourself and get on with it." Eva shocked him out of his reverie. "You'll probably start to bleed again when you wash those crusts off, so use this." She tossed him a can of waterproof skin sealant taken, he noted, from his own kit bag.

While he was tenderly washing the worst of the blood from his face and generally patching things up, he watched Eva strip down to bra and pants, wash out her mouth and repeatedly rinse her hands and face in cold water.

Got to watch it there.

He quickly turned the water on to full for a moment to rinse his entire body and then stepped out and started gingerly drying himself with a white bath towel.

By the time he left the bathroom, Eva was already dressed in clean jeans and a heavy shirt – even new shoes. His bag lay on the floor and Eva was rummaging through it. "Here..." She threw a pair of running shorts, trainers and a t-shirt in his direction, "...this is all I can find for the moment. We should get moving."

While Bruce rapidly pulled on his minimalist clothing, he couldn't help but be amazed at Eva's transformation.

I just pray that she'll be able to keep it up.

Following Eva to the van, Bruce shivered as the sleety wind cut through his light running kit. He chucked the bags he was carrying in the back and then climbed in behind the steering wheel. "Call your guys now," he requested as clambered in on the passenger side, "but put the call through the repeater in my house in Switzerland. Those folk were already hacked into your pharm's secure coms, so we have to assume others will be too."

While he drove to the exit of the car park and sat waiting for Engel, it occurred to him that his captors might well have been recording everything.

Too late now to check, but maybe best to play safe.

"Ah, Eva, when your team gets here, ask them to avoid touching any of the communication kit, just torch the place."

They sat in silence for ten minutes until, just as Bruce was starting to worry, the IWU van emerged from the murk and drove past in front of them, the tiny red-haired driver almost lost behind the wheel. Bruce counted to twenty and then pulled out behind it, noting that the road was otherwise empty in both directions. After a couple of kilometers, Engel turned onto a busy autoroute, with Bruce closing up behind. After a further ten kilometers, a rest stop was signposted and Bruce flashed the van in front.

After they pulled to a stop in a large car park, as far as possible from the toilets where the only other cars and trucks present were sitting, Bruce clambered awkwardly out and hurried to meet Engel. The small ninja had already opened a side door of her vehicle and Bruce heaved the single, heavy transport container free and dumped it in the back of his truck. Doors slammed and they were moving, Engel sitting in the front, on the other side of Eva.

Only after they rejoined the autoroute did Engel finally burst out, "Okay, what the fuck has happened to you two? You both look fuckin' awful." She stopped in surprise as Eva turned to her, wrapping her in a close embrace.

"We can tell our stories later," Bruce broke in, "but the big problem now is to get out of here without picking up any tails."

"Shouldn't be a problem," Engel responded, muffled by the taller girl's hug. "I'm fairly sure that this vehicle is clean and there's no sign of anyone behind us. In this fuckin' miserable weather, there's no chance of spot picking us up, so there would only be motorway monitors..." she paused in reflection, "...which they'd need to be very smart about to be able to nail us down."

"They're smart enough, no doubt about it. They've had me nailed since I arrived in Switzerland. We can't even be certain that they haven't managed to bug us somehow, they've got very good kit." Bruce glanced to see Eva nodding into the small woman's shoulder. "Even if they don't have a bead on us that way, their profiling is almost miraculous. They seem to be able to predict my every move."

"Told you that the first minute we met," Engel responded smugly.

Bruce coughed theatrically.

"If not the first minute, then when we first had a chat," she corrected herself. "Bottom line, though, they can certainly read you like a book."

"That's our number one problem now," Bruce agreed. "I can think of a number of options, for example back to Basel, fly straight out from Strasbourg, out from Paris, whatever, but I've got to assume that these bases would be well covered. What do you think?"

"This strategic stuff isn't my usual line of mischief, but what about we just drive for a bit. Pull into the next town and I'll get us some new wheels. Then just head somewhere crazy: Latvia or Lithuania or one of those other places that don't really exist anymore."

"Changing cars, we should definitely do that. The problem is that the opposition also knows that you're involved. At least some of them do. Our ace is Eva. They seem convinced that Professor Flynn is dead and I'm not sure that the presence of Drndarski was ever leaked out of your pharm. The killers we met certainly seemed to discount her..." Engel's head jerked free to stare fiercely at him, "...which we'll tell you all about when we get breathing space. For now, Eva, what would you do?"

The tall girl straightened up with a sniff and inelegantly wiped her nose on the back of her free hand, keeping the other round the shoulder of her diminutive friend. "A new car is definite, but I'd buy or hire one – not steal it. Then I'd get somewhere out of the way and just hole up for a couple of days."

Bruce looked at Engel and raised an eyebrow. "Sounds pretty damned good to me...not what I'd do at all. If we can lay low for a day or two, it'll really complicate things for the search demons, as the options to be examined increase exponentially with time. The key will be to lose all possible traces before we hide out."

He set the autopilot and projected a road map onto the windscreen. "In twenty k we can turn onto that high-speed transeuropean. It's payage, but we can use an anonymous credit chip. The weather..." he projected an overlay, "...is particularly shitty in the direction of Paris, so we head in that direction."

A map of the sprawl of Paris suburbs appeared. "Okay, Eva, pick a name."

"Mmm, Chantilly. Sounds like a dessert or a cocktail or something."

"Good enough for me. I'll program that in. Eva, access some databases – passive stuff only – and find somebody who is selling a car that you fancy. Anything at all, as long as payment is through a third party site. If possible, get him to transfer the key to your palmtop and leave it for pickup by a station somewhere, as if we will be arriving by train."

"Engel, same thing for digs. Somewhere in the vicinity of..." the map expanded and he glanced at Eva.

"Rouen."

"Rouen, it is. Somewhere outside town and private – not a big chain."

"Gotcha." Engel started her search.

Bruce sagged back as aches and pains built up; the last traces of the slowdown finally burned out of his somewhat feverish system. At least the girls were both busy at present, which would keep them from worrying about the danger they were in. He closed his eyes, replaying again the explosion of the ambulance and the young Indian being gunned down in front of him. Tears seeped silently from his eyes and down his ruined face before he gradually drifted into a light doze.

***

The rest of the trip was a bit of an anticlimax after the

frantic pace of the first part of the day. Bruce woke up only when roughly shaken by Engel, who frowned at his groan of agony and slapped a painkilling derm on his neck. *Now why couldn't she have applied that before waking me?* he wondered absently while the pain receded to a dull throbbing.

"Where are we now?" he mumbled, seeing that they were parked in front of some kind of massive edifice of light-colored stone. It was already dark and sleet was turning to snow, which was beginning to accumulate on the surrounding grass. However, the balustrades of the grandiose frontage were well lit by searchlights.

"Fucked if I know. You set up the autopilot," an uninterested Engel responded. "The sign read something about some kind of stables, but it looks a bit big for that. Maybe a Museum of Stables," she speculated wildly.

"We've been here for a bit. Eva insisted on going to pick up the car alone, as she's the one they don't seem to be looking for. I wasn't happy about it at all, but she is right. She'll drive past a twenty-four hour hypermarket place we saw coming in and pick up some new togs for us. You look like a particular dork, travelling in a blizzard in shorts and a vest," she couldn't help adding with a wan smile.

"I guess Eva's filled you in during the drive."

"Most of it." The small redhead looked grim. "There are certainly some very fuckin' evil sick fucks out there." She looked worried, but suddenly brightened up. "Big Blondie didn't see how you took down the nutter with the gun, but she did mention that you pissed yourself."

Bruce groaned. "Not actually pissed myself. Well kind of – more pissed on myself." He stopped, noticing that he was beginning to babble. "Anyway, what happened was..." he hesitated to order his thoughts, and then started from the ambulance explosion and told the entire story.

When he finished, Engel looked directly into his bloodshot eyes with a look of evident concern. "I'm not sure how much Eva really took in. She didn't mention the ambulance to me or say much about how the wee Packie got killed. She seemed most worried about not being able to help you...blaming herself for freaking out. We need to have a long talk to the girl."

"I'm telling you, I was bloody freaking out myself. That pair of psychos were seriously fucking scary. I could easily have..." he broke off as their car was lit by headlights and an ancient delivery van pulled up beside them.

Eva jumped from the driver's door and turned to pull out a couple of large carrier bags. She then scurried into the back of Bruce's truck, entering along with a blast of cold air and a swirl of snowflakes.

"Okay, folks," she announced cheerfully, "I have denims and trainers for everyone." She started pulling out blue jeans, shirts and jackets and throwing them forward. "It was a special sale," she explained. "Anyway, anything that could possibly be traced gets left in the truck, which I guess is just about everything..." She pointed at Bruce's laptop. "...including that."

Bruce started to object but was over-ridden.

"Look now, you admitted that I'm the one they don't have a profile of. Are you, or are you not wedded to that bloody laptop, even though it spent ages lying around in the car, bedrooms, the bus and all over the place?"

Bruce nodded sheepishly.

"So it stays. Anything on it you need, copy over onto your palmtop. At least it's not been out of your sight, I guess."

Bruce was amazed, but greatly relieved, by the slim blonde's transformation. He quickly downloaded some personal records and then, with greatest reluctance, set a scrubbing program loose on his laptop. Only then, did he start to change clothes, with the momentary pleasure of watching the tall blonde and the short redhead wriggling out of and into clothing in the confined space available.

After they were changed, Eva rummaged again in one of the bags. "Here it is." She drew out a red bottle and tossed it casually to Bruce.

He groaned again. "Barbeque lighter fluid?"

"For the car." As Eva pushed Engel towards the door she added, "I know, I know...you're also attached to the car. But it's a risk now. It's got to go."

When the girls jumped out, blasts of cold followed by slamming doors, Bruce realized that Eva had been thinking ahead. Not easy to set fire to a modern car without a lot of help. While the girls were struggling together to transfer the heavy DU sample container, he threw piles of scattered clothing onto their luggage and, with great reluctance, dropped his computer on top. He then opened all the windows a couple of centimeters and sprayed the entire contents of the bottle over the insides of the truck. Stepping out, he flicked the igniter on the cap and threw it and the empty bottle onto the back seat before he slammed the door.

With a dull whoosh, the interior of the car burst into flames, fanned by the wind blowing through the open windows. As he jumped into the van, Eva already had it in motion, heading for the car park exit. Bruce glanced back when they turned onto a small road, heading away from town, to see that the blaze was already producing a plume of black smoke. Not the very cleverest idea, he realized in retrospect. *Torching the car was sensible,* but they should have done it somewhere more remote, where it might not be found for a while. Nevertheless, the girls were doing well and the area appeared to be completely deserted, with no traffic in view.

Just hope for the best.

While he settled back to try and find a position that minimized the discomfort from his ribs, Eva waved at a bag lying by Engel's feet. "Food," she announced. "It's all right for those having had long extended French lunches, but my man and I haven't eaten since breakfast."

Only when he smelled the fresh bread was Bruce aware of how starved he was. On the freeway, Eva engaged an extremely basic autopilot that could, at least, manage such major roads. Engel distributed bread and cheese and small cans of French supermarket lager. Bruce ate carefully as his throat was still very painful, which was only soothed by gently sipping the ice-cold beer. *Maybe better even than Calenda,* he mused, amazed that his recent highlights on the beer front had been two such naff brews.

He was dozing again when Eva drove up to the front of an imposing old hotel set in its own grounds and situated about twenty kilometers from Rouen. Engel climbed over him and went to sort out check-in while he peered blearily at Eva. The girl was evidently exhausted, but she shrugged and climbed wearily from the car into the gently falling snow, which was about twenty centimeters thick in the car park. Bruce joined her and they plodded together to the back of the van. He glanced only briefly at the larger container, before covering it half-heartedly with the bag that had contained their evening meal. He lifted the smaller subsample container with a grunt and, taking the blonde's outstretched hand, they walked wearily into the warmth of the hotel.

Well, I really screwed the pooch today. I must have been picking up warning signs subconsciously, but I kept all my worries to myself and so we walked into a trap like total amateurs. I was worried that we might get hurt, but it's a miracle that we weren't all killed. And some of those around us weren't so lucky. Angela was sure that the big boys would back off and that this jaunt wouldn't be as dangerous as the last one, but she's clearly wrong. And we're not out of the woods yet, by any stretch of the imagination.

9 ...I keep looking over my shoulder, but no one is there

Bruce slowly drifted awake and lay unmoving, watching the colors play on the ceiling. Gradually the memories of the previous day replayed and he shivered, recalling his encounter with the murderous American couple. He gently touched his face and winced.

Very tender.

He traced his wounds with the tip of his left index finger, listing the damage.

Nose, around my eyes, cheeks, forehead and scalp. Also throat, he swallowed saliva, *still very sore.*

His hand drifted under the sheets:

Ribs, both sides, very badly bruised.

He didn't want to press harder, so he inhaled deeply.

Hurts a lot, but doesn't really feel as if anything is broken.

A little bit farther down and his hand brushed against his engorged penis.

Nothing at all wrong there, although it does seem to be about the only part of my body that is in full working order.

He tried to remember the previous night, but everything was blank after his arrival at the hotel. Engel checked in, he could remember that, but nothing about the room, getting undressed, or going to bed.

He focused again on the ceiling – the colors now registering as an open fire...beyond the foot of the bed, he concluded while straining to hear the crackle of flames. Yes...and a hint of the smell of burning wood, pine. The ceiling was high, with an ornate chandelier almost directly above his head. Fancy plasterwork around it and, as far as he could make out by the light of the fire, some kind of gilt paintwork.

To his left, a heavy curtain covered a window that showed chinks of grey light around the edges.

Could be early morning, or any other time during the day if the weather was as miserable as it was last night.

He lay close to the center of a massive bed, his body covered with a thin sheet in the pleasantly warm room. He turned his head to the right. His face sank into the soft pillow as he inspected the expanse of white. The sheet was wrinkled and a definite impression was evident in the mattress. He sniffed deeply.

Sweat, but sweet, not mine.

He turned back to watch the colors dance on the ceiling.

I'm not going anywhere for a bit, just lie back and relax.

***

Bruce was dozing, halfway between planning and daydreaming, when a body bouncing onto the bed beside him shocked him awake.

"Wakey, wakey, sleepy-head. Time to rise and shine."

Gasping at the stab of pain from his ribcage, Bruce glared at the cheerful girl. "Fuck off, why don't you? Go to fuck, go directly to fuck, do not pass go, do not collect two hundred francs."

His reaction appeared only to please his tormentor, who bounced up and down on her knees. "Come on. Don't be a grumpy old Beast. We had breakfast and went for a walk and now we're thinking about lunch. Come on!" She pulled the sheet back to his waist. "Oh, nasty." She winced, somewhat subdued as she examined the multicolor bruising of his chest. "Is it sore?" She poked him with a finger and was rewarded by a screamed curse. "I guess a little bit. Anyway, it doesn't look like anything's broken."

"Just fuckin' leave me." Bruce moaned. "Go and eat or whatever and leave me in peace."

Before Engel could respond, hands clamped onto her shoulders and dragged her backwards off the bed. Eva leant forward and switched on lamps above the bed. "Nasty, indeed."

He heard a small intake of breath when she peered at his throat. A feather-light finger brushed his face.

"You've still got something embedded in your cheek. The sealant has just covered over it. We should get that out and reduce the swelling of your nose and that beautiful pair of black eyes you have. We can get the bruising down over the ribs and kill the pain there too."

Eva gently eased the sheet lower, completely ignoring Engel's giggles and Bruce's moan of embarrassment as his erection became exposed. "Left shin also looks very messy. Very bad bruising and the bone may well be chipped. Wasn't that the one you banged up recently?"

Bruce conceded that it was, adding his guess that the resultant reinforcing should have protected the bone.

Eva wasn't convinced. "Anyway, we probably can do without a scan just now. Also get the bruising here down and see how it looks. Maria, it's what today – Monday? So even the little specialist shops should be open. Pop into town and get what we need for Bruce, you know the stuff."

Engel was evidently reluctant to leave, but not prepared to stand up to the new, forceful Eva. She left the room with a muttered, "Big poofter. Just a wee bit of pain...can't see what all the fuckin' fuss is all about—" which was cut off as the bedroom door slammed shut.

Eva stood, looking down at his fully exposed body, and then kicked off her shoes and quickly pulled down her jeans. After unbuttoning the top fastener of her shirt, she pulled it over her head and slipped into bed beside him before drawing the sheet up to their necks.

Bruce raised his right arm and her head snuggled into his shoulder.

They lay together in silence and then the girl stretched a long thin arm to switch off the lights. The fire had died down a little, but the room was still brightened by a warm red glow.

Bruce felt contented, ignoring the odd spasm of pain as a smooth, well-toned torso rubbed against his battered, bruised – and, he had to admit, hairy and somewhat flabby body. He didn't feel any need to say anything and limited himself to stroking her ear with his thumb.

After about five minutes Eva started to sob quietly. "I'm so sorry, Bruce. Sorry about dragging you into this. Sorry that you got hurt. It's really not worth it. It's gone too far. That lovely Indian girl...she was younger than me. That just shouldn't happen."

Bruce kissed her brow while her body shook beside him.

"Even that poor bloody Nariman," she continued. "What the hell was she thinking? She was the poor soldier dying for a cause while the generals were laughing at her."

Bruce sighed as Eva spoke his own thoughts of the previous day.

"Then there are the two guys in the ambulance. I'm not sure at all about them. I see my employer in a new and very unattractive light. Whatever they were going to do, though, they were still young and just the same as Nariman and Rehana...cannon fodder."

Bruce felt ashamed to admit that he had completely forgotten the ambulance crew. "Don't keep on going over all that stuff," he murmured in her ear. "It's all history now that we can do nothing about, so we just have to get on with it. In particular, we need to get ourselves and these samples back to your mum. To do that, we really are depending on you."

"Depending on me?" she cried, her voice becoming shrill. "That's the problem. That's the real problem." She lay silent for a few seconds then continued in a whisper, "I was completely and totally useless. I froze solid when the ambulance was blown up and you carried me around the entire time after that. I sat and watched while Rehana was shot...twice. I sat around while you handled the guy with the gun. I was hiding and crying while that female monster was killing you."

"You've seen what I can do. I work out almost every day with Maria. We've got it all down pat, all the exercises. I was okay last time, wasn't I?" A note of pleading entered her voice. "But anyway, I've lost it now. Totally, totally useless, just a waste of space."

With a twist of his neck, Bruce pulled himself around to look into the girl's face, her eyes hidden by deep shadows. "Come on, Eva. That's just not true. You were in shock for a bit. I was in shock. Our poor Rehana was in shock...and she was some kind of professional in this dirty game. It's not the shock, it's the getting over it that counts. I was also hopeless, didn't do anything at all until I couldn't back off any farther and was forced to react. It's not cowardice to avoid going against a loony with a gun. It's bloody common sense."

He shook his head. "Sometimes, though, there's no option and it really is kill or be killed. You came through, and you came through well. If it hadn't been for you, it's not just both of us, but also Engel and the rest of the IWU crowd that would have been killed. You had the courage to fight back, to pull the trigger. It's something that was hard for you at the time and will stay with you all your life, but you did the right thing, and I'll always be grateful to you."

Bruce sank back and they lay in silence until her sobbing died away and her breathing became more regular. Then Bruce continued, "You've done a lot already, but we've got to keep it together for a few more days. I'm really convinced that you're the key to getting us back home. They know far too much about Engel and me. Every time we've been caught flat-footed, it's because they've predicted my moves in advance. You're our ace in the hole. They can't anticipate your moves because they don't even know that you're a player in the game."

"I suppose you may be right." She turned to him and attempted a smile. "Anyway, your pep talk has done a lot to cheer me up. I do love Maria. I love her to bits. But sometimes it's more reassuring to cuddle up to a big hairy beast..." She attempted to copy Engel's lilt. "...rather than a lovely but very wee and somewhat bony nymphet."

"If it was up to me, I'd take the wee nymphet any day of the week. In fact, I wouldn't pass on even a large nymphet." He squeezed her and grinned.

***

Eva had dozed off against his shoulder, and her dead weight just began to give him pins and needles in his arm when the door bust open, and he was momentarily blinded by the bright ceiling lights, which emanated from the chandelier. Engel jumped onto the bed and lightly kicked the stirring blonde. "What the fuck've you two been up to? I go off to do the messages and you're straight into bed with that useless spaz, ya hoor!"

Another kick caused Eva to jostle painfully against Bruce's ribs. Then she rolled free, bowling the small redhead over and pulling the sheet with her as they ended up piled together on the floor. Engel fought to her feet first and pointed. "I knew it, hiding a big bloody hard-on while the blonde hoor..." she couldn't keep a straight face, "...is wearing a big baggy pair of Winnie the Pooh knickers. Where the bloody hell did they come from?"

She looked at Bruce's cock again "I stand corrected. It's actually just a wee, totey hard-on. Actually, a kind of mini-soft-on. Not at all surprising really, given the state of those knickers. Not even the famed udders could compensate there." A pillow hit her face with enough force to knock the small woman backwards and ended the exposition on the condition of Bruce's wedding tackle.

"I forgot to get clean knickers yesterday and this antiquated place doesn't have instant freshers," Eva responded defensively. "I found them in the back of one of those drawers...and at least they're clean, rather than what that dirty bism there's wearing."

Engel grinned as she slipped beside the tall blonde. "You weren't complaining this morning when I was sitting on your face. If my knickers are dirty, it's mainly from your saliva." She noticed Bruce's involuntary reaction. "Tell you what, though, why don't we share your Pooh ones, there's enough room in them bloomers for the two of us. Ha." With a squeal, she pulled Eva's knickers down to mid-thigh and jumped clear of a slap that grazed her ear.

The blonde stood for a moment with the pants caught at her knees, then let them drop to the floor and stepped out of them. "Yep, a bit on the baggy side." She stood, completely unconcerned by her nudity, looking down at Bruce's erection. "Okay, Maria, let's get started on him. I'm not sure that you brought anything with you that would reduce that swelling, though."

Engel grinned lasciviously, licking her lips in a theatrical manner. "Do you, perchance, want to bet some money on that?"

***

Half an hour later, Bruce felt indescribably better: patched up with Engel's dressings, lotions and potions, his nose straightened back into place, and a chunk of porcelain removed from his cheek.

Everything's taken care of, in fact. Just as well that Eva hadn't taken Engel's bet.

Showered and dressed in his denims, he headed off to join the girls in the hotel bar, a grand room that looked like it must have been a sitting room or parlor in days gone by. Faded pictures in heavy frames covered the walls, mainly hunting scenes by the looks of them. Tables and chairs were a bit of a mishmash, generally the former being battered and scarred by generations of cigarette burns and the latter overstuffed with faded upholstery.

The clientele were equally mixed; two late-middle-aged couples sat at opposite sides of the room, three ancient women conversed at a table, two roughly dressed young men were elbow to elbow at the bar, and a balding man who reclined in a bay window with a tarty young woman.

She could have been his daughter, but almost certainly wasn't, if his hand on her thigh was anything to go by.

Bruce smiled cheerfully, noting all eyes followed him from his entrance until he sat with the girls.

This must be a first. Never, previously, has anyone paid attention to me when this pair was about. Of course, two black eyes, a broken nose and a scarred fizzog will tend to do that.

To his surprise, Engel handed him a menu and offered to get the drinks. After she ordered the pichet of rouge for him and cidre bouche for Eva and herself, he could hear her stage whisper, which carried through the room. "Wife it was. Caught the three of us in bed together. She's not very big, but she really knows how to use a frying pan. Beat him up and chucked him out the house, she did. It's a bit sad, but you've got to laugh, haven't you?"

Bruce rolled his eyes and hoped fervently that her audience understood only French.

It doesn't look like it, though, from the smirks and stares in my direction.

When Engel plumped down with a satisfied grin, reporting that the drinks would be brought over by someone who would take their lunch order, Bruce hissed, "Was that really necessary?"

Engel was unfazed. "Completely," she assured him.

"When you came in, everybody was wondering what had happened and, you never know, some smarty-pants might even have tried to trace you, imagining that you might be some kind of criminal. Now they have the story and it's a juicy bit of gossip, so they don't need to do anything. Clever, eh?"

Bruce stared into space for a moment, and then grinned. "You know, that's a bloody good excuse. I'm sure that you're really just enjoying taking the piss out of me, but that story is truly credible in a bizarre kind of way."

Eva laughed and hugged the small redhead to her, kissing her cheek. "She's not just a pretty face, you know. She has many other talents, apart from Beast servicing." Her eyes twinkled.

Bruce carefully stretched back, with his head cradled in his hands, letting the girls prattled on. Most fun was being had at his expense, but he didn't mind in the slightest.

It feels like before, before the nightmare that was yesterday. If we can just keep this up, we might yet get home and dry without any further problems.

The girls ordered lunch on his behalf and he ate like a pig. Soup, salad, venison sausages with garlic creamed potatoes, cheese and fruit, all accompanied by fresh, crusty bread. The combination of little to eat the previous day, missed breakfast and, in particular, the tissue rebuilders made him ravenous. During the meal, he had polished off three of the little 25 cl pichets of house red – imported from England, he guessed – but felt no influence of the alcohol. The girls, on the other hand, had consumed a couple bottles of cider between them and were getting quite boisterous.

When they rose to leave, only the three old ladies remained in the bar. They tittered merrily as Bruce walked past. From the little that he could make out of their strongly accented French, it appeared that Engel's story had already been elaborated on considerably.

By tomorrow, these old biddies will have me being caught in the bath with two women, three catamites and a cocker spaniel.

The girls preceded him, hand in hand, from the room as he followed gloomily.

***

Bruce was talked into a brief, post-prandial walk in the hotel grounds. The snow had stopped, but a grey, overcast sky suggested more in the offing. Their light trainers were poorly suited to the hard-packed snow on a path that wound through the gardens past a snow filled swimming pool and a desolate tennis court. The temperature was relatively mild, about one or two degrees above freezing, Bruce guessed, so the denim jackets were sufficient. Nevertheless, he made a mental note to get some warmer clothing before they moved on.

He watched the girls build a snowman, but then retreated rapidly as this evolved into the inevitable snowball fight. Hard snowballs were whizzing around at high velocity and he really did not want to test the extent of recovery from his injuries just yet. While he watched from the shelter of the hotel doorway, they looked like a pair of kids, although somewhat unfairly matched for size. Nevertheless, they were clearly having fun: Engel presently standing on one leg and deflecting with her raised foot the snowballs being pitched in her direction.

***

During the afternoon, they remained in the bedroom; the girls wore thick bathrobes while their clothes steamed in front of a roaring log fire. They had searched public news sites, but coverage of the Bure incident was very sparse, implying that it had been a terrorist bomb attack gone wrong. The girls could certainly have obtained more details by active mining, but Bruce insisted that they avoided doing anything that could attract the attention of search demons.

Bruce had, in fact, initially argued for a global search thus hiding their inquiry in generalities that would render the chance of being spotted negligible. This was over-ruled by Eva. "That's the kind of thing you would do and hence exactly what we have to avoid."

Bruce could not fault this logic and nodded his agreement.

Eva had other concerns. "We do, however, have to contact my mother. She's going to have heard about Bure by now and will be worried sick. It won't help that she can't raise us on any of our comm links. As far as we could make out yesterday, she's not a search target but might become one if she crashes about too much. My guess would be that she's going through the pharm at present but, if they don't come up with something soon, she'll be on a flight over here."

After examining a wide range of possibilities, they finally decided on the lowest tech option as having the least chance of compromising either sender or receiver: an encrypted text email attachment sent through a long chain of blind-forwarders. Even though Bruce could imagine no possibility of such a message being traced back to the hotel, Eva insisted that she would drive into Rouen with Engel, who could hack into any train that happened to be sitting at the railway station and send it over the rail network. Bruce was very impressed with this suggestion, which went far beyond his normal levels of paranoia.

The message was edited several times to ensure that there were no keywords that could lead to its interception. The final version was blander than Bruce would have liked, but Eva assured him that it would suffice:

Dearest Mum, we're all doing fine and have managed to pick up everything we needed. We will be out of touch for a wee while and may need to take the long road home. Don't worry. Beauty and the Beast send their love. L&K, E.

It was agreed to get this missive to Angela as soon as possible. Shortly before five pm, the girls dressed quickly in now dry clothes and prepared to set off. "How about picking up some more clothes?" Bruce suggested. "The weather is supposed to clear up a bit tomorrow, so the temperature will drop. Some warmer stuff would be good, in any case, but hats, sunglasses and bulky jackets would be a good precaution, even though the chance of pick-up on a surveillance camera or spot image must be pretty remote. A couple of bags would also be good. We're going to have to fly out at some point and will need to have, at least, hand luggage. Intercontinental travel carrying only a palmtop might raise a few eyebrows."

"And knickers," Engel added as she herded the tall blonde in front of her. "We don't want to risk seeing this one back in the dread Winnie-the-Poohs." She slapped the comely posterior in front of her and slammed the room door.

***

It was almost eight pm when the girls returned. Bruce had been increasingly worried over the last hour and stood at the bedroom window, watching for them. As soon as the battered van drove into the car park, he rushed downstairs. He reached the van while Engel unloaded packages from the back, and he stood, shivering in his shirt-sleeves while she loaded up his arms with their shopping.

Back in the room, Bruce started to chide them for being absent for so long, but was interrupted by Eva. "Don't fret, Brucey. We were shopping. It's a girl thing. Every now and then, especially if things have been a bit fraught, there is nothing better than a bit of retail therapy. Look at Maria. She says she hates shopping. Look at her."

Bruce had to admit that the grinning redhead looked

pleased with herself. This caused a first twinge of foreboding. "Okay, good enough, but we should get down for dinner. It's eight already."

"In time, in time," Eva murmured. "First we get dressed for dinner. Out of those smelly jeans now."

Bruce was about to argue that they could hardly be smelly after a single day's wear, but gave up as a pair of lurid blue slip-on shoes was thrown at him. "You have got to be joking," he exclaimed, before these were joined by elasticated purple trousers and a paisley pattern shirt. "Is this supposed to be a flower-power party night or something?" A small leather tanga was hurled into his face with enough force for his nose to give a slight twinge. This was not the reason for his plaintive groan, however.

Sensing that resistance was futile, Bruce began to peel off his shirt while he watched the women sort out their own clothing. Standing in a sea of packaging, which was scattered around the bed, they quickly stripped off their denims and gamboled together into the en-suite bathroom, slamming the door behind them.

Bruce had caught a glimpse of a bag in Engel's hand as she scurried into the toilet. His feeling of foreboding got stronger.

Bruce had almost fifteen minutes to pace the floor in his colorful costume, peering occasionally into a mirror and grimacing, before the girls emerged, giggling, with their arms around each other. They both had hair and eyebrows dyed jet black and were fully made up with fire engine red lipstick and nail varnish. Artificial nails, Bruce corrected himself. Neither girl had talons like those. Red bras, tangas, suspenders and black fishnet stockings completed the rig-out. The knickers were, however, sufficiently ephemeral to reveal clearly Engel's shaven mons and show that Eva really was a blonde. He sighed as he attempted to subtly readjust his prick, which was threatening to burst from the confines of his under-dimensioned underwear.

After a saucy pose together, hands on hips, the girls helped each other into tight black dresses that zipped up the back. They then squeezed feet into shiny black stiletto heels and posed again, Eva bending down to kiss Engel on the lips, which added greatly to Bruce's discomfort.

Engel on his left, teetering a little on her heels, and Eva on his right, they steered him downstairs. Holding his elbows, they made a grand entry into the hotel dining room. Even fancier than the bar at lunchtime, the long room had windows along one side that looked directly into a tropical theme conservatory. Mirrors covered the other long side, which made the room seem even larger. The far end featured two doors separated by a sideboard piled with exotic liqueur bottles of all shapes and sizes. The high vaulted ceiling was painted with a trompe l'oeil blue sky and fluffy white clouds and featured a row of chandeliers containing ancient incandescent bulbs.

About a quarter of the sixty or so tables in the baronial room were occupied, and all heads turned their direction in response to the high heels clip-clopping on the parquet floor. A dinner-jacket-clad waiter rushed to greet them and flamboyantly led them to a table by the window, which was set for four. Before they could be seated, a second waiter had already removed the extra chair, and a third gathered up the extra place setting. As chairs were held for them, the Maître d' appeared with large card menus and a leather bound wine list the size of a small Bible.

After agreeing to sparkling water and ordering aperitifs – a Fino and two Kir Royales – the staff backed off and Bruce had recovered enough to whisper, "Just what are we doing here? I look like a pimp with a couple of hookers. Very high-class hookers, I hasten to add, but we've been stared at by everyone in the place. It's not quite low profile."

"Low profile?" Eva inquired. "Slip down to the bar for a quiet snack. That's what you'd do?"

"I think so. We'd attract a lot less attention."

"Ha," Engel interjected, "the very point. You would never do something like this. It doesn't match your profile."

"Yea, but, that could hardly be spotted here, just now."

"Who knows?" This time Eva broke in. "Look at us. You would never wear anything like that, unless we forced you. We never wear stuff like this. We both like wearing stuff that's a little bit on the wild side, but we don't go in for this schoolboy wet-dream dick-magnet look."

Bruce reckoned that a lot more than schoolboys had such dreams, but had to admit that the girls had a point.

They often dressed outrageously, but a very different kind of outrageous.

"You're right," he conceded after some thought. "I'm still having difficulty getting my head round this profiling thing. The two of you seem much better at it. I guess I'm too old and boring and set in my ways."

The girls grinned smugly at each other and then Engel added, "Yep, you're just a boring old fart. You also haven't noticed that nobody has paid the slightest attention to your battered kisser. It's not as bad as lunchtime, but you still look like you've gone five rounds with the legendary Mohammed Ali. Your awful clothes – and our lovely legs..." She lifted a hip and showed off the split that ran to her waist, exposing a triangle of thigh above the top of her stocking. "...have been the focus of attention."

The legs certainly work for me.

A waiter approached with their drinks and the girls considered the options available on the menu.

***

Over a much extended dinner – the set 7-course *Menu Gourmandise avec Vins* – they casually discussed possibilities for the following days. Bruce had to admit that the girls' plan for the evening was having an additional benefit for him.

Dressed in these weird clothes, doing something that was so alien under these circumstances makes me more aware of the components of my normal behavior that could be the basis for our opponents' profiling.

They agreed to stay for a further night and leave early Wednesday morning. Eva and Engel had already been looking at maps and decided to dump the van in Rouen and take the train to Le Havre and then a jet hydrofoil to Portsmouth. Originally Bruce had been completely baffled by this choice, but Eva had evidently been doing a lot of careful thinking.

"It's not us that's the problem, it's these samples. There's no way we're going to get depleted uranium onto a commercial flight..." Bruce started to object, but was over-ridden.

"You lucked out one time with cabin luggage. Getting the big sample container into the hold's just not on. Hiring a private jet might work from that viewpoint, but we don't have enough loose credit to pay for it. Any of us could mobilize enough from our various bank accounts, but that might well set alarms ringing. We just don't want to risk it anyway."

Her small partner nodded.

"So here it is. A Caribbean cruise liner, which leaves in time for the New Year party. Sails five pm, if I remember correctly. We book a suite, send our luggage ahead, but we are delayed and miss departure. We'll dream up some kind of story – family problems of some sort."

As the tall girl paused for a breath, Engel took over. "We then just need to get our asses to Nassau, wherever the hell that is, and join the boat when it arrives. We then cruise a bit and jump ship anywhere there's a flight to Bermuda. Smart stuff, eh?"

Bruce was forced to concede that he couldn't see any problems with the plan and agreed that it was not at all the kind of option he would have come up with. "I had been thinking of various ways we could get round scanners, so that we could fly with the our samples..." he started, before realizing that he was just emphasizing the differences between his type of approach and that dreamed up by the girls. "No, you're right, we do it your way."

***

After digestifs and coffee, the extremophile team rose rather unsteadily to their feet and left the room, followed by the eyes of most of the remaining diners and all of the staff. Bruce had consumed a considerable quantity of wine but, due to the high metabolic rate caused as a side-effect of the drugs that were healing his injuries, he felt quite sober although a little dizzy. He placed his arm round Engel's waist, as she was teetering dangerously in her unaccustomed footwear. Eva was a little steadier, but carefully held the banister while they ascended the stairs towards their room.

After the door shut behind them, Engel kicked her shoes into a far corner of the room and wriggled her toes. "Thank fuck for that," she exclaimed gratefully. "Why in Christ's name would anyone want to put up with these fucking things? They're fuckin' painful and you can't walk properly in the stupid fuckin' things. Jesus!"

"They do make your bum look good though." Eva slid her hand over the mentioned part of her anatomy. She kicked her own shoes off and nudged them out of the way, under a chair.

"But I thought you said it always looked good." Engel pouted, pulling up the dress above her waist to allow her butt to be inspected.

"You've got a point." Eva stroked the tight, almost boyish buttocks. "Anyhow, let's get you out of this before you get yourself into a fankle." She started to unfasten Engel's dress.

"Bruce, stop drooling." Eva's sharp command jolted him to attention. "Into the bathroom now and do what you need to do. We need to get this stuff off and some of this mess sorted out."

Bruce stripped, dropping the garish clothes onto a chair that already held his denims. Engel, now wearing only suspenders and stockings, started undressing Eva. Bruce hurried into the bathroom before the physical effect of this display became more obvious.

Bruce took his time with his ablutions, finishing with a shave with a mechanical razor – which seemed to be the fashion in old French hotels – and a cold shower. As he stood in front of an asthmatic single-wall blow drier, he touched his ribs tentatively.

A bit sore, but fit enough to face whatever the girls had in store.

He emerged into the bedroom to find the mess of

packaging and clothes cleared out of sight and the two women – both of them in stockings and suspenders – rummaging about in a couple of small leather bags.

Seeing him, Eva took Engel by the hand and dragged her towards the bathroom. "We may be some time getting all this gunk cleaned off," she commented, rubbing at her lipstick.

Bruce added a couple of logs to the glowing embers and, after a few minutes, when a few flames began to lick over the mossy wood, turned off the light and lay back on the bed under the single sheet. He gazed at the hypnotic patterns moving on the ceiling and listened to the splashes, squeals and giggles coming from the bathroom.

The wheezing sound of the blower fan and then the hilarity seemed to diminish a little. A bar of light cut through the room as the bathroom door opened then cut off with a click. Soft padding sounds of feet on the carpet and then the sheet was gently pulled down to the foot of the bed.

"Schoolboys' wet dream one," Engel announced while she climbed onto the bed and walked with bouncy steps to his feet where the light of the fire better illuminated her body.

"And wet dream number two." Eva bounced to her side and bent down to kiss her friend, their tongues noisily licking into each other's mouths. Still stockings and suspenders, he noted, as they sensually caressed thighs and buttocks.

"And just as a counter irritant, memories of past

pains to take your mind off the present." Engel reached with her teeth towards the shapely breast presented before her.

Bruce pushed himself onto his elbows and peered, aching ribs forgotten. Firelight glistened on a large ring that Engel had caught hold of and was using to pull on a prominent nipple, causing Eva to give a sudden gasp.

Eva's hand slid up the smaller woman's thighs, rib cage and over a small breast to seize a similar ring, piercing a smaller but equally prominent nipple. Engel grunted, rather inelegantly.

"Now," Engel breathed, "we can check out the other two rings. Can you guess where they are?"

Bruce's guess was more of a wish. Very shortly thereafter it came true.

***

The following morning, Bruce's awaking was a replay of that previously. He felt much better, although with a slightly spaced-out, dreamy feeling that was an effect of the rebuilders. Running a quick inventory of his injuries, everything seemed to be fixing nicely, with only the slightest throb from his ribs.

The fire was blazing cheerfully so he guessed the girls must have banked it up when they went for breakfast. Thinking of the girls resulted in a hardening of his erection, while the thought of breakfast made his stomach rumble.

Now if I had a choice of one option, which would I go for?

He swept his hand over the depression to his side and examined the couple of dark hairs sticking to his fingers. Their hair was still dyed black, as he remembered vaguely from the previous evening. He sniffed the faint muskiness from his fingertips and closed his eyes.

No doubt about it, in a pinch I could do without food.

He was still daydreaming when the girls clattered into the room and Engel strode to the window and threw the curtain wide, lighting the room with bright sunshine. "Come on, Beast. You're missing out on a beautiful day."

Eva sat on the edge of the bed. She held a tray laden with coffee, croissants, bread, jam, cheese and a couple of hard-boiled eggs. "We've got some brekky here for you. You must be starving."

Bruce struggled stiffly into a seated position. Engel propped pillows behind his back. The tray was placed on his lap but, before he could start, Engel removed two of the croissants from the pile and threw one to Eva. "These are really brilliant, you know. Full of chocolate. Okay for slim nymphets like ourselves, but not so good for a fat old Beast." She took a fold of his love handle between finger and thumb and frowned.

"Ignore her, Bruce." Eva offered a bite of her pastry. "You'll need to eat as much as possible over the next couple of days. Now, get that breakfast down your neck and then we'll have a look at how you're healing up."

"And you've got to save your energy, so no self-abuse." Engel slapped a bulge in the sheet. "So just stop thinking about these." She pulled her t-shirt tight against her right breast, allowing the faint profile of the ring to be seen.

"As if I could." Bruce moaned as the bulge got bigger. He tried to concentrate on his breakfast but couldn't resist asking, "About those rings...how did you get that done?"

Eva raised an eyebrow. "If you're very lucky you might find out soon. Anyway, Maria, let's find something to do in this place before Bruce knocks over that tray."

After the girls left the room hand-in-hand, Bruce muttered to himself as a mantra, "Don't think about nipple rings. Don't think about nipple rings." While trying to concentrate on his breakfast. "Some fucking chance."

***

After lunch, again taken in the hotel bar, they drove into the center of Rouen, which was busy with crowds engaged in the usual intensive shopping, which seemed an inevitable part of the Christmas holiday period. They parked on a quayside by the river where an array of old sailing ships were tied up and looking mysterious under their blankets of snow. The sky was cloudless and the sun shone brightly on snow-covered roofs and slushy streets. The roads were clear, but pavement heaters struggled with the heavy coating of snow and air temperatures that were well below freezing. Adjacent to the quay stood the large shopping mall that housed their goal: a cinema club showing old 2-D film classics.

While Eva led the way, Engel grumbled, "I really don't see the point in bothering with this old toss. It's bloody mechanical, stone age. Not even got sound. You've got to read everything."

Bruce said nothing, but sympathized completely.

Eva was not to be budged in her resolve. "It'll be good for you. A bit of culture. There's no point in watching something like *Fritz Lang's Metropolis* in some kind of cleaned and polished, 3D, sound-synchronized version. The old projected version in an old fashioned cinema has much more impact. You'll see. And anyway..." She played her trump card. "...there's no way any profile demon would pick this up. This isn't something that you'd normally ever do."

"You are so fucking right there, Blondie," Engel muttered, ignoring the fact of her friend's currently jet-black hairdo.

After the movie, which Bruce, with reluctance, had to admit that he enjoyed considerably, they found a little bar by the riverside. A glass-roofed terrace surrounded by an air curtain allowed them to enjoy the last of the sun, now touching the snowy roofs on the far bank of the river. All three wore sunglasses against the glare and sipped hot chocolate laced with brandy.

Engel had also, despite herself, found the film interesting. "I just cannot believe that movie is well over a hundred years old. A lot of the places looked just like Tokyo. Remember, next to the hotels, there was that one crazy place."

"Tokyo Metropolitan Building," Bruce confirmed. "It's pretty old itself...must be seventy years or so, but I guess that's only half the age of that film. Amazing, if you think of it that way."

Eva sat for a moment then spoke, "Thinking about Tokyo, I've been wondering about how we should go from England to the Bahamas." She noted Engel's scowl. "Bahamas. That's where Nassau is."

"Then you should have said Nassau," Engel muttered.

Eva ignored her. "We get our samples onto the cruise liner and have five days to kill before the boat reaches Nassau."

"Five days?" Engel blurted out. "Five fuckin' days? Does it have fuckin' sails?"

"It's a cruiser, not a power boat. There's no particular rush to get anywhere. It has a stop in the Azores, I think, then somewhere in Florida before Nassau. Whatever, we have a bit of time on our hands before we need to be in the Caribbean."

"I don't see a problem," Bruce said. "Get an evening flight from Heathrow and we can be in New York in plenty of time to dress up for the bells. As soon as possible thereafter, away from the miserable weather of the Big Apple to the sun of the Bahamas. Just about the perfect time of year because the hurricanes will be pretty well over by now. A bit of sun, sea and sand...just the very dab. January to April is the main diving season, so maybe we could get in a bit of scuba."

Eva frowned. "That's what you'd do. So what would I do, not being Scottish? So, The Bells or what's that other thing you Jocks call it..?"

"Hogmanay."

"Yes, Hogmanay. It's not a big deal to me."

Engel and Bruce looked at each other askance.

"So I think we should go to Nassau the long way," Eva prattled on. "Via Asia. It just occurred to me when we were talking about Tokyo. My pharm is weakest in the Far East. That's the last place a profiler, who thinks you two are working for GRW, would expect you to go."

After a couple minutes of silence, Bruce conceded, "Good thinking, Batwoman. That's again right on the button...exactly what I wouldn't do. So, where in Asia were you thinking of?"

"Well..." Eva replied rather sheepishly, "...I thought we could just go to the terminal for intercontinental flights to Asia and just pick one at random. For example, the one with the lowest flight number leaving within a couple of hours of us getting to the airport."

"Right again." Bruce sighed. "No way is that a method I'd ever use to plan a trip."

***

Back in the hotel, they had a light dinner in the bar, all three dressed inconspicuously in their denims. By this time, Bruce's face was no longer attracting attention, with only slight traces of discoloration and puffiness around his eyes. The girls had retained their raven locks and convinced Bruce to start on a beard, so presently he looked somewhat grubby and unshaven.

Upon returning to the bedroom, they started packing in preparation for an early start the next morning when they'd catch a six-twenty super-TGV. Despite how crazy it looked on the map, their optimal rail route involved going into Paris and back out again. Bruce pointed out that it would be logistically much easier to drive to Le Havre and dump the car there, but Eva was adamant. "That's what you'd do, not what I'd do," which ended the discussion.

Everything fit into two rigid suitcases, leaving two leather bags for smaller carry-on items. A large rucksack had been purchased for the main sample container and Bruce added a couple of bath towels and a pair of thick bathrobes.

Got to bulk it out so that its weight doesn't seem overly unusual.

Packing completed, Eva decided to have a last check on Bruce's recuperation and ordered him to strip and lie on the bed. She first examined his face and throat, deciding that the medication had worked well and remnant swelling, bruising and scarring was cosmetic only and would be gone within a couple days. The originally livid bruising over his ribs had also died down considerably, along with associated swelling. As she pushed her fingertips against his left side, however, he grunted with pain.

"Cracked or broken," she concluded. "The drugs you've been on so far will allow you to keep going but, to get you fully up to scratch, we need some high-speed bone-builders. Maria?"

Bruce glanced to the side and watched Engel sort through a small emergency first aid kit of the kind used by climbers, bikers or trekkers in remote locations. Eva went to the mini-bar and brought him a half-liter bottle of sports energy drink. He had finished the bottle by the time Engel had found what she wanted and checked it with Eva.

"All right, we're starting with an activator," Eva explained while spraying a cold liquid that evaporated quickly over his left ribcage. Shaking the spray can after this operation was completed, she shrugged and then sprayed his right side also. "Waste not, want not."

"Now you need to lie there quietly for about ten minutes. I'll just have a look at your leg now."

It appeared that Bruce's assessment of his strengthened bone was borne out; damage had been restricted to the skin and muscle, which was now recovering well.

Engel had added logs to the fire, which was now crackling merrily. She then turned off the main light and dimmed the wall-lights over the bed.

Bruce glanced down and watched her peel off clothes and drop them carelessly on the floor.

Looks like a repeat of last night.

He felt the first beginnings of a physical reaction to that thought.

"Now the builder itself." Eva pressed a derm to his neck. "This is pretty powerful stuff, but we need you to be one hundred percent by tomorrow."

A judder of the bed and all of a sudden a naked quim

appeared above his face. "Just a shame you'll need your beauty sleep, 'cause otherwise we could have played hide the sausage."

Wet flesh – and a touch of metal – slid against his nose.

He inhaled deeply in rapid response to the erotic aromas invading his nostrils. A slap against the side of his neck. "Oh no. You wouldn't. Not fucking now. Please."

As Bruce sank slowly into blackness, wet sultry metal rubbed against his tongue and distant laughter echoed in his ears. Despite such distractions, his last feelings were of unease.

Every time we seem to be through the worst and relax, an unforeseen threat catches us out. What am I missing now?

10 ...Je t'aime

Bruce emerged groggily from deep sleep and looked to the side to see Eva peeling a dermal patch from his shoulder.

"Now, don't you feel much the better for that?" she enquired cheerfully while gracing him with a radiant smile.

Bruce stretched carefully, then with a bit more enthusiasm when he noted a complete absence of pain. Yawning, he twisted his wrists and rotated his neck. "You know, I feel as if I could do with a light workout this morning. Is there a gym in the hotel?"

"There's some basic training machinery in the basement that Maria and I have been using, but it's really rubbishy. Not that it matters anyway. We've got to make tracks. Maria is loading the van at present and has already sorted checkout. We left you to sleep as long as possible."

Bruce now remembered, with a twinge of regret, his last waking seconds of the previous night.

"As soon as you're up and dressed, we're on our way." She pulled back the sheet and pulled him from the bed before pushing him in the direction of the bathroom. "Remember, no shaving." She slammed the door behind him.

Just as well she reminded me.

He rubbed a stubbly chin and hurried through his morning ablutions.

Emerging from the bathroom, he came face to face with the two girls in matching winter suits: heavy jackets and trousers in a pattern that looked like the kind of camouflage used in desert warfare, not exactly conventional, but nothing that would cause particular attention given the current heterogeneity of clothing fashions. He looked at the clothes lying on the bed and grimaced, causing both young women to giggle. Jacket, trousers and boots in a screaming, silky scarlet.

He lifted the jacket to look at the lurid crest of some Thai kickboxing team: a bewildering coruscation of bejeweled dragons, cobra and swords. "Oh, no. Give me a fucking break."

"Nice color, don't you think?" Engel mocked. "We chose it to match our sussies and knickers bimbette kit. You weren't complaining then. Here, look." She tossed him a matching jockstrap.

"Only thing we couldn't find were socks. Will these do?" Eva asked mischievously.

Bruce stared at the socks with the Winnie-the-Pooh motif and had to grin. "Okay. You guys win. Anything at all for a peaceful life. At least you can be sure that I'll divert attention away from both of you."

"That was exactly the intention." Eva smirked.

***

At Rouen main station, they parked the van at the distant end of an underground car park and piled out. Bruce pulled the heavy rucksack onto his back, swaying a little until he found his balance. Eva then handed him the two suitcases. "You wanted some training this morning, so now's your chance." She passed one of the other small bags to Engel and, swinging the other gaily, led the way towards the ticket desk.

They purchased second-class tickets but, following the instructions in the coach plan projected above the platform, positioned themselves to board the restaurant car. Only ten minutes late, which Bruce assured them was very good for France, the train whistled into the station. The carriage door opened exactly as indicated at the edge of the platform. They climbed aboard. Bruce stowed his load in a niche beside the door while the girls entered the busy dining car to search for a seat. Bruce used his palmtop to register Paris as his destination with the luggage security demon before heading off to look for his companions.

At first he saw no sign of them in the packed car, but finally noted Eva waving from the very last table. He walked along the narrow aisle between tables, squeezing past waitresses and other passengers, finally seeing that the women were sitting at a table for four, already occupied by a tall, heavily built young man.

Engel was blatantly flirting with the man, who

seemed disappointed to see Bruce slide into the free seat. "This is Henri," she reported, "who kindly invited us to join him."

And who is not happy to find the talent has a chaperone. Or maybe worried because the chaperone has such a weird taste in clothing.

"Bonjour, Henri. Very nice of you. Well, ladies, have you ordered?"

Service was glacially slow and, by the time they had been served with coffee and croissants, the TGV had already reached the outskirts of Paris. Bruce had started to wonder if they would have time to complete breakfast, but he needn't have worried. The train then crawled, with frequent stops, until it finally reached the new main station in La Défense.

En route, Bruce pointed out the Combat Zones and Ghettoes scarring the suburbs and showed the results of the rioting that had flared in a continuous five-year cycle for half a century. 2042 had been one of the highs; riots during the summer and autumn involving refugee groups fleeing to Northern Europe to escape rising seas and extreme weather in the South. As usual, though, Paris had borne the brunt of the arson and violence. The last fifteen kilometers was on elevated track, at least twenty meters above the ground, but this was also encased in blast-proof Plexiglas, serving its purpose well, based on the evidence of frequent scarring and smoke marks.

Their arrival in La Défense was thirty minutes behind schedule, but they had plenty of time to make their connection as it, in turn, left forty minutes late. For this leg, Eva had selected first-class tickets, and they were able to find an empty 6-seater compartment, which they had to themselves for the entire trip on the quiet train.

They alighted at Le Havre main station and took a free shuttle bus to the foot-passenger departure gates at the ferry terminal. It was almost deserted, matching the car park that it overlooked: a few private cars and coaches, but an almost complete absence of the goods vehicles that normally packed the port.

After purchasing tickets from an automat, they had to wait almost an hour in the dreary waiting hall before the ship was ready to sail. As soon as their gate opened, they boarded along with a couple of bedraggled North-African-looking families who were loaded down with piles of luggage and a group of a dozen youngsters, who had been playing guitars and flutes in the far corner of the waiting room.

Bruce logged the families as refugees who already had the worst part of their journey behind them – getting into Europe in the first place. Of course, the remaining really hard bit would be a job, but anyone getting in nowadays would probably be highly qualified. The kids were probably students, but a bit too clean and wholesome.

He shivered.

Probably rabid God-botherers: there but for the grace of God, go I.

This reverie was broken when they boarded the ship

over a long passageway, which entered high up into the otherwise blank hull of the ferry. Casting his eye along its flanks, Bruce guessed the thing must look a bit like the pictures he had seen of stealth warships of the turn of the century, all blocky and strange angles, somehow reminiscent of ancient ironclads from the American Civil War. Recycling of amazingly ugly – but practical – designs.

The hydrofoil ferry wasn't intended to deflect cannon balls or radar beams, but rather crash through the huge seas created in the Channel by the regular storms. It was the brick-shithouse school of marine engineering. Hugely armored, containing vast quantities of ballast and a nuclear power plant that could supply the needs of a good-sized city: this didn't go over waves – it went through them. It was just about as much a submarine, or torpedo, as it was a conventional surface ship.

They claimed that no weather was bad enough to stop these babies sailing and, as Bruce passed though the wall of the reinforced hull, he could believe it.

The other foot passengers followed the signs to the lounge, while Bruce steered his party towards the bar and restaurant. When they entered a large airy room at the bow of the ship, they were faced with a wall of glass that looked down from a considerable height onto the harbor, which was gleaming wetly in the wintry sun. It was a beautiful day, with only patches of fluffy white cloud and a gentle wind from the northwest. Nevertheless, beyond the breakwater, whitecaps extended to the horizon.

Already a few dozen passengers were scattered

throughout the room, having come up from the vehicle deck that loaded first. Eva led the way into the bar area and selected a table well separated from other occupants.

"Fancy a quick beer and a sandwich for lunch?" Bruce piled luggage onto a neighboring table.

Engel was examining the view on what, on closer inspection, was a projection screen rather than the window it first appeared to be. "I'm not sure that would be such a good idea. It looks pretty choppy out there."

Bruce laughed. "Choppy? Not in the slightest. As far as the Channel goes, this is about as calm as it gets. This brute is well stabilized anyway and, especially when it gets up to speed, it'll be as smooth as a pancake."

Engel looked skeptical, but eventually decided to have a Babycham and a cheese and pickle sandwich – a selection Eva copied. When Bruce ordered at the bar he grimaced at the sweet, sparkling perry:

Enough to make me sick without being at sea.

By the time he returned with a loaded tray, including a pint of Guinness and a packet of cheese and onion crisps for himself, the ship had cast off with only the slightest of jolts and was now gliding smoothly through the harbor. No sound was noticeable over the tacky background muzak – some kind of electric folk of indeterminate provenance – and only a faint general vibration indicated the power that was driving this behemoth forward.

All three watched in silence while they passed through the breakwater and started to accelerate into open water. Initially, waves broke over the ram-like bow but these then became a continuous plume of spray after the ferry gained speed. Faster and faster and then the spray died away when the hydrofoils bit and the huge bulk of the hull was lifted clear of the water.

Engel was curious about how ferries managed to survive, given that there were perfectly adequate road and rail tunnels.

Bruce smiled.

Engle's not really so much younger than me, but young enough to have missed some of the major upheavals of the late twenties and early thirties when I was a kid.

As he explained the series of oil shocks over this time, when the industrial expansion of India and China was peaking, finally forced the move from oil to hydrogen. It was a slow and painful process for road transport industries – involving extensive development of new technology and an entire new support infrastructure. No problem at all for shipping, however, which required only a few locations for re-fuelling and paid minimum penalties for increased weight.

The advantages for shipping became even more significant with the advent of simple, cheap, inherently-safe nuclear plants like the one powering the ferry they were travelling on. It seemed impossible to wean the general public from private cars but, as a whole, surface transportation was now dominated by rail and sea.

Eva followed Bruce's discourse with interest, but Engel was quickly bored, yawning theatrically. "Enough, enough, O Learned One. I think that is more information than I really need about boats."

Bruce tried to interrupt in order to explain the difference between a boat and a ship, but was silenced by a glare.

"This boat, ship, whatever will be arriving fairly soon, so we should get our plans sorted out. We left bang on twelve noon, so we arrive at..."

"Twelve noon," Eva answered, "still an hour difference between France and England, despite all the EU has been trying to do about it for years."

"Decades actually, including a painful Brexit and an even more painful re-entry," Bruce corrected her before the glare shut him up again.

"Okay, okay. We're in at twelve and the other boat sails at five. How are we going to send our luggage over?"

"I'm sure there will be some kind of luggage drop off point," Bruce said.

Eva jumped in. "I've been thinking a bit about that. I think it would be much easier if we took the luggage on board ourselves. Much less chance of anyone, somehow or other, messing about with the samples. No matter how automated the process is, baggage always ends up getting chucked about. What do you think, Bruce?"

Bruce pondered for a moment, then: "Mmm, I think you're probably right. Increasingly I wonder why I ever ended up planning these capers. You've really got a knack for it."

Eva smiled happily and settled back to watch the approaching coastline.

Engel rolled her eyes and looked as if she was going to say something, but was stopped by Bruce's wink and his slight nod towards Eva. Correctly interpreting his intention to keep Eva as occupied as possible, her scowl turned quickly to a conspiratorial grin before she lifter the taller woman's arm and settled her head against a camouflage-covered shoulder.

***

At Portsmouth, everything went smoothly. They disembarked and packed into a taxi for the short ride from the ferry terminal to the separate complex from which the cruisers departed. The driver of the old-fashioned manual taxi was clearly unhappy with the short trip, but cheered up considerably when Bruce doubled the fare to give him a hundred percent tip.

The only potential problem involved confirmation of their reservation at a ticket desk prior to boarding. The reservations had been made anonymously, held by a direct credit transfer. However, unlike a ferry on an internal EU run, identification was needed for the cruiser. If it had simply involved sailing directly to a free port like Nassau, such an identification check would have been fairly superficial. The prior stop in the USA made this much stricter and more problematic due to the notorious leakiness of US government databases.

To minimize risks, passage had been booked only for Eva and this was confirmed using a secondary identity that had been provided by her pharm. Although identified as working for GRW in Glasgow, they had agreed that this would have minimum risks of setting off any alarms, even if encountered by the profilers' demons or other network agents. Bruce and Engel would only accompany their friend aboard and leave directly afterwards.

The registration process went without a hitch, the biometric information downloaded from Eva's palmtop being accepted without question. A porter then appeared. He took the cases from Bruce and placed them on an automatic transfer trolley. Bruce claimed that the rucksack was light and contained a couple of fragile presents, so the porter allowed him to retain it without any fuss. Taking the two small bags from the girls, he led the way up a series of escalators that took them onto the cruise ship and then to the upper accommodation deck.

Following along the thickly carpeted corridor and then into Eva's cabin, Bruce was impressed at how plush and modern the furnishings were.

Certainly top of the range.

The porter set the bags on a stand and informed Eva that the cases would arrive shortly. While Bruce tried to shuck-off the rucksack in a manner suggesting that it was much lighter than it really was, the porter opened a bottle of champagne and pointed out a gilt-framed card inviting passengers to the New Year's ball.

Eva grinned happily when the man left, and then poured champagne into the single flute and also two white wine glasses from the minibar. "Come on now. We don't want this to go to waste. I must say that I'm beginning to wish we were actually going on this cruise. It looks like it would be fun."

"Definitely very swanky," Engel commented from the bedroom adjoining the lounge. "Very nice big bed." She bounced on it. "With some heavy duty fittings." She pointed to rings set into the headboard as the others looked in. "Bondage kit seems to be standard in all the places you take me to, Beast. Are you trying to say something?"

Bruce pointed out that the selection of both the cruise and the cabin had been entirely up to Eva, which did nothing to stop the girls from happily speculating on just what his wildest S and M fantasies might involve.

After finishing their champagne, Bruce and Engel took their leave, kissing Eva goodbye at the door of her cabin for the benefit of any passers-by. Back on shore, they walked out of the port area in the direction of the town center. Enjoying the chance to stretch their legs, they ignored a shuttle bus and several taxi stands, electing to walk the couple of kilometers to the main railway station.

Streets were generally quiet during their walk, becoming busy with shoppers only as they got into the pedestrianized zone that contained the railway station. Opposite the station, they entered a pub and, while Bruce fetched a couple pints of local bitter from the bar, Engel logged into a public vid service and sent their agreed message to the cruise liner. Although it would automatically be relayed on to Eva, anyone interested enough to hack into the cruiser's internal server would be able to find a record of the short missive.

The text-only message would appear to come from Eva's employer in Glasgow, automatic forwarding a search-mail from a fictitious brother. It asked Eva to contact him, with the title line *family crisis*. The contact address would elicit only a short voice message, which Bruce had already recorded, asking her to come home to Irvine as soon as possible, as her mother was ill.

It certainly was not the most sophisticated of ploys but fit with the identity data Eva had logged. It should, in any case, allow her to leave the ship without any special fuss. For a vessel carrying about three thousand rich passengers, many of whom would be rather aged to boot, they had guessed that such events must happen fairly regularly.

Eva and Bruce spent time over their drinks, which was rather easy to do with the rather soapy, insipid brew. Bruce persevered, reminding himself that it was an acquired taste and hoping that the taste bud acclimatization process would go a bit faster. Engel gave up less than halfway and opted for a half of cider and a packet of peanuts, "...to take the bowfin' fuckin' taste of this shite away," as she colorfully expressed it.

They had both been sitting with empty glasses for fifteen minutes when they spotted Eva emerge from a taxi at the drop-off point in front of the station. Bruce pulled Engel to her feet and hurried her out of the pub. On reaching Eva, he took over the two small bags she carried and rushed her into the building. "We're cutting it very fine, but there's a fast train to London in about two minutes. Platform three."

Eva strode along behind him. "Sorry about that, Bruce. It just seemed a waste of good champagne not to finish the bottle." She grinned at Engel, indicating that the apology was less than sincere.

"I don't see what the fuckin' rush is all about," Engel complained as she scampered along, half running to keep pace with the taller woman. "It's not as if we've got to catch a particular plane or anything."

"It's just Bruce's way." She grinned. "At least here we can let him off the leash for a bit."

They reached the train with only seconds to spare then sat for ten minutes until it finally drew out of the station. Bruce cursed under his breath. "Just as bad as the sodding French. All the fucking technology in the world, but still can't get trains running on time. They work in Switzerland, work in Japan. Why can't the bloody Brits and Frogs run railways?"

"Don't get your knickers in a twist." Engel peeled off her heavy jacket and stretched, which showed off to maximum advantage the skin-tight, long-sleeved ski vest she wore. Same camouflage theme, Bruce noted, as he peered closely to confirm that it was indeed an item of clothing and not just body paint. His distraction was completed when Eva revealed a matching vest, even more spectacularly displayed on her more curvaceous torso.

Just as well we've got this compartment to ourselves.

Bruce crossed his legs to try and relieve some of the

strain on his under-dimensioned underwear. Even on a high-speed train, it would be a long journey.

***

Rather than transfer between stations in London to take advantage of a fast rail link, Eva elected to take a taxi to Heathrow. Bruce supported this decision, pointing out that Heathrow, as one of the largest airports in the world, was a bit of a zoo as far as internal movement was concerned. Building and rebuilding had been ongoing almost continuously for more than half a century and the maze of runways and taxiways on the surface was nothing compared to the multiple levels of labyrinthine tunnels below.

The trip to the airport was subdued; all three silently relived their frantic transfer through Heathrow six months earlier. Nevertheless, when the fully automated vehicle dropped them at *Intercontinental – Asia Terminal 7*, they perked up noticeably. The girls attempted to guess where Eva's method for randomizing their travel itinerary would take them. To increase the fun, they had elected not to download departure information until they reached the terminal building and to use a selection window based on departures between one and two hours after the moment they arrived.

Bruce was greatly relieved when Singapore emerged as the clear winner; a Singapore Airlines flight SQ 6 would leave in just under two hours, sliding into the far end of their window.

Could have been very much worse as the runner-up was an India Air flight to Mumbai.

Eva purchased tickets at a special standby desk where she obtained first class tickets for about half the normal rate. Although Eva's almost limitless stocks of untraceable direct electronic credit covered payment, the saving warmed Bruce's Scottish soul and lightened his dissatisfaction with the thought of seeing in the New Year at ten thousand meters over the Far East.

Again the tricky step was registration for the flight and subsequent emigration control. Bruce considered how much easier it must have been in the old days when passports were physical documents and one could, in principle, carry around a bag full of them if one had resources for the required forgery. Now a passport was a biometrically identified file on a database. All he needed to have with him was a code number, provided by a palmtop link, that allowed his biometric scan to be compared with that in the database. The problem, therefore, now involved the creation of false records on databases that had some of the strongest protection currently in existence.

The checks within, and access to, these databases had been a battleground between government agencies and civil liberties groups for decades. Typically, there was no international conformity, and the standards of passport security and entry requirements differed considerably from county to country. For anyone, like Bruce, wanting to travel incognito, a balance had to be found in order to choose a database within which a false passport file could be created but which, at the same time, could not easily be hacked by demons searching for travelers with identical biometric data in different databases.

As a compromise, they had decided to travel on Bermudian resident alien passports, which had been produced by the pharm to ease their stay on the island. These had never been used for travel before, so sophisticated background checks would reveal a discrepancy resulting from their appearance in England. This should, however, cause no particular problem for either exit from the UK – as Bermuda was part of the greater EU – or entry into Singapore, which focused on screening out a very long list of undesirables and ensuring that short-term visitors left within thirty days.

Despite Bruce's concerns, again the identity controls went without a hitch and, within twenty minutes of purchasing their tickets, he was ensconced in the plush Singapore Airlines lounge while the girls went shopping within a terminal complex that resembled a mall more than an airport.

The girls appeared in the lounge half an hour later, laden down with carrier bags and two sizeable kit bags. As it was almost 5 pm, they toasted the departure of their samples on the cruiser with champagne before the girls went off to change, taking one of the kit bags with them. When they disappeared into the shower-spa area, Bruce picked up the remaining carrier bags with a feeling of foreboding.

Could have been worse, but not much worse, he

concluded as he rummaged through the clothing: knee-length plaid shorts and a lurid yellow shirt with a prominent golfer on the pocket, completed by tennis shoes in a Black Watch tartan. "My God," he muttered. "Who on earth would ever spend their own money on such tack?" He lifted the other kit bag and set off for the men's toilets.

On the other hand, it's got to be better that this red shit.

Bruce had already changed and started on a second glass of wine when the girls returned still wearing their tight tops but now more demurely covered by open white blouses. Matching khaki shorts and all-terrain sandals completed their outfits. Their hair was still dyed, but now more a kind of chestnut brunette rather than the previous jet black.

I wonder if this dressing up identically isn't getting a bit out of hand, but I'm not sure if it's a good or a bad sign in any case.

The girls inspected him with increasing amusement.

"Don't you think the shoes go particularly well with the Winnie-the-Pooh socks?" Eva asked.

"I still think it's a shame they didn't have those kids' Pooh trainers in larger sizes. The ones with the lights that flash when you walk."

"But then we would have needed a Pooh t-shirt. I only saw those in small sizes too."

"But think about how cute he would look with his little Pooh tummy." Engel patted Bruce's stomach, which was indeed somewhat rounded and draped over the belt of his shorts.

At that point, priority boarding for first class passengers was called and Bruce was happy to break off this conversation in order to organize redistribution of contents between their items of carry-on luggage.

A lounge attendant guided Bruce's party and a dozen or so other passengers to the nearby gate, bypassing long queues of those waiting to board other cabin classes. First class was in the nose of the lower deck of the plane and included both a sitting /sleeping area and a dining area, which was gaily decorated on a New Year theme. The seating was grouped to suit the passengers, with wide spaces between, probably reflecting the fact that the cabin was only filled to about thirty percent maximum capacity.

It makes a lot of sense, utilizing the extra space rather than just flying a lot of empty seats about. Must make the logistics a bit tricky, though."

Reflecting their late booking, the three seats assigned to the extremophile team were at the very front of the cabin, next to the galley, and farthest away from the washrooms, which were at rear of the cabin. A side locker had more than enough room for their entire luggage. After it was stowed, they settled down to yet another glass of champagne while a rather camp steward presented the dinner menu and described the facilities available.

Bruce stood and stretched to examine the other passengers in the cabin. Most were evidently business travelers, who had been working with laptops or jabbering over com links in the lounge and, in several cases, during the entire transfer to the plane. Three Asian men, sitting together in the back row of seats, had already disappeared behind a privacy screen, as had a tall Japanese man who was sitting alone and a loud American couple. Another couple of Asians in business suits, a man and a woman, were seated together, and an extremely fat American businessman sat alone. The remaining passengers were a European family – father, mother and teenage daughter – all tall, blond and blue eyed and speaking a Scandinavian language. Finally, he noted that two seats together, which formed the second-back row, were still empty.

Drinks had been topped-up and doors were about to close when there was a disturbance that caused Bruce's party – and all other passengers who had not retreated behind privacy shields – to turn their heads. A flamboyant couple had stumbled into the cabin. They were loaded down with luggage and shopping bags. The steward and two stewardesses rushed to help divest the pair of their burden, plus heavy fur overcoats, hats and gloves. The bulky outer garments contrasted dramatically with the slim frames revealed within, both clad in tight black garments from head to toe. Dark haired with very similar features, the couple looked somewhat familiar to Bruce, although he couldn't put a name to them. He turned to the girls who were huddled together and whispering excitedly.

In response to a nudge by his elbow, Engel turned and immediately identified his look of confusion. "You don't recognize them, do you?"

Eva leaned over her smug friend. "They're the De

Marcos. Italian jazz dancers who won gold in the last Olympics. Their routines are based on Tae Kwon Do and some other martial arts, mainly Wu Shu or some other kind of Kung Fu. They're really high grade fighters, to boot."

Bruce nodded. "Yea, I think I've heard about them. Brother and sister?"

"Twins. You should see them move. They almost seem telepathic."

"And very nice arses, both of them," Engel added while licking her lips.

***

After takeoff, the first class passengers were invited to come to the dining area where more champagne was served and the steward offered a toast to the New Year, pointing out that it had just occurred in Singapore. Most of those behind the security screens were not eating and Bruce guessed that they may already be sleeping. Unfortunately, the loud Americans did emerge and took places at the next table, where they discussed both work negotiations and personal problems at a volume sufficient to carry throughout the cabin.

Engel was not happy. "Fuckin' Yanks. Why can't they fuckin' speak normally instead of fuckin' shouting all the fuckin' time."

Bruce kicked her shin under the table, despite the fact that her outburst had clearly gone completely unnoticed by their neighbors. "Cut down the swearing. You're supposed to be a civilized Bermudian, not bog-Irish street scruff."

Engel looked taken aback, then belligerent, but finally smiled, to Bruce's great relief. "I suppose you are quite right, Bruce darling," she responded in an awful imitation of upper class English. "I suppose I was most terribly frightful. I'll be good as gold from now on. Honestly, darling." She fluttered her eyelashes at him.

Eva rolled her eyes, but responded in kind with a good impression of the Milngavie accent, which provided a caricature of the West Scottish social climbers. "Well I, myself, never swear. It's a characteristic of the Hoi Polloi and the rest of the Great Unwashed. And, apart from anything else," she grinned at Bruce, "if you swear you will end up in the Bad Fires."

Bruce groaned.

Shit. What've I done? I really think I preferred the swearing after all.

Silly accents continued over an extended dinner that would not have been out of place in a high quality restaurant. Amuse Bouche, French onion soup, salad, steak Marilyn Munroe, profiteroles, fruit and cheese board. A range of excellent European vintage wines and some New World ports matched the gourmet meal.

Bruce felt completely stuffed as he sat, hands on stomach, at the end of the meal. He noticed the background sound of conversation die away as the volume of the previously unnoticed background muzak gradually increased. Turning, he saw that the De Marco couple had risen from their seats and were standing in the open area at the back of the cabin, which Bruce recognized only now as being set up as a very small dance floor.

The music was some kind of electronic, jazzed-up tango. However, Bruce could not categorize the dance itself, which had certainly something of the tango rhythm of continuous change of pace – explosive movements followed by motionless poses or languid stretches. The movements themselves, executed with catlike grace, were more like something out of a paired kata, a stylized combat with flamboyant kicks and punches that were gracefully evaded or deflected. The combination was stunning and, although now a recognized Olympic discipline according to the girls, Bruce had never seen anything of its like before.

The dance reached a crescendo with a flurry of head-high kicks, which were obviously constrained somewhat by the low cabin roof, ending with both dancers back to back, standing on one leg with bodies completely horizontal. Back roundhouse kicks had frozen, each with the heel at the point of contact with the back of a head. The music died away and the cabin was completely silent, apart from the distant muted drone of aero engines and the sigh of air conditioning.

The steward was the first to break from this spell and started the applause, which was taken up by all in the small audience. Bruce realized that he had actually been holding his breath and clapped enthusiastically while he exhaled with a sigh. The dancers unfroze, spun to face each other with matching grins and then acknowledged the applause with small nods. Every movement and gesture were perfectly synchronized.

"Really incredible, poetic almost," he whispered. "I must really have a look at some holos of this stuff. You'd really have to slo-mo it in order to pick out the fine detail. The dance seemed to represent some kind of lovers' tiff, but the ending – was that supposed to represent mutual killing blows, a stalemate or an end to hostilities?"

Eva responded, "The dance is one of their classics and is called The Kiss, so I would guess the last option is most probable."

"Could well be, anyway, I'm certainly going to have a look at some more of this stuff."

"I could make some recommendations," Eva said. "The De Marcos are the best, but there are Irish and Brazilian couples who are also extremely good."

Despite calls for an encore, the dancers split up and the girl, Claudia according to Eva, walked over to the steward and pulled him, protesting volubly, onto the floor. Meanwhile, her brother, Antonio, approached the teenage daughter of the Scandinavian family, who exploded into excited giggles when he offered his hand. Bruce could not help but note that her mother, who was facing in his direction, looked distinctly jealous of her daughter.

The music was now something like a slow, electro-jazz samba, and the steward attempted to dance ballroom-style. Only the agility of the snakelike Claudia De Marco saved her feet from being stomped on and fittings from being bumped into. By way of contrast, the blonde teenager tried something in the De Marco style, gamely whirling and kicking high in the air. The short skirt she was wearing provided no hindrance to her movements and occasional flashes of white knickers titillated Bruce during the higher kicks.

A kick to his shin brought his attention to Engel, who was frowning at him. "Stop ogling the child, for God's sake," she whispered. "She looks about twelve."

"Easily thirteen," he replied with a grin, noting with relief that Engel's silly accent had disappeared without a reappearance of her continuous swearing. "If they're old enough to bleed, they're old enough to—"

"You really are a disgusting old man." She turned to pull a protesting Eva onto the dance floor.

Eva and Engel kicked off their sandals and danced in bare feet, fitting the movements of one of their morning training sessions to the beat of the music.

I must learn how to do this.

Bruce's attention flickered between the dueling brunettes, the sensuous Claudia and the blonde teen's underwear.

Although, if planning to dance this kind of stuff, I'll have to eat and drink a lot less. How do these people dance like that directly after dinner?

The music ended to applause from both dancers and audience. The steward beat a hasty retreat and was replaced by a blushing blonde stewardess. The other two couples stayed together on the floor and were joined by the loud Americans, which left little room on the small floor.

The next dance was an electro-jazz version of a tune Bruce identified as *Girl from Ipanema,* slow enough that the limited space would not cause problems.

One of the De Marcos is probably setting the music program. This must be one of their known pieces, as both of them are leading dances that seem to be based on Kung Fu Sticky Hand training.

He thought back to when he tried it, pairs of students with their right hands in contact and trying to use this single point of contact to unbalance each other. The dance maintained the principle of continuous hand contact, but attempts to topple an opponent were replaced by sliding body-to-body contact with a partner.

The young blonde was clearly in rapture, as the slim Italian slid his body against hers. Bruce grinned when he noted that she smiled salaciously in her mother's direction, just before her eyes closed and she rotated her groin against a muscular thigh.

If this keeps up much longer, she's going to have an orgasm in the middle of dance floor.

He smiled at that thought.

Eva and Engel quickly adapted their own dance to this pattern, but the Americans seemed oblivious, swaying gently to the music while the man surreptitiously groped his partner's sizeable buttocks.

After the dance, the floor cleared and the steward announced that they could now celebrate New Year yet again: local time over the Indian Ocean. Over the following three hours of the flight, the dance floor was in regular use while the party continued. Any time things got quiet, Bruce spotted further crew and some passengers from the Business Class cabin being sneaked in to dance.

After his dinner had fully settled, Bruce allowed himself to be occasionally dragged to the floor, ensuring in all cases that the music was slow enough to minimize the risk of him making a complete fool of himself. He enjoyed several dances with both Eva and Engel, although he almost choked when Engel, looking innocently into his eyes during a slow, smoochy number, slid her hand up the leg of his baggy shorts and playfully squeezed his dick. He was released only in response to an increasingly tight nip to her buttocks. “Mmm... S and M.” She pulled his head down and stood on tiptoes to whisper into his ear. “Maybe we’ll have a Happy Hogmanay after all.”

Getting more into the mood of the party, Bruce also danced with the luscious Claudia and the blonde girl, who transpired to be Swedish and was called Ulla. The former was an education for Bruce, being another of the Sticky Hands type of dances. He found that all he had to do was ensure the edge of his hand stayed in contact with that of his partner and she did the rest. Despite this, for the first time in his life, he felt as if he was really dancing elegantly as the lithe, black-clad woman slid like an eel around him.

The dance with Ulla was a different experience; she actually came onto the floor and invited him to dance just as he finished a dance with Engel. He quickly glanced over in the direction of the girl's mother; her father had already retreated to the sleeping area, having failed completely to persuade his daughter to join him. The blonde woman, who had refused to dance the entire evening and was evidently playing chaperone to her daughter, merely rolled her eyes in defeat.

The dance was slow and the tall teenager, who was almost exactly the same height as him, swayed gracefully in his arms. Initially they exchanged names and pleasantries and Bruce began to relax a little. The family was actually moving to Singapore, where her father was about to take up a research position with one of the major bioengineering companies that concentrated in this high-tech hothouse. Based on the way that the girl chattered, Bruce guessed that Engel's original guess might have been correct and twelve years old might be closer than thirteen.

While he thanked her for the dance, the next number started, a revamped version of the classic Je t'aime. She squeaked with delight in a way that confirmed Bruce's suspicions about her age and grabbed his hands. "I love this one," she declared as she slipped into his arms. Swaying languidly, she stuck to him like glue, grinding her body against his while she breathed heavily into his ear. She twisted her hips, so that his hands, held loosely around her waist, slid over the curves of her taut young bum. Bruce frantically moved his hands up to the middle of her back, as a pair of liquid blue eyes looked directly into his and a blonde eyebrow was raised in a blatantly challenging manner.

Christ on a Bike.

Bruce quickly glanced over her shoulder at her harried-looking mother.

If this is twelve, what the hell is she going to be like at fifteen? Her parents are going to be nervous wrecks.

A hand slid over his left buttock while her groin ground against his, to the accompanying groans of *Je t'aime* on the soundtrack. He glanced around anxiously to check if anyone had noticed and observed that the move was clearly arranged to be invisible to her mother. Most attention was now on Eva dancing with Claudia and Antonio dancing with the gay steward. Both couples were evidently getting well into the music, with some very deep kissing going on. The only person who seemed to have noted the girl's move was an extremely pissed-off Engel, who looked like she clearly felt cut out of the action.

Bruce sighed with relief when the dance ended, having managed without causing offence to deflect the young girl's attempts to kiss him. He hugged her and thanked her profusely for the dance, and then she skipped off happily in the direction of Antonio, who had been reluctantly released by his partner.

When Bruce sat beside Engel, she sighed theatrically. "No wonder these bloody profilers always find you. You can be read like a bloody book. You were all over that poor wee lass. Pedophilia, that is. You'll go to jail for that."

"And burn in the Bad Fires," a Milngavie accent added, which announced Eva's arrival at the table.

"Not that you're that much better, you lesbo tart. I

saw you with your tongue down the throat of that De Marco girl. A glance in your direction from any slag and you're in there, like a rat up a drainpipe."

Eva was completely unperturbed and maintained the annoying accent. "Actually she's a lovely girl. Tastes of butterscotch. And a very, very nice tight bottom...as you observed earlier this very evening. In fact, I do believe she's looking in your direction this very moment."

Engel's wrath was completely diverted when she was dragged to her feet and propelled in the direction of the female De Marco.

Eva grinned while sliding to sit beside Bruce. "Maria's going to have an interesting dance. Yes, I knew it. *Je t'aime* is starting again. Claudia is really into piercing and liked my ring." She drew back her blouse to show the ring through the engorged nipple, plainly evident through the thin top. "Both of them, actually." She laughed at the look on Bruce's face. "I told her that Maria had the same set, so Claudia is dying to check them out."

Bruce stared at the squirming women and tried to work out how Claudia could possibly be doing the checking out. He was still none the wiser when the dance finished but, from the look Engel flashed Eva when she returned, it appeared to have been carried out successfully.

Shortly before the party ended, prior to commencing descent into Singapore, a third New Year was announced – that in the UK. The passengers who had remained until the bitter end toasted each other and the cabin crew on the dance floor while a traditional Auld Lange Syne was played as a last dance. While he swayed, rather drunkenly, in the group who packed with linked arms into the limited space, Bruce had to concede that he had actually had a great time and that this would rank as a truly memorable Hogmanay.

Guiding the girls to their seats while the crew tidied up for landing, he gave them a squeeze. "Just a shame Angela wasn't here. Other than that, it's been an absolutely fantastic New Year party. Yet again Eva, a great choice. Anyway, we should hit some detox, to get ready to disembark."

Eva distributed the detox, and the girls went back to silly voices, speculating just what Eva's outrageous mother might have gotten up to with the potential victims available at the party. Bruce let it all wash over him, sitting in a contented haze and delaying the detox until the plane touched down in the torrential rain of Singapore's Changi airport.

I was going to talk to the girls about my worries, but maybe it's just paranoia. What could possibly go wrong in Singapore?

11 ...looking out for a hero

Bruce awoke when a ray of late afternoon sun shone directly into his face. He wiped crusty eyes, which were beginning to water in the bright light just before the sun vanished behind thick cloud. The light had initiated the throbbing that presaged an imminent hangover and so, with a groan, Bruce threw back the sheet and rolled to his feet. The large room contained two queen-sized beds: the one he had been sleeping in, which was considerably disheveled, and a much neater one containing a single hump under the duvet from which two brown-haired heads protruded. Typically, the girls were sleeping face to face, their noses actually touching.

Bruce slumped into the bathroom and searched through a bag containing toiletries for appropriate medication. Extracting a violet capsule, he swallowed it with a mouthful of flat champagne from a glass standing on the sink. He looked at the ultra-modern shower and then the deep Japanese-style bath.

Definitely more like a bath needed.

He started the program to fill it with piping hot water.

The detox pill was already doing its job when he slowly eased himself into the bath, sinking inch by inch as his body acclimatized to the scalding temperature. The water reached mid chest by the time he settled his backside onto the inbuilt ledge and leaned back with a sigh, sweat already streaming down his face and dripping from his nose. He looked though the one-way glass that formed the facing wall and saw that the earlier ray of sunshine was probably the last of the day. Heavy clouds roiled overhead and occasional large drops of rain spattered against the glass.

Bruce closed his eyes, feeling the soak drain residual stresses and strains from his body.

I didn't actually feel noticeably tense beforehand, but now I can tell that the pressures of the last few crazy days have taken their toll. Not that all the action has been unpleasant.

He grinned while reviewing the previous night – or actually morning, he corrected himself. Arrival in Singapore and immigration formalities had been anticlimactic, and Bruce's party had checked into their hotel – a Conrad attached to a sprawling conference center – within forty-five minutes of touchdown. This speed was aided by their early morning arrival time and hand luggage only, which caused a raised eyebrow but no actual comment at the customs control point.

Although it had been 7 am local time – and 1 am according to their body clocks – they had all still been in New Year party mode when they settled into their room. Recognizing that party opportunities would be somewhat limited in early-morning Singapore, Engel had opaqued the windows, called up jazz-dance holos on the entertainment system, set the volume to high and the sound-proofing to max, and then broke into the well-stocked mini-bar. They danced together in twos and threes to the accompaniment of holos that were increasingly raunchy, starting with past Olympic dances and ending with some that got close to the limit of what Singapore's draconian anti-pornography legislation would allow.

In line with the entertainment, the girls had gradually shed items of clothing – or stripped them forcibly from Bruce – during the dances. By 10 am they were again fairly drunk and Bruce was wearing only his miniscule jockstrap while the girls were completely naked, their dancing surrounded by torn items of clothing.

With a lascivious lick of her lips, Engel had selected a version of *Je t'aime,* with an associated holo which had abandoned all dance pretensions and was a simple sex romp featuring two extremely well developed young women and two body-builders, both of whom were hung like donkeys.

Must be some kind of surgical enhancement.

Bruce tried to console himself as the two girls slid against him and, in the background, the body-builders pumped untiringly into what must have been surgically armored orifices.

By the end of this dance, the trio had been sprawled on the bed and Bruce had been relieved of his last item of clothing. As he remembered the details, he could feel his body reacting, despite the heat of the bath.

He had been about to restart *Je t'aime* when Engel

winked at Eva. "Now for your New Year's present," she had announced as she linked her palmtop to the room holo system.

Bruce had levered himself onto his elbows as the faint drum beats announced the start of Ravel's Bolero. The holo was indistinct, clouds swirling in the center of the floor.

Some kind of kinky porn video of Engel's?

As the figures became more distinct, he had been surprised to see that it was the De Marcos and, as Engel zoomed in, it was evident that their usual black attire was, in this case, only body paint. The twins were dancing naked. The girls giggled when Bruce started in surprise. "Special collector's edition," Engel had announced. "Claudia gave it to us as a present last night. Now, look at this."

A close up of one face, then the other. Rings through ears, nose and eyebrows flashed in side lighting, while the bodies gyrated with gradually increasing velocity around each other. As the pace became more frantic, Engel scanned farther down the bodies, blowing up detail in turn of four multiply pierced nipples and two pierced navels. Both the De Marcos had double lines of small rings down their backs, linked by crisscrossed black ribbon. The Bolero reached its climax and the dancers froze with dramatic matching high kicks that were caught in the partner's hand.

Engel maintained the frozen tableau, zooming in yet closer. Claudia's raised leg exposed smooth black-painted mons and the pink of a gleaming open labia. Light glinted off half a dozen golden rings. "Quite a sight there," Eva commented, "more metal than even the well-pierced Mistress McLachlan."

Bruce wondered how she had managed to know that as the viewpoint moved crazily over black-painted skin to focus on Antonio's erect penis. At first, Bruce's only thought had been that, at least, it appeared to have normal dimensions but a further zoom revealed the golden bolt penetrating his glans. "The full Prince Albert," Engel had announced gleefully, as Bruce squirmed. "We've decided to get one for you."

"Actually, it isn't..." Eva had corrected, as the viewpoint moved up the penis to expose a ring curving from its tip, "...this one's the Prince Albert. According to legend, used to hold his foreskin back and keep his penis sweet for Queen Victoria. I reckon that this would be the one for you."

"Over my dead body," he had shouted before the girls decided to tickle him to death. The bed got very messed up over the next quarter of an hour and, as he remembered details, Bruce could feel his erection recover from the thought of the excruciating-looking piercing.

Not at all a bad way to start 2043.

***

Bruce soaked for almost half an hour, the bath maintaining constant temperature throughout. When he finally emerged, he felt quite light-headed and, wrapping a towel around his sweaty body, tiptoed through the bedroom in search of a drink. Unimpressed with the remaining selection in the mini-bar, he ordered fresh grapefruit juice from room service. The drink was delivered within a couple minutes, automatically via the serving hatch beside the bar. He then sat on the end of his bed and sipped from the frosted glass while he watched the tropical storm slowly build up outside the window.

A quarter of an hour later, Bruce stopped sweating and began to feel peckish. The sun had probably set by now, he guessed, but the heavy cloud, underlit by the lights of the city, made it difficult to be sure. Bored by the weather, he called up Engel's *Bolero* holo and played it through a couple times with the volume set low and without the anatomical close-ups. It really was an extremely clever piece, seemed to tell a story that involved a display of incredible athleticism and synchronicity...

...and definitely highly erotic. Enough of this...

He resisted the temptation to play the dance a third time, and instead opted to tidy up and get dressed. A very quick rinse, hair trim and a vaguely Old Spice scented blow dry in the shower and he emerged to examine himself critically in a full-length projection mirror, which allowed a three-sixty degree view of his body that could be zoomed-in on in response to verbal commands.

Residual bruising and scarring on my face and throat are now visible only under magnification; helped a bit by this beard that is almost at the point of justifying the name, rather than looking like a five o' clock shadow. Bruising on my chest was still discernible, but made less noticeable by my Bermuda tan. Shin looks and feels perfectly okay. Unfortunately there seems to be no way of curing this Pooh-tummy as rapidly.

He patted his stomach, and with a sigh, wandered into the bedroom in search of intact clothing.

Dressed in his freshened denims, he stared down at the sleeping girls.

A bit of fun - or discretion as the better part of valor?

The Japanese bath included a small plastic bowl that could be used for the formal washing process prior to bathing. The temptation to fill it with cold water and use it to wake the girls was almost unbearable.

On the other hand, two irate girls might be a bit much to handle. Actually, either one of them would be more than enough.

He jerked back the sheet and exposed the entwined bodies. Engel immediately extricated herself and rolled to her feet without disturbing her partner. Standing on the bed, her blue-green eyes gleamed as she kissed him gently on the nose. “Good choice, Beast. You saved yourself a New Year kicking.”

Bruce staggered back in surprise. “Buggeration. You were awake the whole time.”

“Just since you started playing Bolero. Blondie, however, is still out for the count.” She gave an evil cackle and sped off in the direction of the bathroom.

“Hold it there.” Bruce managed to intercept the naked girl and block her return to the bedroom, noting that she held a large dripping sponge. “Let’s not start something that’ll cause a ruckus.”

“Why not? Start the year the way you intend to

continue, that's what I always say." She tried to wriggle past him while keeping the sponge out of his reach.

Catching the small form around the waist, he crushed her to him in a bear hug.

She looked up in surprise.

"Start the way you intend to continue," he mumbled and kissed her on the mouth. Her resistance lasted only seconds before she melted against him and her mouth opened.

After a long, drawn-out kiss, she arched her head backwards and stared into his eyes. "Grapefruit, my favorite..." she sighed, "...apart from Eva's naughty bits, of course," she added with a grin.

Engel dropped her brow against his shoulder and Bruce stood silently for a moment until he was suddenly pushed to the side and staggered, dropping his small captive onto the thick carpet.

"Can't you folk find anywhere better to copulate?" A naked Eva rushed into the toilet. "Bursting for a pee." The door slammed in time to intercept the thrown sponge that, on contact, sprayed water in all directions.

"Shit, look what you made me do," Engel exclaimed, although clearly amused by this development. "Actually, could really do with a pee myself." She opened the door, followed her tall friend, and slammed the door behind her.

***

By the time the girls had dressed – matching shorts, blouses and sandals – Bruce had scanned the hotel database on eating options. It was now after 6 pm but, having just awoken, they felt that it should really be breakfast time. As a compromise, Bruce suggested an Irish pub in the old dock area, which offered *all-day Classic British Breakfast*. This was situated close to the commercial center: old offices and small warehouses that had been transformed into a maze of restaurants, bars and clubs a half century previously. It also included the closest that puritanical Singapore came to a red-light district: a few rather tame strip bars along with some dubious saunas and massage parlors.

They took a taxi for the short ride from the hotel to the pub, which was in an area of two or three story buildings lying below the massive concrete levee built to combat rising sea levels and the massive storm surges associated with frequent typhoons and tropical storms. Singapore was unusual due to its combination of small size, high population density and, most importantly, great wealth from its diverse range of high-technology industries and role as a shipping gateway to much of Asia. As such, it had been able to engineer against climatic change and thus was the only coastal country that had actually increased its land area since the beginning of the twenty-first century.

Like Tokyo, armored skyscrapers directly challenged the forces of super-charged storms, with similar displays of spectacular, if often ugly, architecture. Also like Tokyo, extensive areas were entirely covered by transparent roofs as protection against high winds but also, for Singapore, the almost continuous rain. Having looked at the statistics, the rainfall here made Glasgow seem dry by comparison.

The manually driven taxi dropped the trio at the door of Mollie Malone's, a classic ex-pat pub of the type found throughout the world. Even though it was still early, the pub was busy, with a wide mixture of Asian, European and North American clientele. Despite the Irish theme, the bar appeared to be manned entirely by Australians, while the waitresses were slim Philippinas who looked similar enough to be sisters.

Bruce led the girls to a table in a quiet corner of the bar where a tiny Asian girl with a name badge claiming she was called Samantha took their order. They all selected the classic breakfast of bacon, eggs, sausage, fried tomato, beans and toast. The girls went for English breakfast tea, but Bruce selected a pint of Guinness, justifying it as an attempt to readjust his body clock.

By the time breakfast was finished and a post-prandial round of stout had been ordered, the pub had filled up considerably. Bruce's party was now boxed-in by a group of a half dozen men in their late twenties or early thirties. They were evidently vying for the attention of three pretty girls seated at a neighboring table. The girls were each very different.

I'd guess Japanese, Malay and Indian despite their strangely dyed and styled hair, but each very sexy in her own way.

It sounded like the lads were in money markets of some kind, boasting loudly of multi-billion-dollar projects and racing classic Porsches at marketing meetings. Their approach failed completely, Bruce was amused to note. When three rather scruffy young Asian guys in motorcycle leathers waved to the girls, they immediately scampered over to join them.

Two of the men appeared to admit defeat, covering their retreat with the claim of a conference comlink in "thirty minutes US."

This on January first?

Bruce rolled his eyes

The brunettes laughed.

They were just finishing their drinks when one of the money men, either getting desperate or perhaps just emboldened by alcohol, approached their table and asked if Engel would like to join them. Engel politely refused, saying she was accompanied then turned to kiss Eva on the mouth. The man retreated immediately, blushing in embarrassment, to the great amusement of his buddies. Bruce sighed with relief, remembering a similar situation in Shinjuku, six months previously, which hadn't ended so peacefully.

Possibly it was this heightened awareness caused by the adrenalin surge when Bruce recalled the fight in the Shamrock pub, or maybe just luck or simple coincidence but, at the moment Engel's admirer turned away, the headline on a news-sheet lying on the floor caught his eye. *Singmed CEO celebrates 90th birthday*. Bruce could feel the hairs stand up on his neck while he bent to pick up the plastic smartsheet. The article described only a birthday party held by one of Singapore's richest and most powerful citizens, but an embedded link provided a brief biography of the woman – Doctor Wing Lee.

The girls were looking at him in a worried manner. Eve asked, "What's up, Bruce? You've gone all pale. I've heard this said before, but never actually seen someone whose blood seems to have drained from their face."

"Looks like you've seen a ghost, in fact," Engel added. "It wasn't that lad, was it? You didn't really think I was going to start a fight here?"

Silently Bruce held the sheet for the girls to read. Both looked mystified, and then Eva's face whitened.

That must be the blood-draining bit.

Engel looked from face to face with growing confusion and concern.

Finally Eva stuttered, "Y-you don't really think... I mean, what are the chances? Surely not?"

Engel's concern rapidly transformed to annoyance. "Surely not fuckin' what? Come on now, give me a break. What the fuck's the matter?"

Eva nodded at Bruce, who leaned towards the girls and whispered at a level only just audible over the background din of the busy pub. "Remember the psycho who nabbed Eva and me? We mentioned that he said that he was working directly for someone. A woman who was very rich and powerful. Who was also very old."

"Yeah, okay. But there are a lot of old, rich bags in the world. Why this one?"

"She's the head of a pharm," Eva answered. "One of

the biggest in the world. They were almost certainly involved in the debacle in May, although we could never prove anything. In lots of areas where my GRW crowd dominate the western market, the east is nailed down by Lee's Singmed."

"Fuck. I just can't believe it. We chose that flight at random."

Bruce was silent for a moment and then sighed. "Bad luck, definitely, but not as unlikely as you might think. If you decide to go east, the very biggest air hubs are Singapore, Shanghai and Tokyo – so it's not beyond simple bad luck. I knew things started far too smoothly at Bure."

"Let's not start with your superstitions about luck." Eva reasserted herself. "We may not have been identified on arrival but, given that Singmed are on their home ground, we have to assume that we've been made by now." She grimaced. "We've also departed from our original plan and ended-up in a Bruce-style dive. Profilers would pick this place up straight away."

Engel nodded and all three could not help glancing around the busy bar. The four men at the neighboring table, in particular, repeatedly looked in their direction – apparently interested in the two women.

"All right," Bruce whispered, leaning forward again, "we blow this joint and head straight for Changi airport. First flight out anywhere. If we walk over—"

"No, we can't do that," Eva interrupted. "We do it my way now. It's the only way to stay ahead of the profilers. So, if we don't fly out of Changi, what are the options? Actually, just think about that for now. We've got to get out of here asap."

Bruce noticed the newssheet still clutched in his hand. He crumpled it and dropped it onto the floor while he rose to lead the girls from the pub.

Superstition or not, our little bit of good luck has been followed by quite a run of bad. Surely it must be time to change again.

He noticed their four neighbors also rising to leave.

Maybe the good luck isn't going to start quite yet.

***

Outside the pub, Bruce hurried into the maze of narrow alleyways, pushing impolitely through groups of pedestrians who often blocked his way. After a couple minutes, Eva caught his elbow and pulled him back to follow Engel downstairs into a basement dance club. Although it was still quite early, the club was already busy, and a number of colorfully dressed youngsters were jumping around enthusiastically on the dance floor.

Bruce followed Eva to the bar where she ordered draft Tiger beer then squeezed onto stools at the end of the bar closest to the dancing. They were forced to speak loudly in order to be heard over the raucous music. Eva frowned. "We may have a breathing space here for a bit, as we seem to have lost those guys from the pub. I don't think it will last long though."

"No way," Engel agreed. "I don't think I've ever been anywhere with so many fuckin' cameras. Every junction seems to be fully covered."

"Singapore surveillance technology is supposed to be top notch," Bruce agreed, "but security is also supposed to be good. I don't suppose we can assume that helps us?"

"Nope." Eva shook her head with certainty. "I know what GRW can do in Basel, so we have to assume that Singmed can do the same here, especially if their CEO is giving the orders directly."

"So how do we get out of here?" Bruce counted options on his fingers. "The most obvious is Changi, but you've already eliminated that. The second would be a ferry. There's a wide range to choose from, but all the international ones go from the central ferry terminal, which is bound to be watched. Private air charter is certainly possible, although the airfield is linked to Changi, and they have a common emigration control database. Fourth would be boat charter. International charters are controlled centrally and are very tightly regulated to reduce smuggling. There must be smugglers around who would take us, but it would be tricky and dangerous to try to establish contacts to them. What else? Railway? Hire car? Anything else is probably too slow." He stared at the ceiling while seeking inspiration.

"Pick up by Eva's pharm?" Engel suggested. "Contact them and cry for help. They could probably mobilize a heavy team with chopper or veetol air transport."

"Maybe doable, but that would take a while to organize and offers lots of chances for com links to be compromised. Only a last resort," Eva concluded. "Um, let's see here..." She scrolled through a tourist information package which was available as a passive download onto her palmtop. "Now that's a thought." She stopped abruptly when Bruce gripped her elbow and turned her to view the men entering the basement.

Three of the men were recognizable from the Irish pub, but two huge bruisers in suits, who looked like bouncers from an up-market club, accompanied them. There was no pretense of subterfuge as they marched in a phalanx, with the heavies to the fore, directly towards Bruce's small group. This was noticed by the barman, who cast a worried look in Bruce's direction, but caused no impact on the seething dancers.

The men fanned out as they neared and one who Bruce identified as the loudest of the moneymen came forward. "Doctor Roberts, it would be best if you just came with us now. If you try anything stupid, you or one of your female friends could end up getting hurt." His very proper English accent vanished in a gurgle, as Engel whirled forward and kicked him in the groin with enough force to lift him from the ground.

Without thinking, Bruce lifted his heavy beer glass and smashed it into the face of one of the bouncers approaching from his left. He attempted to emulate Engel, but was rewarded only with a shock of pain as his foot came in contact with some form of armored underwear. Although he didn't drop, the kick did cause the big man to grunt with pain. Thus encouraged, Bruce played on his advantage and stepped forward, punching upwards with all the force he could muster, the heel of his hand contacting his opponents chin.

The man's head snapped back and he dropped like a log, his head smacking the edge of a table as he fell.

He's not going anywhere soon.

Bruce spun round to check on the others.

The other big man was lying on his back with Engel kneeling on his throat. Blood poured from a smashed nose, and one arm lay at a very unnatural angle. Another man was actually spinning backwards in midair, obviously in response to a kick delivered by Eva. The last man stood directly behind the tall blonde and struggled to pull a huge gun from a shoulder holster.

With a scream of anguish, Bruce threw himself towards the gunman, already convinced that he would be too late. The scream did seem to have an effect; as the gun was pulled free, it swiveled around to face him. A flare erupted, simultaneous with a deafening explosion.

A*t least it isn't Eva getting shot again this time.*

He blacked out.

***

Bruce realized that he could only have been unconscious for seconds when he came to, seeing Eva crouched by his side, pressing a dermal patch against his neck. The look of worry vanished from Engel's face as he turned towards her. He became aware then of the background din of screams, breaking glass and splintering furniture, requiring Engel to shout, "Come on you total ponce, get your arse in motion. The bullet missed by a mile and you only bumped your skull when you hit the deck. Can't possibly have harmed anything that fuckin' thick."

Eva pulled him to his feet and he could now see the backs of the throng who were fighting to escape from the affray up the narrow steps. He tried to ignore the piercing pain from the left side of his scalp and peered at the gunman, who was lying at his feet. Bruce was baffled for an instant, until he noted the thin shaft protruding from the man's eye. There was remarkably little blood, but clearly this was what had killed him.

Engel was now taking charge of things, putting an arm around the taller woman and shouting to Bruce. "Back door. There's got to be one."

Bruce vaulted over the bar, almost landing on the barman who was huddled on the floor. He had obviously been listening to what was going on, because he pointed towards a dimly lit storeroom as soon as Bruce looked in his direction.

In the back of the storeroom, Bruce found a ladder leading up to a hatch secured by a couple of massive bolts. These slid easily aside and the hatch dropped open with a loud clang. Bruce quickly climbed through and found himself in a dark and dingy dead-end alley, which evidently served for deliveries to the establishments that backed onto it on both sides.

Bruce helped the girls climb up to join him and then started to head cautiously for the lighted end of the alley when Eva stopped him. "Where are you going?"

"Out of here pdq. In a couple minutes, both the cops and the Singmed folk will be buzzing around here like flies round shite. They might expect us to head towards the airport or the hotel, so we'll set off in the direction of the commercial center..." He was about to say more, but it dawned on him that any move he might suggest to elude their pursuers was likely to be already identified by the profilers.

"We can't do any of those things..." Eva pondered, "...so that means we just have to stay here. We need to lie low for twelve hours or so anyway. You two wait here for a minute. Don't move. I'll be back in a tick." She strode quickly past him, out of the alley and around the corner, heading away from the increasing noise of the customers who had emerged from the club and were evidently milling around in the street.

To try to take his mind off worrying about what Eva might be doing, Bruce turned to Engel. "That was a crossbow bolt in that guy's eye, wasn't it? How on earth have you been able to carry a crossbow around with you?"

Engel mover closer to him and took his arm in her hand. "Don't be a daft tosser, Beast. There's no way I could be carrying that wee toy with me, very nice though it is."

"But I saw the bolt."

"Indeed you did, you observant old Beast you," she mocked him. "But the fact of the bolt does not prove the presence of the crossbow, as that Meiringen druggie guy would say," she finished smugly.

"Okay, smart arse, what does the fact of the bolt prove?"

"It proves that, although I had to leave the crossbow in my shipping luggage, which is probably still in your house in Switzerland, I was sensible enough to take a couple of the bolts with me as a kind of wee souvenir." She looked momentarily uncomfortable with this admission. "Anyway, I've practiced throwing them just like darts. The ceramic points and the D U body make a lethal combination...literally as you've just seen. Pure dead brilliant. Just a shame I didn't have a chance to dig that one out, so I've only got one left now."

"Love, I'll buy you a bloody quiver-full if we ever get out of this." Bruce pulled her to him and gave her a squeeze. They stood together silently while police sirens approached and their concern for Eva grew.

***

Bruce had almost decided that, regardless of Eva's instructions, he was going to go looking for her. However, a door near the blind end of the alley opened with a squeal of rusty hinges, and a shaft of bright light cut the gloom like a knife. Bruce had automatically pulled Engel into the shadows of a doorway, but quickly emerged in response to a call from Eva. "Come on, you two. Stop cuddling in the dark. Get in here."

They hurried into a brightly lit corridor. The door slammed behind them and Bruce detected the snick of electric latches closing. Eva waved them forward, around a bend, up a steep staircase and towards a heavy door, which was clad in red leather secured by heavy brass studs. Eva rapped on the door and it opened silently inwards to a waiting room containing a half dozen large armchairs upholstered in the same red leather. Four other heavy doors led from the room. An unattended bar was its only other feature. The walls were adorned with faded Chinese-pattern wallpaper, and the floor was covered in a thick red carpet, which was rather threadbare in places.

Bruce glanced at Engel, who had obviously also recognized the setting, before turning to Eva. "I can guess where we are, but what are we doing here?"

Eva smiled wanly. "It's all I could think of in the spur of the moment. This place caught my eye when we were running towards that last place. *Happy Joy Massage Parlor.*"

"I would guess with a name like that they service mainly Japanese and Chinese salarymen," Bruce responded. "Anyway, how did you get us in the back way?"

"I talked to the boss lady and said I was an escort with a very rich, famous and kinky client. I implied that you're some kind of American politician from the Bible Belt who doesn't want to be seen in this area but also doesn't want girls seen around his hotel room. I've paid triple rates in advance for her two naughtiest girls, for the entire night in their best and kinkiest room. There was no problem arranging to sneak you and your other escort in."

Bruce was speechless, while he exchanged amazed looks with Engel. Finally he found his voice. "With all the bad luck we've been having, I wondered when it would finally turn. Just about getting shot in the head was a pretty crap ending to the evening, but all of a sudden things are looking up. The two of you and the house's two best girls? Yodel-odel-ey-ee-oo."

Eva cleared her throat. "Um, the girls are finishing with other clients at the present and should be here in ten minutes or so. I just need to clarify things." She looked uncomfortable. "I mean you had just been knocked out. I rushed in here and just... Anyway..."

"Come on, out with it girl. What's up?"

"Well, you see, the boss lady wanted to know your exotic kink. I just reacted." Eva took a deep breath. "I told her you were into watching Caucasian and Asian woman making love... Well, actually, not so much making love as being very obscene with each other. It was all I could think of at the time. The girls are the wildest lesbians she's got."

"Yodel-odel-ey-ee-oo," Engel cheered. "Happy days are here again." She pranced in front of Bruce, swaying her tight bottom, which received a slap as she passed Eva.

"We're not actually going to do anything with the girls though. I mean, they're prostitutes."

Engel looked mystified. "And? Just means that they're professionals in the shagging business rather than amateurs. Yodel-odel-ey-ee-oo."

"Maria, don't tell me you've paid to have sex with a whore."

"Not with a girl," she conceded. "It was always easy enough to get that without paying. I did six months military service, though, and it's a really bad idea to fuck your fellow squaddies. The men, anyway. I had a couple really good pals and we'd have a girls' night out together. Hire ourselves a nice, clean, well-built lad and shag his brains out. Much, much easier, safer and more fun than going to the fuss of picking up somebody."

"We were based in Wales, you see," Engel added as clarification.

Eva stared at her, speechless, then: "You are a dirty wee bitch. I cannot believe you paid a man to have sex with you." Eva turned on Bruce, who had been happy to be out of this conversation. "Bruce? You haven't, have you?"

"I travel a lot," he confessed sheepishly. "I also don't do the kind of work that involves meeting a lot of women. This gig is so exceptional that it is bizarre – in an incredibly good way." Bruce felt that he was beginning to ramble due to embarrassment, when Engel saved him.

"I really don't see what the big deal is anyway. I mean it's just a job. There are some nasty things going on in the weird sex business that I wouldn't want to think about, but usually it's just a man – or a woman – doing a job. I can think of a lot worse jobs. "Can you imagine spending your whole day in a sewage works? Fuck that!" I'd rather be paid to shag any day of the week."

Bruce felt obliged to support the petite woman. "Taken together with porn, it's one of the biggest industries in the world economy. As Engel says, there's a nasty end to it, but that's the same with every big industry.

We've recently seen what Big Pharm can get up to. Ninety-nine percent of the legal sex trade is just harmless fun. The market supplying a demand."

Eva slumped into one of the chairs. "It looks like I've been leading a sheltered life. I must say that I've just never thought about prostitutes before."

Engel sat on the arm of the chair and leaned to put her arm round the taller woman's shoulders. "Don't you worry, my dear." she winked at Bruce. "You don't need to bother about anything. I'll make the sacrifice and shag them both." The laughing girl leapt to her feet to avoid a slap to the thigh.

***

As the banter between Engel and Eva continued, Bruce was relieved to see that it had managed to divert the girls from consideration of their plight.

We've wandered blindly into the lion's den and getting out intact is going to be very tricky.

It was almost a half hour before one of the doors opened and a svelte, middle-aged Malay woman appeared with a small Chinese girl in each hand. "This is Mee-ling and this is Tina." She smiled at Bruce, but turned to address Eva, continuing in flawless English. "Have a wonderful time and buzz me if there is anything that I can do to increase your pleasure. Now the girls will take you to your room." She backed out of the door with a bow and vanished.

Bruce watched the girls as they approached. They

were both wearing extremely short white Baby Dolls and matching frilly knickers. Mee-ling's hair was in a pigtail, which fell almost to her waist, while Tina's hair was paged. It was hard to estimate their ages: could have been anywhere between twelve and thirty. Given their air of confidence, though, probably at the upper end of the range.

"Follow me." Mee-ling put her arm around Engel's waist and led the way through the door opposite the one they had entered. Tina followed, holding Eva's hand. A bemused Bruce followed at the rear. Both the Chinese girls were roughly the same height as Engel, with similar slight builds. Mee-ling, however, had rather large breasts, which appeared somewhat incongruous on her small frame.

As the women turned into a room on the left, at the end of a long corridor, Bruce appraised them.

Eva's classically beautiful, maybe better suited to her natural blonde hair but still stunning as a brunette. I wouldn't call Engel beautiful in the same way, but definitely pretty. By comparison, the Chinese girls are rather plain. Nevertheless, both are attractive at some kind of basic level. Cute, that'd be the name for it.

Bruce raised his eyebrows when he entered the room then closed the heavy door behind him. A huge circular bed covered by purple satin sheets dominated the room. To the side, steps led up to a hot tub, behind which a holo projection simulated a window into a similar room. There appeared to be six well-oiled girls rolling around on the bed seen through this window.

Beside the tub was an open niche containing a shower, toilet, bidet and wash-hand basin. On the opposite side of the bed, a wooden frame like a Saint Andrew's cross stood against the wall, draped with a complex array of ropes, chains and pulleys.

Christ, you'd need a fucking degree in mechanical engineering to operate that contraption!

To the side of this device sat what looked like a gynecological examination chair, in front of which stood a table displaying a range of dildoes, vibrators and similar equipment, some of which he could only guess the way it was used.

What an incredibly well equipped massage parlor, absolutely everything except a massage table.

Engel beamed as she inspected the furnishing. "Yodel-odel-ey-ee-oo, indeed, Beast. If you don't have fun here, it's not for lack of kit." She lifted a long, flexible, double ended dildo of huge girth and waved it at Eva. "Catch a swatch of this beauty. Christ, it brings tears to my eyes just thinking about what we could do with this."

Eva looked distinctly uncomfortable and her unease increased when Tina reached up to start unbuttoning her blouse. Before she could protest, Engel came to her side and stood on tiptoes to kiss her cheek. "Relax, for Christ's sake. It's not going to be an ordeal. It'll be fun. Look, the girls are well into this. It's got to be much better than getting rogered by big, hairy beasts." She grinned at Bruce. "Honest, satisfaction guaranteed or your money back." Another smirk in his direction and she turned to draw the nightdress over the head of the well-endowed Mee-ling.

As the night progressed, Bruce's original annoyance at Eva's arrangements evaporated, discovering pleasures of voyeurism beyond his wildest imaginings. Eva's original reluctance also vanished quickly in response to Tina's expert ministrations.

After an initial oral exploration of each other led to a set of very noisy orgasms, which also appeared genuine in the cases of the Chinese girls, the women huddled together in a giggling heap on the bed. With a rush, they converged on where Bruce sat on the steps of the hot tub and pulled him to the floor, undressing and tickling him at the same time. It only took seconds before he achieved his own release; a well-lubricated Engel sitting on his face while someone, he guessed one of the Chinese girls, carried out some very skillful handwork.

The girls then scampered back to the bed, leaving Bruce panting on the floor. As they started writhing about again, Bruce noticed the time: not yet nine o'clock. "Christ," he mumbled, "we've still got eleven hours to go. I reckon I've got more chance pegging out tonight from a heart attack than as a consequence of anything else on this jaunt so far."

Please let that be true. It looks like paradise here, but outside it's hell and I've not a clue how we're going to get out of this jam.

12 ...like a virgin

Bruce was awakened by his palmtop alarm and he rolled off the bed in search of it – finding it still clipped to the belt of his trousers, which were hanging from one of the arms of the bondage frame.

I wonder how they got there.

He cast his eyes over the naked bodies sprawled on the other side of the gigantic bed. Engel was awake, following him with her eyes while she lay with her cheek against the buttocks of one of the Chinese girls. The other Chinese – Mee-ling it seemed to be – slept head to toe beside Eva.

More accurately nose to pubes.

He tried to recollect if Eva's blond bush had caused any comment, but such details were lost in the myriad of sensations experienced over the last twelve hours.

He tried to remember what time he had finally fallen asleep. He had strained to stay awake as long as possible, reluctant to miss an instant of this unique experience.

I must have dosed off about two – so around six hours ago.

The four women had still been going at it hammer and tongs, he remembered with admiration of their stamina.

While he collected his clothing, a pat on his bottom informed Bruce that Engel had arisen. "I'll just utilize the facilities while you wake the sleeping beauty. Remember how she didn't want to have sex with prostitutes? Fuck me, she's fucking insatiable! At least I know now what to get the girl who has everything for her birthday."

Bruce watched the androgynous form pad towards the exposed toilet and then, with a shiver, turned to the bed and gently rubbed Eva's shoulder. The woman woke with a start, involuntarily burying her nose in the crutch of the gently snoring Mee-ling. Turning onto her back, she gazed into his eyes and stretched, unashamedly showing off her large breasts to best advantage.

"What a beautiful morning," she exclaimed.

"I don't know about that. I'll bet you ten to one that it's pissing down with rain at present."

"Well it looks pretty good from my viewpoint." She turned her head to view Mee-ling's silky black pubic hair and Tina's tight bum. "In fact, I think I can remember just where we left off." Her pink tongue followed the cleft between the sleeping girl's buttocks.

Bruce seized a shapely foot and pulled the grinning girl to the edge of the bed. "Enough, for Christ's sake. I can't believe that even you can still be in the mood for bonking. Go and find your clothes. And remember, you've still got to tell us your brilliant plan for getting us out of here."

"Ah, the plan. Just a minute." She found her shorts on the floor and extracted a slim wallet from the back pocket.

Extracting a couple of patches, she stripped off the backings and pressed one gently against the buttocks of each sleeping girl, following each administration with a kiss to the anatomy involved.

"Okay, that'll just ensure they sleep soundly for the next couple hours. They probably would have slept in any case, because they must be pretty tired." Her face took on a distinctly dreamy look.

A sharp crack and she yelped and swiped at the retreating Engel.

"Just testing that they are sound asleep, honestly." She caught a head-height kick and forced Eva to hop to keep her balance. "Yes, I must admit that I've also got a fine view this morning, but the Beast is right. We should get moving as soon as you tell us where we're going."

When released, Eva returned to searching for clothes while she explained. "I was looking through the tourist stuff, when I saw tours on offer in a vintage seaplane. It's also available for charter, apparently. It's based at the maritime museum, which isn't far from the hotel we were staying, just at the mouth of the river."

Bruce stood silently, trying to think of a better alternative to Eva's plan. After a couple minutes, he admitted defeat. "Can't think of any reason why that shouldn't work. Engel?"

"I think it's bloody brilliant. She's not just a blonde lesbo sex-machine, you know, even if she often acts like it." She dodged a thrown sandal.

"The only difficulty will be getting there, avoiding all

these bloody cameras."

"I think we can manage that, Bruce. I'll get the Mama-san to organize a limo pick up at about ten to nine. If we go directly to the seaplane office, we'll be there just after it opens. Like the museum, they're open every day of the year, but I can't imagine them being too busy early on the second of January."

"That should work," he conceded. "Let's get dressed and see if we can scrounge up some coffee somewhere."

"Good idea," Engel agreed. "Also, see if we can find some nosh. I could eat a horse."

"How about a couple beavers instead," Eva suggested, raising an eyebrow in the direction of the bed.

"Jesus." Bruce sighed. "You're getting as bad as Engel. You used to be the shy, polite one. Kicking around with her is having a bad influence on you."

"Don't worry your sweet little head about a thing," Engel said in her artificially gracious voice. "We're going be as polite as anything, aren't we?"

"Yes indeed, darling," the Milngavie accent answered. "We will be polite as anything, so we will. No more mention of naughty things, like vaginas."

"Certainly not...nor those horribly vibrating things which are shaped like a gentleman's naughty bit."

"No, no, it would be very impolite to talk about those...or what they feel like in your vagina."

"Or in your bottom, for that matter."

Bruce groaned.

It's going to be a long wait for our transportation.

***

At quarter past nine, the trio arrived at the *Vintage Flight Experience* office in their automatic limousine, windows set to one-way. Two Malay girls in navy blue uniforms, which seemed copied from the ancient poster for BOAC on display behind them, were drinking coffee and looked up expectantly as the party entered the small office situated in the museum entry hall.

Eva took charge as the options available were presented. The emphasis was on short half-hour trips, which played up the excitement of taking off and landing on water in an eighty year old aircraft. *Given Singapore's almost continual rain, opportunities for sightseeing will be rather limited, though.*

More exotic options involved trips to some resort areas in Malaysia and Indonesia that had been leased by Singapore and now were very popular destinations for those wanting to escape from the city-state to somewhere with fewer people – and much less rain.

One of the special trips on offer was to Kuantan, a resort on the east coast of Malaysia, just over three hundred kilometers north of their present position. A package provided champagne flights both ways, two nights' accommodation in a Shangri La luxury hotel and entrance to the World Jazz Dance Championships, which was being held there at present.

Eva immediately selected this option. "I knew there was something else in the back of my mind when I saw the bumf on these charter flights. I'm sure now that Claudia De Marco mentioned Kuantan, but it's only now clicking into place."

The receptionist explained that this trip would only be confirmed if all eight seats on the plane could be filled. So far only two seats were booked, but with their party this now made five. She was fairly sure that the remaining places would be taken within the next few hours and asked for their hotel details.

Eva made it clear that this was not what they were looking for and requested rates for payment of the remaining three places and the earliest possible time for departure. One of the Malay girls contacted her boss, apparently the pilot, who was one of the owners of the company, while the other tried to contact the couple that had already reserved seats on the flight. Within ten minutes, details had been sorted out and Eva transferred credit to pay for three jazz dance packages and three additional single flights. Take off was set for ten thirty and Eva's party was offered free tickets for the museum.

With an hour to kill, Bruce was keen to have a look around the museum, but Eva vetoed this. "Too many cameras," she insisted. "I'm fairly sure that no profiler would ever predict us hanging around a museum in our present circumstances, but we're just too recognizable for some pattern-scanning demon with access to security cameras. The chance would be small, but it's just not worth it. Have a coffee instead."

Bruce had to concede Eva's point. "True enough. We

certainly don't want to risk leading anyone here, as this flying boat idea is a cracker. It seems better and better, the more I think about it. Kuantan has been effectively ceded to Singapore, so this is classified as internal transport and has no identity check requirement. Of course, once we're there, we still have to get out of the country. I have this sneaking suspicion, however, that you already have an idea about that."

"I do now. Look at this." Eva handed over a smartsheet brochure on activities on offer in Kuantan.

Bruce took the sheet and, with a quizzical look, activated the indicated link labelled *shopping*. While he scanned down the list, Eva pointed to the strangely titled *Black-run heli-shopping* and the penny dropped, confirmed when he opened this further link. "Day trips for duty-free shopping in Kuala Lumpur. Absolutely perfect. Now don't tell me that you have just now come over this by accident. My multi-D project planning kit would struggle to find such an obscure link."

Eva shrugged her shoulders and grinned at Engel. "I've always been the intuitive type. You've said before, Bruce, that the main problem today is information overload. Too much data is available, so you need special experience and tools to be able to make use of it. You're very good on technical problems that can be solved in a logical manner. I seem to be able to do something similar for less well-defined problems. Unfortunately, for me, the analysis seems to be carried out at a subconscious level, so answers emerge without the approach to derive the solution being obvious. Believe it or not, I used to have lots of problems at school because of this."

"I don't care how you do it, as long as you keep on coming up with the goods like this."

***

While they awaited the arrival of the other two passengers, the extremophile team speculated on what they might be like. Bruce was beginning to wish that they had simply chartered the entire plane, as he had initially suggested. Eva had, nevertheless, been insistent that they should minimize actions attracting more attention to themselves: the payment for the three vacant seats was already sufficiently unusual to be a talking point for the receptionists.

"It could be the De Marcos," Bruce suggested idly and was met by a barrage of derision.

"Don't be daft, Beast. They're competing this evening," Engel threw in. "There's no way they'd be hanging around on spec for a trip like this."

"And they must be clear favorites. They travel with an entourage." Eva shook her head decisively.

Bruce attempted to defend himself. "But they were alone flying out here."

"Alone in first-class, sure. You don't think their road crew, press, etcetera travel in first class, do you? Some might be in business, but I would guess most would be back in toilet class with the rest of the plebs."

"Anyway," Engel concluded, "now that you bring it

up, I'm fairly sure I remember Claudia say something about flying on directly somewhere. It must be this Kuan-whatsit place."

"Okay, okay, I concede. Silly idea. It would have been too much of a coincidence anyway. The chances must be..." Bruce ground to a halt and the girls burst into laughter as their fellow-passengers entered the small office: the Scandinavian woman and her jailbait daughter from their New Year flight.

The girl gave a distinctly childish squeal of delight when she spotted them while her dour mother looked even grimmer than the night before. She was, however, pleasant enough as she greeted them. "Hello again. Small world, isn't it? I guess you're also going for this dance thing. Ulla has been driving me crazy since we arrived. I only booked this just to keep her quiet. I didn't think they would actually fill all the seats."

"Mother, that's a terrible thing to say. She doesn't really mean it. I wonder who else is on our flight," a clearly excited Ulla babbled.

I'm not sure mum is going to be happy when she finds that we're fully responsible for the trip taking place.

Luckily, by the time everyone had said their helloes, one of the receptionists came to lead them to the plane.

A covered walkway led along a pier, at the end of which the flying boat was moored. A gangplank extended from the end of the pier to a doorway in the side of the plane, just in front of the left wing. The few steps from the cover on the jetty to the aircraft were enough for them to receive a good sprinkling of rain, which was falling steadily from a leaden sky.

The Malay girl offered them free choice of the seats, which were on either side of a narrow gangway. The Swedish girl selected the front seat on the right while her mother sat opposite. Bruce sat behind the mother, although the view from his window was somewhat obscured by the wing and floats. Engel sat behind him, with Eva opposite.

They settled into old fashioned but surprisingly comfortable leather seats, and the receptionist, who apparently also served as air hostess, arrived with a tray of glasses filled with champagne and orange juice. Ulla was offered a drink first and helped herself to champagne, causing an immediate squabble with her mother. A compromise was quickly reached, when the Swedish woman agreed, with a long-suffering sigh, to take the champagne glass after some had been added to her daughter's orange juice.

Bruce eventually received his champagne, and the girls were organizing their own *Morning Glory* mixtures when the pilot emerged from the cockpit. Bruce was amused to see that the chubby red-faced man with the handlebar moustache looked like a caricature of a vintage pilot or an escapee from a film about the Battle of Britain.

He really should be called something like Biggleswort h or Smythe-Boddington to fit this image.

Bruce was even more amused, although a little disappointed, when he introduced himself in perfect

Oxford English as Captain Carlo Chung.

Obviously a fanatic, Captain Chung welcomed them aboard and gave them a potted history of their aircraft. Bruce was greatly surprised to find out that it was a Swiss-built plane, being unaware that there had ever been an aero industry in his adopted country. Originally, this *Pilatus Porter* had been configured with skis for high altitude transportation in Nepal, but had been completely rebuilt as a seaplane by an eccentric millionaire who owned an island in the Andaman Sea. When he went bust in the crash of the mid-thirties, the state of Singapore had received the airplane from his estate and it had been then purchased by a group of collectors who completely rebuilt it and supported the establishment of the charter company.

After he finished his spiel and disappeared back into the cockpit, Engel leaned forward to whisper in Bruce's ear. "Sounds right fuckin' dodgy to me. This fuckin' thing's twice as old as you...and look at the shape you're in. Not only ancient, but put together by a bunch of amateurs. Fuck me! Even the driver looks like he's having his day out from the loony bin. I think a boat would be a fucking much better idea."

"A bit late now." Bruce turned to grin at the girls. "We're casting off now." Their hostess threw a tether to the other receptionist, who was now waving cheerily from the end of the pier.

"I just hope we've got fucking parachutes, that's all."

"Parachutes?" He laughed. "You're not likely to need them. When these babies crash, it's almost always during takeoff or landing. The biggest risk is hitting a floating log or something similar. If they hold together at all, the tricky thing is getting out of the sinking plane. If you want to improve your chances, an aqualung might be the thing to have."

Eva picked up on the joke, having to shout as the engine noise rose to a deafening roar, which caused the entire plane to vibrate and start a cacophony of secondary rattling and buzzing throughout the cabin. "Don't worry, Maria. Look at this thing. What is the chance of it staying intact in a crash? More likely it'll just fall apart while taxiing." As if to confirm her point, the plane started to judder as it turned into the wind and accelerated, floats banging as they bounced over the choppy water.

Engel was white faced as she pushed back into her seat and closed her eyes. Bruce and Eva grinned at each other as the rapidity of the banging noise increased and, after a surprisingly short time, died away when the flying boat eased into the air and offered an instant panorama of the harbor area before climbing into a low-lying cloud.

The flight to Kuantan took almost one and a half hours, a fact that served only to increase Engel's concern. "Are you sure that's fast enough?" she enquired. "I've driven cars much faster than that. Trains are, what, two, three times quicker. Won't it just stall or something?"

Bruce assured her that this old plane would fly happily at speeds you could just about get up to on a racing bicycle and was able to divert her attention with the view from the windows when the clouds finally cleared about halfway through their flight.

They followed along the eastern coast of Malaysia, which was obviously suffering from the effects of increasing sea levels, made even worse by the consequences of surges from frequent tropical storms. The only exceptions to the picture of drowned and deserted roads, towns and industrial complexes were the occasional Singaporean enclaves: gleaming concrete and glass monolithic hotels surrounded by golf courses, swimming pools and artificial beaches, all enclosed within massive protective sea walls and levees. Most included small airfields and all had large ferry terminals and marinas clearly visible from their cruising altitude of just above two thousand meters.

When they started their approach into Kuantan, he noticed this resort was somewhat bigger than those passed previously. It extended about three kilometers or so along the coast and around half a kilometer inland. The massive protective walls around the complex had, however, resulted in extensive erosion around them so that the resort was effectively a peninsula at high tide, connected to the mainland of Malaysia only by a narrow isthmus.

Geography reflecting political reality.

To Engel's evident relief, the landing was feather-smooth on the mirror-flat surface of the enclosed lagoon. They taxied to a pier on which a girl in uniform was waving. When they approached close enough to make out details, she appeared to Bruce to be a clone of the receptionist left behind in Singapore, but she wore dark sunglasses to combat the glare of the tropical sun.

Their hostess coordinated mooring with the girl on the jetty and the sound of the engines died away. The pilot appeared again and shook hands when they left and stepped into the blast of heat on the gangway.

At the end of the pier, two golf carts waited. Bruce's group was led to one, where the hostess repeated to the driver Eva's original story, that luggage for this party had been sent separately. They waved at the Scandinavians, who were waiting at the other cart for their luggage to be offloaded, and then drove off to their hotel.

The Shangri La was located near the northern-most end of the resort and was shaped like some kind of Aztec ziggurat.

At least the kind of thing that some architect, blown out of his head with hallucinogens, might consider Aztec glass and ceramic pyramids to look like.

The golf cart drove into the basement level of the hotel and directly into a goods elevator that whisked them up to the thirteenth floor, which appeared to be the uppermost level of normal rooms. The fourteenth contained executive suites while the entire fifteenth comprised the presidential suite and the sixteenth was the *Sunset Bar.*

The golf cart proceeded along a service corridor and then a radial aisle to deliver them to the doors of connecting double rooms. The driver, who had been chatting away continuously for the entire trip, simply programmed the doors for them and left, evidently pleased with Eva's generous tip.

The group entered the left-hand door and strolled through the large, airy room with its king-size bed and onto the balcony. This extended for the full length of the room, separated only by a glass wall. They were looking southwards, over the length of the resort and its array of hotels. There had clearly been no attempt to impose any kind of common style, and imaginative design seemed to have aimed only to ensure that no hotel had any architectural feature in common with the others.

A classic example of the Las Vegas approach to resort design.

The girls elected to annex this room, so Bruce peered through the connecting door into an identical room with an identical view. "Here we are again with no luggage. This constant shopping is getting a bit tedious."

"What do you mean tedious?" Engel frowned. "I don't recollect you actually doing any yet. Eva and I have been doing it all while you sit around on your fat arse."

"Not a problem, anyway," Eva interjected. "As I'm going to choose all your clothes for you."

Bruce's loud groan instantly caused Engel's face to brighten.

"But we can do that afterwards. First some lunch, although my body doesn't seem quite sure if it should be breakfast or dinner. I must say that I'm seriously thinking about changing my mind and trying one of those body-clock resetting pills."

"Let's go to the bar on the roof," Engel suggested,

leading the way to the door.

After walking along the plushly carpeted corridor, they reached the exterior *inclinators* that ran at an angle up the edges of the building. While they travelled up the southeast rim of the hotel, they had an additional view of the beach and an enclosed area of flat blue-green water within the protection of the sea defenses. On the other side of the wall, choppy sea extended to the horizon, dotted here and there with small boats and, in the distance, the hazy outlines of blocky bulk carriers and fast-moving ferries.

The elevator brought them out at one corner of the wide terrace surrounding the square bar. The outer perimeter was completely open where patrons wearing swimsuits populated tables. Extremely skimpy in some cases:

I guess mores are a bit more relaxed in these resorts as compared to the rest of Singapore.

The blast of heat was already causing Bruce to sweat, very aware that his denims were completely inappropriate for Kuantan temperatures, which must be in the high thirties.

Even the girls wilted under the tropical sun, so the party hurried into the inner zone that was protected by a sun shield and an air wall that maintained air-conditioned coolness. The transition, associated with a drop of about fifteen degrees when they passed through the wall, caused them to gasp.

The group found a free table at the relatively

unpopular west side of the busy bar. The instant they seated themselves, a holo menu appeared in the center of the table, diverting their attention from the landward view from the hotel. They had hardly completed their lunch order, two types of Dim Sum and mixed sate, when a small barman in a neat brown uniform appeared to pour Tiger beer into frosted glasses. They had time to clink glasses and have a first sip of beer when a waitress in a similar uniform appeared with their food.

"I'd certainly give ten out of ten for efficiency," Bruce stated as he activated an anti-sound privacy screen. "The facilities are definitely state of the art, with gratuitous use of staff, just to add that special feeling of luxury. Not that staff would be expensive here. I'm sure they all come from over there." He pointed to the shantytowns in the distance.

Over a drawn-out lunch, plans were made for the rest of the day. First of all, shopping for clothes and some pieces of hand luggage: the girls agreed to handle this. Thereafter, there was some extensive debate over Bruce's suggestion of a swim, Engel's desire for a workout in the gym, and Eva's preference for a massage. Considering that the dance competition did not start until eight thirty, Eva back-calculated that they would be able to fit it all in, and hence, it was agreed that the girls would also pick up some swimwear and training kit.

Bruce headed off to the girls' room after lunch, to await their return from a shopping expedition to the mall in the ground floor of the hotel. He stripped off and lay on a padded sun lounger, sweating in the intense heat. He closed his eyes for a little snooze, mulling over Eva's proposal for the trip back to the Caribbean.

Three flights away from Nassau, could it really be that easy. From Kuala Lumpur, it would be about twelve hours travel. And about twelve hours time difference. Now does that mean we arrive exactly the same time that we left?

He was wondering how that worked for the two different options of flying east or west when he drifted off to sleep.

***

Bruce was shaken awake by Engel who posed in front of him, one hand in the air and the other on her hip. "What do you think of it?"

"Your body? Okay, I suppose, if you're into emaciated boys. I definitely prefer Angela..." He rolled to the side, almost managing to avoid a kick that just scraped one buttock cheek. "...or Eva, for that matter."

"Stop waffling, Beast. I'm not asking about my beautiful body, which we all know is devastatingly attractive to all men and quite a few women, I hasten to add. Not my gorgeous bod: my swimsuit."

Bruce screwed up his eyes. "By God, you actually are wearing something. I thought it was just a trick of the light."

Engel resumed her pose. "The mall had a *Wicked Weasel* shop. Well named, ain't it? Truly wicked."

Bruce had to concede the point. The postage stamp of translucent material left absolutely nothing to the imagination. From a distance of less than two meters, Bruce could not even see the strings that held it in place. As he sat up and pulled the prancing girl forward for a closer look, he was sure he could make out the profile of her intimate body jewelry.

"Ah, wait a minute..." Realization dawned. "Your nipple ring's gone." Bruce was very aware of mixed emotions, not knowing whether he was predominantly relieved or disappointed.

"Eva thought it might attract a bit of unwanted attention here. If you weren't half blind, you might also have noticed the hair dye's gone."

"Right enough, you are indeed a redhead again. I can't help that I never find hair noticeable; above the waist, anyway."

"You'd be able to see better if you just wanked less. Anyway, come on and see Eva's suit." She pulled him to his feet and dragged him into the bedroom.

Eva emerged from the bathroom, now a blonde again. She spotted the others. "That's a great shower. You can select sunscreen strength and get a spray before the blow dry. Very sensible."

"Now you can't fool me here. No way is she wearing a swim suit." He looked in admiration at Eva's trimmed pubes.

"Of course she isn't, dick head." Engel rolled her eyes in the direction of a bemused Eva. "Blondie, get into your swimming kit."

Within seconds, Eva was wearing a matching tanga,

which was accompanied by a similarly microscopic bikini top. In response to Bruce's raised eyebrow she explained, "I wanted to keep the nipple ring in, so I thought I ought to get a top."

Moot point. Bruce noted that he could quite clearly make out the profile of the ring through the diaphanous material.

"I suppose you also picked up something for me. What've you got this time?" he asked with a feeling of foreboding.

Engel pointed towards the bed, which was heaped with shopping bags. "Top bag there...yep, the blue one."

Bruce lifted a suspiciously large bag and drew out a huge pair of baggy swimming shorts; black with a pattern of pink elephants. He held them against his waist. "Jesus, girls. How the hell can anyone actually swim in these? How fat do you think I am, anyway? You'd get two of me into these. In fact, my gut would fit into each leg."

As his complaints were only increasing the girls' amusement, Bruce gave up and allowed himself to be issued with an equally baggy t-shirt covered with crude drawings of female breasts which were compared to different fruits. "I can't wear this." He groaned.

"It's dead brilliant," Engel countered, pointing. "As you can see, I would be peaches and Blondie here would be watermelons. Giant watermelons."

Eva threw a t-shirt at the small redhead. "Peaches? No Chance. Cherries would be a possibility, but only because they don't have redcurrants. Now I would be the peaches, or maybe cantaloupes."

Bruce found sandals in the same bag as the shorts. "All right, let's get kitted up. You two might just be acceptable on the beach in those rig-outs, but you'll need something for going down in the lift. I think there should be beach robes in the bathroom."

He gathered up his new clothes and those still lying around on the balcony and retreated to the neighboring room, noting that the girls' banter veered off in his direction.

"I guess maybe a Banana?"

"Wrong shape. Maybe a German sausage?"

"That's not a fruit. Anyway, if it was a sausage, it'd be something smaller...one of those weenie things."

"You mean a wiener. Could be. But if it was a fruit—"

Bruce demonstratively slammed to door as he left the room.

***

On the beach, the women peeled off their flimsy wraps – the beach robe idea hadn't gone down well – while Bruce looked around with baited breath. No particular reaction. The girls were certainly at the extreme end of the distribution, but there were many women of all shapes and sizes sunbathing topless or wearing very small tangas. In fact, as he gazed appreciatively over the sea of flesh – white, yellow, brown, black and a myriad of shades in between – he couldn't help but notice that women predominantly populated the beach.

The female to male ratio must be two to one, or even slightly more.

Despite the crowded beach, there were only about a dozen people in the water along the stretch of about four hundred meters in front of their hotel and, of these, most were paddling or promenading along the water's edge, rather than swimming.

While the girls' attention was elsewhere, Bruce quickly whipped off his shorts to reveal his small jock strap and made a dash for the water. "No way I'm swimming in those baggy shorts," he called over his shoulder while he stumbled into the rapidly deepening water and transformed a fall into a shallow dive.

After a couple powerful strokes, he was already deep enough to tread water then turned to look for the others. He caught a glimpse of spray and blond hair as his head was pushed under, and then he fought to hold his breath while he clawed his way to the surface.

Time for a gulp of air as a squirming body clambered onto his shoulders, and then he was dunked under again. Because he was less surprised this time, he allowed himself to sink through the crystal water to stand on the firm sandy bottom while he looked around, grateful for the foresight that had led him to select a pair of swimming contacts from the selection of goodies available in his hotel room. A meter or so above his head, he could clearly see the girls circling on the surface.

If not for the fact I'm getting seriously short of breath, my first wish would be for a camera. Now it's my second wish, after an aqualung.

Bruce sank farther into a crouch and then straightened his knees explosively, shooting his body out of the water like a rocket and landing on top of a surprised Engel, who was pushed under, now wriggling and beating on him. Eva carved towards him like a shark, but he managed to push Engel into her path before stroking rapidly towards shore. He stood when the water reached chest depth and twirled to defend himself.

A smiling Eva and a distinctly unamused Engel were treading water, aware of his present tactical advantage. "So what's all this about?" he asked petulantly. "You almost drowned me there."

"Don't be a baby, Bruce," Eva answered. "It was just to teach you a lesson. We've agreed that I make the decisions on clothing, so you stick to them."

"Oh, come on. We're just having a swim. There's no way this increases the chance of a profiler picking us up."

"It's just the principle of the thing. Anyway, you just swallowed a mouthful of guaranteed sanitized-for-your-protection seawater. It'll just act as a reminder for you in the future."

"Don't listen to Watermelons, there. If I get a hold of you again, you'll swallow more than—"

The blonde pushed Engel's head underwater. "Sometimes that girl just opens her mouth too much." Eva laughed and took off in a racing crawl - soon pursued by a much less elegant, but obviously determined, Engel.

Bruce gave a silent prayer of thanks and set off in a

more relaxed crawl, heading in the opposite direction. The rhythmic swim was soothing as he paralleled the shore at a distance of about fifty meters from the beach. The sandy bottom was almost featureless apart from the occasional seashell.

Probably artificial, something for snorkelers to aim for.

The water was warm – in the high twenties – and he felt that he could continue swimming for hours.

A bit boring though, not like swimming in the ocean back in Bermuda. A lot cooler there, but much more to see.

After he turned to swim back the way he had come, he decided that the entire experience was just like a large swimming pool, rather than being in open water.

When he emerged from the water and looked over to where the girls were sitting on towels, he noted that they were talking to a couple of women. After rapid blinking reset the contacts for air and his vision cleared completely, he recognized the Swedish woman and her daughter.

The mother, who was clad in a bikini that was, by the standards of the beach, rather modest, exchanged pleasantries with the girls. It appeared that many of the jazz dance packages were based in the Shangri La, which explained the large number of women in the hotel.

Ulla was wearing a much skimpier swimsuit, but was clearly not happy about it. She started to mumble something in Swedish but, in response to a glare from her mother, swapped to English. "Look. They've got *Wicked Weasels*. I told you it'd be okay here. I certainly don't need this." She defiantly pulled off her bikini top, exposing a pair of beautifully pert young breasts.

Now, those I would call peaches.

When he joined the group, Engel glared at him. Bruce easily interpreted this as a *stop staring at the young girl's tits* sort of a glare and grinned in response, annoying her further with a surreptitious wink.

While the Swedish woman turned to greet him, Ulla blurted out, "Even him. See? Even men don't wear big panties on the beach."

Bruce could feel himself blush when he suddenly became aware of his minimalist swimwear. "I don't always wear trunks quite as small as these," he spluttered while struggling to clamber, still wet, into the baggy shorts and getting sand over everything. "They're just for swimming, you see. Only ones left in the shop," he finished lamely while the girls giggled and even the Swedish woman smiled at his antics.

First time I've seen her smile.

The Swedes wandered off to find a spot closer to a beach bar providing some kind of background muzak. Bruce watched as the girl slipped behind her mother, allowing her to bunch the fabric of her bikini bottom into the crack of her bum unnoticed by her parent. Bruce watched the swaying buttocks disappear into the crowd and sighed.

Quite a handful there, in more senses than one.

***

A half hour lying in the sun, continually being teased

about lusting after pre-pubescent girls, a quick visit to the rooms to pick up some kit, and then Bruce was leading the way into the hotel gym. Eva had been disappointed to find that the luxury hotel did not possess a dojo and that it was also not possible to reserve a training room. However, the receptionist assured them that there would be no problem, as the training facilities were little used during the day.

The gym consisted of two connected rooms: one containing a range of high-tech training machines and the other wooden-floored for aerobics and similar group exercises. As promised, the gym was almost empty, containing only two very fat women who were walking at a sedate pace on running machines, apparently managing to both hold a conversation and watch the different soaps playing on holos that faced the machines.

It never failed to amaze Bruce how many fat people he encountered, especially in countries like the USA, the UK and many Caribbean islands, where it almost seemed to be a national stereotype. It was true that powerful pharmaceutical lobbies kept weight control drugs expensive and hence obesity was still widespread amongst poorer communities. Nevertheless, there was no justification for anyone who could afford to stay in such a hotel being so massively overweight. He grimaced at the sway of the elephantine buttocks.

Must be a lifestyle choice as these folk probably spend a lot more to combat the detrimental effects of obesity than it'd cost to avoid it in the first place.

The aerobics room was deserted. Eva darkened the

windows to the rest of the gym. The girls stripped off wraps and sandals and dropped them on a pile of mats at the back of the room. They wore matching grey skin-tight shorts and tops. Bruce had been provided with knee-length shorts and a vest of the same material.

He had decided that the girls must have finally tired of the silly clothes joke, but then noticed in the mirror that, while he went through a short warm-up, stretching of the material resulted in it becoming increasingly translucent. He opened his legs wide, bent at the waist to put his elbows on the floor and looked through his legs at the mirror that comprised one wall of the room.

Fuck! Enough stretching and they are completely transparent.

The girls were searching through racks of aerobics gear, discussing possibilities of being able to use them as weapons. Eva found a weighted bar about two meters long, which she reckoned would do, while Engel brought a pair of light hand weights over to Bruce. "Here you go, Beast. Think of them as knuckle-dusters. It's you and Blondie against me."

Bruce tried to protest that he only wanted to do some gentle kata to loosen up, but to no avail.

"You've got to help Watermelons," she insisted, "to make it last a bit longer before I kick her butt." A loud crack echoed through the room as Engel's raised foot blocked a vicious blow aimed at her head.

Definitely the same material used for their shorts – and clearly no underwear!

He only had time to observe this before he threw himself to the side to avoid a kick to his gut.

As the sparring continued, it was clear that Engel had a considerable advantage. Both Bruce's hand weights and Eva's heavy pole made satisfying noises as they were blocked by the redhead's panzering on the sides of hands and feet, elbows and knees. Nevertheless, the extra mass slowed down their movements, allowing Engel to easily beat back every attack.

Bruce and Eva drew back panting while they circled around, trying to maintain their opponent in a position directly between them. A relaxed Engel rotated between them with the slightly head-down stance that maximized her peripheral vision.

We're tiring quickly and will soon be on the receiving end of the attacks.

He caught Eva's eye and warned her of an attack with a slight nod of his head.

Stepping forward to punch left handed towards the side of his small opponent's head, he made no attempt to avoid the block by a surgically armored elbow that sent a shock up his entire arm. Engel was already moving to respond to his expected follow-up with his right, when she jerked her head backwards to avoid the weight hurled at her ear with a twist of his wrist.

Eva was fully prepared to capitalize on this momentary distraction and the bar walloped across the small woman's shoulders, propelling her forward. The stumble was turned to a fast roll, which brought her to her feet in time to duck a second thrown weight, leaving her open to the pole which thumped into her midriff, throwing her onto her back.

Engel bounced to her feet from a shoulder spring, just able to block the bar descending towards the crown of her head. However, she had no defense against Bruce's sweeping leg, which caught her behind the knees and sent her crashing onto her back, though she attempted to break her fall onto the hard wooden floor.

Bruce dropped on his victim before she could roll clear, kneeling on her left shoulder and attempting to find a lock on the wrist of her immobilized arm. His body was hunched, braced against counter attacks from Engel's free arm, but she was far too preoccupied using it and both legs to defend against a rain of blows from the tall blonde.

Bruce managed to get a grip on a small hand, which fit easily within his, and started to twist the wrist. "Give up? We've got you now."

"Fuck off." Her arm jerked back and forward, but Bruce had a firm grip and he twisted the wrist further, rewarded by a grunt of pain.

Eva was plainly enjoying herself, swinging the pole in a whistling figure-eight that was hardly slowed by the blocks by Engel's legs and free arm. "Come on, Redcurrants. I thought you were supposed to be beating me up."

"What in the world are you doing to that child? Stop at once! I'll call security."

Bruce twisted to see the doorframe filled with one of

the huge women, her obese companion peering timidly over her shoulder. Enormous breasts heaved in a silver shell suit, possibly indicating that the irate woman was building up to come to Engel's aid.

The split-second of distraction was, however, all that the talented martial artist required. A carbon fiber reinforced foot caught the side of Bruce's head and her arm pulled free of his grip. A second blow to the side of his head, this time with the heel of her right hand, knocked Bruce backwards onto the floor, where he lay dazed.

Helplessly, Bruce watched the small ninja fight to her feet, slip inside the whirling stick and throw the blonde over her hip. Engel emerged from this move holding the pole with its tip against Eva's throat, who tapped her right palm against the floor to acknowledge defeat.

A gasp reminded Bruce of the spectators, who were now looking shocked by the sudden change in the situation. Engel piped up with a grin. "Thanks, missus, but if I want any help, I'll ask for it." A foot kicked painfully into his side and he curled into a ball, protecting his head with his arms. "And that's for throwing stuff about the place."

Bruce watched a strange combination of embarrassment and irritation replace confusion on the big woman's face before she withdrew from the room. Her evident attempt to express annoyance at Engel's lack of courtesy by slamming the door was defeated by inbuilt damping, which slowed the door's movement so that it closed with only a gentle sigh.

Bruce clambered to his hands and knees while Engel pulled Eva to her feet and then replaced the bar. When the girls started sparring bare handed, Bruce crawled to a corner of the room where he could do some stretching exercises, well out of the way of the flurry of punches and kicks. As Engel stood on one leg and defended herself with a series of leg blocks, he realized that, yet again, he was missing out on another fantastic photo opportunity.

After half an hour, the girls reluctantly finished their training. They pulled Bruce to his feet and dragged through the now empty gym towards the spa area, which abutted onto it. Eva had booked parallel massages for the three of them: formally the package was an *Ayurvedic four hands* massage for a couple, but she had negotiated a deal where Bruce would get the full four-hands treatment while the girls would split one.

Two hands each, I guess.

The spa was a huge complex that included every imaginable kind of beauty treatment: saunas, steam baths, mud baths and strange aromatherapy and color therapy rooms. It was very busy, almost entirely with female clients, so Bruce attracted a number of stares while his group was led to their massage room.

They stripped and showered in an alcove off the main massage area, which contained two marble slabs and a wooden massage table; the last had evidently been added in response to Eva's special requirements.

Two diminutive Malay women led Bruce to the central slab, while a taller Malay settled Eva on the other slab and a young, Chinese-looking woman helped Engel onto the wooden table. Bruce lay on his stomach and closed his eyes as the four hands worked together in perfect synchronicity, releasing tension and soothing aching muscles while the scented oil was rubbed into his skin.

After half an hour, he was brought out of his light doze to be turned over and the entire procedure started again on his front. Legs, arms, chest and face were gently manipulated while Bruce daydreamed, paying only slight attention to the girls who were chatting to the massage therapists.

He was slowly beginning to pull himself awake, in preparation for the end of the massage when, from either side of the slab, hands slid down his chest, over his stomach to the side of his groin. Surprise turned to shock as the small fingers stroked his testicles and the shaft of his rapidly stiffening penis. His head jerked to the side and he looked directly into the depths of Eva's blue eyes.

Before he could say anything, she shushed him with a finger to her lips and whispered, "The girls said there was a special service, if we wanted it. Seemed a shame to miss out."

Her eyes opened widely and her head pressed back against the pillow; then her back arched and she emitted a low groan.

Bruce twisted his neck to see that the tall blonde had her legs bent, knees hanging over each side of the massage slab, while the tall Malay's fingers were working busily between them.

"Jesus suffering Christ on a fuckin' bicycle," he whispered under his breath.

This girl has been totally opposed to prostitution her entire life and is now paying for sex for the second time in twenty-four hours.

He closed his eyes again and was now also aware of Engel's heavy breathing. This awareness vanished quite rapidly, when the sensations from his own massage became more intense and the sounds of his own building orgasm drowned out those of his companions.

***

To Bruce, the rest of the afternoon and evening passed in a blur. They dressed for dinner and, for the first time, he felt that the clothing wasn't selected as a joke aimed at him. Simple white cotton slacks and shirt that matched the surprisingly demure white shorts and blouses the girls wore.

While they strolled along the covered walkway, darkness descended, the night air cooled by overhead fans to maintain a pleasant temperature in the mid-twenties. They headed towards the convention center, near the midpoint of the resort, where the dance competition was held. Bruce felt distinctly content, wending his way past boutiques, bars and restaurants, one girl on each arm and both on their best behavior while they window-shopped their way towards their goal.

Just before reaching the jazz dance venue, the girls

reached agreement on a Hard Rock Café for dinner. Comfort food was called for, they decided, selecting burgers for themselves and recommending a *pig sandwich* for Bruce. As a starter, they shared a huge portion of nachos; Bruce cautiously picked at a few of the chips with their thick coating of sauce, cheese, sour cream and guacamole, but the girls made up for him, eating as if they had been starved for a week.

Beers were polished off with the starter and Bruce selected a strange-sounding Chinese Cabernet Sauvignon to go with the main courses. They agreed that it had little resemblance to anything they had previously encountered claiming to be a Cab Sauv, but not unpleasant and a reasonable complement to their junk food.

Taking their time over coffees allowed them to finish in good time to enter the hall just before the seven thirty start of the competition. They had assigned seats near the front of the balcony, giving a good view of both the stage and the huge projection holo above it, which would provide close-ups and slo-mos of the action, according to programs selected by the competitors themselves.

The large hall was filled to capacity, and Bruce was unsurprised to find the Swedes seated beside them. When they arrived, Ulla seemed unhappy to find Bruce bracketed between his two companions but, within minutes, she was happily chatting jazz dance to Eva.

Engel used this opportunity to brief Bruce on what to expect. This final included twenty couples selected during regional qualifying rounds. They would all dance together for two set pieces. Based on points awarded by a panel of eight judges, the ten highest scored would then dance individually – music and arrangement of their own choice, with a five-minute time limit.

Formally, the competition would end with the winners dancing another piece but, according to Engel, tradition was that, when this finished, the two other pieces previously danced by the winners would be repeated, and members of the audience would be allowed to join them on the stage.

"All very well," Bruce commented, "but you're not going to get us up there."

Engel grinned mischievously. "If a certain tall blonde not a million miles away from here makes up her mind otherwise, I'd just love to see you trying to stop it."

Bruce groaned. "Maybe we could suggest going to a brothel instead. Do you think that'd work?"

"Could well be a possibility. Should I ask her? Probably the Swedish kid would want to tag along. Maybe you could divert her spoilsport mum."

Bruce rolled his eyes, but was spared further torture as the hall lights dimmed and the introduction of the competitors commenced.

Having no knowledge of this sport, Bruce was surprised to find that three of the competing couples were pairs of girls and one a pair of boys. The Japanese couple was particularly confusing as, from their names, Michiko and Hiroyuki, they were clearly girl and boy, but he would be damned if he could say which was which. In response to his question, Engel had given him a despairing look and informed him that it was, "...obvious to even the most onanistic of Scots that the delicate Japanese posing to the left was a girl." Even using his palmtop to further expand his view of the holo image, however, didn't convince him.

The first group dance was set to something that appeared to be a cross between trad jazz and reggae – the kind of thing that should have been cacophonous, but managed to provide a perfect background for an exciting dance in which partners were repeatedly thrown high into the air. From Bruce's viewpoint, all the pairs appeared to dance flawlessly, but the spread in points awarded, accompanied by slow-mo highlights of particular performances, evidently focused on subtleties that were beyond him. At the end of this round the De Marcos were tied in the lead with couples from Germany and New Zealand.

The second round featured a piece of music that was like a speeded-up samba and a dance sequence that Engel informed him was based on the Brazilian *capoeira* martial art. The flashing punches and kicks were more like the dances Bruce had seen the De Marcos perform previously, and hence, although he again could see little difference between the performers, he was unsurprised when the Italians moved into a clear lead after this dance.

The individual dances were performed in reverse order of position after the second round, so the De Marcos came last. By the time they appeared, Bruce had been completely overwhelmed by the wide range of music and dance style and had increasing respect for the judges, who showed remarkable consistency in their marking of the performances. Although there were some obviously partisan groups, the level of applause from the audience also matched the scoring well, making it seem to him that he was the only one in the huge hall who didn't fully understand what was going on.

The rapturous applause following the De Marcos' dance was confirmed by the scoring, which put them well clear of the second-placed Brazilians. This was obviously the highlight for Ulla, who was bouncing on her seat with excitement, clapping and letting out piercing whistles, looking her age more now than at any previous time.

The award ceremony included the top five placed couples and featured holo highlights of the performances involved. Thereafter, the stage cleared, leaving only the De Marcos, lit by a single spotlight. Bruce felt a shiver of gooseflesh as the drumbeats introducing *Bolero* became gradually audible in the silent hall. Their signature piece, Bruce guessed, as the now-familiar dance commenced.

After the crescendo of the dance's climax, there was a moment of silence followed by an explosion of clapping and stamping. Bruce found himself on his feet, part of the standing ovation that lasted for several minutes. When this began to die down, the Swedish girl squeezed past her mother and rushed off, evidently heading for the stage.

"Let's beat the rush," Bruce suggested, inclining his head in the direction of the nearest exit. To his great surprise, Eva nodded and they made their goodbyes to

Ulla's mother and reached the exit, just as the first dance was being introduced.

They strolled back to the hotel arm in arm, Engel in the middle this time.

With the differences in size, this must – at least from the back – look like a child walking between her parents.

The girls were chatting excitedly, reliving favorite moments of the evening. Clearly too excited to sleep, they persuaded Bruce that a nightcap was needed, so they agreed to his suggestion of the rooftop bar in their hotel.

The bar was much quieter than at lunchtime, and the group easily found a table at the edge of the terrace near the southwest corner. The outside temperature was pleasantly warm, with a distinct hint in the air of the typically tropical sweet-sour of decaying vegetation. Their view emphasized the dramatic contrast between the neon strip of the resort and the darkness of the mainland, punctuated only rarely by the amber glow of villages and shantytowns and the pearl necklaces of streetlights along connecting roads.

While they sipped Calvados, Bruce found a gap in the girls' conversation. "It was a great evening, Eva. I'm just a bit surprised that you didn't end up on stage for the last dances. Not that I'm complaining, though," he hastened to add.

"I would have liked to, but I thought discretion was the better part of valor." She smiled at the confused looks on her companions' faces and continued. "Ulla, I mean. I had a bit of a chinwag with her during the evening. She was telling me how much she adored Antonio De Marco and how much she wanted to lose her virginity to him. She's a very forthright girl," she expanded in response to Bruce's horrified expression.

"I told her that I suspected that she was the wrong sex to appeal to that boy and that she would probably have more success with Claudia. The girl's amazing. She was completely unfazed. All she said was ´Okay, I'll try my luck with her, if I don't get anywhere with him´."

"Amazing," Bruce agreed. "But why did this require a hasty retreat?"

"We got on to discussing sex and she asked if I had ever made love to a woman. I wasn't going to lie to the child, so I told her that I was a lesbian. She was extremely interested and wanted to know details. She's still a virgin, but convinced already that she's AC – DC. I might have accidentally mentioned that you were inclined in that direction, Maria." Eva looked sheepish. "Anyway, I thought it best to escape before you started getting interrogated on your love life."

"Fuckin' right. I do not do sex education for wannabe Swedish nymphets. Jesus. How does her poor mother put up with it?"

"It gets worse. The girl is now convinced that we are a kinky sex triangle and is keen to get together with us if she can sneak away from her mother."

"Right then..." Bruce coughed. "I guess we double lock and barricade the bedroom doors tonight. We could end up in jail."

"That's not a problem here. There's a big Muslim community in Singapore, so the age of consent is twelve Ulla told me. She's determined to lose her virginity here, by fair means or foul, before she returns to Sweden."

"Even if it is legal, it's still not kosher, as far as I'm concerned."

"And we thought you were into schoolgirls." Engel batted her eyelashes and attempted, rather unsuccessfully, to look young and innocent.

"Yes, well, maybe – but significantly older schoolgirls. Fifteen or sixteen, at least. Well, maybe, at a pinch, a well-developed fourteen year old..." He ducked a beer mat flicked in his direction by a smiling Eva.

After they finished their drinks and wandered back to their rooms, the girls speculated on just what the wild Ulla might be like in a couple of years. As ideas got more outrageous, Eva proposed that it might be worth keeping in contact. "We could meet up with her and take her to that brothel. It could be a celebration or something, maybe for her sixteenth birthday," she suggested.

Until Bruce kissed the girls goodnight and reluctantly left their room, the brothel idea was being fleshed out in more detail. Bruce rolled his eyes to heaven.

They're beginning to sound half serious.

Quarter of an hour later, he was lying in bed, beginning to drift off despite the sounds coming from the next bedroom through the connecting door. Engel had referred to him as an onanistic Scot: her vocabulary seemed to be improving while Eva's degraded. In any case, even the good Onan himself would be truly knackered trying to keep up with the strains of this trip.

It would be good just to relax and go with the flow, but that was clearly not an option.

We're still on the home turf of someone who clearly has no scruples about multiple murders, even if they take out innocent bystanders. Even then, how could she or her minions possibly catch up with us now? I can't think of how it would be possible, but I'll let my guard down only when we're safely back in Bermuda, which should be very soon now.

He should have been reassured, but was still worrying when sleep finally claimed him.

13 ...going home

Bruce awoke to early morning sunshine flooding the airy room. He lay for a moment, reviewing their plans for the day. On the move again. It would have been good just to chill out in this place for a couple days, but Eva was correct; they had to get out of Singapore before Doctor Lee's searchers inevitably caught up with them. Eva had already reserved three places on the 10 am shopping trip to KL.

He crawled from the bed, stretched and then padded through to the girls' room. He slid between the sheets of the bed and spooned his body against Engel who, as usual, was sleeping nose to nose with her lover.

From the small twitch on contact with her body, Bruce was sure that the small redhead was awake. He stroked her slim, muscular flank and whispered into her ear, "Just going down for a swim. I'll be back in about a half an hour. We should get our shit together so that we can get out of here by nine thirty at the very latest. Luggage will be bit tricky. We can't take much, as we are supposed to be on a shopping trip. On the other hand, it shouldn't be so minimal that we'll attract attention when we check in for an intercontinental flight. Think about it."

With great reluctance, he peeled free of the small woman and went off in search of his swim wear, trying not to think about Engel's approach to wakening her partner, which had started by nuzzling against a very shapely breast.

***

Refreshed by his swim, although the water was actually a little too warm for proper exercise, Bruce returned to his room to find the girls had already placed a backpack containing all of his clothing on his bed. They had ordered breakfast from room service and were enjoying it on their balcony. Both completely nude, he observed, glancing into their room. He quickly showered the salt water off and, with a towel round his waist, joined the women for coffee and toast.

No random flights this time, Eva had decided. Bruce examined the options she had narrowed down to: a Virgin Intercontinental flight to LA or Confederate Airlines to Dallas Fort Worth. "Well, my choice would be clear. Virgin's a top airline and they fly a new hypersonic airbus on that route. I've never even heard of this other crew, but they're certain to be one of these ephemeral companies that come and go in the States. Literally, fly by night operations," he joked lamely.

Engel rolled her eyes. "If you prefer Virgin, I guess that means we need to take the other one."

"Are you sure about that? This is Dallas fucking Fort Worth we're talking about. Regularly voted the worst international airport in the world – and I can assure you that takes some doing, if you consider places like Karachi or Almaty."

"It can't be so bad, surely," Eva remarked. "It's in the South, but it's still the USA."

"Texas has been pretty bad ever since the Gulf coast evacuations, and Dallas is definitely the armpit of Texas. I've always been able to avoid the airport, but it is supposed to be the wart on the arsehole which is Dallas...if I can mix my physiological metaphors."

"Be that as it may, it seems to be our best bet," Eva insisted. "Timing is perfect; the shopping heli lands directly at Kuala Lumpur's international airport. We just need to lose the transfer to the limos that meet us there and get over to international departures to check-in within a half an hour...tight, but doable. I can confirm the bookings just before we land, so it's just security due to us being in transit from Singapore to the States."

"When we don't get the return heli flight, our day exit passes will be automatically converted to Singapore departure records, which are bound to be picked up by Singmed. By then, we'll be well under way. It should work. Okay, we should get moving...and we'll be somewhat less noticeable if we are wearing clothes."

***

The trip to Kuala Lumpur went completely to plan; so smoothly, indeed, that Bruce's superstition about the consequences of runs of good luck began to worry him.

They received some strange looks when they boarded the busy jet helicopter with well-filled backpacks, but these were not so far beyond the size of some of the huge handbags carried by the predominantly female passengers as to cause comment. Similarly, their rather feeble story, which involved meeting up with some friends in transit before making their own way to the shopping mall, was accepted without comment by the two tour guides, who shepherded the shoppers towards a special immigration desk for one-day visitors.

Within two hours of touchdown in Kuala Lumpur, the extremophile team was in the air again, flying in an antiquated, long-range, sub-sonic 747. Bruce guessed the plane must be over four decades old, and the shabby furnishings implied there had been little refurbishment over this period. First class was upstairs in the small bulb of the *megatop*, but appeared only slightly less disreputable than the rest of plane. There were twenty old seats, five rows of four, which reclined into horizontal beds. Only two of the seats in the back row were occupied by a couple Asian men with the builds of sumo wrestlers; they appeared to be travelling together but were both sleeping when Bruce's party boarded. The business class cabin appeared to be similarly devoid of passengers, but economy class was reasonably busy; more than half-full, Bruce estimated.

Eva led the way to the front row and settled down at the window, with Engel beside her and Bruce on the other side of the aisle. After take-off, the girls swapped places and Eva accessed onboard coms, while a dowdy hostess took drink orders. She worked her way through the range of options for further transfers to Nassau, based on their estimated flight time of sixteen hours. With Dallas fourteen hours behind Singapore, this gave an arrival around three in the afternoon of the same day. All options required at least one further flight transfer, with shortest travel options needing two transfers.

Eva postponed a decision until after lunch. Despite Bruce's forebodings, the lobster that he selected was very tasty, and the accompanying Malaysian industrial Chablis knock-off was surprisingly pleasant, even if served a trifle too cold. The girls were also well pleased with their steaks and pronounced their copy-Zinfandel to be perfectly drinkable, a tribute to the abilities of flavor chemists rather than vintners.

Bruce was savoring a pseudo vintage port when Eva gasped and pointed at the display on the reactivated coms holo. A mail entry to Doctor Bruce Roberts and party with identified sender *Singmed* was flashing a priority flag.

On Bruce's shrug, Eva activated the link after first setting a privacy screen for their party. He wasn't sure how effective the security on this ancient aircraft would be but, in any case, the Asian men still appeared to be sleeping soundly and the hostess had vanished into the small galley.

The instantaneous flicker of synchronization of Eva's palmtop with the plane's internal holo system was replaced by head-and-shoulders projection of Singmed's aged CEO. She spoke clear English, with only the very faintest trace of an Australian accent. "Doctor Roberts, I am, as I am sure you know, Wing-yun Lee. I apologize profusely for the over enthusiasm of my security staff. I was completely unaware of their actions and they far exceeded their remit in their behavior towards you. They will be strongly disciplined." The old woman looked severe. "The survivors of this fracas may well consider their deceased comrades to be the lucky ones."

Bruce tried hard to find any trace of true emotion in a face that clearly owed more to cosmetic surgery than nature.

"In any case, I can only assume that you came to Singapore to meet with me. You are evidently very resourceful, more so than I had expected. I was very surprised that you managed to best Mister Bush and his partner. I previously considered them amongst my top operatives."

Bruce was momentarily confused then realized that she must be referring to the psychopathic couple from Bure.

"I can only surmise that Bush somehow let it slip that I have a good idea what you possess and I am prepared to pay a lot for it. An awful lot. Maybe the idiots in my security service have frightened you off, but please reconsider. The reply option on this message will allow you to contact me directly, at any time. I strongly recommend that you take advantage of my offer. After we negotiate terms, I will arrange a chartered flight to bring you back to Singapore. But make no mistake about it; you will be met in Texas in any case. I will have the late and very much lamented Professor White's secret at any cost."

Eva looked at the others in turn and then exhaled noisily. "Phew. She doesn't mince words, does she? We can't have escaped from KL with much time to spare. What do we do now?" She looked to Bruce.

"Our only advantage is, maybe, that she has added one and one to make three. This Doctor Lee obviously thinks that we would only have gone to Singapore if we were thinking of changing sides...an obvious mistake, especially given our Miss Maiden's past history."

Engel stuck out her tongue at him but, ignoring the rude gesture, he continued. "I can't really see how it helps us much, though. No matter what we say, we're going to have a welcoming party in Dallas. I think we're getting in above our depth here."

"Do we scream for help then?" Eva asked.

"Despite the fact that the last help GRW provided turned out so catastrophically, I don't think we have an alternative. Okay, Eva, let your security folk have the key elements of the story. Get them to set up a heavy team, plus a private jet, at Dallas. Make sure the plane has plenty of range, just don't give them any destination. Maybe imply Hawaii, but no specifics. Engel, anything else?"

"Make sure they're tooled up for both the Singmed and local teams. If half of what I've heard about Dallas is correct, two opposing heavy squads heading for the airport will draw local gangs like a fuckin elephant with diarrhea draws flies. It's going to get messy." She thought for a moment then added, "Also make sure they have protective kit for us. The old fuckin' Lee witch may want us in one piece, but the local neds may be less picky."

While Eva contacted our security liaison in Basel, Engel crawled over her to sit on the arm of Bruce's seat. "We've got to watch Eva," she started without preliminaries. "She's not doing quite as well as it looks on the surface. She was just getting over Bure when there was that fucking rumble in Singapore. She might be trying to drown it all out with constant wild sex..." She hesitated in response to Bruce's raised eyebrow. "...not that I think it's a bad way to handle things. But anyway, she cries in her sleep."

Bruce looked into the small woman's eyes then pulled her into his lap and gave her a hug. "Don't worry. We'll keep her between us. It'll be a quick rush through the airport, with the paid heavies doing all the work. What happens afterwards though? That's what we need to nail down."

Engel gave him a quick peck on the cheek and then roughly jerked herself free. "Worried?" she whispered. "Who's worried? Just try not to fuck up, for a change."

That's probably as close to a thank you as I'm ever likely to get.

He waited until Eva had finished with Basel and then brought up his next concern. "Girls, I think we have to assume that our opponents will be throwing everything they can at us now. All hell will break loose when we land, but we also have to expect that I'll be traced back to Bermuda, if this hasn't been done already. Doctor Lee thinks your mother is dead, Eva, but this doesn't mean that she's in the clear. We should get her out of Hamilton."

Eva smiled wanly. "Funnily enough, I've been thinking exactly the same thing. What about if I get her to meet us in the Bahamas?"

Bruce thought about this suggestion for a bit, waiting to see if Engel would raise any objection. "I can't see a problem with the idea, the difficulty is going to be contacting her and ensuring that it doesn't simply act as a signpost pointing in our direction. We can do everything we want to encrypt and redirect a message, but they know we're on this plane. I can't think of any way that we can be sure the message won't be intercepted and read."

"If we use an open, common access notice board that Angela scans, we can ensure that the message can't possibly be traced to her," Engel contributed.

"That bit's okay, but they will also be able to read it if they can follow our comm path. How can we possibly pass on this information without any chance that our destination will be compromised?"

Eva looked worried for a moment, and then her face lit up with a smile. "Nul problem. How about this?" The plain text message appeared suspended in the air:

Mum, take the job you were thinking about immediately, see you there, L&K, E.

Bruce peered at the message then glanced at Engel, who shrugged, plainly mystified. "It's certainly cryptic enough. I've been living with you gals for six months and I haven't the foggiest about what it means. Are you sure this'll get your mother to Nassau?"

"Certain. I'll explain it later." She then proceeded to program the most complex encryption and transmission route she could think of.

"All right. That's out of the way now," Eva announced after she sent the message.

"Fine, O Mysterious One, despite the fact I've no idea what you're up to." Bruce grumped. "Anyway, how do we get to Nassau to meet her? We've got a plane waiting in Dallas, but how do we get to the Bahamas without giving the game away?"

"I've also got an idea for that." Eva's eyes twinkled mischievously. "Just get me to the plane and I'll take it from there." She turned to Engel, and the girls started to whisper conspiratorially.

Bruce could have attempted to eavesdrop, but decided to let Engel take care of things.

If there's anything I need to know, I´m sure that she'll let me know in good time.

The feeling of tension, in anticipation of action to come, began to make him feel squeamish.

Not good enough, I need to be in top form when we disembark, despite the long flight and yet another change of time zone.

He rummaged in his wallet and selected a restorative relaxant. Thereafter, he was still nervous, but his concerns seemed somehow less pressing. A mere ten minutes later, he drifted off into dreamless sleep.

***

The flight had only one hour left to run when Engel shook him awake. The hostess was standing by his seat with a tray of what he guessed was breakfast, although the local time would be more appropriate for a late lunch. He struggled to bring his reclined seat to an upright position, while at the same time rubbing sleep from his eyes.

"Good one, Beast." Engel handed him a glass of ice-cold grapefruit juice. "You've been sawing logs for ten hours straight. Thank fuck for anti-sound. Anyway, time for a last meal before we get stomped." She smiled and left him with this cheerful thought.

While Bruce gradually came fully awake, tension again started to build up, turning his stomach acid. He forced down a rather soggy cheese roll with a couple of mouthfuls of bitter coffee and then placed the tray on the unoccupied seat next to him and adjourned to the small toilet to freshen up.

A bit basic and on the shabby side, but clean.

He rinsed his mouth with a minty solution and then splashed cold water on his face.

Definitely not the breeziest that I've ever felt, but much the better for that long nap.

The girls were heartily tucking into *huevos rancheros* when he returned, reminding him of his stomach's delicate state. Trying to ignore them, he sipped the remnants of his juice and initiated calming breathing exercises in preparation for landing.

Trays were soon cleared away as the approach to Dallas-Fort Worth commenced. Bruce glanced through the window. Grey, overcast skies lay above an apparently endless, grey suburban sprawl. The higher buildings of downtown were visible in the distance as black shadows on a grey backcloth.

A picture representing the word drab.

The landing was smooth and, while they taxied to the gate, an announcement was made apologizing for a delay in deplaning. Just as this announcement was being made, the hostess came over to Bruce and informed him that his party would leave the plane first. This message was clearly overhead by the sumo wrestlers, who muttered angrily to each other in what sounded to be Korean.

There were stares from the couple of passengers in the business cabin when Bruce's team was led through to leave from the front exit. Waiting in the transfer passageway for them were two heavyset uniformed police officers – both looking extremely pissed-off.

The taller of the two addressed Bruce. "Okay, you're Roberts I guess?" On Bruce's nod, he continued in a southern drawl, "I don't know what kind of shit is going on here and, to tell you the truth, I don't wanna know. The terminal has been ordered clear, so anybody out there is aware that it's their own risk." He glared at Bruce, making it clear that he was not happy at all with this arrangement.

His partner continued, a similar drawl, but strangely high pitched for such a bulky man. "You have exactly half an hour to get airborne and out of here. After that, we just flush the entire terminal with riot gas. You really don't want us to do that, boy. Also, any sign of firearms – anywhere – we gas the joint." He looked at the taller cop, obviously checking if everything had been covered.

"That's it. Thirty minutes. If I were you, I'd get my sorry fucking ass moving. Pardon my French, ladies." He touched a finger to his Stetson and the policemen turned to board the plane, presumably to hold back disembarkation for the indicated half hour.

Bruce shrugged and chucked his backpack onto the floor while the others followed suit. "Here we go, another set of luggage lost. Let's follow the man's good advice and get our sorry asses in gear."

Bruce led the way along the passage at a fast walk, followed by the striding blonde, causing the small redhead to jog in order to keep up in the rearguard position. When they entered a buffer waiting room, Bruce ground to a halt and gazed in horror at the mass of very rough-looking individuals packing the area. Before he could master a first shock of panic, Eva pushed past him and approached a tall woman dressed in combat fatigues. She was well over two meters tall, Bruce estimated, with the heavy build indicating some kind of power sport – or maybe another ex-gladiator.

The big woman spoke first. "Eva, Maria and Bruce...my name is Elizabeth and I'll be looking after you for the next little while. Welcome to Dallas-Fort Worth." She laughed pleasantly, a contrast to the grim appearance of the men and women standing behind her. "First things first. Wilson will get you kitted up, so strip off any loose clothing and get into that body armor. Move it. I'll update you while you get tooled up."

Eva was already pulling off her blouse when Bruce glanced at Engel, picked up her shrug and then hurried to strip down to underwear and then pull on the one-piece suit of a grey smart fabric, which first appeared somewhat baggy but shrank to fit snugly in response to his body heat. He accepted a pair of combat boots, which appeared to be made of the same material, but turned down an offer of a helmet with integrated visor, selecting instead protective goggles.

The leader of their escort spoke as they dressed. The GRW team was lucky; they had managed to get thirty operatives in place before the terminal was sealed. She wasn't sure of exact numbers, but estimated than the Singmed opposition couldn't number more than twenty.

"Basically, we should be fine..." she summarized, "...except that there are an unknown number of members of local gangs between us and them. Here." She handed Bruce's party red bands, which they pulled over their foreheads – or in Eva's case over her helmet.

"Anybody without one of these ain't one of us and is fair game. Don't hesitate to defend yourselves...there are no civilians out there. You shouldn't actually need to do anything. We will be all around you. But, just in case, help yourself to the tools of your choice." She indicated an open chest filled with a glittering array of weapons. Bruce couldn't help notice Engel's feral grin as she rushed forward to load up with the fruits from this cornucopia of instruments of grievous bodily harm.

"We're ready to move out as soon as you are armed. Your transport is at gate *B32*. It's about half a klick. The Singmed team is waiting there. Third parties may appear out of the woodwork at any time. One last warning. Your armor is a compromise between protection and mobility. It will stop a lot, but you're not invulnerable. Stay out of the way of sharps or fast-moving blunt instruments. If you do get hit, scream. We've got a couple of medics, those guys with the white helmets." She pointed to two large colored men, one who was a light brown but the other so black that his features were difficult to make out. The medics were both heavily armed, clearly intended to cause as much damage as they were able to repair.

Elizabeth pulled down her visor and walked towards the door into the main terminal building, her team fanning out silently around her, no doubt responding to instructions that Bruce was sure she was continuously broadcasting on a tight comnet. For an instant he was annoyed that they had been excluded from this communication, but then it occurred to him that he would probably be unable to make sense of the messages passed between members of this evidently professional outfit. He was sure that their redoubtable leader would let him know anything critical, as and when required.

As they entered the main concourse, the ancient terminal building curved out of sight in both directions.

The gate they had exited from was labeled *B65* and their group turned right; gate numbers counted down on their right, and empty shops, bars and restaurants lay on their left.

The entire building felt weird because of its emptiness. A bit Marie Celeste-like, given that many restaurants and bars were lying open with abandoned food and drinks scattered around. Even this weirdness could not hide the dirty and bedraggled appearance of everything, though. Many of the retail units were boarded up, trash lay around everywhere, possibly due to the fact that fires seemed to have burned in all of the scattered rubbish bins, and all available surfaces were covered with graffiti.

Just before gate *B55* they encountered their first signs of life. A gang of about a dozen long-haired men in dirty motorcycle leathers stood in the middle of the passageway, blocking their path. As the GRW team approached, the gang leader with lank blond hair, a bushy beard and evident paunch, called out, "Just hold on there, Sweetie," evidently spotting Elizabeth as the one in charge. "There's a lot of very fucking mean mothafuckas waiting on you, just along the way a bit. You don't want to be getting your boys all tuckered out before they got to do some fucking hard fighting. Now all I'm asking is a miserable ten fucking thou to go away. Call it a toll, if you like. Now what do you—" His eyes glazed over as a throwing star materialized in the center of his forehead. While he toppled backwards, his gang unfroze and scattered towards a burger joint, but various missiles brought four down before they could reach cover.

Three of Elizabeth's team, two armed with small crossbows and the third with a complex compound hunting bow, kept the gang pinned down while the rest of the party hurried past the restaurant. This first encounter seemed to act as a signal, however. Increasing numbers of bodies began to emerge from both sides of their path, to mass in front of them. This time they clearly did not represent a single gang and remained in separate clumps, everything from individuals to the largest group of about twenty Hispanics, with about equal numbers of men and women, in black and red gang silks.

The total number of our opponents was about fifty, but from the jostling and jeering going on, it looked like they were about to start fighting with each other at any moment.

"Now would be a good time to speed up," Engel whispered, slipping a purple pill into her mouth.

"Jesus, this must be serious," Bruce subvocalized as he swallowed his pill. He had never before seen Engel use combat drugs. He glanced at Eva, who seemed to be echoing his thoughts before she also slipped something into her mouth.

As the drug took effect, Bruce felt calm and his movements seemed to slow down to a more manageable speed. A first exchange of missiles, predominantly fired from the GRW side, and then the groups rushed at each other and met with a clash of metal. Bruce drew his katana and threw away the scabbard. Engel cocked the small crossbow strapped to her right wrist and drew nunchaku from her belt, swinging them lazily from her left hand. Eva carried tonfa fighting bars, batons held by a side arm, in both hands.

Action was fast, furious and, from Bruce's viewpoint, completely chaotic. Chains and flails, usually enhanced with ceramic cutting edges and possibly poisoned, seemed the weapons of choice for most of their opponents. Although they had weight of numbers and some advantages of local knowledge, lack of coordination and discipline meant they were no match for Elizabeth's professionals, who were cutting them down with awesome efficiency.

The exception to this generality was the Hispanic gang. They held back until the first wave of attackers had spent themselves against the wall of GRW steel and ceramic, before charging directly towards Bruce's party, brandishing broad-bladed Chinese swords. Now the fighting was much more balanced, and the GRW team began to take losses.

Bruce was momentarily blinded by a gush of blood as the man beside him, one of the medics, was completely decapitated by a scything blade. The goggles cleared just in time for him to see the same blade cutting down towards the crown of his head and only his pharmaceutically enhanced reflexes allowed him to drop to a crouch while bringing up his own sword in time to deflect the blow. When his assailant stumbled towards him, unbalanced for an instant, Bruce drove forward at the exposed throat and drove the ceramic-edged Japanese blade up into his opponent's brain. Only as he jerked the blade free and the body collapsed on the ground in front of him, did Bruce become aware that he was looking into the face of a girl in her late teens or early twenties.

Despite his chemical support, this revelation shocked Bruce into a moment of immobility, sword held loosely at his side. This was dispersed only as a screaming figure in red hurled towards him. While he struggled to bring his sword into a defensive position, the body flipped backward as a crossbow bolt blossomed in the young man's ear. Simultaneously, the end of one of Eva's batons crashed into his brow.

Another gang member jumped into the gap in the GRW wall, but was immediately felled by Elizabeth's kick to his throat. On his knees as he choked, he received the coup de grace, a slice acroos the neck with a huge hunting knife, wielded by the remaining medic, the very black one.

The entire melee could not have lasted more than about a couple of minutes, when their opposition finally recognized that their position was hopeless and individuals began to turn and run. Within seconds, battle transformed to route; those who could escaping into the shelter of establishments out of the path of the advancing GRW team, leaving the field of combat to the screams of the injured and the bodies of the dead.

Elizabeth quickly took stock. Her team was down to eighteen fully functional fighters, three wounded but mobile, two very seriously injured and seven dead. One of the injured had extensive head injuries and was unconscious, while the other had lost a leg below the knee. Elizabeth looked grim as two of her team cleared up wounded opponents, beating down any still mobile and slapping dermal patches onto any immobile or unconscious. She had a short whispered conversation with the black medic and then the team formed up and moved on again.

Bruce glimpsed over his shoulder and saw the medic hold the arm of the crippled man while he slapped a derm against his neck. Moments later, the wounded man slumped bonelessly to the ground, and the medic hurried to catch up with the rest of his squad.

There was no further organized resistance before they reached the vicinity of gate *B32*, although occasional flurries of missiles flew from the shadows. One more of Elizabeth's team was injured when he was struck in the shoulder by a heavy DLC-coated, DU throwing knife, which easily penetrated his light body armor. As the medic pulled the blade free, Bruce heard him mumble, "Must be one of ours. No way any of these mothers going to be carrying no expensive blades like this. If he picked up the blade back there, got to be very fuckin' seriously pissed with us, to throw it away just like that."

Bruce saw that the medic had a good point and Elizabeth's rather callous treatment of her wounded was probably fully justified. In the beginning, the GRW team had the great advantage of being prepared to use missiles

– basically throwing away very expensive weapons. No way that these gangs would throw stuff like that, even if they had it, unless they were pretty sure of being able to recover it. Sure as fate, however, scavengers would be following in their wake; becoming increasingly well armed as they progressed. Unless they started squabbling amongst themselves, they might eventually realize that they could gain a lot by turning these weapons against their original owners.

When they finally approached a group of sixteen black-clad figures arrayed around *B32,* they were greeted by a hail of crossbow bolts, knifes and throwing stars. Although one figure on the GRW flank dropped to the ground, and there were a couple of other minor injuries, the effect of this barrage was much less than Bruce had expected.

Realization dawned and he shouted at Elizabeth who was marching forward in front of Eva, deflecting projectiles with a small circular shield made out of some kind of transparent material. "They're under strict orders to get Engel – I mean Maria – and me alive. They can't be sure in a lot of cases just who is who, so they have to go for non-lethal shots."

Bruce did not have to say more. On some silent command from Elizabeth, the entire GRW team sprinted into the attack, leaving only two of the four walking wounded to protect the extremophile team. Although GRW had an advantage of numbers, the Singmed fighters were fresh, and overall, the groups of fighters seemed evenly balanced. Over the next five minutes, the pace of combat gradually slowed as the teams were whittled down by attrition and most combatants began to accumulate injuries.

For an instant it looked like GRW was faltering when an ox of a man, who dwarfed even the tall Elizabeth, managed to catch her with a blow to the face using a huge quarterstaff, which sent the GRW squad leader flying into a wall in a spray of blood. The lack of her coordination caused a moment of confusion, during which the quarterstaff laid low the black medic who was trying to reach his commander.

The giant raised his staff above his head, preparing to crush Elizabeth's skull while she struggled to pull herself to her feet. He smiled in anticipation and it seemed to Bruce as if the battle had frozen to watch this act. While the staff scythed down, this look was transformed to shock and then horror as both his arms appeared to come apart just above the elbows and blood gushed from the severed stumps.

Only then did Bruce notice the slim Asian woman who had ghosted to her leader's side and followed up her initial attack with a return cut which sliced through body armor like butter and disemboweled the screaming man. After he dropped to his knees, shrieking while attempting to hold his insides in place with the remnants of his arms, the woman coolly silenced him with a cut that removed the top half of his head.

Although still leaning against the wall, blood pouring

from her face despite the bruised medic's attempts to provide treatment, Elizabeth clearly was back in control and GRW appeared to be regaining the upper hand, even though only very slowly.

Bruce glanced at Engel and indicated with a pointed finger the individuals beginning to appear behind them as the GRW and Singmed squads wore each other down. "This is going on far too long. It's got to end now." He turned to Eva, who was standing between the two injured GRW heavies. "We've no choice. It's now or never. Ready?"

Eva nodded and Bruce noted the look of grim commitment on her white face, before he turned and, with a screamed "Hai!" charged into the fray.

At this stage of the fight, the sudden onrush of three fresh fighters had a devastating effect and the Singmed defense collapsed. Bruce managed to divert the attention of a wiry Japanese man who had been involved with a long sword dual with GRW's swordswoman, giving an opening that allowed her to thrust her sword deep into his chest. Together, she and Bruce then descended on a Singmed couple, who were sparring with Elizabeth and the medic, and cut them down before they were even aware that they were suddenly outnumbered.

Within seconds, the pitched battle had become a mopping up operation, and Elizabeth used her palmtop to open the armored door that allowed access to the departure gate. After the last of the GRW injured was helped through, the door was closed and sealed, and only the faint rattle of projectiles hitting its other side could be heard over the sigh of air conditioning in the shabby transit lounge.

Elizabeth led them down a narrow stairway and unlocked a door that allowed access to the greyness of the open air. She pointed at the strangely shaped aircraft parked on the tarmac. A ladder led to an open hatch. "Your transportation, ladies and gentleman. I hope you enjoyed your brief stay with us and will consider using our services if you ever pass through Texas again. We will just wait here for our pick up, so you folks have a nice day." She turned and disappeared, locking the door behind her.

"Shit." Bruce spat. "Is she bloody cool or what? We've had twenty minutes of the worst bedlam in my life and that woman still sounds like an airhostess."

"Fucking amazing," Engel agreed. "That was one truly fuckin' tough squad. Thank the great and holy fuck that they were on our side."

"Time to get airborne." Bruce turned to Eva. "You had a way to get to Nassau untraced?"

The tall blonde looked haggard, but she forced a wan smile. "Indeed, I have a cunning plan, my Lord Blackadder."

Bruce and Engel looked quizzically at each other, without the slightest clue what she was talking about.

***

As they walked towards the airplane, Eva turned to Engel, whispering, "You know what you have to do, don't you?"

"Come on, for fuck's sake. Of course I know *what* to do. I just don't have a fuckin' clue about *why*."

"And Engel's got the advantage," Bruce interrupted, "because I'm also clueless about the *what*."

Engel immediately cheered up. "Worry not, dear Beast. You are usually clueless, so you should be used to it by now. And remember, what you don't know about, you can't fuck up."

Bruce would have put hands in his pockets in resignation, had he any pockets. Instead, he concentrated on flicking his sword to remove blood and then giving it a final wipe on the sleeve of his already blood-splattered suit.

Maybe it was a bit rash to throw the scabbard away, as it was a beautifully balanced weapon. Hyper-sharp.

He realized that shoving the bare blade through his equipment belt was not an option.

The girls entered the ultra-modern looking plane ahead of him, and he dropped back to look at the strange material of the fuselage in more detail. It felt silky to the touch, hard but definitely not metallic. *Probably textured smart ceramic or ceramic fiber resin. Certainly stealthed and probably chameleon skinned, with a lot of other active and passive anti-tracking goodies*

He took in at the indistinct lines of the blocky craft.

Specialist design for smuggling or spying. A good start, but not enough on its own to ensure a clear getaway from a determined pharm with major resources of money, political power and, especially, computer processing capacity.

A bumping noise drew his attention, and he saw Engel backing out of the narrow door to the cockpit, dragging a supine form in a white uniform behind her. She pulled the floppy figure, which Bruce could now identify as an airhostess, to the hatch and, with a shout of, "Catch," let the girl fall out towards the ground.

Bruce automatically extended his arms and, with a grunt, caught the falling woman and eased her onto the tarmac. "Shit," he complained as he straightened up. "I've pulled a muscle in my back. If you're going to be throwing girls at me, couldn't you make it smaller ones?"

"Your wish is my command. Number two coming down." Engel and Eva tossed out the slumped form, which they had been holding by the armpits. Again Bruce made the catch. Although the middle-aged woman who landed in his arms was certainly significantly lighter, he overbalanced and fell backwards, landing painfully on his bum with her on top of him.

As he moved the woman off his chest and struggled to his feet, glad of the protection provided by the smart body armor, he noted that this woman's uniform indicated that she was the pilot.

Bruce stormed up the ladder and was immediately pushed towards the cockpit by Engel, who started the process of withdrawing the ladder and closing the hatch. "Okay," he started as he entered, "what exactly was the point of taking out the pilot? I don't give much for our chances of sneaking onto another flight in this airport and I don't even want to think about making our way through Dallas on the surface. What..?" He stopped as he finally noticed that Eva was strapped into the pilot's seat and waved him towards the co-pilot or navigator position.

"Can you fly one of these things?" he asked in amazement.

"I've never flown one of these, but I've flown planes. Flown one, you've flown them all."

"Really? You've got that much flying experience?"

"Not actually in the air," she confessed, "but loads of simulations. There's no significant difference between virtual reality and real reality."

"There's a hell of a lot of difference in the consequences of screwing up." He buckled in as indicated. "So what do you want me to do?"

"I asked for a top of the range smuggling job," she started, confirming his previous suspicions, "but I don't know how all this stealth stuff works. We won't switch it on until we pass out of US airspace, so you have until then to work it all out." She flicked a couple of switches and the plane began to move slowly forward. "But before you do anything else, try to find a route to runway *E11*, while I get our clearance for takeoff."

Engel came in to peer over their shoulders, before latching the cockpit door open and settling in a seat in the front of the cabin. "Good afternoon ladies and gentlemen," she called out in a good imitation of Elizabeth's rather nasal tone. "As we prepare for takeoff, please stow away all luggage and place your seat backs in an upright position. In particular, samurai swords and other weapons should not be allowed to block the passageways."

Bruce grimaced as he remembered that he had simply dropped his katana on the floor to buckle in and had completely forgotten about it thereafter.

Not the kind of thing you want to have flying about the place in the event of a bit of turbulence.

Once Bruce had found the GPS taxi route, Eva steered the plane confidently onto the short runway and took off smoothly in a blast of acceleration that pressed them back into their seats.

They climbed rapidly through clouds and emerged above them into the brightness of late afternoon sunshine.

Less than three quarters of an hour since we touched down in Dallas, but long enough in that hellhole to last me a lifetime.

He turned to Eva. "Well done, love. You are indeed a woman of many talents."

"Indeed," Engel added. She had slipped silently into the cockpit behind them. "Not only a tireless blonde sex-bitch. Then again, have you ever had sex while flying a jet?"

"Don't even think about it, you two. First of all, Eva, will you definitely be okay landing this thing?"

"The entire flying thing's a complete con anyway. Pilots have only been in planes for PR purposes for half a century. A combination of protectionism by pilots' lobby groups and the general public's fear of flying, I suppose. You could automate the entire commercial fleet tomorrow and you'd just reduce costs and improve safety. It's just like cars. In lots of places we still have human taxi drivers. Now what kind of nonsense is that?"

Bruce had to concede Eva's points but, even with his technical background, was not sure that he would be happy being at a height of ten kilometers with a robot under control.

"Fine, I can go with that. The stealthing looks straightforward and I can give you the entire shooting match as soon as you say the word. But is that going to be enough? We'll be monitored to the Gulf and then we disappear. The Americans won't give a shit, as long as we don't return to their air space while stealthed, but we've still got to land somewhere."

"We curve round the south of Florida and then directly to Nassau, stealthed the whole way. The old international airport there has been derelict for years, but we've got veetol capacity, so we can land okay. It'll be a little tricky, as I think we'll just catch the tail of tropical storm Sigma," she admitted, "but I'm sure I can do it. I've plenty of time for running through a few sims before we get there. The storm is actually good, as it'll give us further cover."

Bruce didn't share Eva's confidence about carrying out tricky maneuvers in bad weather based only on VR games experience, and Engel looked positively green at the thought. Nevertheless, this wasn't his main concern. "This could all work, but they'll be combing the entire area for us. We can't just assume they'll accept that we've vanished without trace. Crashed or something."

"Correct, indeed, Doctor Watson. That's why a stealthed plane will appear off the Yucatan Peninsula, land in Cancun to refuel and then fly west over Mexico before stealthing. Much later this will be repeated in Fiji. And so on for the next few weeks. There'll be changes in flight crew, but the back passenger cabin will be kept blocked off. No matter how good the searchers are, the possibilities expand exponentially over time. So I don't think there's really much risk of finding us in the Bahamas by tracing the plane."

Bruce was stunned. "This is completely amazing. Awesome. But how on earth have you been able to organize it? Is there no way that it could be leaked somehow?"

"I don't think it'll leak. My mother will actually have set up the details herself and I hope she'll be in Nassau by the time we reach there. She can explain when we meet, but you can try to work it out as an exercise in the meantime. Anyway, set up the stealthing routine so that I can engage it in..." She examined her instruments. "...forty-five minutes. Maria, if you've got nothing better to do, I could murder a glass of champagne."

Bruce arranged the stealth settings as requested and sat back to sip his glass of champagne. No matter how he wracked his brains, however, he could not conceive of any way in which Eva could have passed Angela all the information she would need to set up this convoluted plan.

***

The flight was uneventful, even if a little bumpy while they skirted tropical storm Sigma, which was currently just below hurricane strength. It was dark and overcast, with occasional squalls of rain as they approached Providence Island, still with full active and passive stealth camouflage operational. With a flight path from the north, there were only a few scattered lights visible and no indications of either conurbations or streetlights.

After Eva slowed the plane to a hover over the featureless darkness of the abandoned airfield, she clapped her hands and punched the air. "Yes. Oh, what very clever girls we are...my mum and me."

Engel shouted from behind, where she had been strapped in since first traces of turbulence had been encountered. "What's going on? What are you so fuckin' clever about this fuckin' time?"

The holo comlink that had just appeared in the cockpit was duplicated at the front of the passenger cabin while Eva called back, "Line of sight laser link. She's here."

Angela appeared as head and shoulders in high res 3D. "Eva, darling. God, I'm glad to see you! Are you okay? I can see Bruce with you. Is Maria there?"

"Everything's fine now that you're here, mum. But we can go over all our adventures later. Have you got landing coordinates for us?" A short pause. "Right, perfect, I've got all I need now. Just stay well clear, I've never landed one of these things in real life."

Engel's moan carried into the cockpit along with a heartfelt, "I'm sure you really didn't need to remind us about that. Are you sure there are no fucking parachutes?"

Eva grinned at Bruce. "Piece of piss, honestly."

The plane wobbled from side to side in an alarming manner as they slowly dropped towards the invisible runway. Bruce gulped, but spoke up with more confidence than he could really say that he felt. "Sure, no problems. I have complete trust in you. All the same, would landing lights not be a good idea?"

"Nope," Eva replied. "Even though the chances of lights being spotted here and now are probably minute, it's still not worth the risk, as they don't contribute anything to help me land. Passive IR does just as good a job, if you feel that you want to see where you're going." She threw up a false-color overlay that showed the approaching tarmac in front of a couple large hangers. "Visuals really are just there to make passengers comfortable."

"What the fuck's wrong with that?" a small voice squeaked from the back. "Though a parachute would make this particular passenger even more fuckin' comfortable."

Bruce could make out a large bulky vehicle drawing to a halt in front of the nearest hanger. "I guess that's Angela."

The comm holo reappeared. "Of course it's me, lad. Who else would it be? Now, stop distracting my girl and let her get that thing down in peace."

This command was enough to completely silence her companions while Eva set up the final approach. Then she sat back with arms folded while the plane dropped the last fifty meters. "Look, no hands!" She grinned at Bruce.

A muffled query uttered from behind resulted, but Bruce felt it was better not to explain to Engel what was happening at this particular moment.

Touchdown was obvious only as a slight bounce of the suspension taking the weight of the plane and a change in the almost subliminal hum of the stealthed engines. Angela appeared again. "Very nice job, love. Just roll it straight into the hanger facing you. You need to watch out, though, there's a lot of junk lying around in there."

Approaching the black entrance, Eva conceded that here a bit of visibility would be useful and switched on nose and wing lights that lit much of the large hanger with their powerful beams. Two partially dismembered planes blocked half the hanger's interior: small propeller-driven jobs that looked to date from the last century. There were also two derelict buses of similar antiquity; broken windows reflected back the searchlights where the vehicles sat forlornly on flat tires.

Eva managed to squeeze the jet between the buses. The sound of tires crunching broken glass was picked up easily by the external microphones, and she found a space to park the plane beside a row of stretched white limousines. The cars – there were probably a dozen or so – were sitting on blocks and were covered by dusty transparent sheeting. Bruce had no idea at all what possible use such huge vehicles could have had on this small island. In any case, it had certainly been a long time since any of them had moved.

Bruce moved aft to open the exit hatch while Eva shut down the engines. Engel appeared much happier after she scampered down the ladder to terra firma, scrunching her eyes against the glare of the plane's powerful lights. "Christ, I would kneel and kiss the ground, so I would, if it wasn't all covered with glass and oil and shite."

The sweeping headlights and the sound of crunching glass, warning of Angela's approach, cut off further comments on the state of their surroundings. Bruce had already disembarked and Eva was emerging from the cockpit, when the bulky van screeched to a halt beside them, and the large brunette exploded from the driver's door.

She halted for a moment, staring at them. Bruce suddenly realized the contrast between Angela's tight white tube and slippers, which positively gleamed under the actinic spotlights, and the bloodstained combat gear that they were clad in. A shout of "Mum" unfroze the tableau, and Angela barreled past Bruce and Engel to catch her daughter as Eva half-clambered, half-fell down the ladder.

As the women hugged each other, Bruce felt Engel lift his arm and place it around her slight shoulders. She looked up into his eyes. "Partner, haven't we done good this time? You didn't even fuck up very often." The smile and the arm squeezed around his waist completely removed the sting from her words.

***

Two hours later they were cleaned up and dressed in the fresh clothes thoughtfully supplied by Angela. They sat together on the terrace of an old and somewhat shabby villa that overlooked a beach identifiable only by the sound of surf. Sheets of rain plunged into spotlights to dash against the invisible air wall that protected them from the mounting fury of the storm.

It was just after nine, but the extremophile team's body clocks were confused, and they were wary to add resetting drugs on top of their recent combat pharms.

Local Kalik beer and cheese sandwiches are going down well, regardless of what meal my stomach thinks it is.

Angela took the lead in explaining the last part of their journey to Bruce and Engel. "It's a bit like Eva and Engel playing these *what if?* combat games. You know, how would a small woman with a knife defend against a larger opponent with a sword? Eva and I have talked a lot about different scenarios, different cases that might mean we have to lose ourselves. We've been doing it since this rejuvenation project got hot, long before we met you two. Naturally, we've refined the ideas since we set up in Bermuda, particularly focusing on the mid-Atlantic and Caribbean area."

Engel asked, "And just when have you been doing all this plotting? Why didn't we know about it?"

"We usually used to sit in bed and chat at times when you were off satisfying Bruce's carnal lusts," Eva answered with a smile.

"Couldn't have had much time for it then. No fuckin' staying power, the sad old Beast. Not like Blondie thunder-thighs here." Engel slumped on the sofa beside the tall girl and laid her head on Eva's lap.

Bruce silently rolled his eyes while Eva refused to respond to the redhead's banter. "In particular," Eva went on, "we looked at ways to use GRW support to get back to Bermuda, in case there were any problems with the Bure sampling."

Angela took over, anticipating his interjection. "Yes, Bruce, we know you don't like depending on them after the earlier screw-up. This was only a backup, remember, just in case your own schemes came unstuck. We came up with the stealth plane switcheroo idea quite early on. It's not so difficult really, GRW regularly moves people and material to and from places where they would rather keep things hush-hush. They have a fleet of these jets, probably a couple dozen. As soon as Eva set up a stealth pick up from Dallas, I knew what was going on and could take care of the rest."

Bruce was annoyed at having been left out of the planning, but he could clearly see the advantages of this approach, considering his own maxim of distributing critical information on a need-to-know basis only. GRW support could only be set up via Angela or Eva, so there was no need to bring himself or Engel in on it.

Bruce saw Engel nodding in his direction, apparently following his thought processes and confirming his silent conclusions. "Okay, I can see how all this works, but I can't see any way that you could know we were heading for Nassau. We didn't know ourselves until Eva had her cruise ship brainwave. Her message to you gave no hint about our destination."

Eva smiled coyly. "You remember we were talking before about how I plan things. I couldn't say at the time why I selected Nassau of all places, but it all clicked when you asked me to get my mother to meet up with us."

Bruce strained to remember the message. "The job. Something to do with a job."

"Exactly, lad. Not just a pretty face, are you?" Angela beamed as if a prize student had just solved a tricky problem. "I've been getting rather disillusioned with my present employer. From what I hear about your adventures, you're also less than happy with some of the things going on. Big industry has always been a bit rough, but the pharms are getting out of control. I clearly can't do anything to change the way they work, but I don't have to be part of it. Vote with my feet, as it were."

Bruce was stunned. "Would they let you? I mean, these folk play very rough. They'd really let you just take your ball and leave?"

"I don't know what *taking your ball* implies in Glasgow, but I've been negotiating a range of options for a while. On receiving Eva's message I simply confirmed one of these, the one I had favored recently, actually. I'm taking an indefinite sabbatical...with Eva, of course. GRW will continue the work ongoing in Bermuda and will take over all my files on this project. They will continue to provide any further support I request and, in turn, I commit only to work for them if I return to a commercial position. Oh yes, they also have first refusal on anything patentable that I might develop."

Bruce frowned. "I suppose they do get quite a lot out of it, when you put it like that. Support for you, and even helping you disappear, is a kind of protection of their investment. But you still haven't explained about the job. What on earth is there for you on a half drowned island right in the middle of hurricane alley? I mean, look at this place." He waved generally in the direction of the steel shutters and thick concrete walls that formed part of the storm protection system for the blocky building.

"Nassau has actually been a base for anti-aging research for well over half a century. I've been formally offered a job to administer a large research grant from an anonymous benefactor. Informally, I'll also be allowed to play in the labs, along with my appointed project research associate." Angela pointed at Eva.

Bruce sank back in his large armchair and glanced at Engel, who looked equally bemused, but was clearly leaving the search for clarification up to him. "I just don't know how your beautiful daughter does it, but she plans intuitively better than my best software. If I can base an expert system on her thought processes, I could clean up in the multi-D MAA market."

"And if you could clone her body, you could clean up on the lesbo-sextoy market," Engel added with a salacious lick of her lips.

This last comment caused a raised eyebrow from Angela, but she refused to enquire further. Instead she followed up with, "Sex toys. What a good idea to relax you after all your toils and tribulations. There's a hot tub out there, which must be fun in this pouring rain. Let's go."

Angela set an example by bounding to her feet, pulling her single item of clothing over her head, throwing it to the floor, and setting off with determination through the air curtain. Engel was already helping Eva out of her blouse when Bruce slowly levered himself wearily from his seat with a shrug of resignation. He had a feeling that the action in the Jacuzzi was going to go on for some time, if past responses of his teammates to combat de-stressing were anything to go by.

The two naked girls disappeared, squealing into the rain while Bruce finished undressing. He looked down.

My brain might be mush, but at least one single organ was raring to go. Whatever it was that Eva had picked up in Singapore, it seemed to be contagious.

He grinned and, with a gasp, ran into the downpour.

Epilogue

Bruce took a giant stride off the back of the boat, holding his mask and mouthpiece in place while he plunged into the amethyst water in a welter of bubbles. Bobbing back to the surface, he looked around in time to see Eva diving neatly in behind him, closely followed by a much less elegant Engel. He raised the tube that let air to escape from his jacket in his right hand, allowing him to slowly sink in the crystal clear water.

While he slowly sank deeper, he held his nose through his mask and snorted to reduce the pressure on his ears. A few meters deeper and he repeated the process. Bruce looked upwards, and blew out through his nose to clear some water from his mask. Watching the sleek silver forms jetting towards him, he was beginning to regret his decision to go for the *vintage dive* option.

He shrugged to adjust the bulky buoyancy control jacket, which also secured the heavy cylinder of compressed air onto his back and tightened the belt holding lead weights.

It seemed like a great idea at the time, when I explained it to the girls.

The cruise ship had docked a week ago, and Eva had

fetched the luggage left on board. They had watched from the windows of Angela's new office while the massive ship left without them the following day. The professor had insisted on doing the initial work up of the samples, instructing Bruce to keep Eva and Engel amused while they unwound from their various ordeals.

"It's *James Bond* dives," he had explained. "Remember, in May, we visited the bar in Hong Kong that had been used for these old films?"

"You mean the one with the girl with the big tits?" Engel had inquired.

"The very one. They filmed several Bond films here, as well, mainly underwater sequences because the water is so clear and the coral is very colorful. I thought it might be a laugh to have a look at the sites used...wrecks and stuff. Best of all, you can dive in the old kit with compressed air, just like in the old 2D films."

So here I am, listening to my breathing in this noisy aqualung and needing to clear the bloody mask again.

Engel had insisted that there was no way she was going to be equipped to go diving in an antiques shop and elected for a smart body suit with a small jetpack, which allowed her to fly between the coral heads like an underwater Jetson. Eva chose a similar suit but, like Bruce, had selected conventional swim fins. Both girls were breathing from small bottles of compressed oxygen as part of small rebreather sets strapped to their chests.

A fraction of the size and weight of my kit, but, as I made the original suggestion, there was no way to back down. Too bloody macho for my own good.

He cleared his ears yet again and followed the girls towards the first wreck.

The *Tears of Allah* was a surprisingly featureless, rusting hulk with open hatches and gaping holes ripped in its side, which allowed access to its inner zones. Bruce watched enviously as the girls cavorted through the wreck like a couple seals, but he was very aware of the bulkiness and vulnerability of his low tech equipment and limited himself to peering into the holes in the coral-covered hull.

The second wreck, according to the dive description, had originally looked like a sunken plane – but now was a vaguely pyramidal pile of coral, swarming with a myriad of varicolored fish of all shapes and sizes. With the eye of faith, Bruce spotted something that looked as if it could have once been part of the landing gear, but closer inspection was precluded by the emergence of the head of a large eel. As the evil-looking face glared at him balefully, he decided that discretion was certainly the better part of valor and withdrew.

He was momentarily surprised when a hand grasped his elbow, but relaxed as he came face-to-face with Engel, who pulled him towards the third wreck. The small woman was evidently annoyed by his lack of comlink – another victim to his drive for authenticity – while she dragged him along in time to see a large barnacle-encrusted turtle emerge from the passenger cabin of what could have been a small inter-island ferry. Eva was slowly finning in its wake, following its lazily flapping course in the direction of the *Tears of Allah*.

After forty minutes, Bruce was getting low on air and, despite the water temperature of twenty-seven C, also getting a little cold when he turned back towards the dive boat.

Well, it's winter.

He started his precautionary safety stop at a depth of five meters. His train of thought was rapidly disrupted, as he was forced to cling to the anchor cable with one hand to maintain his decompression depth and fight off the girls' attempts to pull down his swimming trunks with the other.

By the time Bruce had clambered awkwardly back on board, the girls had already stripped off their suits and were removing beers from the small fridge. Engel turned to him just as he removed his mask and was splashing his face with water to remove strings of snot. "Yuck, that's truly disgusting, Beast. No way are you ever going to get me to wear anything where you risk drowning in your own snotter."

The naked blonde pressed a cold can of beer against a small bottom and was rewarded with a squeak of shock. She tossed the beer to Bruce before enfolding the struggling girl in her arms. "You know, diving with this kit really is fun. We'd quite like to do a bit more, wouldn't we?"

The redhead's wrath had evidently been successfully diverted. "Yeah, this is fuckin' pure dead brilliant. But we don't really need the suits, do we? It's not really so cold."

"I suppose not," Bruce responded. "The suits also provide buoyancy control, but a couple of kilos on a weight belt and some breathing control would do that. You'd be warm enough, if you didn't stay in too long and kept moving."

"That's what we thought, so let's have a go tomorrow. This fuckin' sex maniac here..." Engel pulled gently on Eva's nipple ring. "...wants to see what an underwater orgasm feels like. Want to come? You could be our lifeguard, save us from marauding sharks driven into a frenzy by copious love juice. Fancy it?"

Engel turned away to search for a beer without waiting for an answer. While he struggled to divest himself of the clumsy jacket, he decided that, if the girls were serious – which he was afraid they were – he'd need to get the absolute best kit available.

Something with an inbuilt defibrillator, as I reckon that my risk of a heart attack under those conditions is significantly greater than being bitten by a shark.

***

Over pre-prandial drinks, the girls were still planning dives, heads together while they scanned profiles of different sites. Angela sat comfortably sprawled against Bruce, evidently pleased with their new interest.

"Looks like this could keep them out of trouble for a while, although their approach to diving is exotic, to say the least." Bruce smiled. "We certainly could do with a bit of R and R before our next sampling trip."

The statuesque professor looked uncomfortable. "I don't want any further sampling trips. The carnage associated with this last jaunt has helped me make up my mind." She took a deep breath and continued, "I've already done some work on your Bure samples. They're even closer than the Japanese ones, but the extremophiles show only very slow aging at best, without any trace of the immortality we were hoping for. I have an extract that appears to transfer this longevity feature to higher animals, but there's no trace of rejuvenation. I think this is more than enough, although this last piece of work is one part of the project that I haven't yet transferred to GRW. I really need to think about it some more."

"How much work would you need to do before you have something that would work on humans?" Bruce inquired.

"None. I've shown that this works already."

"How?" Eva broke in as she stood, displacing a startled Engel. "Who was the Guinea Pig?"

"I was." The buxom scientist was clearly amused at the shock on the faces of the sampling team. "It's very clear, the aging process has restarted, even if it is very slow."

"But why on earth?" Eva squeaked out. "It might be slow now, but it was effectively zero before. Why'd you do that?"

"I didn't like the idea of watching my daughter and my friends grow old before me. I'm still not sure that the world is ready for great longevity, but increasingly certain that effective immortality is a very bad idea. Anyway, this is what I'm going to be thinking about over the next couple years in my Nassau office."

***

"There is some good news and some bad news, Beast," Engel whispered into his ear while Bruce sat on the terrace after dinner. "And the bad news is that you're going to have to watch Eva and me repeatedly making wild passionate love."

Bruce felt his eyebrows lift in surprise as he squeezed the coffee mug between his hands.

It's either a dream or I've finally started to hallucinate from over-indulgence in alcohol.

Not daring even to turn round, he prodded her onward. "That's the bad news? The good news has got to be a real cracker."

"You're going to father our children," Eva squealed, causing Bruce to jump in his seat, almost spilling his coffee.

How on earth do they manage to move so silently?

Bruce wondered about this before the sense of her words sank in. He spun round to face the grinning girls, the tall, blonde Eva towering over an almost childlike, red-haired Engel. "What on earth are you two gibbering about now? I'm telling you, unnatural sex...against the laws of God and man...is really doing your heads in. Good regular heterosexual bonking is what you girls need."

"It's fairly straightforward," Engel continued, "we

just want a wee favor. Not even you could fuck it up." Engel glared at Eva who was spluttering.

Bruce sank back in his seat, sipped coffee and made a show of drumming the fingers of his left hand on the window ledge.

They were going to make a theatre out of this and there's really nothing I can do about it.

He endured five minutes of innuendo before the core of their proposal emerged.

Now that Angela was convinced that her serum worked, the extremophile team had to think about the consequences of using it, should they choose to do so. This was more critical for Eva, as Angela was convinced that this treatment would slow the degeneration that resulted from the injuries she'd sustained during their first sampling trip.

As discussed over dinner, the main thing to be considered was the probable complete loss of fertility. As Angela had noted, "At seventy-five, this was never a problem for me, not that I had any thought about the consequences at the time. Eva is just thirty and thus she has to think a lot about whether she really wants to give up entirely on the chance to have kids."

This was what led to the girls' idea. If Eva was going to bank some ova, she had decided that she wanted Bruce to bank sperm as the chosen father. Not to be outdone, Engel had decided to do the same.

"So that's our idea," Eva said. "But we think it would be a real shame if you had to have a wank over a porn mag in order to produce the goods. Much more romantic if you were watching us making love...and probably a lot more productive too!"

"I even agreed to provide manual assistance," Angela added from somewhere to his left, causing him to jump.

Jesus, for a big woman she can certainly move as quietly as the others.

Pushing aside this distraction, he stood to face Angela. "Surely you can't be serious. This is your daughter we're talking about."

"Bruce, dear," she responded with an air of exasperation, "don't be so bloody prudish. This is the 21st century, not the dark ages. We have biological controls that make all the old religious prejudices, which may have been sensible enough when we were hunting aurochs, completely meaningless now. I spent too much of my youth on the academic treadmill to be able to fit in a proper love life. In any case, that was back in the old AIDS days when most sensible folk were too scared to have casual relationships. By the time that AIDS and similar pestilences had been cured, I was too old and respectable to get into the new sexual revolution."

Angela looked at Eva wistfully. "As you must be aware, I was in my mid-forties when I finally had Eva – and that was a full IVF job, which finally had to be brought to term in a surrogate womb. I can tell you, it's not fun combining the strain of menopause with that of bringing up a child as a single mother. I always tried to get as close to Eva as possible, to compensate for our difference in ages. I also encouraged her to take full advantage of her youth in our sexually permissive environment...to avoid missing out on all the things I did."

"And now the age difference is gone," Angela exclaimed, throwing her arms wide in a gesture which threatened to burst the fabric already straining to contain her formidable breasts. "I fully intend to take as much advantage as possible of the wild, decadent lifestyle available these days. Or, I suppose, available to all who are lucky enough to live in the right country."

There's not a thing I can say without appearing even more of a sad case.

Despite his attempts over the last couple decades, the traces of his fundamentalist Catholic boyhood remained like an albatross round his neck.

You can take the boy out of the Church, but getting the Church out of the boy was a much harder job.

"So, Beast..." Engel drew on tip-toes to whisper in his ear. "What do you think? It's got to be your wildest of wet Freudian dreams. Live, hard-core lesbo floorshow while you get your meat beaten by a mother substitute."

As he leaned down towards her, he whispered back, "If Angela hears your mother substitute crack, we'll see whose meat gets beaten." He straightened up. "Yeah, okay, whatever you lot decide. I don't know why you bother asking me, anyway. You always get what you want, regardless."

"Asking? Asking? Who was asking?" Engel responded at normal level. "We were just informing you of our decision."

"I think it's kind of sweet, really," Angela contributed. "It adds a bit of intimacy to the normally clinical process of IVF. It's a kind of extension of being present at a birth...being present at a surrogate conception. And when you think of it, conception is a much less messy process than birth."

A novel use of the word sweet. In fact, I'm not sure that the bit about messiness is correct, based on our experiences over the last few weeks.

"Oh, and by the way," Angela added, "you should get yourself into my bedroom now. I have it in mind to give you a good shagging, just to check that all is in working order."

In response to Bruce's look of shock, Eva and Engel linked arms and thrust their groins towards him with a chorus of "Yodel-odel-ey-ee-oo."

***

Angela sat on the bed beside him, gently stroking his developing erection. "You know, the girls also gave me a copy of that Singapore holo."

Christ on a bike, she'll have a duck fit if she sees her daughter with a couple of Chinese prostitutes.

"I especially liked this bit." Eva appeared before them, life size in glorious 3D. She was blindfolded and tied to the bondage cross. Her panting began to turn to squeals as Engel tightened screws on her bloated nipples, and the two Chinese girls knelt under her, working hard with a pair of large vibrators.

Jesus, I've heard of broad minded parents, but this is bloody ridiculous.

"I managed to get these." She handed over matching nipple screws. "But do you have any idea where we could get one of those bondage thingies?"

"Anyway," she continued while she guided his hands to the erect nipples crowning her huge breasts. "Shut your mouth. You look silly gaping like that."

He applied the screws and gave them a twist.

"Now that's the stuff, lad. Tighter now. Tighter. Mmm." She grunted inelegantly and fell backwards, opening her legs wide to expose her gaping, wet vagina.

"Come on, lad. Now. I want to try out this clit ring that Eva sorted out for me. It's supposed to maximize the sensation of penetrative intercourse." Angela's cries began to drown out those of her videoed daughter,

My God, I hope she doesn't find out that penile piercing is also supposed to increase the woman's pleasure. What'd she do to me then?

Even this painful thought was not sufficient to decrease his rigidity as he rode the bucking woman to her ear-splitting climax.